HELEN'S TOMORROW

Helen, daughter of middle-class mill owners,
defies her mother when she marries 'beneath her'.
And when tragedy strikes she is left widowed and
penniless with two young daughters to support.
Determined not to accept charity from her
remorseful, guilt-ridden mother, Helen finds
success when she returns to her job in antiques.
But she is not prepared for the spiteful ways and
bitter reprisals of her sister, Laura or the unwanted
attention of greedy mill hand, Jack. During a visit
to a London exhibition Helen's dreams are
shattered once more and, during a traumatic
incident, she unexpectedly meets surgeon, Charles
Ravel. What will tomorrow hold for Helen?

HELEN'S TOMORROW

HELEN'S TOMORROW

by

Shirley Heaton

Magna Large Print Books
Long Preston, North Yorkshire,
BD23 4ND, England.

British Library Cataloguing in Publication Data.

A catalogue record of this book is
available from the British Library

ISBN   978-0-7505-4574-7

First published in Great Britain 2016 by Aphrodite Publications:
Amazon Edition

Cover illustration © Ali McGuire by arrangement with
Shirley Heaton

Published in Large Print 2018 by arrangement with
Shirley Heaton

Magna Large Print is an imprint of Library Magna Books Ltd.

Printed and bound in Great Britain by
T.J. (International) Ltd., Cornwall, PL28 8RW

To my darling granddaughter, Sarah for her constant support and enthusiasm

My grateful thanks to Ali McGuire for producing such a vibrant front cover.

Chapter 1

1948

Startled by the sound of boots on the garden path and the loud hammering on the door, Helen's anxious thoughts came to an abrupt end. She reached for the door handle but the knock was repeated sharply and the handle began to turn. Taken aback, she stood rigid as the door began to open slowly. A waft of cold air streamed into the room. Her eyes settled on the image – a short, hunched figure in a dark overcoat and bowler hat. He stepped over the threshold and pushed his way in. It was Boothroyd.

'Rent,' he announced, taking a derisory glance at the doormat and scraping his feet roughly over it. 'Caught you in this week, I see,' he sneered, closing the door behind him before fixing his gimlet eyes on her breasts. Subconsciously, Helen folded her arms across her chest. If it was cheap thrills he was after, he'd come to the wrong place. But she was puzzled. It was Tuesday. Rent day was Wednesday. This wasn't Boothroyd's usual time. Had he made a special effort to catch her in this week?

He sidled closer. With a flash of resentment Helen frowned and backed away. If only she could expose him for the sham he was. An obnoxious little man, he puffed himself up to look the gentleman, bragging and putting on an act as though he owned the property, yet he was nothing but a door-to-door rent collector. She shuddered at the thought of his touch or lurid suggestions. She certainly didn't intend putting up with his familiarity, not now, not ever. But she might have to humour him, anything to prevent eviction for non-payment of rent. Last week she'd been short of money and ignored his knocking. But the rent had to take priority this week. The Family Allowance covered it.

'Sorry I missed you last week,' she said taking the ten shilling note and sixpenny piece from beneath a glass ashtray on the mantelpiece. 'Here's the two weeks' I owe. I'm up to date now,' she said with finality, lifting her chin in a determined effort to fend him off, a false smile developing on her face as she handed him the money. That was that! She'd settled her debt and now she wanted him off the premises, quick sharp.

'Pity we couldn't come to some arrangement, Mrs. Riley.' He smirked. 'I knew you were in last week. I heard one of the kiddies coughing.' Helen didn't respond. There was no point disputing the fact when she knew he was right. He edged closer, his stale breath causing her stomach to lurch. Slipping his arm around her waist, his fingers began to roam. 'You know what I mean don't you, lass? A bit of that-there wouldn't go amiss.'

Digging her elbow into his chest, she pushed him away roughly, her eyes ablaze with disgust. What was it with this obscene little man? 'Don't even think about it! I'll pay the rent the legitimate way thank you very much! And I'll not put

16

up with your advances. If you continue, you'll have my husband to answer to,' she threatened, determined to have her say whether it put her in his bad books or not.

Boothroyd smirked. 'I do like a spirited woman,' he confessed, stepping closer again. 'You say I'll have your husband to answer to?' He shook his head. 'He's too busy looking for work to be bothered about you, lass. But seeing he's short of brass perhaps he'd be glad of a small contribution.' He stared, glassy-eyed, licking his already wet lips in anticipation. 'I know I would.' He reached out and tried to pull her close and as he did so Nell, the little Jack Russell, jumped up and down at the door, yapping and clawing at the panel. There was someone outside.

Helen turned and the door suddenly burst open. Jim stepped inside pointing his finger and striding towards Boothroyd. 'I heard what you said,' he shouted staring the little man in the eyes and digging his finger into his chest. 'A contribution? I'll give you a bloody contribution,' he added as Boothroyd tried to back off. But Jim lashed out and stuck his fist on the offender's cheek. 'Don't ever give me cause to do that again, do you hear?'

Boothroyd reeled backwards, missing the sideboard by a whisker and falling with a heavy thud. But he roused himself in an instant, struggled to pull himself round and eventually staggered to his feet. 'You won't get away with this,' he wailed, rubbing his head vigorously and heading for the door. He pulled a handkerchief from his pocket and dabbed the blood from his split lip. Apparently still dazed, he reeled slightly before backing

17

away, a look of malice mantling his face. After steadying himself he turned and, without another word, he left the house, slamming the door behind him.

Helen listened to the scuttling of boots down the garden path, her heart thumping loudly and echoing in her ears. In a cloud of unwarranted guilt she turned to Jim. 'Thank God you came, darling.'

'He won't try that again,' Jim vowed, taking her hands in his. 'Don't blame yourself, lass. You wouldn't have to struggle if I could get work.'

Helen looked into his eyes and a touch of nostalgia descended. They met for the first time in 1938 when she worked at Waxman's Antiques and Jim had a regular job at Benson's. Proud and upright, he was a fine, handsome man with black curly hair, the image of his father who'd brought his family over from Dublin after the First World War.

Reining in her thoughts she sighed. This was no time for reminiscing. She reached for the tea caddy and tipped two scoops of tea into the brown earthenware teapot before pouring on the boiling water and setting it down on the hob to stay warm. A tiny frown developed on her forehead. Jim had been out looking for work, and judging by the look on his face it was obvious he'd been thwarted yet again – another disappointing day. She must give him the chance to tell her the outcome for himself.

'How did it go?' Her voice was light, her tone falsely optimistic. With an inner dread she anticipated his words.

'There's nothing out there for me, love.' He took off his khaki greatcoat and cap, slinging them on the hook behind the door. Slipping his arm around her slender shoulders, he gave her a peck on the cheek. 'I'm lucky to have you,' he said and, as he stooped to sit, shoulders slumped.

Helen searched his face lovingly as she smoothed her hands nervously over her shiny, chestnut hair which was pulled back into a horse-shoe roll, framing her face. 'Did you try Brockle-hursts?'

The ensuing silence was ominous. Jim dropped his elbows to the table and held his head in his hands. 'They don't want me.' He paused. 'Nor do Hargreaves. What else is there?'

Winding her arms around his strong back she squeezed him fondly. The business of losing his job at Benson's had sapped him of his self-respect. It had been difficult for him to cope in the weaving shed once his army days were over. His war injuries had held him back. His problems started when the cold struck. With two fingers missing from his right hand and the early onset of arthritis, the prognosis was grim.

Helen urged herself to lighten up and examine the positives. Her mind drifted once more to the past. She had stood firm against Mother who had strongly disapproved of her daughter's relationship with Jim. She constantly maintained that Helen was a cut above the likes of a mill worker who would be lucky to provide the basics, let alone the luxuries. But what did Helen care about the middle class life? It meant nothing to her. All she needed was Jim. And she stuck by him.

When his call-up papers arrived and he was sent to Narvik, Mother continued her campaign of attrition. And she was outraged when, during a short leave, Helen and Jim married at the registry office. Within days Jim was called to the front line. Ten months later, only weeks after Jessie's birth, he returned home safely. Within a couple of years Sylvia was born and their happiness was complete. Mother had still not forgiven Helen and it was now 1948. Although Jessie was six, Sylvia four, neither of them had ever set eyes on Grandma.

Helen pulled her thoughts up sharply. She must stop dwelling on the past. Her husband needed her full attention. 'How about a cup of tea, Jim?'

Jim nodded as Helen filled a mug and placed it in front of him. 'The meal's nearly ready.' She smiled. 'We're not too poor to have a decent meal,' she reassured him, her happy memories having strengthened her resolve to keep him buoyant. She opened the sideboard drawer and took out a red and white checked tablecloth. Jim lifted his elbows as she shook it out and smoothed it down on the table.

Jim frowned. 'Is there something burning, love?' He sniffed and moved his head from side to side trying to detect the offending odour. Helen didn't reply but she looked up as the door to the front room flew opened and Jessie bounded in.

'Come here, treasure,' Jim said, his eyes filled with tenderness. 'Where's our Syl?'

'I'm here,' the little one cried, trailing behind.

Both girls ran towards him and he squeezed them before turning to Helen again. 'Did you hear me, love. There's a smell of burning.'

'The pie is just about ready, darling. It's not burning,' she replied brightly, quickly side-stepping an issue she knew she couldn't avoid much longer.

'That fire needs mending first,' Jim observed, standing up, reaching for the coal scuttle and slipping quietly outside to the shed. Frozen to the spot, Helen stared after him and the girls slipped their skinny arms around her hips. She held her breath. He would have to know sooner or later, but now wasn't the best time.

Seconds later he stormed back inside and, with a surge of sudden anger he bellowed, 'What the hell's happened to our Nell's chair?' He pointed to the little dog and nodded to the corner of the room where the old chair usually stood, the one Nell always claimed.

'It was an accident. I can explain.' Arms outstretched, she stepped forward and tried to calm him down.

Jessie, now inflamed with guilt, fought to control her tears. 'Daddy, it wasn't Mummy's fault. It was mine,' she admitted, averting her eyes and gazing at the fire.

Jim dropped the scuttle onto the hearth and pulled Jessie into his arms. He bent down and his face softened. His voice was caressing as he gently stroked her hair. 'How do you mean your fault, treasure?' He turned to face Helen. 'What's going on, lass? What's Jess done?' he snapped, his tone accusing.

Helen felt he'd spoken more sharply than he'd intended, but before she had a chance to respond, Jessie started to wail.

'We were messing about, Daddy and I poked a piece of paper in the fire. But it was burning my

21

fingers. I dropped it on to the chair. I didn't do it on purpose.'

'Where was Mammy?' Jim frowned before turning to Helen, his voice heavy with disgust as he banged his fists down on the table. 'My God! You didn't leave the kiddies in here alone did you?'

'I only went to the Post Office, Jim. I was no more than ten minutes. I needed the Family Allowance to pay the rent. Don't blame them,' she said as she tried to appease the situation.

'I'm not blaming them! What do you think you're playing at leaving them? It's a wonder the whole bloody place didn't go up in flames.' His anger got the better of him and he pushed his chair back with such violence that it rocked and hit the cupboard behind him, sending a vase crashing to the floor.

'I'm sorry, Jim. It was my fault,' Helen admitted, knowing the best remedy was to humour him. 'Calm yourself love,' she added as she opened the oven door of the Yorkist range which gleamed mirror-like through its layers of black lead. She drew out a cream enamel dish and set it down on a side hob. A rich beefy aroma issued from the brown pastry-crust topping the pie. 'This'll do you good, Jim,' she ventured, her tone encouraging. 'Sit down, darling.'

Jim bowed his head and covered his face with his big sinewy hands. 'I couldn't eat it. Not just now, love.' His reply was pettish.

'We'll get by. Don't worry.' Her voice dropped to a whisper. She hardly believed for herself the promise she made, but they must stay optimistic for the sake of the girls.

Jim gave a heavy sigh. In one hasty movement, he jumped up and dragged his greatcoat from the hook behind the door, pulled it roughly over his broad shoulders and slipped it on. 'I need some air. I need to think.' He shrugged and the two little ones, sensing the tension, looked at him coyly. 'Come here my lovelies,' he murmured, appearing a little mollified. He held out his strong arms to enfold them, kissing and squeezing them both. 'Behave for your mammy now,' he begged, his eyes glistening. 'I won't be long.'

Helen sensed his feeling of inadequacy, the futility at not being able to find work and his frustration at not being able to provide sufficiently for them. Nothing could go right for him. She put arms around him reassuringly.

'Don't go getting your death of cold in this weather. Do you have to go, darling?'

'Stop fussing, lass.' He gazed into her face for a long moment. 'Sorry I shouted,' he said quietly, kissing her gently on the cheek. 'It's getting me down. You shouldn't have to leave bairns. It's not your fault. I should be able to support you.'

Before Helen had the chance to reassure him, he opened the door to a rush of air and closed it quickly behind him. The clatter of his boots on the path echoed in her ears before fading away to silence. She thought about what had happened earlier. She hated leaving the girls but it was pouring with rain and Jessie's Wellington boots were too small. She had placed the guard in front of the fire and warned the girls to stay away. But Jessie, obviously wanting to show off in front of

23

little Sylvia, had moved it.

Helen had rushed back from the post office but the minute she saw their tear-stained faces at the front room window she knew something was wrong. When she opened the back door she felt Nell's warm body squeeze past her legs as clouds of acrid smoke billowed towards her. She struggled valiantly to lift the blazing chair, tossing it into the back garden. Once outside with the girls enveloped in her arms, they watched the flames strike out maliciously, licking greedily at the chair's frame, the exposed springs tinged with blues and purples from the intensity of the heat. Helen agonised. But it would be getting dark by the time Jim was home. The time to tell him would be later when he'd relaxed. But he'd discovered the chair before she'd had the chance to tell him.

She sighed. If she hadn't gone to the post office she would have been two weeks' rent in arrears. She didn't want Jim to find out. That would knock his confidence completely.

But now this! He'd gone off in a huff before she had time to coax him not to leave.

Jim's feet were leaden as he trudged wearily down the steps at the front of the house, his demeanour anguished, his handsome face creased with concern. He was finished. All he was doing was dragging Helen and the girls deeper into poverty and misery. How could he keep on believing in himself when there were no jobs to be had? He'd be better off out of it. He stuffed his hands into his greatcoat pockets, pulled up his collar and set off towards the canal, trying to brush the thoughts from his mind. The cold, miserable rain dripped from the peak of his cap on to his chin and trickled down his neck. He pulled the already damp muffler tighter to stop the water from seeping further.

He regretted the way he'd snapped at Helen. After all, she was the innocent one. His heart lurched. It was his fault she'd had to leave the bairns alone. She wouldn't be short of money if he had a job. That was the real choker. It wasn't as though he was a shirker. All he wanted was a job, any job to bring in a wage.

His mind drifted. His pals had envied him when he married Helen and he felt immensely proud when he reflected on the way she had defied her parents. It was common knowledge the lads thought she was way above his class. What a picture she was, her rich, dark brown eyes lively and challenging, her mouth always ready to break into a smile, and her shiny, chestnut hair framing her face. She was stunning.

His anxiety returned and his thoughts became tangled. He tried to unravel them and concentrate on what was important. There was one thing for certain. He should have told her more often how desperately he needed her, although he couldn't have tried harder to provide for her. The consolation was that she was happy with that. She'd given up the middle class lifestyle, the comfort, the clothes and the luxuries. He reprimanded himself. He shouldn't have been bickering. He must put matters right and convince her he'd not meant what he said.

But the depression was back in a flash. How

25

could he cope? He carried on walking, his head facing the muddy ground beneath him. And when he reached the canal he stopped and stared into its murky depths. He could end it all here and now. But he quickly dismissed the idea and kept to the tow-path, his pace becoming slower as myriad thoughts drifted through his mind.

He barely noticed his old workmate, Fred Jarvis passing by and calling out, 'Lovely weather for ducks!' Fred's face was aglow. 'Penny for 'em!' he ventured and, despite his inebriated state, he must have realised something was amiss when Jim hadn't replied.

Jim looked up. 'Hello, Fred. I was miles away.'

'I thought as much. How are things on the job front?' Fred asked. 'Anything doing?'

'Nothing different,' Jim continued dolefully. 'I don't know where to turn next.'

'Something's bound to turn up. Give it a chance.'

Fred's optimism spilled over from his merry state. He seemed a little unsteady on his feet but he was in good humour.

They crossed the bridge and passed Walkers Engineering. Jim looked up at the building. They'd nothing for him either. But what good was it letting Fred know how he felt, letting his misery show?

'I'll be as right as rain when I get back to my Helen. I might try Huddersfield next. I've heard there's jobs there.' The sudden intervention by Fred had served to clear his mind.

When they reached the viaduct Fred turned and slapped Jim on the back good-naturedly.

'Well, I'll bid you goodnight, old pal. Keep your pecker up,' he said, stepping out jauntily towards the main road, occasionally sidestepping to keep his balance. Jim pondered on Fred's hard streak of honesty and kindness. At times abrasive, drinking too much at the Black Swan and talking too much, yet his pal was the salt of the earth.

Jim continued under the viaduct and climbed up the railway embankment. It was muddy up there and he kept on slipping but after a struggle he pushed himself over the brow and wiped his feet on the grass to remove the heavy mud from his soles. Having let common-sense prevail and sharpen his perception of the situation, he decided he needed to get back home out of the rain. It would do no good for him to pick up a chill. He needed to keep fit to carry on his search for work.

Ridding his mind of the negative thoughts, he walked along the railway sleepers, taking the shortcut he'd taken when he was a lad. It triggered memories of his childhood, of the times he and his brothers had played dangerous games. Smiling to himself a feeling of optimism surged through him and, quickening his pace, he knew once he saw Helen and the girls, he could cope afresh.

The sound of a train approaching disturbed his thoughts. He turned and looked in horror. It was speeding towards him. He made to jump clear of the line. But his boot was caught between the sleepers. He tried frantically to free it. But it wouldn't budge. In a state of panic he bent over the line and attempted, without success, to drag his foot from his boot. The London express loomed before him, hitting him full on. He fell to the ground like a drooping puppet.

The brakes went on and the train screeched to a halt further down the track. The driver jumped from his cab and stared back. Anger gave way to bewilderment as he ran to where Jim lay silent and still. When he stopped and looked down at the victim, the inflamed colour drained from his face. He started to vomit. 'Bloody hell,' he said. 'What have I done? I never saw him!'

Several passengers opened compartment windows and, curious to see why the train had stopped, stared down the line to where the body lay crumpled. One of them jumped from the train and dashed over to where Jim lay. Taking in the extent of the injuries, he grimaced and shuddered visibly. Jim's legs were horribly crushed; he was unconscious and appeared not to be breathing. The passenger slipped off his jacket and placed it over Jim.

'We need an ambulance right away. Poor devil didn't have a chance,' he said, staring at the train driver who had started to shake. 'Nor did you, pal.' He patted the driver on the back. 'Calm down. It wasn't your fault.'

A thin, bony woman ran purposefully from a house next to the railway line and on to the cinder track. 'We saw what happened. My husband's calling an ambulance.' Her gaze fell to the ground. 'Is he all right? He doesn't look too clever to me.' She peered more closely and shook her head. Narrowing her eyes suspiciously she averted her accusing gaze towards the driver.

The passenger, now on his knees stared up at the woman. 'It'd be a help if you'd see to the

28

driver, missus. He's in a terrible state of shock. Poor lad couldn't stop quick enough,' he explained. 'A cup of sweet tea might do the trick.'

The woman seemed to pull herself up sharply.

'Aye, I can see that. Come on, lad,' she said, a more concerned look on her face. 'Sit on this wall. Wait there while I go back and make you a brew.'

The passenger lifted Jim's arm. It was limp. And then he tried in vain to take a pulse but there was nothing. He cleared his throat awkwardly, shook his head and directed his conclusion to the onlookers. 'I think he's had it.'

Chapter 2

Laura Conway glanced at the menacing clouds as she sat on the wooden bench waiting for the bus to take her to Potters Moor. The warmth of her fine camel coat settled around her, reflecting the air of middle class living to which she was accustomed. Her matching hat was tilted forward framing her pretty face. Thomas, the younger of her two boys, stood beside her, his navy school cap cocked jauntily over his face. In a world of his own, he traced his name in the dust with his shoe. As the bus approached she straightened his cap, pushing aside his fair hair which flopped untidily from beneath it.

'Come along, Thomas,' she said briskly as she handed fourpence-ha'penny to the conductor.

'One and a half please.'

The bus rumbled through Kidsworth stopping close to her childhood home. She pointed. 'That's where Mummy and Aunt Helen used to live,' she announced proudly, recounting her fond memories.

They left the village and Laura gazed absently through the window. The cold February sun had pushed the clouds behind it, and was shining now on the crystal clear windows of the large Victorian houses sitting high upon the hill. In the fields it cast vague shadows on the vivid yellow carpet of primroses clustered beneath the trees. The willow catkins hung down heavily, and the rooks with their glossy plumage squawked stridently, swooping between the branches of the high trees that stood naked against the skies.

They stepped off the bus at Potters Moor, avoiding a frozen puddle at the roadside. Her regular Tuesday visits could be a chore but she always fulfilled her obligation.

When Kirk Grange came into view she was puzzled by the knot of people huddled at the end of Mother's drive. She quickened her pace and turned to Thomas. 'I think something's wrong,' she said, a guilty edge to her voice reflecting her earlier resentment. The onlookers turned and parted to let her through. She shuddered visibly when she saw an ambulance parked close to the front steps and two attendants carrying a stretcher. Her stomach churned violently. 'What's happened?' she asked, her mouth trembling, her body rigid with tension.

'Afraid there's been a gas leak, love.' The

shorter of the two attendants nodded stiffly at the stretcher. 'Is Mrs. Sarah Dorrington related to you?'

Aware of the rumbling undercurrent from the spectators, Laura felt a sudden surge of panic and an unnatural stillness surrounded her as she struggled to reply. 'She's my mother.'

'She's in a bad way, love,' he quoted solemnly. 'Better come with us, missus, but we can't take the lad,' he maintained, pointing to Thomas.

One of the neighbours, a kindly-looking soul, stepped forward. 'Come along young man. You'll be fine with me.' She placed her arm around the boy's shoulders. Turning to Laura, she added, 'I'm Mrs. Butcher – number fifty three. I'll take care of him. Your mother's a good neighbour of mine.'

Laura recognised the woman and turned a strained smile towards her. 'Mother has mentioned you. I'm so grateful, Mrs. Butcher.' Feeling useless and empty, she stepped into the ambulance, aware she needed to gather her strength. The attendants pushed the stretcher quickly into place, grabbed an oxygen mask and placed it over Sarah's face.

Laura stared blankly ahead. 'She will recover, won't she?'

'We may have caught her in time,' he said, his gentle efforts to rouse Sarah without response. Laura held her breath and her stomach fluttered when she noticed that, apart from the vivid lipstick daubed on her mother's lips, her face was pallid.

The Clifton General came into view and the

ambulance stopped. The attendants whisked Sarah inside and a staff nurse took Laura's elbow, steering her towards a row of wooden chairs. 'Sit here, dear whilst we see to her?'

Laura stared at the green fabric screens opposite and took a deep breath. She must remain positive. If anyone had a fighting spirit it was Mother.

Minutes later, Sister appeared. 'Don't get upset,' she said, patting Laura's hand in a kindly gesture. 'Your mother's pulse is strengthening.'

Laura sighed and, after what seemed ages the screens parted and a young doctor emerged, smiling. 'She'll be fine,' he said gently and his announcement gave Laura a glimmer of hope.

She gave a sigh of relief. 'I'm so grateful to you.'

The doctor continued. 'She's still drifting in and out of consciousness but her pulse has strengthened. We're confident she can be moved to the ward. Do go up and see her for a few minutes, but not for long. She'll need constant supervision.'

All was quiet in the ward as Laura sat beside the bed. 'Talk to me, Mother,' she whispered, her voice filled with urgency.

The staff nurse entered. 'Any joy?'

'No. I'm afraid there's no response as yet.'

'She needs plenty of rest. It'll probably be an hour or more before she comes round fully. Maybe you'd fancy a cup of tea. You could come back later.'

Now exhausted Laura had a desperate need to contact her husband, John. Retracing her steps towards reception, she searched for a public telephone. At first the line was engaged, but after making several frantic attempts, she heard the pips and pressed button A. 'Mavis, Mrs. Conway here. I need to speak with my husband urgently.'

'Sorry, Mrs. Conway, he's in an important business meeting,' the girl drawled casually.

Laura was taken aback. She had supreme confidence in her husband for his support, and she needed to speak to him right now. 'Then interrupt the meeting, Mavis. As I said, it's a matter of urgency,' she directed sternly. The girl could be insolent at times.

John came to the telephone. 'What's so urgent, Laura? I'm in a meeting.'

'It's Mother. She's in the Clifton General. There's been a gas leak. She's unconscious and I'm worried, John.' Laura's words were almost garbled.

'I'm on my way, darling. Don't upset yourself. I'm sure she'll come round.'

Laura listened to his heartening words but she seemed barely capable of logical thought and, when he arrived, relief swept through her as he reached out to comfort her. 'Don't worry, my love. You know Mother is a survivor,' he whispered.

'I hope you're right,' she urged, but the prospect was crushed by doubts. 'I feel so guilty. We should have been there earlier.'

'You can't blame yourself. It's no good looking in retrospect.' John brushed his lips against her cheek and squeezed her tightly.

Sister's voice broke into her thoughts. 'Your mother's come round, dear. She addressed me as Mrs. Bean. Does that mean anything to you?' She frowned and smoothed down her starched apron.

'That's strange. Mrs. Bean is Mother's cleaning lady. She must have been at the house earlier.'

Laura took hold of her mother's hand. 'Mother, it's me, Laura. Can you hear me?' she asked, waiting in paralysed silence.

Mother's eyes flickered. 'I'm fine, darling,' came her feeble reply. 'But so tired.'

Relieved at this reaction, Laura added, 'You gave us all such a shock, Mummy darling. I don't suppose you remember what happened.'

'I haven't the foggiest,' she mumbled.

'Maybe it'll come to you later,' Laura said, happy that at least Mother was conscious.

Sister re-appeared and gently steered Laura away from the bed. 'You can safely leave your mother now. She's very tired.'

Laura nodded. 'I'll come back later,' she said, turning to John. But her mind started to race and her problems seemed to multiply. 'I must contact Helen and tell her what's happened,' she whispered.

John took her arm and led her out to the car. 'You're much too tired and we must collect Thomas. Contact her tomorrow. I'm sure Mother will be fine now.'

Laura knew she was putting it off, but she felt drained of energy. Perhaps she could handle it better tomorrow after a good night's rest. John was right. It had to be tomorrow.

Helen clasped her hands on her lap and began to fidget. The later it became, the more she fretted. The accident with the chair had upset Jim and a streak of guilt attacked her. She glanced up at the clock on the mantelpiece. It seemed to be ticking louder than ever. Jim never stayed out this late. She stared at the fire grate with its dying embers and a cold draught wrapped itself around her. She shivered. Surely Jim wouldn't be long. He wasn't in the habit of spending his money on drink and anyway she knew he hadn't the price of a pint in his pocket. Time elapsed and despair tore through her. Midnight, quarter past. An ominous silence enveloped her.

Suddenly there was a sharp knock on the door. Her heart began to beat erratically. The knock was repeated, the second time louder and with more urgency. Nell started to yap and, in a state of panic, Helen called out, 'Who is it?'

'Sorry to call at this time of night, Mrs. Riley. It's the police. We need to talk to you.'

She jumped up so quickly she trod on Nell's paw. The dog yelped. 'Sorry, Nell,' she said, patting the dog's head before struggling to pull back the heavy bolt. She opened the door fractionally and a glaring beam of light spilled out revealing a uniformed officer. 'What is it?' she asked, her voice wavering.

'I need to come in, love.' The sergeant pushed open the door and stepped inside, running his index finger around his shirt collar in discomfort. 'Sit down, love. It's bad news I'm afraid.' His thin, straight lips barely moved.

Helen stared and her brain became numb. A kind of paralysis seemed to set in. 'It's not Jim, is it?' The sergeant gently helped her to the chair. She perched on the edge and looked searchingly into his face, her eyes revealing confusion.

35

'I'm afraid it is.' The officer took off his helmet. 'Jim Riley was knocked down by the five o'clock express from London. It's taken since then to identify him.' He swallowed hard. 'He had no chance, Mrs. Riley. Died straight off.' He paused. 'In the circumstances a blessing if you ask me.'

Stunned and in a state of shock her body was completely devoid of sensitivity. 'I don't believe it,' she wailed, but tears wouldn't come. 'It can't be true. You must have the wrong person. It's not Jim. He'll be back in a while. I know it.' Adamant, Helen stared ahead and her eyes became glazed.

'Come on, love. The constable's asked the woman next door to come round.'

In a complete daze and at her most frightened Helen turned. 'Would you mind taking the girls for me, Maisie? I must go to the police station and get things cleared up.' Her voice was brisk as she tried to remain level-headed in order to get to the truth.

'Don't worry, love. I'll take them back with me.'

Dazed and in a state of shock, Helen took her woollen coat from the hook in the hall. There must be a mistake. It couldn't be her precious Jim. She stepped into the cold night air, the biting wind attacking her body. Darkness folded around her as the police car stood there menacing, beckoning her to step inside. She felt empty.

'Come on. Let's get you down there.' The sergeant's words echoed inside her head. He took hold of her elbow and gently helped her into the back seat. 'Sorry but you'll need to identify him.'

Despite her courageous determination to prove him wrong, her heart began to thump heavily in her chest as she climbed the steps to the mortuary.

'Let's get it over with,' he whispered.

'It won't be him,' she stressed but inside she knew the time for the moment of truth was imminent and, as the sheet was lifted, her false expectations were shattered. 'It is Jim.' Her tone and expression held little emotion. Stunned, she stood in silence, wrapping her arms around her slender body. The nightmare refused to end.

The sergeant drew her towards the waiting car. Her eyes became glazed and anguished as the bitter blow hit her. She began to sob quietly but then the sob changed to a loud wailing. She had tried to reconcile the situation but failed. Time could never dim or heal her pain. Jim was her world, her everything. Would she ever recover from her loss?

There was a chill wind blowing as Laura and John approached Kidsworth. Laura didn't relish the thought of telling Helen about Mother's accident knowing she may refuse to visit after Mother's bitterness towards her. There were barriers between them even Laura couldn't penetrate. 'Are you all right, my love?' John glanced towards his wife.

Laura gazed back, feeling fragile. 'I think I can cope.' She gave a faint nod and, putting on a brave face she walked slowly, tentatively up the steps towards the front door. The house appeared desolate and the bedroom curtains were still drawn, but despite the ominous stillness surrounding her, she rapped on the door and waited. There was no reply. The only sound she heard was the dog yapping. She tried the door but it was locked and when she stood on tiptoe to peer through the window it was obvious there was no-one at home. She hurried down the steps, almost slipping on the thawing ice. In a state of panic, she opened the car door.

'That's strange,' she whispered. 'I thought Helen would have been in. It complicates matters,' she added and, before she could continue, she heard a voice behind her. She turned. It was the woman next door yellow-stoning her freshly scrubbed front steps. Laura looked with disdain at the metal curling pins glistening through the woman's bleached hair.

'Are you looking for Mrs. Riley?' The woman removed a cigarette from her mouth and pushed herself up from her knees. The imperious look she gave was enough to shake the disgusted look from Laura's face.

'Yes I am. Do you know where she is?' she replied shakily, suspecting the worst.

'It's her old man. Don't know exactly what's happened. She had to go down to police station.' The woman paused. 'Are you her sister?'

'Yes I am. Did she tell you anything more?' Laura climbed the remaining steps and faced the woman.

'As I said, that's all I know,' she spat out the words with a shrug.

'Thanks for your help,' Laura replied politely yet firmly, now desperate to get away.

She was about to step into the car when the woman added, 'By the way, her two girls are with me. They'll be as right as a bobbin,' she promised. She lit up another cigarette, drew hard as though her life depended on it, and continued her stoning.

'It's dreadful news, something to do with Jim. According to the woman Helen's gone to the police station.'

'What's happened?'

'The woman didn't elaborate.' She turned to John. 'I hope Jim isn't in trouble.' She gave a heavy sigh. 'Helen should never have married him. Surely she's got enough on her plate without this.'

'Hold your horses, darling. You're jumping to conclusions. You say the neighbour didn't elaborate. But what exactly did she tell you?'

'That something had happened to Jim.' She shrank back into the car sea. 'After the accident with Mother, I can't take much more.' Her eyes were blank and lifeless as she gazed back at the house.

'We need to go along there and sort it out.' John's voice was firm.

The station was minutes away and John drew up outside. 'I'll find out what's happening,' he said and Laura followed.

The duty sergeant appeared promptly at the front desk. 'Can I help you, sir?'

'It's my sister-in-law, Helen Riley. I believe she's with you. It's something about her husband. My wife and I are anxious to know what the problem is and if we can help.'

The sergeant gave them the stark facts. 'Her husband was knocked down by a train. Died straight off.'

Laura gasped.

'She's identified him at the mortuary,' he continued, 'but we couldn't take her back home the state she's in.' He turned his gaze on Laura. 'You say you're her sister?'

Unable to utter a word, Laura nodded.

'Hang on. I'll tell them you're here.' Not waiting for a response, he turned and disappeared.

'I never expected this.' John squeezed Laura's shoulder and swallowed whilst Laura shuddered and, in a state of anxiety, clung to him.

But then she shook herself free and held herself erect. 'I'll be fine, John. I've got to cope.' Her voice was soft yet despairing, but she had to be strong for Helen's sake.

'Be brave, darling. She'll need you more than ever now.'

The colour left Laura's already pale cheeks. She took a deep breath and, still unable to speak in case she broke down, she made a massive effort at self-control. Breathing deeply and concentrating, an inner strength took hold of her.

The sergeant came back. 'I'll take you in, love. She'll need plenty of moral support.'

Chapter 3

Laura slipped an arm around her sister's shoulders and whispered, 'It's me, Helen. I'm here for you.'

Helen stretched her arms towards her sister. Her face was swollen and blotchy, her eyes red rimmed. 'How am I going to tell the girls? And how can I go on without Jim?' She brushed the tears from her face and stared ahead, her eyes now

40

blank and unfocused.

Calling on all her resources to comfort and support her sister, Laura hugged her. 'I know it's going to be hard coming to terms with losing Jim and I'm so, so sorry, darling. But I'll do all I can to help you. We'll face it together,' she promised in a voice heavy with sorrow. Taking a deep breath she added, 'Why not come home and stay with us, just for a while. We'll collect the girls on the way.'

Helen struggled to cope with her grief and she nodded her agreement.

The journey back to Emley Street passed in silence. Laura collected the girls and they squeezed into the back of the car. But Jessie, always sensitive, became pensive. 'What's wrong Mummy?' she wailed, pressing Helen for an explanation.

'Wait until we're back, Jess,' Helen replied, her voice unsteady.

'Has something happened to Daddy?' Jessie persisted.

Laura intervened. 'Leave it for now, darling,' she whispered, 'until you're back at Aunt Laura's.' Jessie's eyes misted over.

They turned into Clarendon Road and once at Crossgates, John swung the car into the drive. The children spilled out on to the wet grass which glistened in golden streams of winter sunlight. The chilling moisture splashed their legs. Laura slipped an arm around Helen's tense shoulders, aware she would be anxious about telling the children.

Helen sat between the girls on the sofa when she

41

broke the news to them. Jessie's brow furrowed and Sylvia's eyes betrayed her apprehension. They were noisily tearful, asking a multitude of questions, some of which Helen was unable to answer.

'We must carry on as best we can girls, just the three of us now. We loved Daddy and we'll miss him but let's make him proud of us.'

When Laura studied Helen's brave face now wreathed in sadness and apprehension, a feeling of unease came over her. Mother's accident came to mind and she knew she would have to tell Helen at some point. But not now! And then there was the business of money. How would Helen manage to fulfil her promise to the girls with no job and no income? But they would cross that bridge in the very near future.

After the post mortem there were whispered rumours based on warped and malicious gossip. Some of the local women maintained Jim had taken his own life after a deep depression brought about by his wife's excessive financial demands. After all, as far as they were concerned, Helen was an outsider. She was not one of them.

On the day of the inquest the evidence pointed to an 'open' verdict, and when a psychiatrist came to the stand, he inferred Jim may have committed suicide whilst the balance of his mind was disturbed. But Helen, outraged and devastated at a suggestion based on mere speculation, found it impossible to accept. Jim had always been mentally stable and he loved his family too much to have done such a thing.

But Fred Jarvis was determined to tell his side

of the events and quell those vicious rumours. He took to the stand and provided more evidence.

'Mr. Jarvis, I gather you were with James Riley the night he died. I suspect you were probably the last person to see him alive,' the coroner suggested.

'That's right, sir, and I can say without a shadow of doubt Jim Riley could not have taken his own life the mood he was in. Fair enough, losing his job didn't help, but when I left him, he was keen to get back home to the wife and kiddies.' Fred was determined to put the story straight.

'Would you say you left him in an optimistic mood, ready to seek work?'

'I would, sir. He said he'd try Huddersfield next.'

After a short recess Helen's spirits were lifted when the coroner announced, 'Death by misadventure.' And she managed to drag herself back from despair and rid herself of the earlier stigma. She left the inquest in the certain knowledge Jim had cared for the three of them to the very end and that his death had been an accident.

The funeral took place a week later, and the weather was as depressing as the occasion. A silent mist swirled around the little churchyard in Kidsworth where Jim was laid to rest. Helen thanked the many colleagues from Bensons, and Jim's pals from the army who turned up to show their respect. But she felt a stab of disappointment that Mother had not deigned to attend, even for appearances sake.

Helen's thoughts triggered memories of the time she had first taken Jim home. She recalled that look of contempt on Mother's face. Jim, bright but with no public school education – a pre-requisite in Mother's book – was a mere mill-worker with a thick northern accent. He was far beneath Helen and totally unsuitable.

Her thoughts were interrupted when mill manager, Ben Lawler, approached her. 'I'm so sorry to be here on such a sad occasion, lass. You know we all admired Jim.'

'Thanks for your kind words, Ben and for your support when Jim was fighting for his job. We were both very grateful for everything you did.'

Ben mentioned several of the men Jim had worked with and, as Helen became engrossed in the conversation, his sudden concerned enquiry led to considerable confusion in her mind. 'By the way, how's your Ma? Out of hospital yet?' he asked. 'Nasty business that.'

'Sorry, Ben but I don't know what you're talking about. I don't understand,' she said, a heavy frown lining her forehead.

Ben's face reddened. 'Oh good God! I'm so sorry. I seem to have put my foot in it.' He looked to the ground and shuffled his feet. Taking both her hands in his, he confessed, 'I thought you knew.'

'Knew what, Ben?' She was becoming more and more confused by the second.

Ben cleared his throat awkwardly. 'About the accident. Didn't your sister tell you?'

'No!' Helen shook her head.

'I expect she didn't get a chance. I'll take you across. It's better if she explains,' he added, trying to placate the situation.

Despite the news of Mother, Helen managed to get through the day without further setbacks. 'I'll visit Mother as soon as I can,' she said. But she was still hurt by Mother's attitude, especially denying the children. That was unforgivable.

'Sorry we didn't tell you earlier, but you know how it is. No time seems to be the right time.' Laura took Helen's hands and squeezed them. 'It's just over a week since she was admitted. I think she'll be home soon. I know it's going to be difficult for you to face her after all these years, but she's desperately sorry for the way she behaved. The business of the gas leak has brought everything into perspective.'

'It may be too late for apologies, Laura. I'll see her, but that's all,' Helen promised, biting her lip as loving thoughts of Jim flooded her mind. Life was so unfair.

Sarah Dorrington awoke in a bed that was hard and unfamiliar. She was aware someone was sitting there but she was unable to figure out her whereabouts. She narrowed her eyes, taking in the shape. It was a man and, on closer scrutiny, she realised it was someone in uniform.

'Mrs. Dorrington? PC Clarke. Can you hear me?' he asked in his gentlest tone.

'Of course I can hear you. I'm not deaf,' she snapped, peering at him in exasperation, resentful at his patronising tone.

'You've had a nasty turn. It's a miracle you're still alive,' he said, tactlessly. 'Do you remember anything about it?'

'What on earth are you talking about?' she

asked, anger making a hard line of her mouth. She liked to be in control of her own life. It was disconcerting not knowing what was happening.

He leant over more closely. 'We need to find out why the gas tap was turned on. Do you remember feeling faint? Perhaps you passed out and knocked the tap as you fell.' He mouthed the words, almost soundlessly, giving her his own version of how it may have happened.

'My last recollection was of Mrs. Bean offering me cakes she'd made. After that I can't remember a thing,' she replied, more calmly now.

'Is Mrs. Bean a neighbour?'

'She's my cleaning lady,' Sarah explained curtly, looking at him with thinly disguised irritation.

'Was she with you at the time then?'

'I've already told you. She came along with cakes for me.'

'Perhaps she can throw some light on the incident. Where does she live?'

Sarah gave him Mrs. Bean's address and as he walked away she stared after him. They'd been on about a gas tap being turned on and she couldn't recall a thing. But, despite everything, she did feel lucky to be alive.

Her early life flashed before her. She dwelt on her working class roots and how her father, a staunch Methodist, had disapproved when her modelling career was launched. But she defied him and, when she met William, she was completely besotted. After a whirlwind courtship, they married and, having taken a step up the social class ladder, her happiness was complete. But when she discovered Helen was walking out with

46

Jim Riley, she maintained the family image was tarnished.

But, after such a fright, she regretted it all now. Her life could have come to an end. She'd had a lucky escape and, having dwelt on her memories, she realised what a hypocrite she'd been. The guilt swelled inside her and she was determined to make amends in some way or other.

The voice of the nurse broke into her thoughts. 'Visitors, Mrs. Dorrington.'

The word 'visitors' triggered a reaction. She snatched the hand mirror from her locker and held it up to her face, quickly applying lipstick before pushing the mirror back. Her makeup and hair had always been immaculate. 'Fine feathers make fine birds,' she always stressed in her own distorted version of the well-known adage. This was still her motto as she almost reached her sixtieth year.

Suddenly she looked up. She was startled. Her two girls, Helen and Laura were standing beside the bed. Her eyes moved slowly from one to the other.

'Oh, my darlings,' she cried, her voice wavering, her eyes shining with tears. Her dream had been broken. It had been eight years since she'd seen Helen and that was at Daddy's funeral. But how vulnerable she looked now.

'What a foolish woman I've been.' She muttered her thoughts out loud before turning to Helen.

'Darling, I'm so glad you've come. I've missed you terribly.'

Helen bent down to kiss her. 'I've missed you

too, Mother.'

Sarah clung to her, reluctant to let her go. 'This business has brought me to my senses,' she added. 'You will bring Jim and the girls to see me, won't you? I'm so sorry the way things have gone.'

Helen's rapid interjection stunned her. 'It's too late to make it up with Jim. I've lost him, Mother,' she replied sternly, facing Sarah with the truth.

'How do you mean, darling?'

'It was an accident,' Laura told her. 'He was knocked down by a train.'

Helen interjected. 'It's a long story and I don't want to go into detail, not just now.' Her voice wavered but she tried to remain calm.

'Dear God. I can't believe it,' Sarah mumbled out loud. Horrified at Jim's fate, she put her hands to her face and smoothed her flushed cheeks. 'I'm so deeply sorry, darling.' Riddled with guilt, she spluttered the words and swallowed noisily. The silence lasted a long moment. 'Please let me help you,' she offered.

'There's nothing you can do,' Helen announced, her flat voice reflecting her mood. She changed the subject. 'How are you anyway?' she asked, her voice softening now in obvious concern for her mother.

'I'll get by, darling. I've asked them when I'm going home, but no one seems to know.' She pulled herself up in the bed. 'You will bring the girls to see me won't you Helen?' she begged. 'I've wanted to see them all these years but my pride has held me back. I've been a stupid old woman.'

Sister interrupted their conversation. 'Come along now ladies,' she chivvied as she walked briskly past. 'It's time for your mother's beauty sleep.'

The sister's caustic comment gave rise to Sarah's mumbled aside and, knowing there would be no joy in pleading with her to allow her girls to stay longer, she took hold of Laura's hand. 'Thank you, darling, for bringing Helen.'

Laura bent forward and kissed Mother on the forehead. 'Relax now and don't try persuading Sister to let you go home. You'll be discharged when the time is right.'

'Oh, do stop fussing, Laura. I know what I'm doing.' Turning to Helen, she whispered, 'Look after yourself, darling.'

'Goodbye, Mother. I hope you're soon well, and do be patient.'

Sarah frowned. Would she ever see her grand-children? Helen's comment had an air of finality to it. Perhaps she wouldn't visit again.

'Why did you leave her, Mrs. Bean?' PC Clarke sat down and placed his helmet on the table beside him.

'She asked me to put kettle on and make a cup of tea. I'd made her some butterfly buns. She's always said she liked them.' Agnes Bean stared ahead as if in a trance, her usually bright and lively eyes now a dull amber colour.

'Go on,' he pressed, hoping to delve deeper.

'I thought I'd pop over, but to tell you truth, I felt a bit faint when I got there. I didn't stay for a cup of tea; I left.' She broke off abruptly.

'After just a few minutes?' He seemed annoyed at having to probe to discover the truth.

'As I said, I felt faint. I've had a few dizzy turns lately. I'm better out in fresh air.' She spat it out with finality as though she'd suffered enough questioning.

'What about the gas tap then? How come that was left on?' He was insistent.

'Nothing to do with me,' she protested. 'Do you think I'd leave a kettle on the stove with the gas turned on and no light?' She stared blankly ahead.

'I'm not saying that, but it's been a right sorry mess. Mrs. Dorrington was unconscious down at the General. She's all right now, but who knows what damage it's done.' He removed his helmet from the table and placed it on his knee, rubbing the top of it as he spoke. 'I might have to ask you to come down to the station,' he said as he finished off his cup of tea. 'The sergeant might want to interview you.' He brushed the crumbs from around his mouth.

'Oh, I hope I'm not going to be in trouble. I haven't done nowt wrong.' Her face was aflame with worry as she looked down at her green and cream plaid slippers.

'I'll be in touch anyway. Thanks for the tea ... and buns. They were grand,' he returned flippantly, but not without a smidgen of suspicion in his eyes.

Aware that, since Jim's death, she'd existed almost in total oblivion, Helen made a determined effort to talk to Laura about the future.

'I've decided to ask for a job with Mr. Waxman,' she said, her voice tremulous.

'What about the children? You'll need someone

to look after them,' Laura replied.

'I wondered if you'd have them, Laura,' she asked, her eyes pleading. 'My only alternative is Maisie and I'd rather not ask her.'

'I couldn't do anything without John's agreement.' She frowned. 'And how do you think the girls will feel having only recently lost their daddy? Are they going to think they're losing you too?' Laura's explanation was plausible but Helen persisted.

'I'll explain. I'm not prepared to accept charity, certainly not from Mother. If you decide you can cope I'll pay you.' She was adamant as she bit her lip, knowing this could be a sticking point.

'That's out of the question,' Laura declared. 'John wouldn't allow me to accept anything.'

Despite her insistence, Helen still had her doubts. Laura was right. How could she expect the girls to understand? But she had no intention of telling them yet. For now her main aim was for the girls to feel loved, and she was determined to do all she could to help them through this sad period. Her decision made, she knew the money the men had collected at the factory would last a while longer, but she must take care not to leave herself short.

In the evening when the children were in bed, Helen relaxed in the sitting room at Crossgates. Laura followed her through, drawing the curtains against the chill of the March evening, and sitting down beside her. 'I've spoken to John. He thinks it's a good idea for me to have the girls, but only on a temporary basis until we come up with some other solution. And he'll not hear of any pay-

51

ment.' Laura smiled. 'So that's a start.'

'I'll pay you back in some other way. I'll always be grateful to you.' Her eyes glistened as she hugged her sister. But then she added, 'I haven't even applied for a job yet. Mr. Waxman may not want me back.' She beamed valiantly, putting on a brave front.

'He'll snap you up, Helen. With all your experience he'd be a fool to refuse.' She opened the walnut cocktail cabinet. 'Let's drink to the future.' Taking out two crystal sherry glasses, she poured out the rich amber liquid and handed a glass to Helen. 'Here's to new beginnings!' she ventured, raising her glass and toasting her sister's future.

Helen's stomach flipped but she put on a brave face, lifted her glass and acknowledged the toast. She would never get over losing Jim. She missed him desperately. Her love had never wavered and she must draw from that the strength to succeed somehow – for the sake of the children.

'How wonderful to see you, Helen.' Vincent Waxman's face beamed with affection.

Helen smiled. She reckoned he would be in his fifties now but, apart from the wrinkles seaming his lively face, he'd changed very little.

'I was sorry to hear about Jim. I know how close you two were,' he added.

Helen caught her breath and her eyes revealed her sadness. 'That's true. It was such a shock.' She paused and lightened her voice. 'But I'm here to ask you a favour. Is there any chance of a spot of part-time work? I'm sure I'd pick up the threads. I really do need to keep the wolf from the door.'

'It's fairly quiet just now.' He sighed. 'I could possibly manage three hours a day two days a week. That would give me the chance to visit the salerooms. Would that help?' He stroked the bald patch at the front of his head and slicked down the little hair remaining.

'That would be lovely, Mr. Waxman. But are you sure?' She could hardly believe her luck.

He nodded. 'Let's drop the formalities. Do call me Vincent. How about starting tomorrow?' he offered. 'I have an appointment with the accountant at ten. Can you be here for half past nine?'

'I certainly can,' she replied. The girls would be at school which meant Laura's help wouldn't be needed, not yet. That would simplify matters.

Next morning Vincent left the shop as soon as Helen arrived. It was good to be back and she was content winding her way through the clutter of stock. Vincent was choosy when it came to buying. There were some nice little pieces, like the pair of green lustres decorated in tans and blues, the pretty glass-domed clock and the matching ornate vases with scrolled handles. But she was surprised the prices had remained fairly static since she'd left all those years ago. There were also the Art Deco items, a new vogue with its simple geometric designs thought by some to be a relief from the elaborate styles of the Victorian period. But many of these items held little value. They were made for the mass market, some from plastic. Despite the lull in demand for antiques, the wealthier classes were still discerning in their tastes.

Time passed quickly. Half a dozen customers came and went and before she realised it Vincent was back. 'How's it gone?' he asked.

'I've sold a cut class vase, managed the full price for it too, and the piano stool you had over in the corner,' she said, rubbing her hands together.

'Well done. You've made an excellent start.' He crossed over to the counter. 'I'm pleased you're back at the shop, Helen,' he told her. 'It's good to have someone to discuss the pieces with.'

'It's certainly given me something to focus on,' she murmured sadly.

'I understand completely after your loss, my dear. Although it is some time since I lost Pearl.'

Helen didn't comment. Hopefully she could try to take her mind off losing Jim, and since she wished to help with the successful running of the shop, she made a suggestion. 'Do we have a complete inventory of all the stock?'

'I'm afraid I haven't had time to sort that one,' Vincent announced. 'I must say it would be useful.'

'Then that's what I'll do, starting with furniture.'

She busied herself cataloguing the items, her mind completely engrossed in the task to the exclusion of everything else. Except that from time to time she thought about Jim and of a future without him.

Chapter 4

'Helen!' Vincent Waxman's voice penetrated her thoughts.

'Sorry, I was miles away,' Helen confessed.

'I'd like you to help me do a spot of buying. Your knowledge on the porcelain front is broader than mine.'

Her experience was in sales not buying. But she had been back at the shop for four months and the prospect sounded exciting. 'I'd like that, Vincent.'

'That's settled,' he continued. 'There's a sale at Ripley on Wednesday, viewing Tuesday. Can you make it? I'll sort out cover for the shop.' He rubbed his hands together in anticipation. 'There could be some gems from the Clifton Manor clearance. You knew Sir James had passed away, didn't you? The executors are putting everything up for sale.' His enthusiasm mounted.

'That sounds promising,' Helen replied.

It was several days later when, in a dusty corner of the shop, Helen spotted a small Rococo style sugar bowl set, its scrolls and curves producing a delicate effect. Surely this was worth more than the marked price of two pounds fifteen shillings and sixpence. The shell volute lid with the natural-looking flower paintings was typical of the Mennecy factory.

Vincent had obviously believed it to be a good

copy rather than an original. But porcelain had been Helen's main area of study at college and she was convinced the set was genuine. When she turned over the sugar bowl and noticed the mark 'BR' on the underside she reckoned that if the set was a copy, someone had gone to a great deal of effort to try authenticating it.

The minute Vincent arrived she approached him eagerly. 'Have you checked the authenticity of the china set over by the window? I'd say it was a Mennecy with the 'BR' incision.' She carefully picked up the bowl and turned it over.

'But the Mennecy mark is 'DV', my dear – Duc de Villeroy,' he explained gently. A diplomat in all respects he obviously did not wish to offend Helen or dispute her findings.

'That was the earlier period,' Helen maintained. 'Later when they moved to Bourge-la-Reine the mark 'BR' was incised,' she added excitedly.

'But of course,' he replied weakly, and she realised he was probably unaware of the history. 'Would you take the pieces from display and put them in the cabinet at the back? We'd better not sell them until we clarify things.' Helen removed the set wondering if Vincent believed her or was he merely humouring her? With that in mind she decided to check things out.

Town Square was busy as she crossed into Romley Road and headed for Kidsworth Art College. The gentle breeze feathered her hair and whispered over her skin as she looked up at the thin clouds scurrying across the sky and painting it with streaks of white. At least the wind should keep the rain at bay until she was back at Laura's.

The college entrance, redolent with that familiar smell of oil paint, met her as she pushed open the great oak door. It brought back happy memories. Fine arts had been her love and had led her to the study of porcelain. With breathless fascination she selected a tome and flicked to the chapter on Mennecy. The marking had changed with the factory move. Her heart fluttered with excitement. Once they had obtained proof of authenticity, the set could be valued.

Vincent clapped his hands joyously when she told him. 'That's amazing!' he declared. 'I shouldn't have missed it but, to be honest, I didn't know about the change in marking.'

With a broad smile on his face later in the week he announced, 'I've had the Mennecy set valued. You were right. It is genuine. I've decided to put it into auction and split the profit with you. After all had you not noticed it, I would have sold it for peanuts.'

'You don't have to split the profit, Vincent.' She smiled as she crossed to the cabinet and looked carefully at the set. 'I'm your employee.'

'I don't make offers lightly. That's my decision.' He glanced at the large open diary on the desk. 'We'll put it into the sale next week – with a reserve of course.'

Helen could scarcely believe her luck. 'I can't wait to see what it brings.' And, itching to tell Laura, she left the shop, her heart racing at the prospect. If the set went at the reserve price, she would far better be able to make ends meet with the extra bonus.

She quickened her pace, but, as she neared the

house, she noticed John's car was not in the drive. The front door was open and Laura was standing there, her eyes red-rimmed.

'Good Lord, what on earth is the matter?' Helen reached for her sister's arms and pulled her close, stroking her hair. 'It's not the children is it?' she asked, holding her at arm's length and searching her face.

'It's John. He's left me.' Looking frail and ashen, she leant against the doorframe, anxiety filling her eyes. 'He's gone off with one of his rich clients, Clarissa Brooksbank.' Helen was puzzled. John had always been the shoulder for Laura to lean on when things went wrong.

But despite Helen's wholehearted support, as time passed, Laura fell into a deep depression. And with no further explanation from John, day after day she tried to stop the tears but they flowed profusely. 'Why, Helen, why?'

Jack Bean, tall and ruggedly handsome, his mousy hair unkempt, pondered over his next move. He'd always fancied Helen Riley and if Jim Riley was anything to go by she seemed to like a bit of *rough*. Not only was she a looker but her family, her ma that is, had pots of money too.

There was no doubt about it Riley had been a right lucky blighter but, now he'd popped his clogs, Jack felt it was his turn to move in. Enough time had passed to make an approach as far as he was concerned.

He looked down at his grey flannelette shirt and home-made fair-isle pullover. He decided he needed to spruce himself up. His idea was to bump into Helen, as though by accident. With no man to warm her bed, she'd be feeling lonely. And he could soon put that right.

They were on short time at work, something to do with an order they'd lost. He'd already covered two of his three days and it was his morning off, but he'd forgotten to book it out. He slipped across to the mill to let the clerk know.

'I'm off today Maureen.' Jack gave her a wink.

'I'll let Mr. Charlesworth know. You'll be in tomorrow won't you, Jack?' Maureen stared adoringly. She had a soft spot for him. In her book, they were two of a kind.

'Aye, lass, don't fret. I've got to earn a bit to pay me way, and for me social life.' A mischievous grin spread across his face as he spun around and took the wooden stairs two at a time. He felt as fit as a flea.

He entered his ma's house in Newport Street and climbed the bedroom stairs at a fair old lick. It was obvious she hadn't heard him otherwise she would have been rushing around like a blue-arsed fly to put his cooked breakfast on the table before he'd barely had time to take in breath.

A blast of cold air hit him as he entered his bedroom. The damp and the chill cut into his bones and he shivered as he opened the door of the shabby oak wardrobe. He took out a dark navy jacket, laid it on the bed and picking up his grey flannel trousers from the back of the chair he slipped them on. Clutching the edge of the maroon candlewick bedspread he rubbed it briskly over his highly-polished black lace-ups. That did the trick; he could see his face in them.

59

He tucked the corner of the bedspread, now lightly smeared with black shoe polish, under the mattress and took the silver-backed hairbrush, the one his Uncle Wallace had bought for his twenty-first birthday, from the glass tray on the tallboy. Carefully applying a spot of Brylcream he brushed his hair vigorously, parting it at the side and slicking it down neatly. He was ready for the challenge.

As Helen headed towards the shop the warm sun caught her face and gave her a pleasant glow. Her head echoed with excitement at the thought of the forthcoming sale. The set had given her the buzz, not that the money Vincent had promised was inconsequential.

Her silver grey pin-striped suit was a little shabby now but her black patent leather shoes and matching handbag were still in good condition. The little black hat she bought for the funeral was tilted forward, the veil pulled over her forehead and the satin bow draped to one side enhancing her high cheek bones.

Glancing absently at the sparkling shop windows and preoccupied with thoughts of the new opportunities within her reach, at first she didn't hear his voice. But eventually, despite the noise of the traffic, it penetrated her thoughts.

'You're a million miles away, lass.' It was Jack Bean, a wide grin spread across his face. His measuring glance swept over her body as he gently took her hands in his and squeezed them. He maintained eye contact and in serious voice continued, 'I'm sorry about what's happened.' He pulled her closer.

'Thank you Jack. I appreciate your kind words.' She smiled weakly but, unaccustomed to his over-familiarity and aware of his nearness, she stiffened. His eyes were far from calm and the emotions swirling in their depths were too complex for her to decipher. She felt uneasy. When she drew herself slightly away he maintained his grip and his fingers tightened on hers.

'If there's anything I can do for you, you've only to ask,' he said breathing thickly.

She managed to slide her hands away from his grasp, and hoping to reflect an air of casual lightness, she lifted her voice. 'That's kind of you, Jack but we're coping fine at the moment.' She paused. 'I must dash.'

He caught hold of her hand again as she started to move away, his smile now brimming with sensual invitation. 'Don't shut me out, Helen. I meant what I said,' he urged impetuously, determination etched clearly on his chiselled features. But as he turned away and disappeared into the crowd, his image remained emblazoned on her mind.

The bell tinkled as she entered the shop. 'Good morning Vincent,' she said, her lively tone reflecting her mood.

Vincent stared, wide-eyed. 'You look a treat, my dear,' he said, smiling warmly. 'You're bound to make an impression at the saleroom.'

'Thank you for the compliment, Vincent. It does help to boost my confidence.'

'Mrs. Brumfitt will be here at half past ten to keep an eye on things. As soon as she arrives I'd like to get away,' he urged.

At ten fifteen the door opened and a poker-faced woman almost tripped over the threshold as she stumbled in. 'Upsy-daisy,' she said, a smile touching the corners of her mouth. Helen suppressed a giggle.

'You're in good time, Gertie,' Vincent observed, looking at the clock on the wall.

'I left early to get me shopping done cos shops are closed Wednesday afternoon,' she replied, barely stopping for breath. She slipped off her coat and slotted her head through a floral pinafore. 'There we are,' she concluded ready to start her cleaning.

'We'll do a spot of viewing before the sale starts, Helen,' Vincent suggested, taking his fawn raincoat from the stand, folding it carefully and placing it over his arm. He ushered her out of the shop and into his new Ford Popular car.

The saleroom was crowded with every kind of buyer, the well-to-do Potters Moor residents, the genuine antique dealers and the second-hand merchants. After waiting patiently the sugar bowl set was introduced and the interest in it was far more than Helen had ever expected. The bidding began and her excitement mounted. Much to her astonishment it continued until eventually two parties were in the running, Major Smythe, a well-known Potters Moor resident, and two smartly-dressed young men, neither of whom Helen recognised. One of them outbid Major Smythe and there was an undercurrent of mumbling in the room when the set went for well over the reserve price.

Vincent turned to her. 'There you are my dear,'

he said. 'We've made a tidy profit on that one, thanks to you.'

Helen was elated. Her share of the proceeds would provide a tidy little nest egg she could fall back on when the occasion arose.

Laura returned from dropping the children at school, the churning in her stomach constant. Her weight had plummeted since John had left and, on the few occasions he'd visited to see the children, he'd still refused to discuss their relationship.

Wrapping her arms around her slim body, she stared into space, her primary need being to escape, to get away from it all. The easiest way was to go back to bed. But unable to rid herself of the feeling of inadequacy, she pulled thoughts together. That was not the escape she needed; that was not the answer.

Determined to shrug off her depression, seconds later she was donning her mackintosh, galoshes and silk head scarf ready to set out towards the soft, rolling hills that encircled the village of Chatsbridge. The fresh air would be good for her, and the walk would give her time to rationalize her thoughts.

The grass towards the foothills was spongy and the morning air was scented with the perfumes of wild flowers. The sunlight glistened silver on the wet grass, its warmth penetrating her face and giving her a brush of comfort. A double rainbow appeared above and lit up the sky with a vivid, iridescent glow. But as she climbed, a band of cloud began to gather and lingered over the hills.

Her mind reverted to the past, as it often did these days and, savouring the moment of silence and the stillness that came with it, her thoughts rushed to her darling John. He was as handsome as she was beautiful. Everyone had remarked on the match; they were the perfect couple. But that was in the past. She had been a good wife to John, but had she become too complacent? Had she taken things for granted? Maybe she'd been too placid, too dull. Maybe it was excitement he was looking for. Perhaps she should have been more demonstrative.

But what was the use trying to analyse the situation. The future called. She must face up to reality. The way she looked at it, she had two alternatives. The first was to do nothing, to continue her role as a mother and see to the needs of the children. But where would that get her? When the boys were at school she would spend the majority of her time alone, fretting. The alternative was to take a job. But what would happen to her children, and Helen's two girls? How could she let Helen down after her own sad loss? But she had to do something to take away the hurt.

Her thoughts were interrupted by a rustling noise behind her and turning quickly, she was confronted by Jack Bean, his mouth curving into a sensual, insidious smile.

'I thought it was you, love. By gum you're a right bonny pair, you and your lass.' His rough voice vibrated through her as he caught his breath and moved closer. 'What's this I hear about your old man leaving you? He must be wrong in his bloody head.' He came closer still, his breath now in her face.

With a feeling of repugnance at his sudden appearance and his familiarity, Laura backed off. 'Hello, Jack,' she stuttered. 'I didn't realise it was common knowledge, but what brings you here?' Her heart began to pound. He scared her.

'Had a bit of business to attend to earlier on. Thought I'd come up for a bit of fresh air on me day off.' Stuffing his hands in his pockets, he swaggered alongside her and a thick rain-cloud of mist enveloped them. 'But what are you doing here?' A little unsteady on his feet, he pulled his hands from his pockets and spun round to face her.

'I needed the air too. I wanted to get out and be on my own.' She averted her gaze. There was something threatening about him. She could feel the hair on the nape of her neck stand up, and her mouth went dry.

'That makes two of us.' There was an ominous tone to his voice, a tone Laura feared. He moved closer and placed his arm around her shoulder, gripping her fiercely.

'What are you doing?' she said, sidestepping. But she slipped and tumbled on to the wet grass. And before she could push herself up, he was on top of her, his arms around her, his body pressing down and covering hers. She panicked even more.

'Is this what you wanted?' he asked, his eyes thinking her in lustfully. 'No need to scream. There's only you and me up here.' He thrust his warm lips on hers, his animal need for her becoming more certain.

Nausea spread within her and, making one last attempt to rid herself of him, she lifted her knee and thrust it violently into his groin. He groaned out loud, his face drained of its inflamed colour. Laura's muffled sobs were almost inaudible as she jerked herself away from him, her face contorted in deep revulsion. Knees bent, he rolled on the grass and cried out in pain. But still his gaze was menacing.

She quickly dragged herself to her feet, slid roughly on the grass, and steadying herself, she clutched at her mackintosh, setting off at an ungainly pace down the hill. She shivered both through shock and the cold dampness which had penetrated her body.

'Don't think you're too bloody grand for me, lass,' he called after her but she was too much in shock to respond and she continued to run.

She shuddered visibly, stumbling and slipping on the wet grass, desperate for home to remove any trace of Jack Bean from her body. Nobody must know what had happened.

But what she felt within her was an icy thirst for revenge!

Chapter 5

The taxi drew up outside Kirk Grange and Sarah grasped Laura's hand before stepping on to the drive. Her pace was slow as she gazed absently at the garden and she was taken in by its beauty.

'What a wonderful show this year. Mr. Coleman has done me proud.' The flowerbeds, crowded with marigolds, petunias and pansies, their beaming faces searching the sun, were a mass of vivid colour.

When she caught her reflection through the front window, she noticed how flatteringly indistinct it was. That was how she liked to look, good even though superficially. Once she was on top of things, she would be back to her old ways, making the very best of her appearance. Perhaps she had let herself go recently but her illness had meant her social calendar had been empty.

She continued to feel lethargic and that strange sensation tormented her each time she entered the house. Her mind reverted to the problem of the gas tap and she was unable to reconcile how she could have been so careless. Was she going senile? She hoped not.

Laura broke into her thoughts. 'You're welcome to stay with us, Mother. You know we've plenty of room, and the children would love it,' she offered.

Sarah sighed heavily. 'Thank you, darling, but I'd like some time to myself, just to rest.' Her voice was vague. Usually, she enjoyed the children's company, but she was too weary for that. Even her bridge sessions had been put on hold. Her mind was not sharp enough to cope with either the game itself or the comments of her friends.

'You know best, Mother.' Laura passed her hand soothingly over her heavy frown, her eyes shadowed with worry. 'How about a cup of tea?' she continued pleasantly.

Sarah moved into the lounge and sat down on

67

the Chesterfield. 'That would be lovely,' she replied, still feeling nervous about using the kitchen and turning on the gas. Aware that making the tea might remind Laura of the incident, she held her breath in the hope that she would not be given a lecture, yet again.

But that thought suddenly triggered Sarah's memory and amazingly the incident started to unravel in her mind. She remembered Agnes leaving and saying she didn't feel well. Later young Billy Lockwood called to see her as he did on occasion. She always felt sorry for him. One of nine children he was thirteen or fourteen years old and had an undernourished, uncared-for look about him. She offered him a cup of tea and went into the kitchen to make it. But seconds later she decided to offer him breakfast. It was then she caught him opening her handbag and taking out her purse. When she tried to grab the bag from him they struggled. She must have fallen and knocked her head against the table leg.

But she wasn't about to tell Laura of her recollection. There was sure to be another reprimand. The less her daughter knew the better. And, come to think of it, she saw no reason to inform the constable either.

But she realised later how foolish she'd been turning on the gas and not igniting it. She convinced herself she would have detected the smell of gas had Billy not struggled with her. He ran off and it was only much later that she discovered he had taken neither the purse nor the money. She sighed. It was lucky the milkman had called for his cheque and detected the smell, otherwise that would have been the end. She pacified herself with that in mind.

'A lovely cup of tea for you, Mother.' Laura soon appeared with the tea in delicate Victoriana Rose china cups, placing one on the small walnut coffee table next to the Chesterfield.

'That's what I look forward to,' Sarah enthused, sipping the tea slowly and savouring it. 'Not those awful thick mugs they produce at the hospital.'

Laura changed the subject. 'You know Helen's back at Waxman's don't you, Mother?'

'Waxman's? She's obviously determined to take nothing from me,' she sniffed, drawing a long shuddering breath. 'I suppose if she must work, Mr. Waxman is one of the best to be with.'

Their conversation was interrupted by the sound of a sharp knocking at the back door. Laura went to answer it and returned with Agnes Bean in tow. Agnes had a pinched look about her face, her lips a bluish colour as though she was cold.

'It's only me, Mrs. Conway. Thought I'd come and see how your ma's going on.'

'I've had my final check-up, Agnes. And not before time. It's been six months now,' Sarah chipped in, having heard her voice. 'Come and sit down. Are you all right, dear?' Sarah asked, her brow puckering into a frown.

'I'm as fit as a fiddle, Mrs. Dorrington. I've had a touch of angina on an off since last week but it's more off than on now,' she replied optimistically. Her weary shrug told Sarah otherwise.

'Do take care, dear. You do too much for that son of yours.' Sarah was very fond of Agnes and she knew Jack Bean had his mother constantly at his beck and call. She turned to Laura. 'It's three o'clock, darling. If you have to get back, I'll be fine now that Mrs. Bean's here.' She turned to Agnes. 'You're not in a rush are you?' Sarah took control, giving a strong hint that it was too bad if Agnes was in a hurry to leave.

Agnes shook her head.

'Are you sure you can cope, Mother? I could come back when I've collected the children from school.' Laura slipped on her tan swagger coat and matching hat.

'Do stop worrying, Laura. Everything's fine,' she replied almost shooing Laura out and waving her goodbye.

Folding her arms comfortably and turning to Agnes she said, 'Get yourself a cup of tea, dear and tell me what's been happening in the village.'

Laura sighed with relief, gratified Mother had refused her invitation to stay with them. She still hadn't explained about John. But now was not the right time. Aware of Mother's potential re-action, the longer she left it the more reluctant she became to tell her.

The sight of Mrs. Bean had reminded her of Jack and she felt ashamed as though she'd en-couraged him. She shuddered visibly. The inci-dent kept recurring in her mind but she tried to shake the memory free.

She hurried towards the school to collect Helen's girls and she put on a smile as they ran towards her, each clutching a handful of papers. She beamed affectionately as they proudly held them up for her to see. 'They're lovely pictures,

70

Sylvia, and what neat handwriting, Jessie,' she said. 'Mummy and I will look at them together when we're home.'

Twenty minutes later when she arrived to collect the boys she could hear Thomas calling from the far side of the playground.

'Mummy!' He ran towards her, his socks around his ankles, his chubby face searching hers adoringly. 'Is Daddy home yet?' Thomas asked the same question every day. She kissed him gently on the cheek. 'Mummy, I asked you a question,' he insisted, pulling on her arm impatiently.

Colin skulked along behind, his fair hair curling over his brow, his brown eyes unusually dull. He shrugged and a blaze of indignation flushed his cheeks.

'No, darling.' Laura gave no explanation. What could she say? How could she tell them the truth? She suspected Colin knew what was going on, but not Thomas who, at five, was still her baby.

By now the sky was beginning to lose its light and it looked as though a vivid lightning storm might be brewing as they walked the distance from Middleton Prep School to Crossgates. Laura hurried the children along. But the storm came suddenly and torrentially, the driving rain slanting almost horizontally into their faces as they entered the drive. John's car was parked outside and the boot was gaping open.

'Daddy's back,' Thomas shouted gleefully.

John was gazing out at the inclement weather when they reached the front door. Laura stared subconsciously. His smoky grey eyes seemed bigger than usual, giving him a look of innocence

71

as he pushed his thick, dark hair away from his forehead. Despite everything, she still loved him.

Seemingly aware of her thoughts, John darted a furtive glance then averted his eyes. His hair ruffled in the wind as he dashed out in the driving rain. As if in a trance, Laura watched him as rain trickled from her nose and dripped down her jacket. Her stomach churned relentlessly and her head felt fit to burst. She continued to stare unashamedly, her heart racing in her chest. But he had betrayed her. He had almost destroyed what remained of their love. As far as she was concerned, that had to be the end.

'When are you coming back?' Thomas pleaded.

'Hello, big boy.' John ignored the plea and, taking Thomas in his arms, he stepped into the hall and swung him around. He set the boy on his feet. 'Mummy and I need to have a little chat, darling,' he reasoned, scarcely looking at Laura.

'Come along, Thomas.' Laura pushed him gently through the hall, ignoring John.

'Laura, we need to talk things through,' he said, searching her face for a reaction. 'That's why I'm here.' He closed the door quietly behind him.

'I assumed you were here to collect some of your clothes,' Laura replied icily.

'Not at all,' he said, and they stood facing each other. Laura's usually lively face was full of worry and pain. But Colin was still there and he looked nervously up at his father.

John turned to him. 'Sorry old chap. I didn't mean to ignore you. It's just that you're almost grown up now,' he said, his face flushing in embarrassment as he squeezed Colin's hands and patted his head. Laura thought it a weak excuse, but she didn't express her feelings.

As if sensing what was needed, Colin took his brother's hand and led him into the kitchen. Laura and the girls followed, and she filled four tumblers with home-made lemonade. 'Play quietly in the sitting room. I need a word with Daddy,' she said gently.

They went into the dining room and sat facing each other like two strangers.

'Laura, believe me, I'm sorry this has happened.' He paused. 'You know I still love you, please remember that. But there's no easy way to explain it,' he stuttered. 'I don't know what came over me.' He spat out the words as if he had rehearsed them, hesitated for a moment and then continued.

'Clarissa came into my life just after Jim died. She wanted me, she flattered me – I suppose that's why I was taken in. You neglected me, Laura.' With a pettish look on his face he averted his eyes.

There was a time when she would have been taken in by such a comment and such a look, but not anymore. 'I see. So it's my fault?' she huffed. 'How can you say you still love me after what's happened?' She hid her contempt behind narrowed lips, determined to keep her cool now that she had started a new life. After the attack that morning, she no longer needed a man. And there was no way John would upset her ever again.

'I'm torn in two, Laura. Clarissa says she can't live without me.' He hesitated for a moment. 'She tells me that if I leave her, her life will be in ruins.

What can I do?'

'You mustn't disappoint her.' Laura's reply was laced with sarcasm. 'What's the problem John?' she asked, aware that her behaviour was totally out of character.

'I want to come back, but I can't make a decision. My mind's in turmoil,' he confessed, his eyes misting over.

'I don't think you have a choice in the matter. I don't want you back.' Her words didn't come easily nor were they said in an act of bravado. If he thought he could play games with her emotions he was wrong.

Obviously shaken by her frankness, his mouth dropped open and his grey eyes registered their disbelief.

'I'm sure we can come to some amicable agreement for you to have access to the children,' she continued. 'The last thing I want is for them to suffer,' she said gravely, now completely calm and composed.

'You've got it all wrong, Laura. Just because I'm concerned for Clarissa doesn't mean I don't love you. I always have and I always will.' Panicking visibly at her cool and relaxed manner, he tried to charm his way out of the trouble, waffling on with a weak and insubstantial explanation.

Laura seemed to lose all respect for him. He was certainly helping her to come to terms with the situation. 'As I said, we'll make some arrangements for the children.' She was perfectly calm. 'And by the way, I'm thinking of taking a job which means I'll need a nanny to look after them until I'm home. I take it you'll agree to pay.' She pushed herself up from the chair and looked down at him, her hands on her slim hips. Once again, she detected his panic and he quickly stood up and confronted her. How handsome he was with his strong, regular features. She watched him as he stood there pensively, and her heart skipped a beat. She felt a warm blush slip through her body. But she stood firm, she controlled her urges.

'Now look here, darling. I don't think you know what you're saying. Sit down and we'll reason it out,' he replied, the words tumbling out.

'I've reasoned it out, John and made my decision,' she said crisply. 'All we need now is to sort out your access to the children,' she added, her words giving finality to the situation. She turned and walked towards the hall door. 'Come along now, boys. Daddy has to go.'

John reached out and slipped his strong arms around her waist, trying to spin her round to face him. But she refused to budge. 'Laura, darling, don't do this to me. You're breaking my heart.'

'You've already broken mine John,' she sighed, 'irreparably.'

'Don't go yet, Daddy.' Thomas started to snivel. 'You haven't played with us.'

John stared accusingly at Laura.

'Daddy will take you out at the weekend, won't you Daddy?' Laura stared back, daring him to refuse.

'I'll pick you up on Sunday at ten o'clock, both of you.' He squeezed Colin affectionately. Colin looked away, not wanting to be caught with tears in his eyes. John gave Thomas a kiss and held him close. He let go and smiled. 'Be ready,' he said and he walked towards the front door.

'Please reconsider,' he whispered to Laura. 'It can't end like this.'

But she left him alone with his thoughts and as he approached the car he turned, giving her a last begging look. He wanted it all. But that wasn't possible. Laura wanted to run to him, put her arms around him, to be close once again. But she was strong now, stronger than she had ever been.

'Helen, I'm not offering to buy you the house,' Sarah Dorrington, veiled in seven years' guilt, insisted. 'I'll still own it. It's not charity.' She was aware she was on shaky ground.

'Mother, I can stand on my own two feet. We're perfectly happy where we are.' Helen's voice was cool.

Sarah recognised her daughter's emphatic gesture. She was just like her father, refusing to give in. But surely she could forgive her own mother, allow her to make up for the lost years. But, wise enough to drop the subject for now, she muttered, 'As you wish.' She smiled. 'How are you finding the job at Waxman's?' She tried to keep the conversation light, yet she wanted to probe and to find out as much as possible, especially about Helen's financial circumstances.

'I'm really enjoying it. We sold a beautiful china set last week, one Vincent hadn't recognised as being of much value. We put it in the sale in Clifton and it brought quite a tidy sum. Vincent split it with me.' Her eyes sparkled with pleasure. 'I've decided to put the money on one side for now. So you see we're not on the bread line yet.'

'I'm delighted for you, darling,' Sarah said but, judging by her tone she was obviously not interested in Helen's success and she changed the subject again. 'Don't you think Laura's looking peaky? I've tried to find out what's wrong but she gives nothing away.'

'It may be my fault. She is looking after the girls as well as Colin and Thomas.'

'It's more than that; I know it is, but what?' Sarah's tenacity kept her delving.

Helen stood up. 'I must leave now. Is there anything you need before I go?'

Sarah, constantly filled with remorse at her earlier behaviour towards Jim was at least grateful Helen had accepted her back. 'Thank you, darling but Mrs. Bean's coming today. She can sort me out.'

Helen pulled open the door, and the air was cool as she stepped into the hall. A picture on the wall caught her eye, one she hadn't noticed before. It was the most aesthetically pleasing watercolour landscape she'd seen since her college days. She scrutinized it carefully, guessing it to be a Jongkind, one of the Impressionist painters. But she was unable to make out the signature clearly. She left the house but she couldn't resist checking it out and she hurried towards the college. It was becoming a habit, but so exciting bringing alive her thirst for knowledge. First the china set and now the picture.

It was already dark and gloomy and the yellow translucence of the lights shone down on the street which was vibrant with life and full of bustling people. The traffic was heavier than usual, making it difficult for Helen to cross the road and she dodged between a Lipton's van and a motorbike and sidecar, carefully picking her way through the stationary traffic held up by a tram spilling out its passengers. Once across, she dashed up the stone steps, entered the library and moved to the section on watercolour.

The tome was heavy and she struggled to lift it down. She flicked to the chapter on Dutch artist, Jongkind, the one she believed had painted the landscape. But she was wrong. It was not his work; the style and colours were different. Within the chapter, reference was made to a contemporary of his, Camille Pissarro, a Frenchman. There was no reference to that particular picture when she skimmed through the pages, but having studied his style carefully she felt certain it was his work. What she needed to establish was the authenticity of the picture. Was it an original or a very good fake?

Laura laid the table for six and returned to the kitchen, the succulent aroma of roast lamb bringing Colin in from the sitting room.

'Is it nearly ready, Mummy? I'm starving,' he wailed, his brow creasing. He had such a huge appetite these days; it was a major task filling him.

'It won't be long Colin. I'm sure Aunt Helen will soon be here.'

It was not usual for Helen to stay for dinner but Laura had asked her specially. She needed the chance to discuss her own future and she was toying things over in her mind when Helen arrived looking excited.

'The Pissarro picture in Mother's hall, the land-scape, is it genuine or just a copy?' Helen's eagerness spilled over, a flush rising sharply to her cheeks as she rubbed her hands together and stared enthusiastically at Laura.

'I know very little about it, Helen. It was one Daddy bought just before he died. Mother will surely be able to throw more light on it.' Laura's voice was flat. Inwardly she resented Helen's enthusiasm, but she was curious to know why it should be so special. She continued. 'Is there any particular reason why you've picked on that one?'

'I fell in love with it immediately I saw it. I adore the work of the Impressionists.' Helen fumbled with her buttons, slipped off the coat and hung it on the hall stand. She stretched to ease the tiredness from her spine. 'There's no clear signature on the piece and I've tried to check out the artist.'

'You'll need to talk to Mother,' Laura replied, showing her lack of interest by closing the subject sharply. 'Are you ready for the meal, Helen? The children are starving.' Colin was back under her feet and so hungry his face was a picture of misery.

'Yes, of course and it smells wonderful. Sorry I've been so long,' she offered following the children into the dining room. 'Hello my cherubs,' she whispered, and they laughed, turning and clasping their arms around her hips and squeezing her.

Sylvia looked up. 'Are we going home after dinner or are we staying here, Mummy?'

'Would you like to stay?' Laura intervened, having primed them earlier on the possibility.

'Yes, yes,' they chorused in unison.

The roast lamb was delicious. Laura had excelled herself. John had always been impressed by the way she conjured up a variety of delicacies. Pudding was scrumptious too; cinnamon flavoured braised apricots served with custard. The children asked for seconds which delighted Laura. In her role as wife and mother it had always given her great satisfaction to see them relishing their food. That had been her forte, until now. But things were about to change. The thread of irritation running through her convinced her that never again would she be an appendage to any man. She was no longer prepared to be patronised. If Helen could play the businesswoman, she could too.

After the meal and when the children were tucked up in bed she poured two glasses of sherry and only then did she broach the subject of the future.

'It's not that I need the money, Helen, but I do need a new and satisfying interest. Most of all I need to feel wanted again, especially after what's happened.' She perched nervously on the edge of the chair, her animated gestures reflecting her determination to make something of herself.

'I understand completely,' Helen replied. 'You've no idea how much I'm getting out of being back at the shop. It's so exhilarating. I think I'm better with the children too.'

Helen's support was exactly what Laura was looking for. 'I've mentioned it to John, but of course, he's not in agreement – he thinks my place is in the home with the children and all that business. But I'll not give in, Helen,' she returned bitterly, relaxing a little more easily in her chair. 'I've suggested to John that I take on someone to look after the children – pick them up from school, prepare a meal and so on. Again he's not happy about it.' She paused and swallowed nervously before continuing. 'And that brings me to the problem of Jessie and Sylvia. I feel awfully mean, but I really can't do both, look after them and hold down a job,' she explained, now preoccupied with her own future.

'Don't worry, I understand. You have yourself to think about now. I'll sort out my own problems.' Helen smiled, apparently reluctant to dampen Laura's enthusiasm as she took a sip of her sherry. 'How about if I pay half and we share a nanny?'

On the surface, it seemed a mutually beneficial solution, but Laura was against the idea. 'I'm sorry darling, but I'm adamant John takes responsibility. Sharing would complicate matters. Maybe you could do the same and set someone on,' Laura added flippantly.

Helen realised that was a non-starter. It would be difficult hoping to employ someone to work at her rented house in Emley Street and she felt a gnawing in the pit of her stomach as the awful realisation dawned. She was back where she started with no-one to look after the children. It was bound to lead to her giving up the job and her mind struggled to hold on to that crucial fact.

'Have you thought seriously about the sort of job you might apply for?' Helen asked, pulling her thoughts together but anxiety sharpening her voice.

'You know my flair for interior design – I thought I could offer my services.' Laura's face now held a look of confidence.

'That sounds wonderful,' Helen replied with genuine admiration for her sister.

'After the dreariness of the war years, there could be several people in Potters Moor and Chatsbridge who could be interested.' She smiled as she picked up the poker and stirred the bed of coals glowing in its centre. The bright, flickering flames cast dancing reflections on the pale walls and the silence between the two sisters lasted for a long moment, disturbed only by the coals settling in the grate.

Despite her own problems Helen was attuned to her sister's feelings and was keen to support her. 'The sort of people you're talking about would probably regard quality antiques as a status symbol, an investment too. I recently saw Major Smythe bidding for our porcelain set. His wife probably sent him for it. I could suggest items to complement the decor if that would help.'

'I don't want to take on too much all at once, Helen. I'd prefer to start on my own.'

'Just a thought, nothing more,' Helen replied digesting Laura's comment and realising she had not given the offer any consideration. Laura had always managed to get her own way. As a child, she was the one who could twist Mother around her little finger. Of course she took after Mother who had that technique too, especially with Father.

Marrying John had been a popular move. John was one of the partners at Bentley's solicitors,

Laura his secretary. Apparently they had an instant affinity for each other. Mother was delighted at the catch, constantly trotting out her theory that Laura was the one with common-sense. John, who came from a middle-class family, had a promising career with prospects and money in the bank. His credentials were good. Conversely Helen's love for Jim had been infinite and her determination to marry him, with or without Mother's approval, was an invincible force.

She pulled her thoughts together as Laura opened the sideboard drawer, took out a card and handed it to Helen.

'This is my first stab at a business card. What do you think of the design?'

Helen reached across and read it carefully. 'It's super. Laura Conway, Interior Design. It sounds grand.' She smiled. 'I do hope it works for you,' she said with genuine concern.

'I don't want to advertise. Mother would be furious. So I've decided to ask Bernard and Wini-fred Wallace if they'd mention it to their friends. You know the number of parties they have,' she offered, slipping the card back in the drawer.

'Good idea.' Helen paused. 'By the way, have you told Mother about John?' she asked, the comment prompting Helen into mentioning her earlier conversation with Mother.

'No. I haven't. I can't face telling her, although I know I must do so at some point in time,' she admitted, a frown sketching her face.

'She thinks you're looking peaky. She'll chip away until she finds out what it is. If I were you

I'd get it over with.'

'I'll think about it. You wouldn't come with me would you, Helen?' she begged.

Chapter 6

That familiar smell of roses permeated the hall as they entered Kirk Grange.

'How lovely to see you both.' Sarah patted the sofa beside her, inviting the girls to sit down. 'You're looking serious, Laura. I was saying to Helen how peaky you looked.' She searched Laura's face for some explanation.

'I have good reason,' Laura confessed. 'You're not going to like this, Mother,' she continued, the words escaping in a soft whisper. 'John has left me for one of his rich clients, Clarissa Brooksbank.' She sighed, her voice now surprisingly controlled. She'd done it, confronted her strongest critic, Mother. Now for the battle!

Sarah's face became tight with anger and a blaze of indignation stained her cheeks pink. 'Good grief, woman. Clarissa Brooksbank? She's older than you.' She shook her head in amazement and gave a bitter, mirthless laugh. 'What are you doing about it? You've tried to get him back I hope.' Her voice was mocking. 'In my book,' she continued, her voice laced with sarcasm, 'men don't leave their wives if things are right at home. Dear God, I could understand a younger woman, but Clarissa Brooksbank!'

'Don't go on, Mother. I don't want John back. It's quite some time since he left. I've ridden the storm. Forget it,' she stammered.

But the revelation had rocked her. 'Forget it! How am I going to face my friends at the Bridge Circle? It's scandalous. What are they going to think, I ask you?' She didn't try to disguise her petulance as she gazed sourly at Laura.

'It's none of their business. You must tell them so.' Helen was concerned to protect her sister and determined Mother would not upset her further. 'If you're going to make things more difficult for Laura, then we'll leave,' she threatened politely.

'Don't do that,' Sarah was quick to reply. 'But surely you can understand how upset I am.'

Helen folded her arms and shook her head. This was Mother's way, the drama and the blackmail. 'It's not about you and your friends, Mother. It's about Laura and John.'

As a gesture of defiance Laura stood up and walked towards the door, impatience shimmering through her. 'I can't take any more. Really I can't.' Her eyes glistened and she brushed at them impatiently, darting a look at Mother, who opened her arms and walked slowly across to her. But the shadow on Laura's face remained.

'Sorry I've gone on, darling. I won't mention it again until you're ready to talk.'

'I'll hold you to that, Mother.'

There was a period of silence until, to Laura's relief, Helen changed the subject and steered the conversation to the picture. 'The lovely landscape in the hall, Mother, how long have you had it?'

'Daddy bought it when he went to London with Clifford Paxton. I've never been quite sure of the artist; the signature seems a bit blurred, a bit faint. Why do you ask?' She frowned, hesitating as if recalling that moment.

'I was taken by it when I spotted it the other day. Is it an original?' Helen stood up and went into the hall where the picture hung. 'It's delightful. How long have you had it?'

'It's the last thing Daddy bought me Helen. I wouldn't want to sell it, if that's what you're thinking.' Her brow furrowed even more.

'I'm not asking you to do that, Mother.' She touched the picture lovingly.

'If you're so fond of the picture Helen, I'd like you to have it. It'll still be in the family.' She beamed fondly.

'Oh, I couldn't. Not when it's one of the last things Daddy bought you.'

'I insist, darling. It's the least I can do when you're so fond of it,' she said, starting to lift the picture down from the wall.

'Let me do that, Mother. It's far too heavy for you.' Helen reached up and lifted it down, gazing as though mesmerised. It was even more beautiful than she had realised. But she needed some indication of Laura's agreement to Mother's offer and, flashing a quick glance towards her, Helen noticed she had a slightly peevish look on her face. Aware that Mother usually favoured Laura, a moment of indecision prevented Helen from responding immediately. But common sense told her to take it. It was Mother's wish. 'I'll bring you a replacement from the shop. But are you sure you want me to have it? I won't let it go, I promise,' Helen replied, elated and smiling joyously.

'My decision's made, darling. Take it.' She flicked the back of her hand towards the picture. 'It was never one of my favourites.'

Back in Emley Street Helen hung the landscape over the china cabinet in the sitting room, away from the fire where the smoke might cause damage and discolouration. She stood back to admire it.

But the following morning her thoughts suddenly turned to her dilemma and the awful realisation dawned. Her sister had left her in a terrible plight. It would be a major problem continuing with the job with no-one to look after the girls. She must tell Vincent about her predicament. There was nothing to be gained by prolonging the matter.

She adjusted the oval mirror above the sideboard and gazed vacantly as she brushed her long hair, struggling to fashion it into a horseshoe roll. She left the house and headed for the bus stop. The bus was early and within minutes she was opening the door to the shop.

She may as well get it over with. 'I'm afraid I have some bad news, Vincent.'

'And what's that, my dear?' Vincent looked up as he played nervously with his tie.

'Laura has decided to start a job and she can't have my girls out of school hours or when they're on school holidays. I'm sorry, Vincent. It looks as though I'll have to leave,' she admitted.

She was surprised when he seemed relaxed about the news. 'Surely we can work something

87

out between us.'

'Really!' She sighed with relief.

'Of course. I'm not going to lose you now.'

'Thank you so much, Vincent,' she added, her frown giving way to a smile. 'You know I'll make an all-out effort to fit in.'

'Think no more about it,' he stressed.

Helen's focus turned to selecting a replacement for Mother. She chose a framed Monet *Water Lilies Pond,* the one arched with a Japanese bridge. 'I'd like to buy this for Mother. I know it's just a print, but she adores Monet.' Helen swung the picture round in her hands to face Vincent.

'Good choice, Helen. You can have it at cost,' he replied casually.

'Thank you, Vincent. I'm sure Mother will be delighted. I can't afford an original watercolour, not even one painted by a local artist,' she admitted.

When she'd finished work at the shop, she took the brown paper parcel to Kirk Grange. Mother tugged at the string, opened it up and stared, her face aglow with pleasure. 'That's better. You know how much I love Monet, darling. Hang it in the hall for me will you?' Helen took the picture through and Mother followed, rubbing her hands together gleefully. 'It fits in beautifully. I'm delighted.'

'I can't stay, Mother. I must collect the girls from school.' She needed to catch the next bus to be back in Kidsworth in time for the children. 'I'm really pleased with the Pissarro landscape, Mother. Thank you so much once again.' Helen bent and kissed her on the cheek.

'As far as I'm concerned, darling, it's a deal.'

Agnes arrived early at Kirk Grange and hung up her coat on the hall stand. But she was puzzled when she realised the landscape picture was missing, the one Mrs. Dorrington had bequeathed her in her will. Not that she liked the picture any more than the others, but it was worth a bob or two. When Mr. Dorrington bought it as a present for his wife, Agnes had heard him telling a friend of its value. After Mr. Dorrington's sudden death, in view of what she'd heard, Agnes was more than rapturous about the picture, knowing the story behind it. Mrs. Dorrington, apparently unaware of its value said, 'If you like it so much, Mrs. Bean, I'll leave it to you in my will as a token of my gratitude.'

But now it seemed her promise had been forgotten and that the token of gratitude was no longer on offer. In its place was a flowery picture. But she couldn't ask Mrs. Dorrington outright what had happened to the other picture, although there was no reason why she couldn't give her the hint.

She busied herself cleaning the sitting room carpet ith the new Hoover vacuum cleaner. There was no sign of the picture in there and, once upstairs, she checked the main bedroom. It wasn't there either.

After a quick flick around the other three bedrooms with a duster she rummaged in the cupboards and under the beds to see if the picture had been tucked away. But still there was no sign of it.

She just couldn't get it out of her head. Mrs. Dorrington had definitely promised her the picture. And she deserved it after the way they'd treated her Godfrey at the mill, calling it early retirement when really he'd been given the sack.

Back downstairs, Agnes decided to try another ploy. 'I like the new picture,' she announced, flicking the feather duster over it.

'Yes. It is lovely isn't it? Monet's one of my favourite artists.'

That was the end of that. There was no explanation.

Aware that Mrs. Dorrington seemed a bit forgetful these days, Agnes wondered if maybe since the gas leak her memory had deteriorated. She sighed. Come what may, she was determined to get to the bottom of the mystery, although if it had been sold or given away, the terms of the will would be meaningless.

'Well, I'll be off,' Agnes called through from the kitchen, realising all her efforts had been futile.

'Just a moment, Mrs. Bean. I haven't paid you.' Mrs. Dorrington followed her through holding out her hand with the four shillings and sixpence she owed Agnes. 'Thank you very much, dear.'

She hadn't forgotten the money so how come she'd forgotten her promise to leave Agnes the picture?

The three twenty was the last bus before the schoolchildren flooded out. Agnes knew if she missed it, the next one would be full. She was out of breath when she reached the stop but her spirits were raised when, in the distance, she saw the red single-decker approaching. It stopped;

she climbed the high step and plonked herself on the side seat.

'You're looking tired, Agnes. Been cleaning have you?' Gertie Brumfitt, sitting at the front of the bus, bobbed her head around the pole and called out.

'I've just finished, Gertie.' Agnes feigned a smile. Gertie could be so common at times. Fancy, calling out down the bus and letting the whole world know her business! 'Come and sit here next to me,' she mouthed, poking her finger on the seat.

Gertie picked up her shopping basket and trundled down the bus, almost reeling with its movement but managing to steady herself. 'I haven't seen you for ages, Agnes.' Gertie shuffled her ample bottom into the empty space and jiggled about with the basket on her knee. Before Agnes could reply, Gertie continued. 'I heard about the gas leak.' With a hungry look on her face, she waited for Agnes to give her rendition.

'Nasty business. But Mrs. Dorrington's all right now, thank goodness,' Agnes replied, cutting the topic short. The gas incident was the last thing she wished to discuss.

It was quite a trudge from the bus stop. She was tired and the business of the picture was starting to get her down. And she wished she'd never told Jack about it. He always had to poke his nose in. She stumbled. She must get her shoes off soon. They'd told her at Wilsons shoe shop they were soft leather but the way they were pressing hard on her bunions made her wonder if it was all sales talk. She traipsed towards the corner of Hardwick Street and noticed a bobby on point duty. It was

PC Clarke. Hoping she'd seen the last of him, she scuttled along head down. Proper nuisance he was asking all those questions. She pushed open the back door and it caught on Jack's bike.

'What've you brought that thing in here for?' she scolded loudly as she looked down and saw the mud on the front tyre. 'It's no good me putting me back into scrubbing the floor when all you do is mucky it. Have a bit of gumption Jack!' She sighed through pursed lips as she placed her shopping bag on the kitchen chair, unlaced her shoes and carefully eased them off. 'Ee, I needed that,' she said, breathing heavily and whistling through her teeth as she rubbed her feet vigorously.

'Stop your nagging, Ma. Saves bus fares this does.' He tapped the front tyre.

Agnes limped across to the fireside chair, sat down and stretched her toes on the rag rug, revelling in its comfort. 'It's gone, Jack,' she blurted, expecting Jack to read her thoughts.

'You what?' Jack was used to this kind of thing. 'What the heck you talking about?' He dipped the inner tube into a bowl of water on the floor. She spotted him.

'You can stop that! I told you I scrubbed the floor this morning. Can't you do it outside?' she ranted, staring at the wet marks across the green marble-effect lino.

'Stop wittering. Shan't be long.' He dried off the inner tube and chalked it up. 'What was you saying, Ma? What's gone?' he asked, continuing to repair the tube.

'Picture, that's what. I've searched high and low. It's nowhere to be seen. I hope she hasn't sold it.'

Jack looked up but gazed blankly. Her words seemed to take a few seconds to register. 'The one she left you in her will Ma?' He frowned. 'My God, she'd better not have. We've got our hopes stitched up on that picture. It's worth a fortune,' he growled between clenched teeth. He tipped the bowl of water down the sink. 'She might have given it to one of girls. I don't think she'll have sold it, Ma,' he continued lightly, trying to mask his apparent anger.

'Why should she give it to one of lasses? She knows she's promised it to me.' Agnes sulked, allowing the resentment to build up again.

'Stop panicking. We'll get to the bottom of it. Leave it with me,' he vouched, a flicker of amusement replacing the fury in his eyes, his lips curling into a malicious sneer.

'And what do you think you can do about it?' Agnes stood up, hands on hips, worried now she might have overstepped the mark once more by telling him too much.

Jack tapped the side of his nose a couple of times with his forefinger. 'Never you mind, Ma. I said leave it with me,' he insisted as he took his jacket from the hook behind the door and put on his cap.

He assembled his bike again and wheeled it out into the back yard. He needed to look into the business of the picture. If the old bat had given it to one of the lasses, he hoped it was Helen. Now that he'd mucked his ticket with the other one, he'd no chance of getting it back. But if he visited Helen, maybe he could find out exactly what was going on. Of course he'd have to be careful not to let her know he was checking up.

Mavis next door was unpegging her washing from the outside line as he walked down the path and crossed the yard. He gave her a look of contempt as he set off down the street whistling, thinking to himself that she'd probably been doing a bit of 'entertaining', as she called it. They must be wrong in their bloody heads paying for it. He'd either get it for nowt, or do without. That was his motto.

Helen hurried towards the bus-stop. The girls were due out of school at half past three and when it finally arrived, she sat down on the lower deck and considered the situation. She still had her job, she didn't have to leave the girls with anyone and she had the precious landscape. For the first time since she had lost Jim, she felt a sense of security.

The girls were waiting at the gate as she rushed towards the school. 'Hello my cherubs.' Helen kissed both girls and they smiled up at her. 'How about if I buy you sherbet dips for being good girls,' she suggested, offering a penny to Jessie and that brought an even bigger smile to her face.

When they reached the shop she pushed the two girls inside. Jessie placed the penny on top of a pile of newspapers on the counter before reaching across for two sherbet dips.

'That's right,' the assistant said, smiling. 'Two sherbet dips, ha'penny each?'

'Don't open them until we get back or the sherbet might blow away,' Helen warned as the wind pressed down on them.

Nell was barking excitedly as they reached the door. 'She's waiting for us, Mummy,' Sylvia cried, clapping her hands gleefully and almost dropping the sherbet dip on to the path.

Helen soon set about cooking braised liver and onions in the side oven whilst the girls started to do a jigsaw, a portrait of Princess Elizabeth and Philip Mountbatten, a present from Grandma. The evening meal was late and by then it was almost bed-time.

'Please, Mummy, just a few minutes to finish the jigsaw,' Jessie begged.

'Half an hour but no more or you'll not get up for school tomorrow. And you won't finish the jigsaw tonight, darling.' She laughed.

Once the girls were tucked up in bed, Helen read *Cinderella* to them and when Sylvia was sound asleep Helen kissed Jessie and went downstairs where she picked up the fair-isle cardigan she was knitting. The pattern was complicated and she had to concentrate to make sure she didn't mix up the coloured yarns. But no sooner had she started than a loud rapping on the back door startled her.

'Who is it?' she called as she approached the door.

'Me,' was the response. The voice was muffled and one she did not immediately recognise. She put on the chain guard for protection, turned the key and the latch went up. There on the doorstep was Jack Bean. He gave Helen a beaming smile as she slipped off the guard and opened the door wider.

Jack stared hard. There was no doubt about it she was a beauty, a right cracker if ever there was one, even with that poker face telling him she was not best pleased to see him. But, controlling his lust, as he knew he must after the fiasco with that posh sister of hers, he smiled and looked her squarely in the face. 'I told you I cared Helen. I just called to see if you're all right.' He stepped over the threshold and into the living room.

'You made me jump, Jack,' she replied, not looking particularly overjoyed to see him. But he could work on that. One step at a time.

'Sorry about that.' He moved across and stood on the hearth rug in front of the fire, rubbing his hands together at the anticipated warmth. 'It's a bit parky tonight. A cup of tea would go down well. It'd warm the cockles,' he said laughing.

'Of course, Jack. I'll put the kettle on,' she said a little reluctantly, turning towards the fire and placing the heavy black kettle on the hob.

'I won't stay long. I wondered if there was anything I could do for you,' he continued. She didn't reply but she smiled and seemed to relax once he'd spelled out his reason for calling.

Whilst her back was turned, Jack surveyed the room. He was surprised she'd stayed in a place like this. It was no better than his mother's house, comfortable but basic. His ma had told him Mrs. Dorrington had offered to buy Helen a house nearby. But Helen had refused it. Women! They weren't easy to understand at the best of times. But he'd soon get the measure of this one.

He looked across at her and smiled sardonically, thinking to himself it was time he had a handsome dollop of good fortune. What he could do for Helen was nobody's business! But he needed to bide his time. No good stepping in like he had with the other one. He'd been a damned fool, rushing it like that. He'd have to learn to keep his trousers buttoned.

'Are you sure there's nothing you need doing, love? Kids' shoes mending? I'm a dab hand at cobbling.' He gave her a sidelong glance and, rolling his eyes in an exaggerated fashion, he started to laugh.

'Jack, you are a joker.' Off her guard, Helen joined in with his infectious laughter. 'Thanks for the offer but there's nothing at present.'

'Your ma seems to be pulling herself round,' he said as she handed him a cup of tea.

'Help yourself to milk and sugar, Jack,' she offered, passing him a spoon. 'Yes. She's improving daily.' She picked up the milk jug and, slipping off the blue beaded cover, she handed it to him.

There was a call from upstairs. 'Mummy!'

Helen dashed to the bottom of the stairs. 'What is it darling?'

'Mummy, come up,' the child whimpered.

'Coming darling.'

Jack heard her footsteps on the stairs. He stood up and strained to peer into the front room. There it was – his ma's picture. Elated, he breathed a sigh of relief. At least that was solved. He knew what he was up against now.

Deciding not to outstay his welcome, he drained the tea from his cup and pushed himself up from the chair, moving towards the door. Within seconds, Helen was back downstairs again.

97

'Sorry about that, Jack. It was Sylvia. A nasty dream but she went straight off again.' She looked across at the empty cup. 'Are you going already?'

'Yes. I'll be off now, love. I just wanted to make sure you were alright,' he repeated before taking hold of the door handle. He turned, once more taking in her beauty. He'd make her want, that's what he'd do. He'd take things slowly. 'Take care now,' he said. 'I'll call again.'

Chapter 7

Laura's first commission came from Bernard and Winifred and, filled with excitement, she sallied forth armed with sketch pad, and wallpaper and fabric swatches borrowed from Kingston's. 'I have several ideas,' she offered.

'I can't wait to see them,' Winifred confessed.

Laura proudly flicked through the pages of the sketch pad pointing out designs she'd prepared in advance. 'If we remove the dado and picture rails,' she said, hoping not to offend them by criticising their dark floral wallpaper, 'we could give the walls a panelled effect with simpler lines. I suggest autumn shades.' She handed over the designs.

Winifred studied them. 'I like this one, Bernard,' she said, pointing to her favourite.

'Did you say autumn colours, Laura? How about the carpet? Rust – don't you think?' he pressed, wanting to put his own stamp on things.

'I thought predominantly gold, Bernard,' she

replied tentatively, keen to please but wishing to make a success of the scheme.

'A good alternative,' Bernard was quick to point out. 'I was talking to Gordon Bristow at the club yesterday,' he added. 'He reckons Dora would be interested in your designs. He likes to please her. She's not very bright but she suits Gordon to a tee.'

Laura stopped herself from replying adversely to his chauvinistic comment. Business is business and the customer is always right apparently. 'Excellent. I'd be delighted to help. I'll contact Dora.'

Bernard gave a slow, judicious nod, and it crossed her mind what a patronising, egocentric prig he was.

After leaving the Wallaces to digest her proposals, Laura called on Mother. The boys would be in bed and Phyllis, the new nanny, would have everything ready for the following day. She was lucky to have found Phyllis who had previously worked for Lady Winterbourne.

Laura was elated with the start she'd made and she gazed up at the sky which glowed with a flush of golden peach. The long, hot days of summer had brought forth a profusion of flowers and their perfumes lingered in the evening air. A kind of serenity wrapped itself around her and, delighted, she dwelt on the first reactions to her new venture. It was the start of her new life.

Sarah thought it odd that Agnes kept referring to the landscape she'd given Helen. But she pulled her thoughts together when she saw Laura walking along the drive.

'It's so good to see you, Laura darling,' she said, hugging her daughter affectionately.

'Just a quick visit, Mother. I've been to the Wallace's. They've asked me to re-style the sitting room and I think they're quite pleased with my designs,' she explained smugly.

'I don't approve, darling.' Sarah's response was deliberately cutting. Reluctant to listen to Laura's account of her progress, she shook her head. 'Why you have to resort to going out to work, Laura, I will never know. Daddy would not have approved.' Sarah's eyes betrayed her lack of enthusiasm.

'Mother, don't start again. You know it's not the money. It's a case of retaining my sanity,' Laura snapped.

'But how will you manage to buy material for the curtains? Your customers will need to give you coupons.'

'They're clients, Mother not customers. And don't you think I haven't thought it through? You know the likes of Bernard will 'acquire' the coupons somehow,' she said, giving a knowing look and smiling. 'And I've a feeling the government is hoping to abolish them next year.' She sat on the sofa. 'Don't try putting obstacles in my way' she stressed. 'It won't help. My mind is made up.'

'You've made your point, darling,' Sarah answered a little wearily, changing the subject abruptly, as was her wont when things became sticky. 'Dr. Jenkinson popped in to see me the other day. He thinks I needed a break. I thought maybe Harrogate. I wondered if you'd come with me, darling, especially now you have Phyllis to organise the boys.' She managed her pleading look.

Laura was quick to respond. 'Sorry, Mother. I'm going to be rather busy now I've committed myself to Winifred and Bernard's decor.'

Sarah sighed. Gone were the days when she could dictate her wishes. Middle age, she refused to call it old age, was something she couldn't get used to. During the last few months, especially since the gas episode, she'd felt more lethargic than ever. And the constant hints that she'd been negligent didn't help.

'Apparently Gordon Bristow has shown an interest in having designs prepared for Dora. It's so exciting, Mother.'

Sarah gave a slow blink. What was new? Laura was in her own selfish world. Maybe she had been spoilt. And Sarah couldn't deny she was partly responsible, Daddy too. But then John had come along and it continued.

'If that's what you want, Laura,' she replied, flat-voiced. It went through her mind that a daughter of hers going out to work was degrading. Helen had to work out of necessity. But Laura had always been John's appendage, the lady of the house, the smart one and Sarah failed to understand her reasoning. And what did she mean by 'keeping herself sane'? She could do that by persuading John to come back. 'Have you seen John this week?' she asked, desperate for the two to reconcile their differences.

'He called in yesterday. He's taking the boys away for half term.'

'What on earth has got into you, darling? I'm

101

surprised. I'm sure John would have welcomed your company if only for a week.'

'He probably would, Mother, but after the Brooksbank affair, he's on his own,' she said, folding her arms defiantly.

'Men do tend to stray from time to time. You must turn a blind eye to it, darling; it's not important, merely matters of the flesh, nothing more. I would imagine the woman is feeling deflated now that he's dropped her.'

'I've lost all respect and trust in John and that's the end of it. And as far as the Brooksbank woman is concerned, who cares?' She smiled bravely. 'I must leave now, Mother. I hope you get someone to go to Harrogate with you. How about Gloria Mason? She's always game for a trip,' she offered, lifting her voice to a more vibrant level but averting her eyes, obviously embarrassed she couldn't support Mother on this occasion.

'We'll see, darling. Don't worry about me. And take care.'

Laura waved as she left and Sarah wandered back inside. If it wasn't enough worrying about Helen's situation, she now had Laura's problems too. Women were supposed to be cared for by their men. Whatever happened she must keep up her campaign of attrition.

'I'd like you to come to the saleroom with me, Helen. You have such a nose for class items. After the Mennecy find I trust you implicitly where porcelain is concerned.' Vincent smiled and turned to face her.

Helen laughed. 'You make me sound like an

expert. The sugar bowl set was a lucky find. But I would enjoy more involvement.'

'Then it's settled,' he said, a satisfied look on his face.

Excitement built inside her, but when she realised the next sale was during school half-term, disappointment curbed her enthusiasm. Who would look after the girls?

By a lucky coincidence she bumped into Mary Grant, an old friend she hadn't seen since Jim's funeral.

'How are things, Helen?' Mary asked.

'Fine until now,' Helen replied, explaining about her job with Vincent. 'But I'm in a predicament. Vincent wants me to visit the showrooms with him during half term. But I'll have to turn him down. I don't have anyone to look after the girls.'

'I'd love to look after them if you think I could manage.'

Helen perked up, surprised at Mary's kind offer. 'Of course you'd manage. They're well behaved.'

'Then you can count on me,' Mary concluded.

Helen was delighted and it was a popular move for Jessie and Sylvia. They whooped with joy when Mary arrived and, with a cursory wave, they barely noticed Helen leave.

Vincent was already at the shop when she arrived. 'We'll get off,' he said, collecting his overcoat and bowler hat. 'It'll give us time to check out the lots.'

The saleroom was vibrant with life and they inspected the lots, checking them against the catalogue. 'I'm expecting some choice items and we've chosen carefully,' he said, 'but I'm afraid

103

we'll need to exclude some of the lots we've ear-marked. My cash flow won't stretch to bidding for them all.'

'That's a pity,' Helen replied, pausing for thought before coming up with an idea. 'What about my Mennecy nest-egg? It's still in the bank – for a rainy day.' She turned to him. 'Would that help? You can't afford to miss out, Vincent.'

'It would indeed. But are you sure?'

'Never been surer,' she vouched.

'It would solve my problem, and I'd be happy to make a written agreement for the amount you're prepared to loan or even invest in the business.' He nodded. 'It would be a pity to miss out.'

His acceptance of the offer brought a swift surge of colour to her cheeks and she felt a stirring of emotion in her chest that this was maybe the fresh start she'd been hoping for.

'I wasn't expecting an investment in the shop, Vincent. But that would suit me best if you're sure,' she said and, brimming with hopes and ambition, she was keener than ever to secure the lots.

'It's a deal. We'll share the cost.'

Vincent's suggestion excited her, and she sat beside him, happy for him to do the bidding. At the start, she found the process nerve-racking, but gradually she relaxed and found the whole experience so stimulating it gave her an enormous buzz.

At the end of the sale after securing the majority of the lots they'd indicated, Helen gave a cry of delight. 'We've done it, Vincent!'

Vincent smiled warmly. 'Yes, I'd say we've had

a good measure of success.'

Back home in Emley Street, Mary and the girls were busy painting pictures when Helen entered the house.

'How's it gone, dear?' Mary asked, her small face shrouded in what appeared to be a permanent frown. But she looked up and the furrows softened.

'It's been wonderful, Mary.' Helen was bubbling with excitement as she took off her coat. 'Once the girls are in bed I'll tell you all about it,' she said.

'I'd love to hear, Helen.' Mary pulled her bottle green cardigan over her small bosom, revealing the neatly darned elbow of one of the sleeves. It was some time since she'd gone out to work. A spinster and a private woman, she'd been cooped up for so long caring for her elderly mother that her confidence had long ago seeped away.

Helen took from the cupboard half a bottle of sweet sherry. 'Just a little tipple, Mary and you'll sleep like a log tonight. Do give it a try.'

Helen poured the sherry, and handed Mary a glass, wondering what sort of life she'd led, always at her mother's beck and call.

Mary, pale-skinned with large innocent eyes, took the glass and, hands shaking lifted it to her lips. 'I've not tried it before.' Tentatively she took a sip and suppressed a giggle. 'Oh, my goodness. What would Mother have thought?' she said, smiling and gulping down the remainder of the tawny liquid rebelliously.

Helen almost collapsed in helpless laughter as she watched Mary drain her glass. It was then an idea came to mind.

'I have a proposition to make, Mary. Hear me out, but do be honest with me,' she said, realising Mary would be apprehensive. Watching her carefully before she broached the subject she added, 'I'd like to know what you think.'

Mary swallowed hard. 'Of course, Helen.'

'Now that you live alone I've been thinking maybe we could help each other. Mr. Waxman has offered me a small share of the business, not a full partnership you understand, but the amount I've invested should generate a reasonable profit once we begin to sell at realistic prices. That gives me enough responsibility to warrant spending more time at the shop and the salerooms.' Mary became more attentive as Helen continued. 'I know you love the girls and they obviously adore you.'

Mary looked down to her feet. Praise was difficult to accept. Most of her life she had been criticised by her mother.

'Would you be willing to spend the weekdays here, be part of the family, look after the girls and the house with me? I'd pay you as much as I could afford, and we'd be company for each other.' Helen took a deep breath, knowing it was a lot to ask.

'Oh, I don't know that I could cope, Helen. I'm getting on sixty now, love.' She fiddled with the buttons on her cardigan, averting her gaze.

'Of course you'd cope,' Helen insisted. 'Please think it over. I couldn't trust anyone else,' she said in all sincerity.

Mary smoothed her hands over her skirt nervously, pulled at her cardigan and buttoned it up with shaking fingers. 'Yes, I'll think about it, Helen. It's kind of you to ask.' She slipped on her gabardine coat and belted it loosely around her skinny waist.

Helen stood up to see Mary to the door. 'Thank you for helping me out. I'll call and see you later in the week,' she promised, a strong feeling of optimism causing her to smile as Mary stepped over the threshold. If only she could get things sorted, she could have a stab at making a success of her work in the antiques business.

They counted the day's takings, checking twice to make sure it was correct – up eighty pounds on the week. If they took ninety five they'd done extremely well but one hundred and seventy five had to be a record. Things were looking up. Helen knew what the public wanted and the shop's high reputation was spreading rapidly.

The shop bell tinkled unexpectedly as she was about to slip on her coat and go to the bank before it closed at three.

'Hello, darling.' It was Winifred Wallace. 'How are you?'

'Lovely to see you, Winifred. I'm fine,' she replied. 'How's the decor going? Laura told me all about it.'

'It's wonderful. Bernard and I are delighted.' Her stance exuded confidence. 'Laura has re-designed the sitting room in autumn shades and I'd like a jardinière to tone in. Can you help?' She focused on the window display where a selection of jardinières took her attention. Helen followed her gaze.

'The Chinese one at the front is delightful but the shades are not quite right. Come and have a look at the other two.' Helen led Winifred to the display, but before they reached it she stopped. 'I know where there's a Chantilly I could possibly get hold of for you. The background is cream and the design sage green and bronze. It's adapted from the Arita style. From what you say, it would probably suit you down to the ground.' She paused. 'The only thing is, it's a genuine collector's item and it would be rather expensive.' It was worth a shot. She knew the jardinière was at Margot Platt's, a classy antique shop in Leeds. There would be a mark-up to take into account, but Helen knew the price Leonard, Margot's buyer, had paid for it at the saleroom.

'That would certainly interest me, Helen. What sort of price are we talking about, dear?' Winifred was not one to stint where money was concerned. After all, Bernard liked to spoil her now and again.

Helen gave Winifred a rough indication of the price. 'I know it's expensive but it's a beauty.' Helen's enthusiasm came from her genuine regard for such fine porcelain. 'If it's still available I could probably bring it here on approval. What do you think?'

'I'd like that. If it's right for us, I might just be tempted to buy it. Give me a call when it's available.' Taking out her kid gloves from the crocodile skin handbag, Winifred carefully smoothed the wrinkles from the backs. As she left, Vincent returned to the shop and when Helen told him of her plan he rubbed his hands gleefully. 'I must say, you've got what it takes, Helen.'

But Helen cautiously pointed out that the deal was not yet sealed.

Helen strode down the station platform, a combination of apprehension and a real sense of adventure in her step. She walked briskly into City Square. Leeds was unfamiliar to her but she had visited Margot's shop many years earlier and she had a good idea where it was. A tram rattled past and she crossed into Park Row and on to The Headrow. The shop was nearby in Briggate. She looked up at the dark blue lettering on the window and the scrolled sign picked out in gold. It was a far cry from Vincent's humble little shop. But if business continued to boom, one day they might own something similar.

Margot had long since retired and Leonard Baxter managed the shop. The sound of the bell brought him scurrying from the back as she entered.

'This is a surprise. How did the saleroom go for you?' That was the last time she'd seen him when he'd bought the Chantilly jardinière.

'We did well, Leonard. There were some lovely items,' she said warmly, quickly scanning the room and hoping the jardinière hadn't been sold.

'I'll say. But I'm sure this is not a courtesy visit,' he said patronisingly. 'How can I help?'

'The Chantilly jardinière, Leonard. I was in Leeds and wondered if you still had it.' She held her breath, hoping the answer would be positive.

'Yes, we do as a matter of fact. We've had a lot of interest in it.'

109

She recognised the patter. 'I'd like to take a look at it, please,' she said, her voice deadpan. It wouldn't do to show too much interest. He'd definitely try to up the price.

He went into the back room, returned with the jardinière and placed it on the counter. 'Lovely piece of porcelain isn't it?' he enthused as Helen glanced at it quickly.

'Oh dear. I'm not quite sure about the colour. I'd envisaged gold rather than bronze.' It was exactly as she had remembered it. But he was a cunning fox and two could play his game.

'Well, it's there if you're interested.' Leonard looked a shade disappointed.

'What's your lowest price, Leonard, just in case?'

He pursed his lips and drew in breath noisily. She was ready for his ploy. He passed on an inflated figure, obviously knowing she was aware of the saleroom price. 'Our overheads are high and we have to earn a crust.'

A crust? She gave him her offer, a low bid, knowing she might lose the purchase.

'Come off it, Helen.' But he didn't give in. He bartered. 'That's my rock bottom price.'

'You drive a hard bargain, Leonard,' she moaned. 'I don't suppose you could let me have it on approval? I'm not sure the colours are right.'

'Seeing it's you...' Flattery had done the trick. His grin almost reached his ears and he purred with satisfaction.

'I'm sure Vincent will be able to collect it tomorrow morning. If you could have it packed ready for him, he could park outside. We are covered for insurance purposes.' A thrill of satisfaction and pleasure stirred inside her and now all she needed was to convince Winifred of its suitability and its value as an investment.

Helen was ecstatic when Mary surprised her with the good news.

'That's wonderful, Mary. Let me show you the room. It's basic but I'm sure you can do something to make it your own.' She slipped an arm around Mary's slender shoulders, led her through the front room and upstairs, pushing open the first door on the landing. 'It hasn't been used for some time and I'm afraid there's only lino on the floor but everything is clean, and I've aired the bed,' Helen said apologetically.

'It's grand, a nice size compared with mine at home. I've two rugs that would match and a nice candlewick bedspread to go with them. They were Mother's,' she explained, stretching her neck to peer through the window. 'And there's no house overlooking the room either.' Her perpetual frown lifted and her glittering blue eyes shone.

Helen ushered Mary downstairs. 'When can you start, Mary? The sooner the better as far as I'm concerned,' she said, laughing.

'How about tomorrow?'

'Tomorrow? I can't believe my luck. I thought I was being optimistic thinking maybe next week, but you're strides ahead.'

Mary picked up her shopping bag. 'I'll get off and start sorting things out. I've had a word with Sandy Ruddick. He says he'll cart my things across tomorrow afternoon. The horse will be ready harnessed after his milk round.'

'You've taken me seriously, Mary. That's excellent getting Sandy to sort things for you.'

Helen closed the door and gave a little skip, feeling a real sense of achievement.

'Mummy, you're being silly,' giggled Sylvia.

'I know, darling. But isn't it exciting that Aunt Mary's coming to stay with us?'

Best stewing steak and kidney was cooking in the oven rather than the cheaper scraggy neck end. Today they deserved a treat. Momentarily, Helen stared out of the window in a pool of silence, memories of Jim flooding her mind. Whatever happened, she would never stop loving him.

Her thoughts switched to her new resolve. She would suggest to Vincent that the stock needed stricter control to maintain a regular turnover and release capital for further investment. And there were some items that had been hanging around for ages and wouldn't sell unless they reduced the prices.

A tiny, mellifluous voice brought her up sharply.

'Is Aunt Mary coming tonight, Mummy?' Sylvia jumped up and down excitedly.

'No, darling, but she'll be here tomorrow. You'll be a good girl, won't you?' She laughed as she chucked Sylvia under the chin. 'Mr. Ruddick is going to bring her things across on his horse and cart. You may be lucky and meet them. Aunt Mary tells me he has a very friendly horse called Peggy.'

'Who's going to come to school for us, Mummy?' Jessie started to fidget.

'What a worrier you are my precious.' She bent down and kissed Jessie's cheek. 'Why, me of course. Aunt Mary needs to be here early to see to her things. But we'll be back from school before Sandy comes with the cart.'

Helen felt Jessie relax. The girls were more important to her than anything else and, although Mary would be there to help from now on, Helen was determined not to become too involved at the shop at their expense.

Chapter 8

'She's got it. It's in front room.' Jack casually dropped the news on Agnes.

'You could do with a good wash an' brush up,' Agnes observed, scrutinising him.

'Are you listening Ma? I said she's got it,' he stressed.

'Who's got what?' Agnes screwed up her face as she deftly wound up newspaper twists and placed them in the coal scuttle ready to light the fire the next day.

'Helen. Who do you think?' His ma could be dopey at times.

'Don't give me your cheek! What's she got? Do you think I can read your mind?' she echoed impatiently.

'Picture, Ma. What did you think I meant?' he snapped, annoyed he hadn't explained it more clearly.

'It's taken you long enough to let me know. When exactly did you call in?'

'Don't get huffy, Ma. I called in Friday but the last thing we want is to start fussing. Take it easy.' Jack liked to keep her in the dark. After all, either the picture or the money would be his eventually. If he played his cards right, he'd get the lass and the picture.

'What's your next step, our Jack? We can't ask her for it?' Agnes smiled stiffly.

He could read her like a book. She didn't want to put him off, yet she didn't want him taking charge.

'I haven't thought it through yet, Ma,' he said, drawing hard on his cigarette and exhaling a cloud of smoke. He knew she was curious but she could stay that way. 'As long as we know where it is, that's main thing.' He smirked. 'What you done about it anyway? You said you'd give Ma Dorrington the hint.'

'I've given her plenty of hints, Jack. To tell you truth, she doesn't seem to remember what she promised.' Her mouth trembled as she explained.

'Don't get yourself upset about it. As I keep saying, leave it with me.'

He'd not the faintest idea what his next move would be. It might be difficult if the old girl had forgotten she'd promised it to his ma. They needed to think of a way to remind her of that promise. But how?

The interior decor at Winifred and Bernard's was almost complete and Laura suggested one or two small items to complement it.

'I forgot to mention, Laura dear. Helen's advising me. Actually, I'm waiting for her to telephone about a jardinière that might be suitable.'

Laura saw red! How dare Helen deliberately go against her wishes?

'That's fine, Winifred,' she said, jealousy nagging away inside. 'I think that's about it for today.' She made a valiant effort to disguise her feelings. 'I'll see you tomorrow.'

On her way to the bus stop her chest tightened and the lump in her throat almost choked her as anger welled up. A bitter stab of envy shot through her. She needed to put Helen in her place. Joining Vincent in partnership had gone to her head. And her ideas were becoming far too grand.

She made an effort to calm her nerves and when she entered the kitchen at Crossgates her face was suffused with resentment. Her temper had already been worn to a frazzle through overwork and lack of sleep, and now this business with Helen had rattled her. The sooner they had it out, the better.

She could have vented her anger on anyone as her black mood permeated the house.

It was after seven before the evening meal was over. 'I need to pop out on a business matter, Phyllis. I shouldn't be too long.'

Her mind was a profusion of thoughts as she waited at the bus-stop, the beautiful sunset painting the sky completely lost on her. Now that John had left, she must buy herself a car. Hanging around waiting for buses was time-consuming and, after the incident with Jack Bean, was she safe standing alone in the dark? Perhaps she

115

shouldn't have ventured out at that time of night. The bus drew up.

'Hello Mrs. Conway. How are you?' Laura turned but didn't let her face slip when she saw Gertie Brumfitt sitting behind her.

'I'm fine, thank you, Mrs. Brumfitt. And you?' she said reluctantly.

'Champion! I see Mrs. Riley's doing well at shop. Partner now,' the woman gloated, a wide grin on her face.

Laura stared in bewilderment. This low-life, no more than a cleaner at Waxman's, thought she could rub her nose in it! 'Yes, that's wonderful news, Mrs. Brumfitt,' she replied frostily.

She stepped from the bus and Emley Street loomed in the distance. A strange feeling came over her that something unpleasant was about to happen. Not that she had any fears on settling the score with Helen. She could handle that. A surge of emotion flooded every part of her body and anxiety suddenly tightened her mouth.

Despite knowing that Helen preferred her visitors to use the back door, Laura climbed the steps and knocked on the front door. Helen didn't like the children to be disturbed when they were in bed. But Laura didn't care a jot. Back doors were for tradesmen.

After a second knock, Laura saw the curtains move and heard the door to the vestibule open. Her stomach gave a nervous somersault. That feeling again. She heard the sound of a heavy bolt being released and eventually Helen opened the door.

'Hello, darling. Is everything all right? Mother's

116

not ill again is she?' Laura saw the look of surprise on Helen's face.

'No, Helen. I needed to talk to you,' she said, her stern voice revealing her impatience. She stepped inside, that strange sensation still lingering as she followed Helen into the living room.

'Come through, darling. I have a visitor.'

The door was slightly ajar as they approached. She peered through the gap and couldn't believe her eyes. Jack Bean was standing there, a sneer on his face. She felt the bile of hatred rising in her throat. Everything came flooding back to her.

'You're looking well, lass.' His voice was scathing as he gave a dry, satirical laugh.

Laura felt numb, bereft of feelings. His callousness was chilling. His mouth curved into a vicious smile. She nodded and her lips trembled, her quick, nervous movements born of fear. She addressed Helen. 'I need to talk to you alone,' she said, turning her head away sharply. 'If it's not convenient, I'll call later,' she declared, hoping to put him off with her icy rudeness.

'I'm on me way, lass. I'll keep in touch.' His demeanour changed as he gave Helen a knowing smile, opened the back door and let himself out.

Shaking with anger and frustration, and still reluctant to reveal the truth about Jack Bean, Laura flashed Helen a look of disgust. 'How could you invite such a low-life into your home?'

'How do you mean, Laura? Jack's been kind to me since Jim died. I know you think he's beneath you, a mill worker like Jim,' she said, giving Laura the look she deserved, 'but that's no reason why you should despise him so.'

117

Helen's comment was right on target. Laura did despise him, but she felt a little ashamed that Helen had compared him with Jim. She paced the floor.

'I'm not referring to Jim, and you know that. You're becoming so patronising since you joined Vincent. How long have you entertained the likes of Jack Bean? I was under the impression that you'd disliked him since his contretemps with Jim.' She spoke slowly and icily making sure her words reached Helen clearly and intentionally.

'Contretemps? That was years ago,' she replied, a tiny frown marring her smooth brow. But she was obviously intent on keeping the peace.

'You know what I mean,' Laura replied accusingly, flicking her hand in dismissal. 'But let me get to the crux of the matter. In spite of what we discussed about my business, yes, my business,' she stressed, 'you're determined to get involved in some sort of underhand deal,' she pouted, pointing her forefinger at Helen.

'What on earth are you talking about?' Helen replied, a puzzled look on her face.

'Don't try that innocent look with me,' she said, stabbing her finger in the air.

'Spell it out, Laura. Let's get it out into the open.' Helen stared in amazement at Laura's rebellious outburst.

'You know full well I'm referring to Winifred. You've been giving her advice and organising deals with her behind my back.' The sniping continued.

'That's true, but not deliberately behind your back. Winifred came into the shop last week looking for a jardinière. I told her I'd seen something that might suit and that I'd try to obtain it on approval. Now does that answer you?'

'The upshot is, dearest sister, that I don't for one minute believe you.' Determined not to be beaten, Laura became wild and vindictive. There was no stopping her now, especially after the way she'd been treated. First she'd lost her husband, and then she'd been attacked by the horrid Bean fellow and now her sister was trying to upstage her.

Helen marched across the living room to the back door and opened it.

'I'd like you to leave, Laura and don't come back until you can apologise.' She gently steered Laura out of the house and closed the door behind her.

Laura stood outside in a complete daze. How could Helen treat her so after the way she'd taken her in when Jim died? But she supposed she had laid it on thick. Now she felt bad she'd accused Helen before letting her explain. But it was down to Jack Bean. The minute she set eyes on him, she felt intimidated. It was his fault she'd lost her rag.

Why was she always the one to get hurt? She wandered slowly down the steps to the pavement and, pulling her thoughts together, she realised she'd be lucky to catch the bus. But she made it with only seconds to spare. The thought of Helen negotiating with Winifred returned as did her anger. Helen would not get away with it. Somehow Laura would make sure she got her comeuppance.

'Aunt Mary,' the girls shouted in unison when

119

Mary appeared at the end of the street.

'Is Sandy coming?' asked Sylvia in a voice loud enough to deafen.

'Steady on, sweetheart. I'll need ear muffs if you carry on like that. Look! Sandy's here now with Peggy,' Mary said, laughing. A puppy was chasing the cart and yapping. The horse whinnied nervously and Sandy called out 'whoa' for her to stop. He jumped down from the cart and ambled across to Mary, a beaming smile on his face.

'Right love,' he said, in his Irish brogue. He removed his cloth cap and despite the name 'Sandy', his few remaining ginger strands were scraped across his bald pate.

'Hello Sandy. How are you?' Helen asked gently.

'Proper champion, love, and yourself?'

'Fine thanks,' she added. 'Stand back girls,' she said, gripping their hands tightly, her senses bombarded with the noise of the shouting, the barking and the whinnying. But the girls wanted to stroke Peggy and they moved towards the horse. Helen stopped them. 'Wait until Mr. Ruddick gives you permission, girls.'

Sandy approached them, and Jessie smiled willingly into his face. The faithful horse whickered noisily, now resting after the chase with the dog. 'They're grand bairns,' he said and he gently lifted the girls on to Peggy's back. Their eyes were agog as they stroked her mane and Sandy stood by proudly. 'I think they like my Peg,' he added.

'I'm sure they do, Sandy,' Helen said. She smiled. 'But come along, girls. Let Mr. Ruddick lift you down now. He needs to unload Aunt

Mary's things. We don't want to give the whole street a full inspection, do we?' she insisted, glancing up at the twitching curtains in Maisie's front room.

'Mummy, I really enjoyed that,' cried Jessie. 'Can we do it again some time?'

'We'll see,' Helen replied as Jessie offered Sandy an aniseed ball from a crumpled paper bag.

After collecting Mary's belongings between them Helen took them upstairs. Mary unfolded the two rag rugs and placed them on the floor beside the bed, turning to Helen as she did so. 'There we are,' she said. 'I'll be as snug as a bug in a rug,' she added, laughing.

'We'll do our best to make you happy, Mary and if there's anything you need, do ask.'

Helen made her way back downstairs. How lucky she was to have someone so faithful and trustworthy. Perhaps this was the beginning of good things to come.

With Mary in charge Helen arrived early at the shop the following day. Vincent came back from Margot Platts' with the Chantilly jardinière.

Drawing it carefully from its box he turned it over in his hands to inspect the characteristic milky white glaze. Holding it up to the light, he checked that the translucent colour was a yellowish-green, known in France as *citronne*. 'It's wonderful, Helen. Does Baxter realise it's a genuine Chantilly?' He gave a sardonic smile.

'I'm not sure but it is worth much more than we paid for it – or will be paying if Winifred's interested. We can't afford to hang on to things. We need the turnover. Don't you agree, Vincent?'

She let common sense prevail.

'I most certainly do. Now we're into better lots, we need to buy and sell pretty quickly and release the capital. A quick turnover will help. We don't want to remain static, hanging on to things just in case they come good.'

'They're my sentiments exactly. Shall I give Winifred a ring? I'd like to be here when she arrives,' she said, hoping Winifred would like the jardinière – Helen suspected she would.

'She's your customer. Do that my dear.' Vincent took his coat and bowler hat from the stand in the corner. 'I need to take an early lunch,' he said, grasping the door handle and turning towards her. 'I hope you manage to pull it off.'

An hour later the shop bell rang and Winifred stepped inside, her face flushed with excitement.

'Let me look,' she begged as Helen ushered her into the back room and pointed to the jardinière. Winifred smoothed her hands over the surface of it and stared hard. 'Gosh, it's lovely Helen. The colours are exact. Tell me all about it. I must have the full story for Bernard.'

Helen described the background to the French porcelain and carefully reversed the jardinière for Winifred to inspect the markings.

'Is that the Chantilly mark?' Winifred pointed to the base.

'Yes. Make sure it's insured. The value could soar.'

'What a sweetie-pie you are,' Winifred murmured as Helen carefully packed the jardinière.

But then she suddenly looked to Winifred. 'I take it you've decided on it. Here I am packing it for you.' She gave a girlish laugh.

'Of course I'm taking it. You try and stop me.' Winifred opened her handbag and counted out the money from a stout wallet. 'Cash rather than a cheque, Helen.' She lowered her voice even though there was no-one there to hear. 'Bernard doesn't have to know the exact cost.' She stifled a giggle.

'The value for insurance will exceed the price. You'll need to double it.'

'Bernard will see to that. He'll pop around in the car and collect it this afternoon.' She beamed. 'I can't wait to show it to Laura. I'm sure she'll agree it's a wonderful find.' Helen cringed. That was unlikely, but she ignored the comment.

Winifred left and ten minutes later Vincent returned. 'How's it gone?' he asked.

'I'm in the pink!' she said, hunching her shoulders, raising her arms and popping a kiss lightly on his cheek. 'That's just to say thank you for letting me be involved.'

Vincent touched his face as if he could savour the kiss forever. 'Wonderful,' he said. 'Well now. I have more news. There's a national antiques exhibition in London, Friday and Saturday early October. What if we put Mrs. Brumfitt in charge, just to keep an eye on things whilst we go down there? I've not been to an exhibition before. It would be a first.' He took a white card from his top pocket and handed it over.

She glanced at it quickly. 'Sounds wonderful, Vincent but will Mrs. Brumfitt cope?'

'She'll be fine looking after the place, not to sell.' He smiled. 'You know her reputation. If any-

123

one tries it on they'll be in for the high jump.'

Helen laughed knowing exactly what Vincent meant. 'It'll mean I'll have to ask Mary to stay Friday night. She usually goes home weekends but I don't think she'll mind.' She handed the invitation back to Vincent. 'Leave it with me.'

'We'll stay at The Strand Palace, just the Friday night, of course. I've been there before.' His rheumy eyes shone. 'We'll need to book the early morning express, too.'

The London express! Helen's stomach churned as memories of Jim came flooding back. But, seconds later, she pulled herself round, showing her enthusiasm once more.

'If we arrive Friday mid-morning, we'll have the rest of the day and most of Saturday to look around. It'll be a lovely change for me, Vincent. Thanks for suggesting it.'

A break away from the girls would be relaxing after having to shoulder so much responsibility. And now that she had Mary to help, things were a little easier.

Laura completed the work at Winifred's but said no more about the business with Helen. But before she went home, she decided to call at Kirk Grange. A little stirring would do no harm seeing Helen was now in Mother's good books.

Sensing her mother was in good humour she decided to launch her plan.

'I'm really surprised at Helen. I called in a couple of nights ago and who should be there but Jack Bean. Don't tell me she's going off on that track again. It was bad enough putting up with

124

Jim.' Laura knew the news would disturb her mother.

'How tiresome, Laura. Agnes hasn't mentioned anything. Are you sure?' She looked shocked, affronted by the news, ashamed even.

'Of course I'm sure. He was there. It's high time she tried to better herself. She's not doing those girls any favours. Jack Bean is the lowest of the low. I dislike him intensely.' Laura sat in one of the armchairs, her back straight, her legs crossed meticulously. 'We must do something about it. She needs to be told.'

'There's nothing I can do, dear. I burnt my boats over Jim. I can't afford to interfere again,' Mother mumbled, lifting her hands to her cheeks.

'Then it seems I'll have to sort it,' Laura acknowledged in petulant mood.

'Really, Laura. We can't afford to become involved. It's none of our business.' Mother was shocked. 'What on earth has got into you?'

'You won't be saying that when you hear Jessie and Sylvia coming out with their slack speech,' Laura exaggerated. What rattled her most was that since Jim died, Mother doted on Helen. It was not long since Laura was the apple of Mother's eye after she married John. But since he'd left her, everything had gone sour. And the business with Jack Bean made her feel nauseous. She was getting a raw deal, one she didn't deserve.

The business about the picture annoyed her too. 'And whilst I think about it, I'm surprised you gave Helen the picture. It's probably worth more than you think. You know I've always been very fond of it, but you never offered it to me,'

Laura pouted.

'How can you say that? When you married John, I showered you with gifts.' Mother looked away, wiping at an imaginary tear. But then she frowned. 'It's strange you should mention the picture. I realise now I promised it to Mrs. Bean. It's written in my will as a little bequest to her. I must change it and leave her something else. Maybe the new picture Helen bought.'

'Do you seriously think the picture Helen replaced the landscape with has any real value?' Another dig against Helen would do no harm.

'It's the thought that counts, darling.' Mother looked hurt.

'I bet Mrs. Bean doesn't look at it that way when you leave her the print. But despite that, the landscape is far too precious to leave to a cleaner,' she said with disdain. 'She must have known she was on to a good thing, Helen too.' Laura pulled a face. The very idea of the print replacing the landscape was too ludicrous to contemplate.

'How on earth could Mrs. Bean know anything about the picture? In any case, it's some time since I promised her it.'

'It's not an issue any more. Helen has it, thanks to your generosity.'

That was enough. Laura needed to get away.

She'd gained a little one-upmanship and felt she had Mother's blessing on anything she might suggest to rid Helen of the depraved Jack Bean.

Chapter 9

John's car was in the drive when Laura returned to Crossgates. Her pulse raced. It was so difficult to ignore him or disregard her feelings. The front she had adopted to fend him off was wearing thin. How long she could continue in that vein was a constant worry. Each time he visited she weakened, but she must try to be strong. Apparently the novelty had worn off with Clarissa Brooksbank and John was anxious for reconciliation with Laura. But how long would it be before the next one took his fancy?

As she turned the brass knob on the front door and let herself in, his voice penetrated from the sitting room. Phyllis came through from the kitchen.

'A cup of tea would be nice, Phyllis,' Laura said. The sitting room door was slightly ajar and she pushed it open. John was on his knees playing Snakes and Ladders with the boys. They were laughing together. He looked up and flashed a smile. She fought hard to stave off her unruly thoughts of their past togetherness. Since he'd left, his weight had tumbled, but his much leaner face still shone with that handsome look she had fallen for years ago.

'Hello, John. How are you?' she asked, her manner formal.

'I'm fine, darling, in the circumstances. And you? I hear you're doing exceedingly well with your interior designs.' He pushed himself up from his knees, leant across and kissed her on her cheek.

She turned away. 'I'm surprised you have time to consider me, John.' She shrugged her shoulders before moving towards the door. 'Cup of tea?'

'Please, darling.'

Mother had suggested she write off his short-lived romance as nothing but foolish experience, but considering he'd left her for that woman, something inside stopped her. Struggling to close herself off she'd built a barrier to hide behind.

John followed her into the kitchen. He moved closer. 'Darling, I know I've been a rat. Please believe how dreadfully sorry I am. I'm desperate to come back. I'll do anything. Just say the word. How about if we keep Phyllis on? You could continue to work.'

'Thank you kindly, sir,' she said, tugging an imaginary forelock knowing he was swept by a wave of guilt. 'So you'd allow me to continue working? How magnanimous of you!'

'Why the acid comment, Laura? I'm being serious. Hear me out, please.'

There was a kind of vulnerability about him when he urged her to forget it all and love him like she'd always done. And there was nothing more she would have liked. But it was not as simple as that. He'd hurt her deeply and, whether she took him back or not, he must be punished.

'John, you must understand how difficult it is. I realise I must come to terms with it somehow, whatever the outcome, but I can't get that

128

woman out of my head.' She tipped the dregs of her tea down the sink and turned to face him. 'I'd like you to leave now. I can't cope with any more. I must stay strong to concentrate on my job. I enjoy working and it takes my mind off things.' She paused and swallowed hard. 'It's the only success in my life at the moment and it means a lot to me.' She tried to smile through the veil of tears as she turned and left the room.

After John left the house Laura decided to call on Helen and clear the air. 'Sorry about the misunderstanding, darling. I have a lot on my mind these days. I saw red when Winifred mentioned the jardinière,' she confessed. 'I thought you'd gone behind my back but Winifred put me straight.'

'I understand. I'm glad there's no rift between us. There's too much at stake to argue.'

Now that they were back on speaking terms and Helen was playing into her hands, Laura was in a better position to control the situation especially Helen's involvement with the despicable Jack Bean.

'By the way, you must try to discourage Jack Bean from visiting. I've heard some horrid rumours about him.' Laura was determined to expose him in any way she could, even if she had to fabricate the truth.

'Rumours?' Helen's naive expression spurred Laura on.

'Apparently he has a fondness for little girls. Believe you me, he's the last person you want visiting.'

Laura's innocent comment appeared to take on

129

its own connotations for Helen. 'Oh dear! I know what you're saying.' Helen stared into space.

After an uncomfortable silence, Laura set about her second task. 'I spoke to Mother today. She'd bequeathed the landscape picture to Mrs. Bean apparently. Do you realise how valuable it is?'

'I realise it's an original but I'm not sure of its value. I'm not intending selling it if that's what you're thinking.'

'I wasn't insinuating that. Mother didn't realise its value and she's decided to offer Mrs. Bean another picture in its place.'

'Are you sure, Laura? If she wants it back to fulfil her promise, then that's fine by me. But I do love the picture.'

Helen was picking up the wrong message, and that was not what Laura wanted.

'But we don't want Mrs. Bean to have something so valuable. I'm merely making the point.' Laura knew she was on the right track with her reasoning. 'The point is that it was given to Mother by Daddy just before he died. I think it might have been rather remiss of you to accept it.'

'I see.' Helen frowned and shook her head gently. 'What with the picture and Jack Bean, you've given me plenty to think about. I must decide what to do, and quickly.'

Laura smiled to herself. Her direct and simple approach had worked. Helen would not get the better of her, either in business or otherwise.

Despite Laura's earlier comments, Sarah had no

doubt in her mind that she wanted Helen to have the picture. It was a pity about the promise she'd made to Mrs. Bean but, as Laura said, she owed her nothing of such value – whatever the value was. Surely it was the thought that counted. The question of Jack Bean was a different matter and had a higher priority in her mind. Laura was right. There'd been enough trouble when Helen married Jim. It would be dreadful if the whole unfortunate business reared its ugly head again in the shape of Jack Bean. He was nothing like his mother. At least Agnes had a little decorum. According to Laura Jack Bean was uncouth, although what she had based her judgement on was a complete mystery to Sarah. Laura barely knew him.

She glanced through the bay window and when she saw Agnes approaching she went through the hall into the kitchen. 'Come in,' she called.

Agnes stepped clumsily over the threshold and wiped her feet on the kitchen mat. She took her mauve cloche hat and maroon coat through to the hall, placing them carefully on the stand. Sarah had always been impressed that Agnes came to work in a proper hat. Most of the local chars wore headscarves. It was strange that, according to Laura, Jack was somewhat of a lowlife. How could that be so when Agnes was such a decent sort?

'Morning, Mrs. Dorrington,' Agnes replied. 'Grand day again. Got my washing pegged out. Hope it stays fine,' she said, staring idly at the Monet picture.

Sarah followed her gaze and realised this was the perfect opportunity to mention the picture

131

and get it off her chest.

'I've been thinking Agnes. I didn't realise at the time but I've given Helen the picture you said you liked. But I'm sure you won't mind. The one she's replaced it with is much nicer.' Now that she had broached the subject, Agnes knew the score. Not that it mattered seeing it was in her will. Sarah hoped to outlive Agnes anyway.

Agnes looked downcast. 'I didn't like to say anything, Mrs. Dorrington but to tell you the truth I was disappointed when it went missing. I was well taken with that picture. But you make the decisions,' she replied looking again at the Monet print disparagingly.

Sarah felt bad but she said nothing more. Agnes was obviously upset.

By the time it was ten thirty Sarah was still riddled with guilt over the picture and she decided to make the coffee herself. It might appease the situation a little and maybe she could mention the subject of Jack's visit.

'Coffee, Agnes,' Sarah called from the kitchen.

'That's good of you, Mrs. Dorrington.' Agnes went through and sat down at the table.

'Do have a shortcake biscuit. I made them myself.'

Agnes looked across at the plate and picked the biggest.

Sarah sat down and took a deep breath, needing to steel herself before broaching the business of Jack. Eventually she plucked up the courage.

'This is rather delicate, Agnes, but I feel I must mention it. Laura came yesterday and told me she'd called on Helen. Jack was there when she arrived.' She paused. 'I know it's none of our business Agnes but do you think it right Jack visiting Helen so soon after Jim passed away?' She sighed with relief that she'd managed to get it off her chest.

'I know what you mean, Mrs. Dorrington, but I'm not our Jack's keeper. I didn't know he'd been visiting. I know he's very fond of her but it won't be what you think. It'll be our soft Jack thinking he can help her out in some way.'

Sarah was taken aback, not expecting that sort of answer from Agnes.

'But if you think it'll help I'll have a word with him.' Agnes looked embarrassed.

'No, no, don't do that, dear. If what you say is right, we don't want to interfere.' Sarah was annoyed Laura had complained about Jack and she reprimanded herself for becoming involved. She must learn to keep her own counsel.

When Agnes left Kirk Grange she mulled over Mrs. Dorrington's explanation about the picture. Anxious to let Jack know the outcome she tried to put on a spurt but, being slightly overweight, she found it difficult. Dwelling on the situation she decided once she'd told him she'd drop the subject. There was no use harping on about it anymore.

Puffing and panting, she entered the house and through set lips, she explained the full version.

'What do you think? She's had cheek to tell me she's given my picture to Helen. I can have the new one but it's a cheap article if you ask me. I don't know much about pictures but I can tell it's nothing special.' Agnes was almost in tears.

133

'How d'you mean Ma? What do you know about new one?'

'I'm not daft enough to think Helen could afford one the same price as the other.'

'I told you Ma,' he chastised, 'you slipped up other week. There's no going back now. We'll have to come up with a different plan.' Looking far from happy, he glanced irritably across at her.

Once more they were at each other's throats and Agnes was sick of it.

'It's all right you saying that, Jack. I did what you said but you weren't there. And what do you mean a different plan?'

Jack did the usual and tapped the side of his nose and this irritated Agnes. She turned the tap and filled the sink ready to wash up. Unable to concentrate she let the large tablet of Sunlight soap slip from her hands into the hot water, her mind still on Jack and his furtive ways. She hoped it wasn't another of his smart ideas.

'By the way, I don't think she's pleased you've been calling on Helen. She thinks it's too soon after Jim died.' She hadn't meant to mention it but he'd rattled her with his comments about more plans.

'What the bloody hell has it got to do with her, interfering old bat? She wants to keep her nose out or I'll keep it out for her.'

Jack's resentment made Agnes feel even worse. She'd not intended to inflame him but she'd gone too far again. 'I'd rather you didn't say anything, Jack! I don't think she meant it the way you've taken it. I think she's just worried about what her friends might think.' Agnes tried to back off but

134

Jack was having none of it.

'Bloody stuck up cow. That's all she is. Who do they think they are anyway, bloody royal family? They're no better than the likes of us, Ma. That woman, Laura is the worst. Don't tell me she's had nothing to do with it. She's a right stirrer!' He sighed deeply and shook his head. 'I'll show 'em,' he threatened.

As she met his angry stare, Agnes started to fret. What on earth had she done to deserve this sort of behaviour from him? That picture had caused more trouble than it was worth. Well, maybe not more than it was worth but more trouble than she could put up with. What a palaver!

'Drop it now, Jack. I wish I'd never told you.' She wiped her hands on the tea towel as she finished drying the crockery.

Jack jumped up put on his cap, muffler and bicycle clips before glaring across at her. Agnes looked up at the clock on the mantelpiece. It was half past eight. She feared the worst.

'Where d'you think you're going at this time of night?' she said, self-control concealing the rage inside her. 'Don't you be stirring it! Leave them lasses and their ma alone,' she demanded, pointing a finger at Jack. 'You'll only make it worse if you put your big foot in it.' It was time she told him straight. 'What you don't seem to take in is that I work for Mrs. D,' she flashed, starting to become heated and finding it difficult now to cover her anger. She could feel her face patching over with red blotches. The doctor had told her not to become stressed or over-anxious. It brought on her angina. 'There, you've started me palpitations again. Your Dad was right. You were a selfish little bugger when you were little.' She plonked herself down heavily in the fireside chair. 'And don't start ordering me about again. I've had enough.' She flicked her hand in the air in dismissal.

'Nay, Ma. What you talking about? I'm only going down for a pint to Mucky Duck.'

'And that's another thing. Why do you have to talk so common? It's Black Swan not Mucky Duck!' Relieved she bent over and picked up her slippers from beside the hearth and put them on. If it was only the Black Swan he was going to, that was all right.

'Don't go on, Ma. Get yourself a drop of that brandy out of cupboard and settle yourself down. You'll get nowhere getting worked up.'

He set out along the road towards Helen's place, striding confidently up the garden path. He had his feet under the table now and nothing could stop him from following his plan. There was no need for his ma to inherit the picture. It would all go through legally if he could afford to bide his time. He was sure he was in with a shout. As far as he knew, there was no-one else on the scene.

He knocked at the door a couple of times and no-one answered. He decided to go round to the front door. He knew it might cause a bit of a rumpus. It was like the bloody Bank of England, Helen having to pull back the bolts to open up. But needs must. He knocked again and heard a tiny voice.

'Mummy, there's someone banging on the door.' It was one of the girls.

136

'Who is it?' Helen's voice rang out.

'It's me, Jack,' he replied.

'Sorry Jack. I can't open the door. I've just stepped out of the bath. It wasn't important was it?'

'I just wanted a word but I'll call back tomorrow.' He softened his voice, hoping she'd not caught the earlier sharp edge to it. He smiled to himself. By bloody hell, she'd just stepped out of the bath had she? Pity he hadn't been there to give her a rub down.

He set off back to Newport Street but decided to call in at the pub just to let his ma see that his story was straight. He took out a Woodbine and, tapping it on the packet, lit it and drew hard. He might be able to afford Capstan full strength once he had his feet under the table at Helen's. The way things were going that shouldn't take long.

As he entered the tap room, he looked across the bar and spotted Maureen from the office. She gave him the eye. Her boyfriend, George Bradshaw was standing next to her, leaning on the bar and whispering something in her ear. He went off in the direction of the Gents.

Jack knew she fancied him and he thought he'd have some fun. He winked at his pals and pushed open the door to the snug with his shoulder, a pint of bitter in his hand and a Woodbine in his mouth. Sidling up to her, he placed his pint on the bar and nipped her bottom.

'Ouch,' she cried, her voice taking on a rebellious, girlish tone. Her blue eyes sparkled as she pressed up against him, her cheap cloying scent penetrating his nostrils. He slid his hand around

137

her waist and fondled her idly.

'What the hell do you think you're up to, Bean?' George, broad shouldered and heavy-muscled, confronted him, raising himself to his full six foot two and staring down at Jack.

'Nothing, pal.' Jack backed off. The fat was in the fire now!

Maureen's flirtatious grin turned sour. 'It's all right, George. We were just having a laugh.' She linked her arm through George's and nestled close.

Jack and George had been lifelong friends. They'd been at school together. But Jack knew that friendship ended when one of your pals started messing around with your girl.

'Don't lie to me.' George shook Maureen off. 'I saw the way you looked at him. Outside Bean!' It was obvious George had already drunk a pint or two but, if it came to it, he could beat Jack hollow even in that state.

Jack edged away from the bar. 'Come off it, George. Maureen's right. It was a bit of fun. Forget it.' Jack cringed, expecting George's powerful hand on his shoulder as he returned to the taproom to the uproarious guffaws of his pals.

'Nearly got it in the neck there Jack,' one of his pals suggested with a snigger.

Jack hated being threatened or mocked. He didn't appreciate the joke and he tapped his foot irritably against the bar's footrest as the scowl on his face deepened.

'It was nothing. Silly bugger's drunk! He wouldn't have a chance,' Jack claimed, looking across and giving George a long, slow blink. The

138

idiot thought he had the earth with Maureen, but she was anybody's. Jack knew he could pick her up any day.

Wait until he pulled it off with Helen. Bradshaw could think what he liked then!

Chapter 10

The early train to Leeds was on time but the carriage Vincent chose was almost full, and he insisted Helen take the only remaining seat. There was a gentle buzz of conversation as the train trundled on its way. But Helen was in no mood for talking. She was tired and anxious. It was the first time she had left the girls although, judging by the way they were behaving, whatever Mary had planned for them must have been something special.

Her concern for the girls triggered thoughts of Jim. Until recently, she had been so involved with her work and organising the girls she could barely think straight, but that was before Mary had agreed to stay. It was only now she was able to consider the situation and myriad questions bombarded her mind. Would Jim have approved of her leaving the girls? A pinprick of guilt entered her mind. But she reasoned it through. She needed to work, she needed the money, and she felt certain he would have agreed.

The train picked up speed and started to wend its way through the countryside, its rhythm becoming regular. The day was bright and the early mist had dispersed. Her spirits were lifted when she looked through the carriage window at fields of cows and horses, anglers sitting patiently on the banks of the River Wharf, trees of beautiful russet shades and leaves in vivid colours of bronze and flame carpeting the ground. Despite the long, hot summer, the rich, green pastures were still fresh. The peace and tranquillity of the countryside gave her an immense feeling of gratitude for her children and for the job she enjoyed so much. And that was thanks to Vincent.

She turned from the window and glanced up at him. He was clutching at the strap above his head and she couldn't help noticing he had a look of discomfort about him.

'Do sit down for a while, Vincent,' she begged, but she knew her suggestion was futile. He was too much the gentleman to sit and allow her to stand.

'I'm perfectly fine, my dear. I'm taking in the scenery.' He smiled. He was so kind and generous, and his support was steadfast.

Leeds City Station came into view and a shuffle of people, mainly commuters, moved into the corridors ready to leave the train. But Helen and Vincent remained patiently until the corridor was clear. Vincent collected the baggage and they stepped out on to the platform.

'Do let me carry mine,' Helen insisted, but he held on tight and refused to allow it.

The crowds dispersed and they headed for the London train. The platform was at the far side of the station and they stepped aboard, settling into

140

their seats. Helen took out a magazine whilst Vincent studied the exhibition brochure. But half an hour into the journey he was lulled to sleep by the constant rhythm of the train. Helen woke him gently as they approached King's Cross.

'Oh my goodness. I must have dozed off, my dear; how rude of me!' He shook his head to compose himself and smoothed his hair down, grinning apologetically as he eased himself from the seat.

'Don't worry Vincent. You must have been tired to have slept for so long.'

Despite the queue at the taxi rank minutes later they were on their way to the Strand Palace Hotel and, once there, Helen was impressed by the grand entrance with its marble columns up-holding the huge stone canopy over the steps. The commissionaire tipped his hat and collected their luggage. They entered the foyer through the large revolving doors and Helen took in the enormous gilt-framed mirror set between two Chippendale side-tables. The matching ceiling rose and cornice were intricately patterned in fleurs de lys.

'Wow,' she said. 'How about this for style?'

Once in her room, she quickly emptied her suit-case, placing her powder-blue satin dress, one she'd bought with the coupons she'd saved, on a hanger. Long-sleeved with a fitted skirt, the stylish bow draped from waist to hip gave it that extra touch of class. For their afternoon visit she slipped on the cream woollen dress and matching swagger coat she'd made on her new Singer sewing machine.

Vincent was there in reception when she came

out of the lift. 'Is everything to your satisfaction, Helen, the room and so on?'

'It's wonderful,' she replied as they entered the restaurant. 'Just a light snack for me,' she added.

'Me too. We need to save our appetite for dinner.'

After lunch they headed for the underground. The Exhibition Centre was already thronging with visitors and they slowly eased their way through the crowded entrance into the hall beyond.

The stands displaying porcelain were directly ahead of them. There were Chinese cups and saucers, brilliantly glazed French spice boxes, some on silver mounts marked in Paris, and a selection of teapots in blue sun-face in the style of Daniel Marot. Helen was entranced. She had read about these masters of porcelain but never experienced their work first-hand.

When the crowds began to press forward Helen felt uncomfortable and needed some space. But suddenly she felt a heavy foot on hers. She winced and spun sideways.

'I'm awfully sorry, my dear.' The offender, male, softly spoken and oozing charm was well over six foot tall and, judging by the impact of his tread, Helen reckoned he must have very large feet. His astonishingly blue eyes flickered with amusement as he placed his hand gently on her shoulder and bent to face her. 'I do beg your pardon.'

For a few seconds she stared mesmerised before responding with a half-smile. But after such a reaction she felt foolish and quickly turned away.

Although he was standing behind her, she could feel the intensity of those eyes as she tried to concentrate her attention back on the stands.

Vincent, unaware of what had happened, tapped her lightly on the arm, suggesting they move on. Helen agreed and, determined not to turn as they edged their way to the next stand she tried to close her mind to the stranger.

Soon she was captivated by the collection of small gold snuff-boxes. Over the years there had been a variety of uses for these beautifully decorated items, some used for face rouge, some to hold souvenirs of love-affairs.

'These are exquisite, Vincent.' Her eyes lit up like a child's in a toy shop.

'They'll be highly priced but most are in excellent condition.'

It was then she noticed Vincent looking rather tired despite his short nap on the train. 'How about a cup of tea?' she suggested, pointing to the cafeteria.

Vincent appeared relieved at her suggestion. 'Splendid idea! It's all rather overwhelming, isn't it?' he said. 'There's so much to see.' He dabbed his face with a large white handkerchief as they headed for a table.

When Vincent glanced towards the entrance, Helen followed his gaze. He was looking vacantly at the stranger who'd stepped on her foot. Again she was drawn to him, his fair hair pushed casually to one side of his forehead and his strong jaw line presenting a generous mouth. He was approaching a woman who was blonde, vivaciously beautiful and stunningly dressed. He bent and kissed her lightly on the cheek.

Helen felt her face become taut.

'Are you all right, my dear?' Vincent interrupted her thoughts.

'I'm fine. I was thinking about the girls and Mary. I hope they're coping,' she said but she was aware the actions of the stranger and his woman had upset her, she couldn't think why. Was she jealous? But she was being silly.

'I'm sure they'll be fine,' Vincent assured her.

Her stomach flipped as she continued to stare after the man who was now escorting the woman out of the cafeteria. How could she possibly be affected by a complete stranger? It was so wrong. She should not be feeling that way when it was not yet two years since she lost Jim and she tried desperately to clear her mind of all thoughts of the stranger.

'Maybe we should go back to the hotel. I think we've had our fill for today?' Vincent suggested.

'I think you're right. We still have tomorrow. Thank you for bringing me. It's all very stimulating,' she said, standing up whilst Vincent drew back her chair.

When they reached the underground, the trains were crowded and they had to stand all the way back. Relieved when they reached their destination, they dodged between the traffic and, as they approached the hotel, a taxi was drawing up outside. The stranger and his woman stepped out and climbed the marble steps. The commissionaire greeted them and they disappeared inside.

The spacious hotel bedroom brought back memories of her childhood home. But that was a long time ago. Looking forward to relaxing in the bath after the long journey and the hectic day, Helen relished the comforting warmth of the water but it made her feel drowsy. Her mind drifted to the beautiful antiques and to Jim who could never understand her fascination for them, but he did appreciate her enthusiasm. One thought triggered another and then, oddly enough, the stranger came to mind. But guilt overcame her and, suddenly realising time was passing, she knew she must make a move.

After drying off she took the blue satin dress from the wardrobe and carefully stepped into it. The glossy chestnut lights of her hair shone as she spread her glorious mane loosely over her shoulders. With a final glance, she checked her appearance in the cheval glass to make sure the seams of her silk stockings were straight before leaving the room and pressing the lift button. It arrived, the attendant opened the gate and immediately she came face to face with the stranger, his female companion beside him. With a challenging glint of danger in his eyes, he smiled but the woman appeared not to notice. A flush of embarrassment coloured Helen's face. She responded with a weak half smile and then looked away. He was no more than a flirt. The lift stopped, and without turning she stepped out and made for reception where Vincent was waiting.

'Helen, you look lovely,' he said, his eyes full of admiration. 'It's wonderful our working together again. Let's call this our reunion.' Without waiting for a response, he lifted his hand. 'Waiter!' he called, clicking his fingers. 'Champagne on ice, please.'

'That's rather extravagant, Vincent,' she laughed,

delighted at being pampered.

'Not at all, my dear. We've worked jolly hard these last few months. Let's celebrate our success and hope there's more to follow.'

The young waiter set the champagne bucket down on the stand beside them and made a great issue of popping the cork. Vincent lifted his glass and clinked it against hers. 'Here's to the future, Helen.'

'The future,' she echoed as she took a sip of the delicate, bubbly liquid. 'And we've only just begun!' she added frivolously.

The waiter served the soup from a silver tureen and, absently, Helen stared after him as he returned to the kitchen. It was then she spotted the stranger sitting at a table near the window. His eyes sought her out, and he held her gaze. Aroused by the passion and energy they conveyed, she felt locked inside them. Momentarily she seemed to be absorbed in a different world, but she drew herself away and struggled to dismiss him from her mind.

Her discussion with Vincent centred on business, but eventually she broached the subject of Jim and how much she missed him. In turn Vincent talked about Pearl. It had been six years since her death.

'I should be used to being on my own by now. But it doesn't get any easier especially when you're getting older and you don't have children. Loneliness gets to you after a while.' He looked away wistfully.

'I know exactly how you feel but I have the girls. I'm never alone but I'm often lonely.' But

146

now she felt weary. 'I'm feeling rather tired, Vincent.'

'Me, too,' he confessed. 'It's the travelling. I'll see you in the morning,' he added.

Helen was up and ready by eight o'clock next morning, her interest taken by the Wedgwood Room where breakfast was being served.

'You look rather tired, Vincent. Didn't you sleep well?' Helen noticed his eyes were slightly bloodshot and shadowed by dark rims.

'No I didn't. It was very warm in my room. I'm used to a much cooler temperature.' He smiled gently, making an effort to look lively.

'Are you sure you feel up to going?' Helen was concerned. 'Don't worry about me.'

'I'll be fine,' he said, closing his eyes and rubbing the lids with his fingertips.

Helen felt uneasy. He didn't look well, but she was helpless to pursue things further.

'What's on the programme today?' she asked. 'I'd like to look at some of the pictures and maybe the tapestries if we've time.'

'A couple of auctions by two of the big houses, I believe one is pictures and the other Regency furniture.' Vincent pulled the folded programme from his pocket and opened it.

'Sounds good,' she said, pushing her chair back and slipping on her jacket.

'We must be away by three,' Vincent insisted as they left for the underground.

The centre was buzzing as they pushed their way through to the tapestry exhibition. The many impressive samples woven with richly dyed wools

147

and silks were embellished with gold and silver threads. Helen looked eagerly across.

'The one at the back, Vincent, the pastoral with the blue drapes, is it a Beauvais? Can you read it?' She pressed forward to see the label.

'It is, Helen. Come and stand here. You'll have a better view.'

'They're intriguing,' she said, straining to look closer.

He laughed and said, 'Is there anything you don't find intriguing? You're steeped in the whole business, admit it.'

Helen smiled. He was right. 'I suppose I do get carried away, but there are so many lovely things'

Vincent didn't respond, and after a few seconds she turned to face him. He was clutching his chest, obviously in considerable pain.

'What is it, Vincent?' she asked, her voice full of concern. Noticing the pallor of his skin, she took hold of his arm and gently led him to the back of the hall where a porter from the carpet stand stood up and offered his chair.

'Vincent, what on earth's wrong?' she repeated and she tried to remain calm.

'It's my chest, my arms. Indigestion I think.'

In desperation she called the porter across. 'Please ask if there's a doctor around. We must get some relief for him.'

She undid the knot in his tie but he slumped down on the chair, slipped to the floor and was violently sick. Helen took off her coat, rolled it up and slipped it under his head. By this time a small crowd had gathered. Taking a handkerchief from her bag, she wiped his brow and within minutes she heard a voice from the crowd.

'Move back.'

She looked up. It was the stranger. He stepped forward and loosened Vincent's clothing. 'Let me have a look at him. Gently does it.' He turned to Helen. 'Clear that lot away, will you?' he ordered briskly, pointing to the small group of people. He talked to Vincent but there was no response.

'It's his heart, I'm afraid. He's had a pretty bad attack,' he said, turning to Helen. His manner was caring. 'Is he your father?'

'He's my business partner,' she told him.

The newly-formed crowd moved aside to allow two ambulance attendants through.

'Thank God for that,' he said to one of the attendants. 'Cardiac arrest.' He moved back to give them room to lift Vincent on to the stretcher and, taking Helen's arm, he led her through the great hall to the exit.

Tension clutched at her throat, and she found it difficult to breath. Dazed, she stared down at Vincent's ashen face as he lay on the stretcher. Only moments ago they'd been chatting together, he'd laughed at her enthusiasm. The next minute he'd collapsed. It was so unexpected. She prayed he would survive. At fifty-five, he was still young and should have many more years ahead of him. But all attempts to revive Vincent were futile. Helen feared the outcome, knowing even before the ambulance left for the hospital, his condition was serious.

A feeling of unease swept over her when the doctor shook his head. 'I'm afraid there's nothing more we can do. It was a very severe attack. These things often come without warning,' he whispered.

At first Helen was unable to react. The shock of it had rendered her speechless and the doctor's words failed to register in her mind. And then it came to her as she recalled Vincent's earlier condition.

'I could have prevented it. He said he felt tired this morning, but he was adamant he wanted to go to the exhibition.' After a long pause, she continued. 'Why didn't I do something?' Her confession now turned to sorrow. Reprimanding herself for not having acted on her instincts, her eyes misted over and she seemed almost incapable of striving for control.

'You couldn't have prevented it. Don't blame yourself. It's no good looking in retrospect.' He took a handkerchief from his top pocket and brushed away her tears before placing his arm around her shoulder.

The ambulance drew up outside the hospital and, still unable to take in what had happened, she followed the attendants to the screens. The doctor held her back. 'It's too late, my dear. He's gone.'

Stunned by the doctor's final disclosure, Helen turned to him, her tear-stained face revealing her devastation. She felt too desperate to listen to reason. A rush of emotion sent her swaying and he placed his arms around her, holding her gently. His body felt strong as she clung to him and found solace in his embrace. It felt quite natural to her, the feeling of security giving way to her grief.

Eventually, realising her plight, she drew herself

away. 'I'm so sorry to impose.' The words rushed out. Dabbing her face, she looked up at him and she felt hot blood surge to her face. 'I'm so grateful for everything you've done.'

'I'm afraid I wasn't much use. There was simply nothing more I could do.' He gripped her hands firmly and squeezed them. 'Are you all right now?'

She faced him and felt an overwhelming temptation to slip back into the comfort of his embrace. But she cast that desire from her mind. 'It's been such a shock.'

Her shivers prompted him to take her coat and drape it loosely around her shoulders... 'We don't want you catching cold,' he insisted.

'I'm sorry to have been so rude. You don't even know my name,' she said, her voice hoarse after her tearful outburst. 'I'm Helen Riley.'

'Charles Ravel. Sorry we've met in such unfortunate circumstances, Helen.' He spoke softly. 'I'm not a cardiologist,' he explained. 'I'm an orthopaedics surgeon. I was in London for a conference when I decided to visit the exhibition.'

'I see,' she whispered. 'But what happens now?' Realising the enormity of it all, her anxiety returned. 'I've no idea what to do next.'

'The police will need to be involved. I'll wait with you until they arrive. They'll give you guidance,' he said, his voice filled with tenderness and reassurance.

'I've no idea what the police need to know. There was nothing I could do.'

'It's quite normal with a sudden death, Helen. But, if you're still feeling delicate, I'll stay with

151

you until the interviews are over. It's the least I can do.'

Helen telephoned Laura and asked her to let Mary know she would be delayed. But she decided not give a full explanation. It was better to let them know the sad news face to face when she returned. She replaced the receiver and turned to Charles. It was then she was momentarily caught in the magnetic blue depths of his eyes. She shuddered. But this was neither the time nor the place for that sort of reaction and she pulled herself up sharply.

The police questioned Helen about her movements on the morning of Vincent's death. Charles offered his support throughout, and his sudden departure left Helen with a dulled feeling of disappointment and a range of hidden emotions she found difficult to isolate. What made things worse was that she had no contact address, not that she needed to get in touch with him, but it would have been courteous to thank him in writing for his support.

The pathologist told her that Vincent had suffered a coronary thrombosis complicated by disturbances of the heart rhythm. His condition had prevented any effective heart beat at all. Cardiac arrest had been almost immediate, as Charles had earlier confirmed. There was nothing that could have been done to save him.

Arrangements for Vincent's body to be released proved to be a major headache. Helen had no idea who his closest relative was. But Mr. Marchbank, the solicitor with whom she and Vincent had registered her share in the shop would no doubt sort it out as soon as she made an appoint-

152

ment. Having done everything in her power, she was relieved for the time being the nightmare was over, even though temporarily.

Chapter 11

Laura made her way to Emley Street to pass on Helen's message to Mary.

'I'm sorry, Mary, all I know is that Vincent has collapsed. It was a very brief conversation. Helen wanted you to know she would be late back. I'm sure she'll put us both fully in the picture as soon as she's home.' Laura looked at her watch. 'I must dash. The boys are with a neighbour. It's Colin's birthday today and I promised him a birthday party. I'll keep in touch if there's any more news.'

'Thank you for coming all this way to let me know,' Mary replied, a heavy frown on her forehead. But then she lifted her voice and smiled. 'I do hope the boys enjoy Colin's party.'

Laura had decided the party would not be too lavish, just a few friends, mostly boys and, for Colin's sake, she had decided to invite John. Despite their separation and his recent affair, her heart leapt at the thought of seeing him again and she knew she could never stop loving him. She glanced at the clock. It was only four and he was not due until five. Her mind drifted to Helen. Perhaps she had been too severe, although she felt no discomfort in lying about Jack Bean. She had vowed to pay him back, brute that he was.

Her reflections were suddenly interrupted when Mother arrived and Laura tried not to show her disappointment it wasn't John.

'Hello, darling. I thought I'd surprise you.' Mother closed the door. 'I've brought Colin his present. I know he's going to like it,' she said hastily as she placed a neatly wrapped parcel on the hall table and slipped off her coat. 'Where is he, anyway?'

'The boys are having a game of putting in the garden, Mother,' Laura replied taking her mother's coat and hanging it in the cloakroom. 'This is a surprise. Did you take a taxi?'

'Of course, dear. You don't think I walked here do you?' Laura ignored the comment knowing Mother could be abrasive at times.

'Cup of tea?' she asked, sincerely hoping Mother, whose allegiance lay with John, would be gone before he arrived. It was a well-known fact that women of her era were prepared to put up with the occasional indiscretion, although Lord knows, she wouldn't have had such a problem with Daddy. He doted on her, hence her lack of understanding.

'I'd love a cup, darling.' Mother walked through to the kitchen and gave Laura a hug. 'You look well, my love. Are you feeling better?' She sat on a kitchen chair and played around with her hair, carefully fluffing the ends with cupped hands.

'Much.' Laura filled the kettle. 'You're excelling yourself popping in like this,' she said pleasantly, surprised her mother had taken the plunge, venturing out unaccompanied.

154

'I can't stay at home forever.' She bent and placed her leather handbag on the floor. 'I've been thinking seriously about asking Helen to live with me. I'm not happy about Emley Street. And after you told me about Agnes's son, I can't seem to stop worrying.' Her brow furrowed and she pouted her lips. 'What do you think? I was....' She was interrupted when a voice called out from the hall.

'It's me, darling.'

Laura's mind jumped from Mother's predicament to John as she sensed a haunting reminder of happier times. Then she faced reality.

'Come through, John. The children are in the garden.' She edged past Mother and stood holding the back door open.

But he ignored Laura's hint. 'Hello Mother dear.' He bent and gave her a peck on the cheek. He certainly knew how to charm his women. Laura inched the door open wider.

'John, darling. It's so good to see you.' Mother began to fawn. Laura was furious. What was she playing at? 'Don't you think it's time you two called a truce?' Mother continued. 'This can't go on forever.' She sighed and her words, directed at Laura, contained an underlying note of accusation.

'Mother, please leave it to us,' Laura replied cuttingly, her face becoming flushed and her eyes flickering hotly. 'The boys are outside, John. They're looking forward to seeing you.' Trying to mask her anger, she pointed to the open door.

John faced her. 'I can't help agreeing with Mother. It is time we sorted things out, darling.

155

But as you say it's for us to decide.' He flashed a maddening grin and shrugging his shoulders towards Sarah, nodded in recognition of her attempts to intervene. Mother caught his glance, and gave a smug gesture of acknowledgement.

Laura stamped after John as he took the steps down to the back garden. 'If you think this is how we'll get back together with Mother dictating and you more or less agreeing, then you're sadly mistaken,' she fumed in hushed tones.

He turned to face her, shrugging his shoulders and opening his arms wide. 'Laura my dear, I wouldn't have the temerity to think anything of the sort,' he said pompously. 'I'm merely being polite to Mother. She's only trying to help. Don't blame her.'

'Only interfering you mean. She's good at that,' she sniped, the heated flush of her cheeks subsiding as she turned and stamped back into the kitchen.

'I know you, Mother. You think you can get your own way every time. What's happened between John and me is far too serious for that.'

'I think I'd better be going, darling. It's not my place to be here. I'm only trying my best.' She started to snivel.

Laura placed an arm around Mother's shoulder. 'I know you're trying to do what you think is for the best but please leave me to fight my own battles. Now let's see you smiling again,' she said, taking the handkerchief and wiping away the tears. 'That's better. Now let's have that cup of tea, shall we?'

John came in from the garden, the boys tagging

156

along behind. 'They're wearing me out.' He laughed with his eyes and casting an impish smile in her direction. Dear God, how she loved him. He would never know how much.

'Time for tea.' Laura ushered the children into the dining room. 'Sit down all of you. Colin you're over here.' She pulled out a chair for him. 'Special place for the birthday boy,' she laughed.

The boys bantered with each other as Laura lit the candles on the cake. Colin blew them out, not once but three times whilst John had his box camera poised for the photographs. After the boys had had their fill and the cake had been cut, they slid from their chairs and ran towards the back door, challenging each other.

'I must say, you do them proud Laura.' Mother smiled as she watched them disappearing, jostling for position and almost falling down the steps. 'I'd like to get back now dear. Would you call me a taxi, John?' She turned towards him imploringly.

Laura knew Mother expected John to run her home. It was a good ploy. They could have a good chat and put everything to rights. There was no stopping Mother. She spent her life conniving and using her 'little woman' feminine charms to get what she wanted.

'You know I'm taking driving lessons, don't you, Mother? Once I've passed, there'll be no need for taxis,' Laura stressed, giving a strong hint that she didn't need a man to run her about or to run her life for that matter. Soon she would be independent.

'I don't hold with women driving,' Sarah said

amiably, her point of view invariably slanted to the superiority of men.

'Why not?' Helen's voice held a touch of bitterness and her eyes blazed with defiance.

'You should be relying on your man to chauffeur you around. Daddy wouldn't dream of me driving!'

John, ignoring Mother's opinion, intervened. 'I'll take you back, Mother whilst the boys are playing.' He went through to the cloakroom, took her coat and held it out for her.

'You've had very little to eat, Mother,' Laura complained. 'I'll cut you a piece of Colin's birthday cake. He'd be devastated if you went without any.'

'My appetite's not what it used to be. I have too much on my mind,' Mother replied, a downcast look on her face. She picked up her handbag and followed John, turning to give Laura a hug. 'Don't you be so stubborn,' she whispered. 'It'll get you nowhere.'

Laura handed her the cake. As usual, Mother had to have the last word.

The boys were still outside when John returned. 'Did you have a good chinwag with Mother?' she asked accusingly, the sarcastic tone in her voice reflecting her mood.

'She commented very little, darling. I think she'd already said it all, don't you?' He moved closer. 'Don't you think she may be right? Surely I've done my penance now.'

'It's not a matter of time. I'm not ready to pick up where we left off. Are you sure it's not the flat that's depressing you?'

158

'Of course I hate being on my own, darling. I know I've been a complete idiot. I do love you very, very much, believe me,' he implored, his voice filled with infinite tenderness.

She met his strangely blistering look with a level one of her own. 'If each time you come you're going to work on me, John, then the invitations are going to be few and far between.' She turned and reached up to the cupboard allowing John the chance to put his arms around her waist. She quickly slid the plates into the cupboard and he spun her around to face him. As she looked into his eyes, she almost lost control and gave in.

'Sorry, darling. I will bide my time,' he promised, an expression of desperate apology on his face. He let go and went off into the garden to be with the children. Laura felt a stab of sympathy, but she was too angry and too stubborn to show it.

Jack was persistent. He called at Helen's the following day but was told by Mary Grant that she had gone to London for a few days. Jack looked at Mary with suspicion.

'Gone off to London has she? She didn't mention it. Well, it's not important.' He left Mary standing at the back door, a puzzled look on her face. He smirked. That'll give her something to think about. Things weren't running to plan or as quickly as he would have liked. Although he'd told himself he should take his time and not rush into things, he had hoped she might have given him the come-on by now.

'Yoo-hoo.' The call came as he set off down the steps.

Jack turned. It was Maisie striding out to the top of the steps, hurriedly fastening her headscarf under her chin. 'I thought it was you. I've noticed you calling in once or twice lately. Got something going with missis next door, have you?' she asked quizzically.

Jack took exception to Maisie's tactless comment. It seemed he could do nothing without these busybodies checking up on him. 'What's it to you? I take it you've no objection.' His voice held an edge of resentment. He stepped on to the pavement and turned to face her.

She backed off. 'It's nothing to do with me, Jack. I just thought it was a bit soon with her husband not long dead and buried.'

Jack quickly retaliated. 'There's nothing going on. I'm trying to give her a bit of help, a bit of support, that's all.' He could do without this hussy prying into his business, broadcasting it to all her cronies.

'It was a shame about her Jim. But I saw it coming. Lost his job, see. I don't know how she's coping. And now she's taken on Mary Grant.' She folded her arms. 'God knows how she affords it. All I can say is old Waxman must be giving her a fair old wage.'

Her prattling riled Jack. As far as he was concerned Helen was doing the right thing. What was wrong with her earning a bit of money?

'I haven't a clue what she gets. As I said, I'm just a good friend helping out. As you say, it's nothing to do with us, is it Maisie?' He stared her hard in the face before clearing off down the road towards Newport Street.

Helen travelled back to Kidsworth, finding it difficult to take in what had happened. Having had to cope with losing Jim followed by the gas incident at Mother's, now she had lost her dear friend and colleague, Vincent. Surely nothing else could happen to dampen her spirits.

Lifting her small case from the luggage rack, she set off across the station yard to the taxi rank. In normal circumstances, she would have taken the bus but this was an exception. What worried her more than anything was how she was going to cope in the shop without Vincent. He'd been her business partner in the true sense of the word. They'd shared their thoughts and ideas and made decisions together. Now she would have to cope on her own. But who would inherit Vincent's assets?

She must stop herself from thinking in that vein. She was being selfish. The priority now was to make arrangements for the funeral.

When she climbed the steps to the house Mary was at the door to meet her, the little ones by her side.

'It's good to be home,' Helen whispered as she bent down to greet the girls.

'Mummy! What have you brought us?' Sylvia cried as they both clung to her skirt.

'Sylvia love. Give Mummy a chance to get inside before you start to attack her!' Mary laughed and eased the child away from Helen, ushering the two of them into the front room where she'd lit a fire in the open grate. 'Come along now, dear,' she said, turning to Helen. 'Sit yourself down and

161

we'll have a nice cup of tea.'

'How could I manage without you, Mary? You're an absolute angel. It's Vincent,' she whispered, 'bad news I'm afraid but I'll talk to you later when things are quieter.'

Sylvia climbed up on her knee and Helen took two small boxes from her bag. They were wrapped in pretty floral paper.

'See what I've brought you my little treasures.'

'Oo, Mummy. I love opening presents,' Sylvia cried, ripping at the paper whilst Jessie carefully pulled hers apart, trying not to tear it. Inside each of the boxes were two butterfly hair-slides, Sylvia's in yellow and Jessie's in pink, and two ounces of Cherry Lips for Jessie, two ounces of Dewdrops for Sylvia.

'Thank you Mummy. They're just what I wanted.' Jessie held up the card of slides and opened the bag of sweets. 'How did you know I liked Cherry Lips the best?' She laughed as she popped one into her mouth.

'I like Dewdrops the best.' Always the copier, Sylvia adored Jessie and looked up to her. 'Please, Mummy put my slides in for me.'

'I can put mine in by myself,' boasted Jessie.

Mary came in with the tea tray to which she had added two glasses of home-made lemonade and a plate of iced biscuits. 'You are lucky girls. Now save your sweeties until later. Stew and dumplings tonight, Mummy. We don't want to spoil our appetites do we?' she lectured, handing them each a glass of lemonade. 'Don't spill it or there will be trouble.' Mary beamed at them in admiration.

Later when the children were in bed Helen told Mary exactly what had happened at the exhibition. But she made light of her meeting with Charles Ravel.

'Helen, love, you must have been out your mind with worry.'

'That's true and so sad.' She wiped the tears from her eyes. 'But now I must make an appointment to see Mr. Marchbank. It's important I know who is going to be my new partner at the shop.'

'I can't believe it,' Sarah admitted as she relaxed on the sofa. 'Helen told me Vincent was perfectly all right when they left for London.' She looked up at Laura. 'Sit down, dear. You are staying I take it?' She would never understand why time should be so valuable to Laura these days.

'I'm on my way to Dora Bristow's. She's wild about Winifred's new decor. You know how scatty Dora is. All I know is she's desperate to try something new.' Laura's haughty glance was one Sarah often witnessed. Dora Bristow had no idea what she was letting herself in for, poor girl.

'It's not everyone who can make decisions. Some of us like to rely on our menfolk to do that.' Sarah smiled inwardly. She had always made the decisions, in a subtle way of course. You had to know how to handle your man to do that. Perhaps Laura was too full of herself to realise that Dora had the hang of it. But she'd soon find out.

'So what will Helen do now Vincent's gone? I must go and see her. But I dread going to that place.' Sarah raised her eyebrows and gave Laura an unequivocal nod.

163

'I know exactly what you mean, Mother. It is rather seedy. It's the neighbours I can't bear. They're so rough and crudely spoken.' Her look was not unlike Sarah's. 'Were you serious about her coming to live with you?'

'I most certainly was. Anything to get her away from that place.'

'It would put an end to Jack Bean's visits.' It was the best idea yet. 'Let's go together and combine forces.'

Sarah perked up at Laura's suggestion. Not only would she have the company of Helen and the girls, but it would take them all away from Kidsworth and Emley Street which had always been Sarah's ambition.

Helen pushed open the heavy door to the solicitors' office and rang the bell on the counter. Taking in the musty smell, familiar to such places, she stared across at the highly polished wooden panelling. A spotty-faced girl opened the hatch door and in a sulky, resentful voice asked her name.

'It's Helen Riley. I have an appointment with Mr. Marchbank.'

Almost immediately an elderly gentleman came out from an adjacent office and stretched out a hand. 'What a pleasure seeing you again, my dear,' he said. 'Do come in.' He crossed over to his cluttered desk. 'Now, what can I do for you?'

'I'm afraid it's sad news.' She swallowed hard in an effort to calm her emotions. 'Vincent Waxman, my business partner, died suddenly of a massive heart attack at the weekend. We were at a London exhibition when it happened.'

'My dear, that's terrible. What a shock! It's not long since the two of you were in here'

'That's right. The problem is I've no idea who Vincent's beneficiary might be. Arrangements need to be made for the funeral,' she stressed.

'You've put me on the spot there. Until I'm officially informed of his death I'm afraid the will is confidential. I need the official documentation before I can make a start.'

'But the beneficiary will be my business partner. I need the information as quickly as possible.'

'Who dealt with the death certificate?' he asked.

'St. Cuthbert's Hospital in London.'

'Leave it with me. I'll ask them to put the document in the post tonight. Give me a ring tomorrow, late afternoon. I should know more by then.' He smiled warmly before shaking her hand. 'Do take care, my dear.'

Out in the street, Helen hurried towards the bus stop. It was Wednesday half day closing which meant she could go straight home to the girls. As she stepped onto the bus a moment of panic touched her. If the beneficiary was not identified soon, her future would be more uncertain than ever.

Mary was rolling out pastry for a meat and potato pie as Helen returned. 'You look all in,' she said.

'How did it go? Did you manage to sort things out?'

'Not really. The will can't be disclosed without the death certificate. I won't know the name of the beneficiary until then.' Helen tried to relax in one of the fireside chairs, stretching her feet towards the fire, and feeling weary now that the full truth had hit her.

'Well, I suppose if he's trying his best, you can't ask for more.'

A loud knocking at the front door disturbed them.

'I'll go,' Mary volunteered, trimming the pastry and slipping the pie into the oven.

Helen listened as Mary released the bolts. 'Do come in,' she said. It was Laura and Mother. Helen jumped up to greet them. 'This is a surprise and lovely to see you both.'

Mother approached her with outstretched arms and gave her a hug, her face a picture of grand drama. 'Darling it must have been awful.' Releasing her, she took hold of her hands and added, 'How are you feeling?'

'I'm coping. It was a terrible shock, Mother. I still can't believe Vincent's gone. It all happened so quickly.' Tears sprang to her eyes but she quickly wiped them away.

'You need a break, my love, a chance to relax and get over it.'

'I'll survive,' she replied, frowning. 'But what brings you here?' she added. It was unusual for either of them to visit. There must be something afoot.

'We need to have a chat, Helen,' Laura replied looking pointedly at Mary.

At that moment Mary was taking her gabardine coat from the hook behind the door. 'I need to collect the girls. The pie's in the oven. There's plenty of tea in the pot, Helen.'

No sooner had Mary closed the door than

Laura turned to glance at the chair Helen had vacated, peeled off her gloves, rubbed her hands together in front of the crackling fire and sat down. Sarah sat opposite.

Helen pulled up a stool. 'What's so private, Laura, that you can't tell me in front of Mary?'

'Mary's your hired help, Helen. Does she have to be party to everything we discuss?' Laura replied, her waspish tongue getting the better of her.

'That's not the sort of relationship we have. I don't regard Mary as a hired help. She's my friend.'

'Whatever. But what Mother has to say would affect Mary indirectly and that's the reason we wanted to talk to you alone.'

Mother stepped in. 'I'm not happy you living here on your own, darling.' She paused. 'Give this place up, Helen. I'd love to have you and the girls with me permanently.'

The suggestion came unexpectedly and Helen was knocked off balance. A multitude of thoughts crossed her mind, adding to her confusion. The idea of living with Mother, unable to come and go as she pleased and having to be sociable with Mother's ever-fawning friends, was totally unacceptable and out of the question.

'Mother, it's very kind of you but now I have Mary we're coping very well and enjoying each other's company.'

'Darling, you know Mother and I have never liked your being here. Now you've no excuse to stay,' Laura added, her mouth firm with annoyance.

'I'm my own woman, a free spirit, just as you are, Laura. I prefer to go my own way,' Helen countered firmly. 'We won't be here forever. I intend making a go of the antiques.' The two of them obviously thought they had her up against the wall with their two-pronged attack. In a way she supposed she was rebelling against convention, but Laura was doing that too.

'It would be good for both of us, Helen.' Mother's tone was soft and persuasive her look pleading. Helen had seen it all before.

'I'm grateful for your offer, Mother. It's so kind of you but I'm here to stay, for now that is.' Pushing wispy strands of hair away from her temples, she held her chin firmly in the air. Her decision was made. She needed some solitude in her life.

'Do remember, darling the offer is always there. Think it over and let me know later.' Mother's face eased into a tentative half-smile, and Helen knew her campaign of attrition was set to continue for as long as she felt she had a chance of succeeding.

After leaving Emley Street Laura stopped the car outside Kirk Grange and turned to Mother. 'Don't give up on her. I'm sure she'll change her mind once she realises what she stands to gain.' Laura tried to sound encouraging.

'What do you mean, dear?'

Mother could be tedious at times. It was easy to work out the gains. But Laura couldn't make out whether Mother was genuinely puzzled, or whether she was being contrary as she was prone to being these days.

Laura linked her arm. 'If she came to you, she

168

could dispense with Mary Grant for a start. That'll save her money. What she'll do about collecting the children from school I don't know.' Initially, Laura hadn't given this a thought, but it could fire the argument for Helen to give up the job. 'Once she's with you, she'll not need to work. You'd like that wouldn't you, Mother?' Laura had a smug, self-satisfied look on her face. That scenario would suit her too. If Helen could be persuaded to give it up, Laura would be the only career woman, the one excelling. The thought that it smacked of jealousy passed through her mind, but she cast it aside.

'I can't see her giving up the shop so readily, not now. But you may be right.' Sarah pursed her lips and nodded in semi-agreement.

Laura continued, hoping she was laying the foundations for what might ensue. 'I certainly hope I'm right. It's far too much for her, rushing about like she does.'

'The same applies to you, darling,' Sarah retorted. 'There's absolutely no need for you to go chasing around sorting out other peoples' decorations. It's surely beneath you.'

It came as a shock to Laura, being drawn into the equation. Other people's decorations? Is that how she saw it? A frown replaced her smile and her eyes iced over. She was on the point of snapping back but she restrained herself. Swept with indignation but remaining calm, she proclaimed, 'Decorations indeed! It's professional design work, Mother and you jolly well know it.' She closed the door and followed Mother through into the morning room. Changing the subject, she

169

glanced towards the hall and asked, 'Did you mention the landscape picture to Mrs. Bean?'

'I did. She told me she had missed it. But I promised her the print Helen replaced it with.' She removed her soft, dark sable coat and her fawn kid gloves, handing them to Laura.

'I bet she didn't care much for that.' Laura smirked, taking the coat and gloves into the hall.

'I don't think she did, darling, but beggars can't be choosers, and I haven't gone yet,' she retorted pointedly.

Chapter 12

Helen sat in the waiting room at the solicitors' office. She'd followed Mr. Marchbank's instructions and telephoned. But in a flat voice, he'd asked her to call in at the office. Somehow she was not anticipating much progress. Not surprisingly, when he came out to receive her, his pinched, expressionless face matched the tone of his voice.

'Sorry to keep you waiting, but I need to explain. I received the certificate from the hospital this morning. But when I took Vincent Waxman's will from the safe, I realised it hadn't been updated. His latest beneficiary was his wife, Pearl.'

'But she died six years ago.' This was her second visit. She was none the wiser and baffled too. But she pulled herself back from the brink of irritation when a sudden, fleeting picture of the

170

gentle Vincent was etched in her mind. It was obvious why he hadn't revised the will. When he'd lost Pearl, the love and passion of his life, he'd been desperately upset and thrown into dreadful confusion. He'd simply overlooked it.

'I realise that but my colleague, who dealt with wills, retired due to ill health shortly after Mrs. Waxman passed away. The review must have been overlooked. We offer a service and do try to remind our clients and give advice. I'm afraid it was an oversight. I'm just as surprised as you are.' He fingered the will nervously, turning it over in his hands and then tying the red ribbon into a neat bow.

'What happens now?' she asked as her eyes searched his for a solution. She bit her lip, disappointed at not getting everything cut and dried.

'You're the only one involved at the minute,' he said, his face taut. 'If you agree, I suggest you make arrangements for the funeral and we'll sort out the costs from his estate. Meanwhile, I'll put an advertisement in the newspaper announcing his demise and asking any relatives to come forward. Are you sure you don't know of anyone at all?' He clasped his hands, now looking more relaxed.

She drew in a deep breath, shaking her head. 'Sorry, Mr. Marchbank. It's something we never discussed.' It looked as though this business was going to be extremely drawn out. 'Is it all right for me to carry on as normal in the shop?' She collected her handbag ready to leave.

'It depends what you call "normal", my dear. Don't invest in more stock but by all means keep on selling. I take it you have a stock inventory?'

'Of course. Why do you ask?'

'I'll need a copy to make sure everything's legal. I hope you understand.'

Whilst she accepted it might be necessary, she was reluctant to be accountable to anyone. Her face conveyed her feelings.

'Don't worry, Mrs. Riley. I don't for one minute doubt your honesty.' His words were intended to sound conciliatory. 'It's just that everything has to be accounted for. Could you bring the inventory in and I'll get someone to attend to it?'

'It's the only copy I have, the one I work from. I wouldn't like it to be away for long,' she pointed out, 'and I don't have the time to do a duplicate.'

'Arnold can scribble away quickly and legibly. I'll get him started as soon we receive it. You'll have it back the next day,' he volunteered, his face breaking into a thin smile.

'I'll drop it in tomorrow.' She paused and then continued. 'When will the advertisement appear in the newspaper, Mr. Marchbank?' she asked, aware that she might appear pushy, although after all, her livelihood was at stake. With Mary to pay from her small income, it was essential she continued to run the business successfully.

'It will be next Thursday now. We've missed it for this week.' Pushing back his chair, he stood up. 'I'll show you out,' he offered, gently ushering her into the corridor. 'Don't fret, my dear. I'll try to speed things up and contact you soon.'

Helen called in at the shop and collected the stock inventory. Some of the items could go, especially the leftover prints from the time when money was scarce. They could be reduced and sold off, provided she could continue to run the business in the absence of Vincent's beneficiary.

Helen's mind was still full of questions. She entered her house and reflections of Vincent triggered memories of his sheltered life. She had no recollection of his mentioning a relative other than Pearl. He'd told her he was lonely since her death so surely if he had relatives they would have visited.

The sound of footsteps alerted her to the arrival of Mary and the girls. 'We're back, Mummy.' Jessie ran towards Helen who scooped her up. Sylvia followed suit, pushing herself in between the two.

Mary laughed heartily. 'She'll not be outdone won't the little one.'

After their evening meal and once the girls were tucked up in bed, Helen came downstairs. Mary looked up from her knitting.

'By the way, I forgot to mention. Jack Bean called on Friday night. He seemed surprised you'd gone away without letting him know.' Mary frowned.

'He's the last person I want around. He's been here a couple of times to offer his help but I'd be happy if he'd stop calling. Laura's heard he's fond of little girls.'

At first Mary looked puzzled but then shuddered visibly, a bewildered expression in her eyes. 'That's terrible,' she said. 'It's as well I didn't ask him in.'

Jack heard the news about Vincent Waxman but

173

he couldn't decide whether it was good news or bad. Maybe Helen would take over the shop now, as long as no-one else stepped in and put her nose out of joint. Whatever the situation, it was time he visited again but he'd have to be careful. According to his ma, old Dorrington had said Helen was upset after Waxman had died. What all the fuss was about he'd no idea. But he knew what women were like.

He cycled home from the mill and propped his bike up against the wall in the back yard, opened the door and stepped on to the doormat, wiping his feet vigorously. Better not tread any muck in. His ma could be a terror when she started.

'You're back our Jack! Thought you said you'd pop back home dinner time. Made you a nice plate of black pudding and peas. I had to eat it meself,' she said magnanimously.

'Nay Ma. I can't get back every day. I did a bit of overtime, if you know what I mean,' he joked.

'I hope you haven't been thieving.' Her cheeks reddened and she had an animated look about her. She was cleaning the brasses, the handles on the black-leaded oven, the fender and the hearth-tidy. They shone like gold.

'Don't get yerself upset, Ma. Back of lorry stuff, that's all.' Grinning mischievously, he chucked her under the chin playfully, knowing she was annoyed.

'Don't start your pranks again, you daft beggar or I'll box your ears. I've just about had enough of you,' she said as she pointed a finger at him.

He knew how to get her rattled, but the truth was he'd done nothing wrong, just helped a mate pick up some furniture in the works van.

He devoured the sausage and mash she dished up, scraping the rim of his plate with his knife. 'Any more, Ma?' he asked.

'Don't be putting your knife in your mouth. It's bad manners,' she preached turning to pick up the frying pan. 'It's like feeding the five thousand,' she said proudly, knowing full well how much he enjoyed her cooking.

He laughed loudly. 'And what would you say if I didn't eat it?'

'Don't be so damned cheeky. You're not too big for a cuff around the ear,' she threatened fondly, swishing the palm of her hand gently across the top of his head and missing it narrowly.

'Don't come with your love taps, Ma,' he muttered, dodging her hand again. He pondered. 'I think I'll call in on Helen tonight,' he announced, looking at the jam sponge his ma had placed before him. 'A bit more custard, Ma,' he insisted.

'I wish you wouldn't go there, Jack. I'd rather you kept away.' She frowned and picked up the jug of custard, pouring it carelessly over Jack's sponge.

'Enough Ma. Don't bloody drown it,' he grumbled, mixing it in with his spoon. 'All I've done is tried to help. There's no harm in that is there?' he said, attacking the jam sponge with gusto. 'Bloody 'ell. This jam's hot,' he shouted, wafting his hand in front of his mouth. 'She ought to be glad someone's thinking about their lass. Nobody else seems to bother,' he offered and, before cramming the spoonful of pudding into his mouth, he blew on it vigorously.

175

'I'm not saying she isn't, Jack. It's just the neighbours and that,' she added, scraping clean her own pudding dish so that not a morsel remained. She pushed her heavy body up from the table and went over to the sink, placing the dish under water.

'Don't say Maisie's been spouting off again. Who takes any notice of her anyway?' he complained. He picked up the jug, poured the rest of the custard into his dish and scooped it up gluttonously.

'Don't eat jug as well.' She smiled benevolently. 'Suppose you've had enough then?' she said obviously avoiding any further mention of Helen.

To his ma's disgust, Jack burped loudly. 'Manners, Jack!' she chastised as she turned to the sink to start the washing up.

Ignoring her comment, he set off upstairs to spruce himself up for his visit to Helen's. Dressing quickly he tucked his shirt into his grey flannels and stared vacantly at the faded wallpaper patterned in nasturtiums. He shivered as the biting wind outside splattered raindrops noisily on the window. A bit of luxury was what he needed, not this place with its draughts. If he played his cards right, he could have that luxury, including the takings from the shop, the picture, and there might be a bit of something from her ma as well. He struggled impatiently with his collar stud, a gleam of sweat appearing on his brow but finally he managed it, pressing down the collar and smoothing it around his neck.

'Jack,' his ma called from the bottom of the stairs. 'There's Walter Ellis here.'

Oh, bugger. He'd have to get rid of Walt. He dashed

swiftly down the stairs.

'Ow do, Walt. Going somewhere special in yer best bib an' tucker?' he asked, swaggering across the room and patting him on the back.

'I thought we might make a night of it down at Cock and Bottle.'

'I've summat on, Walt, but I'll be in later,' he promised. With a wicked grin he rolled his eyes and winked at Walt who looked him up and down.

'You bugger.' Walt gave a conspiratorial laugh. 'Who's lucky lass then? Anyone we know?'

'A bit of hupper class stuff. Know what I mean?' he said affectedly, as he mockingly brushed invisible hairs from his jacket.

'Fair enough. See you in Cock and Bottle,' he concluded and with that, Walt left.

Jack slipped on his jacket and made his way on foot to Emley Street. As he approached, he looked around furtively hoping that gasbag Maisie didn't catch sight of him. She'd only cause more trouble.

He'd be firm tonight. Helen would be feeling low after the old lad had pegged it. Careful handling might just do the trick. She'd need someone to give her a bit of guidance, and a bit of the other. He whistled as he stepped jauntily towards the front steps, smirking to himself. He felt as fit as a lop.

A wagon drew up outside the house, and two coalmen stepped out, their bright eyes gleaming out of black faces. *A bit late for them.* Deciding to wait until they'd delivered, so as not to complicate matters, he hung about behind the high wall. *What a bloody nuisance.* They were delivering next

177

door as well. He hoped Maisie stayed up the side path where she was standing, hands on hips, checking the number of bags they were dropping in her shed.

'Left me one short, last time,' she complained.

'We don't do them tricks, love,' one of them said.

Getting no joy from her complaint, she went back into the house and slammed the door. Jack climbed the steps. The front room light was on. Don't say she had visitors. That would jigger the job up. He went down the side path, not wanting to change his habit. She was used to him going to the back door. He knocked briskly and after a couple of minutes he heard the key turned in the lock.

'Who is it?' The voice was not familiar.

'It's Jack.' Straightening his tie and standing to attention, he felt it vital he made a good impression.

The door opened. It was Mary Grant. 'Oh, it's you Jack. I told Helen you'd called,' she said, her voice a little shaky. 'It's Jack Bean,' she called.

Helen came to the door. Jack looked her up and down. She looked a proper Bobby Dazzler. He continued to stare for several seconds, taking in her slender body and that lovely chestnut hair. Oh yes, this one was for him. He pulled himself together.

'Now then Helen. Going to let me in or what?' He stepped over the threshold and on to the mat.

'I'm rather busy tonight, Jack. Perhaps you've heard that Mr. Waxman passed away last week. It's left me so much to think about. Mary and I are trying to sort out the stock.' Her voice was firm, in fact Jack felt it was a bit too firm, considering his relationship with her, at least what it could be.

'Anything I can do for you?' Now that he'd gone and stepped inside the house, he felt a bit of a dope. It was obvious he'd picked the wrong time. But he felt she was making a bit of a fool of him and what that old maid Mary Grant was doing there on a Saturday, he'd no idea. From what he'd gathered she only stayed weekdays.

'Thank you very much Jack, but we need to continue. Maybe some other time,' she said and, in expectation of his leaving, she held the door open.

His back stiffened. 'Sorry to bother you, lass.'

It was as if a barrier had sprung up between them, he couldn't think why. He left and without looking back he walked briskly down the path. Inwardly, he was seething, his anger dark and active. If those Dorrington lasses thought they could get the better of him, they were sadly mistaken. He was usually slow to anger, but once he was aroused, he could be dangerous.

Chapter 13

Charles Ravel walked briskly into the railway station. Heads turned and took in his classic good looks and his suave appearance in the black, velvet-collared Crombie overcoat. He was heading for a four day conference in Leeds on *'Theatre and Post-operative Techniques'*, which was to be followed by a tour of Leeds General and a visit to Woodbridge, a small orthopaedic hospital several miles away. He bought train tickets and, knowing the journey threatened to be long, he bought a couple of newspapers at the kiosk, slipping them under his arm. It was then he spotted Miriam.

'We're in good time,' he said, striding across, taking hold of her case and leaning forward to give her a light kiss on the cheek.

'It's been a rush, darling' she said, moving her bag from one shoulder to the other, her blonde hair immaculately groomed in page-boy style. Beneath her fawn swagger coat Miriam wore a French navy suit in grosgrain.

The train was half empty when they entered the first class compartment. The porter appeared, folded their coats, placed them on the luggage rack and looked expectantly at Charles, who took a shilling from his pocket and handed it over.

'How did yesterday go?' She unbuttoned her jacket and relaxed in her seat.

'It was rather drawn out. The laminectomy became tricky, problems with the anaesthetist, temperamental old so-and-so. The knee was pretty straight forward.' He folded his newspaper back.

'You're going to wear yourself out. You take on too much. After all, Gerald is extremely capable. You should delegate,' she said with an air of authority. 'By the way, I'm meeting Jeffrey for a weekend together. He travelled up to Leeds on Wednesday, for the Cranford Murder trial. He's

180

hoping it'll be finished by Friday.'

'Let's hope all goes well. I'd like to spend a couple of days in Leeds, call on a few friends,' he pondered before continuing. 'It must be wearing this barrister business, thinking on your feet.'

'How about when you make snap decisions, when complications arise in the middle of an op?'

'Well, I suppose each to his own.'

'You sell yourself short every time. You need to start organising your life. Give yourself time to socialise, have some fun darling,' she insisted.

'Don't go on, Miriam. You know the score. I'm happy the way things are,' he said and he stared vacantly ahead.

Once in Leeds they booked in at The Queens and arranged to meet in the foyer at seven o'clock. The reception was at seven fifteen but Miriam had figures to sort out before then.

Charles switched on the radio in his room and heard the announcement that Norway would donate a pine tree for Christmas. It was to be placed in Trafalgar Square. Christmas had not even crossed his mind and yet it was almost the end of the year. He smiled. The youngsters would enjoy seeing the tree, especially after the austerity of the war years.

He buttoned his dress shirt, fastened his bow tie and slipped on his dinner jacket, taking the clothes brush from its hook and flicking it gently across his shoulders. The news continued with an item about the new medium, television, but his mind was brought abruptly back to the evening's reception when he glanced at his watch. It was already ten minutes to seven, and it was not his way to be late for appointments. As he entered the function room he realised the place was already buzzing with activity. He turned to look for Miriam.

'Sorry I'm late, Charles,' she whispered, smiling pleasantly at some of the people she knew.

Charles smiled to himself, aware that Miriam was always professional in her approach. He glanced across at the programme displayed near the door.

He was to be the main speaker during the afternoon of day one, but the following day he would be free. A feeling of warmth and expectancy came over him. That would give him the opportunity to look up Helen at her shop.

The management lectures ran in parallel with the medical conference and Miriam, one of the few women to gain a top position in hospital management, had agreed to spend her free time with Charles whenever possible.

It was nine o'clock before the conferences were over, and the two met in the bar for a final drink before retiring for the night. 'I'm hoping to travel to Kidsworth tomorrow, Miriam. I intend getting in touch with Helen Riley. I left London in a hurry and I would like to see her again and make sure she's coping,' he said defensively. 'Are you free?'

'Not tomorrow.' She paused. 'I know you're fond of her, Charles, but do you know her background? She may be married for all you know.' Miriam was a purposeful woman with her own quiet dignity. 'You know how much I admire you for your professionalism, but more especially for

182

your understated manner. Beyond all doubt you're a surgeon of some considerable note, a rare breed in my book. But I'm concerned for you. You're so vulnerable and I don't want you hurt, yet again.'

'You flatter me, Miriam. But Helen's widowed. It's a very sad story. She told me about it when we were at St. Cuthbert's.' His memory of her was bittersweet, part sadness and part pleasure. A look of anticipation shone from his luminous eyes.

'I've seen that look before Charles. Take care!' Miriam warned, her face softening into a smile.

Charles made enquiries about the shop in Kidsworth, having established it was the only antique shop in the area. He took a taxi there but all was in darkness and the sign on the door said *Closed*. That was bad luck, but not intending to give up easily, he leant forward to speak to the driver.

'Unfortunately the shop's closed but I need to contact the owner. She lives in the area. If you'll drive on I'll enquire at one of the local shops.'

The taxi pulled up outside a parade of shops, but Charles noticed they were all closed. Saturday must be half-day closing in the area. He looked at his watch. It was twelve thirty-eight. He'd obviously missed Helen by a whisker if twelve-thirty was closing time. Not to be beaten, he asked the driver to pull up beside two elderly ladies. 'Excuse me. I'm looking for a Mrs. Helen Riley. She owns the antiques shop. Do you know where she lives?'

183

'Mrs. Riley lives over there,' one of them said, pointing to a row of houses opposite. 'Number fourteen I think,' she added.

'Thank you so much,' he said. He pointed as he spoke to the driver. 'Left at the end, please.'

The driver, obviously puzzled that someone of his type should be visiting this area, gave him an odd look but did as he asked.

Charles climbed the steps two at a time and was about to knock at the front door when someone called out. 'She's out, love. Is it anything important? Can I give her a message?' It was Maisie Blenkinsop.

'Have you any idea when she'll be back?'

'Sorry. She goes to her ma's Saturday afternoons. You'll be lucky if she's back this side of teatime. Are you sure you don't want to leave a message?'

'Thank you for your help, my dear. I'll call again later,' he replied and promptly returned to Leeds.

Maisie, breathless and flustered, stared after him open-mouthed and obviously flattered at being called 'my dear'. She kept a look out for Helen, anxious to find out as much as she could about the smart gent. Later in the afternoon she spotted her.

'You've had a visitor Mrs. Riley. A right smart-looking chap, ever so handsome and wearing a lovely black overcoat with a velvet collar.' Maisie stood on the back step and shouted across to Helen.

'What time was that, Mrs. Blenkinsop?' Helen was puzzled. Surely it couldn't be the doctor who

184

had helped when Vincent collapsed in London.

'I can't remember exactly. I'd say about two o'clock. Anyone you know?' she pried.

'I've no idea who it might have been, Mrs. Blenkinsop. Did he leave a message?' she asked, her heart leaping in anticipation.

'I asked him but he didn't seem to want to give anything away,' Maisie reported, her voice tinged with disappointment.

'Thank you for letting me know,' Helen replied. She was becoming used to keeping a tight rein on her emotions, but the memory of Charles began to haunt her as, with a mixture of wistfulness and embarrassment, she recalled the short time they spent together. It couldn't possibly be him. Why would he come all that way to see her?

'I'd still like to get in touch with Helen.' Charles was determined. 'Would you like to come with me tomorrow, Miriam?'

Miriam looked surprised. 'If you're sure, Charles. I don't want to cramp your style,' she stressed, laughingly. 'But, yes, I'd love to come.'

Charles felt a ripple of emotion and a smile of recollection rested on his lips. He was looking forward to seeing Helen again. In the past true happiness and fulfilment seemed to have passed him by. Some years earlier he'd been badly let down and he'd convinced himself only his pride, not his heart, had been wounded. And he wouldn't let that happen again. But this was different and nothing serious. He could handle it.

The taxi was prompt and took them straight to the shop in Kidsworth. 'I'll go in and make sure

185

she's there,' he suggested, and as he glimpsed the silhouette of a woman through the window, a tingle of pleasure stirred inside him.

As he entered the shop Helen turned to face him. With an expression of joy and surprise on her face, she moved swiftly towards him. Encapsulated in the moment, his feelings towards her were completely irrational. Yet he couldn't deny them.

'Charles. This is a surprise. How lovely to see you,' she breathed, her eyes full of tenderness.

He took her hands and squeezed them, giving her a peck on the cheek and taking in the sweet, intoxicating smell of her skin. A single shaft of winter sunlight shone through the shop window, catching her rich chestnut hair and bringing out the gold and amber lights. His stomach somersaulted. He wanted her too much for comfort.

'What brings you here?' she asked excitedly.

'You, of course,' he replied, his eyes brimming with adoration. 'Just a joke!' he added and laughed. 'Miriam and I are at a conference in Leeds. I've left her outside in the taxi. I'll call her in?'

Helen's face dropped and her voice faltered. 'Please do, Charles.'

Charles perceived a look of disappointment as she backed away and he noticed a kind of vulnerability about her that awoke in him a strong feeling of protectiveness. He longed to hold her close, but he controlled his emotions and went to collect Miriam.

'Helen meet Miriam Jordan, a very dear friend and colleague of mine, Secretary of the Shropshire Hospital Group. Miriam, Helen Riley, the lady I bumped into in London.'

Charles was relieved to see the warm welcome Miriam offered to Helen.

'Bumped into? Engineered I imagine!' she joked good-humouredly, winking impishly and giving Helen a knowing look. Her enthusiasm was heartwarming.

'Miriam. Don't exaggerate.' Charles was amused. She was always sensitive to his needs and he had tremendous faith in her innate common sense, her unconditional support.

'We're still in Leeds tonight, Helen. Back to Oswestry tomorrow. How about dinner? Can you manage it? Miriam, you're invited too, of course.'

'Sorry, Charles. I'm seeing Jeffrey tonight,' she replied, chuckling good-naturedly.

'How about it, Helen?' His eyes were pleading with her not to refuse. She appeared to catch his signal and her face was suffused with pleasure.

'I'm sure Mary won't mind but I'll call you and confirm it? I don't like to take her for granted,' she said, directing her eyes intensely into his.

'Wonderful. I'm sure she'll agree. About seven, then?' Charles was optimistic and felt a thrill of satisfaction that they'd met up again.

Helen broached the subject with Mary as soon as she arrived home that evening.

Mary's supportive attitude was reassuring. 'You only go out once a blue moon, Helen. It's time you had a treat.'

Going out for dinner was certainly a treat and, oblivious to the cold penetrating her bare hands, she set out to the nearest telephone box at the end of the road. Charles was out when she rang the hotel, but she left a message. Her heart sang as she started back to the house and she felt herself flush with pleasure in anticipation of seeing Charles again.

It was her first opportunity to wear the peach shantung two-piece Mother had recently bought from Jepson's as a birthday gift. Helen had not approved at the time, but now she was grateful she had two outfits to wear in the evenings. Adjusting the dressing-table mirrors, speckled with age, she viewed the back of her glossy mane, its glorious curls resting gently on her shoulders. Applying a final dab of powder to her face, she hastily glanced at her watch. It was seven o'clock already.

Mary answered the door and invited Charles in. It was no use leaving him on the doorstep. He had to know some time Helen didn't live the life of luxury.

When Helen appeared looking soft and vulnerable, a devastating smile danced around his mouth and lit his eyes. Immediately she detected the same signal he'd given her earlier and she realised it was many years since she'd been overwhelmed with such feelings. But she was acting like a child and she tried to she compose herself.

'Hello Charles. It was a bit of a rush, but I'm ready now.' A happy smile lit up her face and she slipped her arm through his.

'You look gorgeous, darling,' he whispered, his voice unusually hoarse. 'It's been so difficult without my car but I've managed to borrow one,' he said, pointing to the shiny black Morris on the roadside. 'At least we're not dependent on taxis. I've booked a table at The Beeches. Do you know it?'

'I don't, Charles, but I'm sure it'll be lovely,' she said, searching his face with a gentle gaze.

Eventually he drew up in the car park of a large hotel. 'This is it.' Turning to her, he added, 'I hope you're going to enjoy it.'

'Charles if it were the corner cafe I'd enjoy it. It's wonderful to be taken out.'

As she stepped from the car, he pulled her close, gently taking her face in his hands and brushing a kiss lightly on her lips.

The maître d'hôtel advanced and led them to a table near the window. 'Drinks, sir?' he asked.

'Two pink gins please,' Charles replied and with a glint in his eye, turned to Helen. 'I take it you approve?'

'Why not?' she replied taking in his tall, strong build. He was amazingly handsome and, whilst she was not sure she could accept her attraction for another man after losing Jim, she found herself unable to escape it. Composing herself, she asked him if he'd coped with the backlog on his return.

'I decided to off-load the minor ops,' he replied. 'We eventually caught up, but of course we'll have yet another backlog when I return. But we cope.' He switched the topic. 'How about you?'

She told him of the problems they were having finding Vincent's next of kin. Charles was positive in his reply, showing a strong interest in her future.

During their meal the memory of their meeting

189

and now their reunion brought a smile to her face. 'I haven't enjoyed myself like this for years,' she said.

'I'm so glad it's been a success.' He laughed, pushed back his chair and beckoned for the waiter. 'Let's go, shall we?' He turned. 'The bill, please.'

They left The Beeches and walked towards the car. He pulled her close reluctant to let her go and a low groan escaped his throat. But the years since his relationship with Rita had mellowed him, taught him patience and finesse. He needed to take control for both their sakes.

Helen looked up in anticipation, but he disengaged himself.

'I'll take you back, Helen,' he said gently, opening the passenger door. But judging by her reaction, he thought she seemed disappointed and a little hurt.

'It's been wonderful, Charles and such a change.'

He leant across and kissed her softly. Holding her at arms' length, he said, 'The way I feel about you is much stronger than you will ever realise.'

'But we're little more than strangers,' she replied.

He read the wary expression in her brown eyes, enormous with apprehension. But her husky voice betrayed her and he sensed the feeling was mutual.

He stopped the car outside the house. 'I hope to see you again soon,' he said and he held her upturned face towards him, brushing his lips lightly on hers before he let her go.

Chapter 14

The solicitor stood up and stretched out his hand. 'Marchbank,' he declared stiffly.

'Donald Valentine,' his client announced. 'Pleased to meet you.' He took a seat and rubbed his hands together. 'What's the score, old boy?'

Marchbank thought the fellow obsequious and took an immediate dislike to him. 'You tell me you're related to the late Vincent Waxman. Have you proof of this?' He wanted to get to the point. Either he was or he wasn't entitled to the estate.

'I'm his nephew.' Valentine smiled ingratiatingly. 'Here's my birth certificate. Mother was Vincent's older sister.' He handed over a dog-eared document.

Marchbank smoothed out the edges and placed it on his desk, scrutinizing it carefully.

'Your mother Olive, Vincent Waxman's sister, married Percy Valentine your father?' He posed the rhetorical question and looked up.

'Indeed,' Valentine replied pompously. 'But Mother died last year.'

'I'm surprised you had no knowledge of Mr. Waxman's death until you saw it in the newspaper.' Marchbank decided to pressurise this bounder.

'We didn't get on with him.' The supercilious smirk on Valentine's face annoyed Marchbank. The fellow would have to do better than that.

191

'I shall need your mother's birth certificate to check the parentage and establish her relationship to Vincent Waxman.' Marchbank maintained his mask of gravity. 'You'll need show me the death certificate too. The estate would have gone to your mother had she still been alive.'

'Of course I don't have them here but I could bring them in. What do I stand to gain?' His directness didn't surprise Marchbank who had already detected the greed in Valentine's eyes. He tried to remain objective but, in his mind, he had a picture of that poor little Riley girl.

'Nothing until your relationship is indisputably proven. I'm not at liberty to disclose the contents of the will until then,' he said, putting him in his place.

'Well then, Mr. Marchbank, I'd better toddle off and see to it, hadn't I? The sooner the matter's settled, the sooner I can start to organise my uncle's affairs.' It was clear from his manner that he was untouched by any sentimentality.

As he turned, apparently to utter his farewell, Marchbank interjected. 'I take it you'll not be attending the funeral,' he challenged. 'You've not mentioned it.' Marchbank was appalled at the very idea of passing the estate over to someone who cared nothing for his dear friend Vincent Waxman.

'Never gave it a thought,' Valentine commented casually. 'I suppose it would be the right thing to do, to show my face.' He took a small diary from his pocket. 'When is it?'

'St. John's, Kidsworth. Eleven o'clock Friday the tenth,' he announced formally.

'Pity. I'll have to cancel a luncheon at my club. Such is life.' He opened the door and concluded, 'I'll be back.'

St. John's Church stood grey and gaunt, and in the churchyard the naked trees were silhouetted against the hostile sky. A haze of fog drifted silently around the church, clinging to its very fabric. The morning air was still cool but the sun threatened to penetrate the clouds and burst through. Helen wished it would. The lack of sunshine was depressing enough, especially on the day of a funeral.

A few business friends arrived, most of them familiar to Helen but, as far as she could gather, there were no relatives. The church was almost empty as the coffin was carried through. The service was short and lacked the personal touch. The vicar, a stand-in for Mr. Pleasance, was a dry old stick, boring and lacking charisma. Despite Helen's discussion with him earlier, he made no effort to give a genuine account of Vincent, of his caring and thoughtful ways, and his generosity. She was disappointed.

Outside in the churchyard the air was fresh and the sun threw an orange glow over the backs of the remaining clouds as Helen gave her personal thanks to those who had attended. She invited them back to the Wellington Arms for a light luncheon.

As the funeral car trickled forward, and she was about to step inside a man appeared from the side of the church. He dropped a cigarette to the ground and stubbed it out with the sole of his shoe, staring her in the face challengingly, and stretching out his arm towards her.

'Donald Valentine, Waxman's nephew,' the man informed her self-righteously.

Helen was taken aback, visibly so, and reaching for his hand, she shook it lightly.

'You look as if you've see a ghost. Who are you?' His scornful look irritated her.

'Helen Riley, Vincent Waxman's business partner,' she pronounced crisply.

'Business partner? I knew nothing about a business partner,' he exclaimed, frowning and shaking his head in disbelief.

'I knew nothing about a nephew,' she responded, keeping her calm. 'Vincent never mentioned you.' She was puzzled. She'd had no letter from Mr. Marchbank.

'Marchbank needs one or two documents before he's prepared to disclose the will. I have an appointment tomorrow morning for the reading.' He stepped closer. 'What sort of business is it anyway?' he probed.

Helen shivered in the raw November air. She was certainly in no mood to explain the situation. Not there in the churchyard.

'Mr. Valentine, this is neither the time nor the place for such a discussion. I must get back to the reception at the Wellington Arms. Come along if you wish.' The chauffeur opened the car door and she stepped inside.

At the reception Helen made a beeline for Veronica Brightwell, an old friend she hadn't seen for some time.

'It's such a sad occasion, Helen, and so unexpected.' Veronica took hold of Helen's free hand and squeezed it. 'What a way to end the year.'

'You can say that again, Veronica. I'll be glad when we reach 1950. I'm looking forward to a new decade, a fresh start,' she said. 'I've been meaning to contact you to ask you to look at a picture of Mother's. I think it's a Pissaro but I'm not certain. I know you're an expert on these things.'

'Gosh, I'm no expert but I think I'd know a genuine Pissaro if I saw one,' she maintained. 'I'd love to see it. Landscape I presume?'

'Yes, it is actually, and rather lovely too,' Helen whispered proudly.

'Let me see...' Veronica started, but before she had the chance to continue, they were rudely interrupted.

It was Donald Valentine. 'There you are, old girl,' he blurted. 'You were saying...'

There was a long silence. The two women turned and Veronica looked him directly in the eye.

'We're in the middle of a conversation if you don't mind,' she said brusquely.

Helen smiled knowing Veronica deplored his type, the arrogant, dominant male.

'Sorry Madam.' His manner was ironically servile, grovelling even.

Veronica drew herself up. 'I should think so too.' She scowled and turned to Helen. 'Perhaps you could contact me later?'

'I think maybe that's best. I'll get back to you next week.'

Helen glared at Valentine. Who on earth did he think he was?

Helen was in the shop sorting through the stock when Donald Valentine turned up. Smartly dressed in a pair of fawn trousers and a navy blue blazer, he swaggered in, looking around with unconcealed curiosity. His eyes were almost as dark as his sharply-parted black hair which was slicked down with Brylcreem. He stood erect, his military bearing giving him an air of superiority.

'I didn't expect you so soon,' she said, unable to disguise her disappointment.

'Maybe not, Mrs. Riley, but here I am. Saw old Marchbank this morning. It seems I've got a seventy five per cent stake in this place.' His handlebar moustache twitched as he walked nonchalantly to the back of the shop, picked up a glass vase and gently tossed it from one hand to the other, staring at her defiantly. 'What's this worth?'

'Careful Mr. Valentine. It's cut glass,' she warned, stepping forward, ready to take it, but he held it firmly. The way he'd strolled in as though he owned the place irritated her. Determined not to accept his claim to part-ownership until Mr. Marchbank advised her officially, she said, 'I'm afraid you're wrong on the matter of ownership. I own thirty three per cent of the shop, not twenty five.'

'It's as near as dammit,' he ventured, hiding contempt behind a thin smile. 'I'd like a full stock-take to check out the value of this lot.' He waved his arms in the air. 'Then I'll decide how to play it.' His voice was distant. He placed the vase down heavily on a table.

Unaccustomed to taking such sharp and direct

196

instructions from any man, Helen stiffened. 'Don't you mean we'll decide how to play it, Mr. Valentine?' she emphasized.

'I meant what I said, my dear. If I decide to get rid of the place you'll have no alternative but to follow my instructions.' A cold smile settled on his lips.

Placing his hand in his pocket and giving her a superior look, he added, 'Agreed?'

Helen was furious. How dare he walk into the shop and try to take over? She felt a surge of sudden impatience and her head started to throb.

'I'd be obliged if you'd leave me to continue my work until Mr. Marchbank informs me officially of your sixty six per cent ownership. I hope I've made myself clear,' she offered, aware she might incur his anger. But he had to be brought to heel.

'Careful, poppet.' His response was patronising. 'We don't want you upsetting yourself now, do we?' He smirked, crossed over to the door and let himself out quietly.

It was later than usual when Helen returned to Emley Street. 'I think I may be in for a bumpy ride with Donald Valentine,' she said as Mary poured the welcome cup of tea.

'How do you mean, love?' Mary stood poised, teapot in hand.

'He's been to the shop today and put my back up inflating his share of the business and suggesting he sells it.' Helen raised her eyebrows and with a hint of sarcasm added, 'That's a good start isn't it?'

'Don't let him rattle you. Stay calm,' Mary advised.

'I should have kept my cool but talk about arrogant. He could ruin my career at the shop.' She sat in the fireside chair knowing it was no use worrying. She must wait and see what happens.

Changing the subject, Mary asked, 'Have you thought any more about the issue with Jack Bean?'

'I'm thinking of calling on him and having a word before he comes here again,' she said. 'I can't accuse him but I need some excuse to stave him off. What do you think, Mary?'

'It'll take some courage but you must take the bull by the horns. Tell him it's too soon after losing Jim for men to be calling and that the girls might misunderstand.' Mary was firm in her response.

Helen thought about Mary's advice. She must go and see Jack otherwise she was always going to worry in case he called again. She sighed. Life seemed to be full of obstacles these days. There was nothing straightforward. Why did everything have to be complicated?

Jack came in from outside. 'It's chucking it down out there,' he said and he dashed the raindrops from his flannelette shirt.

'What do you think, Jack? Mrs. D's getting one of them new wireless sets with pictures,' Agnes piped up before slipping her arms through the wrap-over pinafore and smoothing her hands over the front.

'Bloody 'ell, Ma. They must be made of brass,' Jack speculated as he took off his overalls and rolled them up.

'Don't leave your dirty overalls in here,' she

198

stressed. Jack's problem was that he never tried to better himself. Not like she did, especially when she mixed with the toffs. It was no wonder Mrs. D seemed not to like him visiting Helen. If only he could put on a bit of style. 'Did you go to Helen's last night?' she asked, shaking out the tablecloth.

'I did but Mary Grant was there doing stock list with her. I never got no further than doormat.' He shook his head and tutted.

'Poor lass must be in a state. She'll have to do everything now Waxman's gone.' Agnes sighed.

Ignoring her comment, he continued. 'You women are too soft. If you left it to fellas, you'd be right.'

'She's still got the picture then?' Agnes hadn't pursued that business for a while. But it would do no harm just to know it was still safe at Helen's.

'I've no idea, Ma. I haven't been in front room since other week. Don't worry. It'll be right!'

Agnes sighed. Not another of his plans. Don't say he was scheming again.

Helen trudged across the waste land towards Newport Street and the ground was frozen hard. Jack should be home by this time. It was already six o'clock. Tentatively, she knocked on the door and waited. It was a thankless task but it must be done. The door opened. Jack stood there facing her.

'Now then, lass. Nothing wrong I hope?' He left her standing in the dark.

'I'd like a word, Jack. May I come in?' He opened the door wider and grinned sheepishly. She

199

stepped inside. His mother was standing behind him.

'Hello, Mrs. Bean. I haven't seen you for ages. How are you?' Helen asked politely glancing around the room. There was a welcome warmth from the fire crackling in the grate. Helen already felt calmer, ready to face up to Jack.

'I've been lucky these last few months. Had no trouble at all to speak of,' Mrs. Bean explained, putting on her best pronunciation.

Jack rolled his eyes.

'I'd like a word with Jack if you don't mind,' Helen said quietly.

Jack looked puzzled. 'Right, lass. Best come into front room.' He opened the door and she perched stiffly on the edge of the sofa.

'This is difficult for me, Jack.' She paused. 'But I'm sure you realise how I valued your friendship and the help you've offered me, but things are becoming embarrassing. My girls are curious about your visits. Some of the children at school have made suggestions, no doubt having heard comments from their parents.' She took a deep breath. 'It's too soon after losing Jim. I'd prefer you didn't call again, Jack, not for the time being.'

During an awkward silence, Jack stared at her in obvious disbelief. 'Hang on Helen. Just let me get this straight. You don't want me calling just in case folk start talking.' His mouth was set and his voice was filled with outrage. He signalled his annoyance by drawing himself up tall and looking down at her.

'I'm still feeling fragile after what's happened,'

she said shakily as she stood up to leave. Her aim now was to get right away and control her own life.

'If that's how you want it. Suppose it's that nosy bitch, Maisie who's put it around. For two pins, I'd go over and knock seven bells out of her,' he fumed as he drummed a heavy tattoo on the chair arm.

Helen backed off. He had suddenly turned sour. In a contemptuous gesture, he lifted his head and the savagery in his eyes frightened her. But she stood firm, sensing his extreme anger. She supposed she couldn't blame him, but she wondered if he suspected the real reason for her decision. 'Maisie hasn't mentioned a thing, Jack. I rarely see her.'

They stood facing each other. It was clear she'd roughened his sensibility but he seemed to become calmer as, undoubtedly fond of her, he held her gaze. Then, as if embarrassed, he turned away and focused his eyes steadily on the door. 'You know how I feel about you, lass. It hurts me that you seem to want rid of me.'

She witnessed the plaintive edge to his words, the tremor in his tone. It must have been difficult for him to express such a personal statement and, she didn't know why, but she had her doubts about the story Laura had told. He didn't seem that type. But her decision was made. 'Please understand, Jack.'

He looked away dejected but, despite her feelings, those were her final words on the matter. As she opened the door, Mrs. Bean, now looking guilty, moved furtively away. 'Everything all right, love?'

Helen was aware she'd been listening at the door. 'Fine, Mrs. Bean. Just something I needed to discuss with Jack.' She opened the back door ready to leave. 'Nice seeing you again.' Her comment was genuine. She smiled weakly. 'Goodnight.'

She closed the door, bitterly regretting her involvement with Jack. Casual though it had been, she'd handled it badly, and she knew she'd been lax in allowing him to visit in the first place. But now a great weight had been lifted and, as she set off back to Emley Street, her face seemed to lose its tension.

As the door closed behind her, Jack stamped across the living room. 'I don't believe it!' he shouted, a vindictive gleam in his eye. 'She's only told me not to call again. Says she doesn't want folk talking. God knows who that might be,' he growled. He shook his head. 'And after all I've offered to do for her. Ungrateful...'

Agnes stopped him in mid flow. 'Stop your shouting, Jack. Don't be getting yourself into a paddy. I don't want you fratching with Mrs. D's lasses. Cut it out?' she urged.

'She's not heard last of it,' he promised chillingly, running his hands through his hair and sucking it back from his temples. 'She'll be sorry she's given me the push.'

Chapter 15

Laura drove her new car seven miles east to Langthorn, aware that Donald Valentine lived in the area, but unsure of the exact address. Helen had told her of the confrontation with Valentine, of his superior attitude and the opinions he'd voiced. But Laura didn't believe her. The thought of Helen being involved with yet another man rattled her. He probably had a soft spot for her, just like the others, but Laura was determined to put a stop to that. This time she would help the situation develop. If Valentine was on the brink of selling the shop, why not convince him it was the right thing to do?

As she reached Winscote Lane, she pulled up outside a general store and looked up at the unusual storm cloud blackening the sky. It was Friday night and the store was still open. On instinct she ran inside the shop before the first of the heavy drops began to fall. A grey wisp of a woman came out from the back, her shoulders hunched as she huddled over the counter. 'Poor day, love. Looks as if we're in for a right storm,' she forecast.

'I'm sure you're right. Sorry to be a nuisance but could you tell me where Donald Valentine lives?'

'They're up at Bridle's Garth. Turn left at top of Winscote Lane, then right up track. Not been before, then?' she enquired, folding her skinny arms waiting for an explanation.

'No, I haven't, but thank you for the help.' To the woman's obvious displeasure, Laura turned and left the shop. The first spots of rain were falling as she opened the car door and slid into the driving seat.

The house was dominant on the skyline as Laura turned into the long, winding drive thickly lined with rhododendrons. The car crunched over the gravel and she stopped at the front. Stone steps led to the imposing front door and two enormous columns supported the great stone canopy, forming an open porch. Despite her fierce determination to control the situation, a flurry of apprehension overcame her but she climbed the steps and rang the bell. Seconds later the door opened and a man of about thirty, tall and rangy with jet black hair and deep-set brown eyes stood there. He sported a slick RAF-type moustache. His dark eyes lit up.

'Sorry to trouble you. I'm looking for Donald Valentine?' she said, her mouth trembling as she made her solemn enquiry.

'Look no further, poppet. What can I do for you?' His eyes glistened with curiosity.

'I'm Laura Conway, Helen Riley's sister. I'd like a word please,' she said, gathering her confidence. 'What I have to tell you might be of interest.'

He opened the door wider and she stepped into the hall. 'Come through into the drawing room,' he said. 'You say you're here about that little sweetie-pie, Helen,' he paused, 'although she can be rather bossy.' His eyes took in Laura's every contour. 'Chalk and cheese the two of you, but equally lovely.' His mouth twitched in a flicker of humour.

'I understand exactly, Mr. Valentine, she can be over-assertive...'

Valentine intervened. 'Donald, my dear. Do call me Donald. May I call you Laura?'

'Of course.' She paused. 'Mother and I are at our wits ends with Helen.' Laura gave him her own warped version of Helen's determination to remain independent, despite Mother's offers of help. 'She needs the shop like she needs a hole in the head.' Trying to gauge his intentions she held his gaze. 'It might be an idea if you bought her out.'

The contradictory nature of Laura's request appeared to come as a shock to him. 'I would have thought that was the last thing she wanted. She seems awfully possessive of the shop.' His voice was coolly non-committal. He looked puzzled.

'Believe me, Donald, you're right. But she is so stubborn. We must make her see reason. Mother and I are convinced the shop is too much for her. She has so little experience.' Laura's views came over as exceptionally plausible.

'I see. The last thing I want is an obligation to someone inexperienced. I'd rather appoint a manager I could trust to run the business. I had thought seriously about taking her on. She seems a spirited little filly. I'm certainly not interested in buying her out, my dear, not my forte, antiques,' he said, and after a brief silence he added, 'It looks like I've no alternative but to sell after what you've told me. It seems that would fit the bill on both sides,' he concluded, his handsome

205

face expressionless.

'I felt sure you'd understand.' She smiled. 'You do realise Helen knows nothing of my visit and I'd like to keep it that way.'

'Don't worry your pretty head,' he said, a lazy, good-natured smile spreading across his lips as he placed an arm loosely around her shoulder. 'I think we need to sort things out together. Couldn't interest you in dinner at the Devonshire tonight, could I? Short notice, I realise but it would be fun. You look as if you could do with a bit of a giggle, old girl.' He arched a challenging eyebrow.

Laura was in a quandary. It was short notice, but they had hit it off well. 'That would be lovely, Donald.' She beamed even though the speed of her own decision surprised her.

Tuesday morning was busy at the shop. Helen sold five prints, having given a considerable discount to dispose of them. Since her visit to the exhibition, she was determined to offer antiques of a much classier calibre to encourage a more discerning clientele. The bell rang as the shop door opened and she looked up.

'The Dresden set. Is it still available?' Mrs. Barclay, a friend of Helen's mother enquired casually. The set of figurines was in excellent condition and the woman had been admiring it for weeks. She could well afford it, but Helen guessed she was playing the waiting game.

'It is Mrs. Barclay, but I've had quite a lot of interest in it. If you'd like it I could reduce it by three pounds, just for you of course. I know

206

Mother wanted you to have it. It would please her so much.' Knowing the woman would take up the offer, Helen smiled. Three pounds was a lot of money, but she would still make a good profit even taking the reduction into account.

'Done,' replied Mrs. Barclay. 'That's my kind of bargain, darling.'

'Bargain. What kind of bargain?' Donald Valentine echoed as he walked into the shop. 'Helen, my dear, you're not losing money, I hope?' The superior tone of his voice angered Helen, but it was no use allowing him to upset her.

She steadied herself and held back, deciding it would be better to play along. 'Glad you're here, Donald. I'll be with you in two ticks,' she said brightly, turning then to the customer. 'You'd like it delivered I presume, Mrs. Barclay?'

'Yes, of course, my dear,' she replied, counting out the money.

'Wednesday afternoon is the earliest we can manage.'

'Suits me,' the woman replied, beaming as she left the shop.

'That was clever of you, Donald – your comment about losing money on the stock. I knew Mrs. Barclay had more or less decided, but I think that clinched the deal.' She disliked putting on an act but she'd made a hash of things on his last visit and she needed to keep her cool now to placate the situation.

'You think so, poppet?' He shrugged his shoulders and grinned, his manner patronizing.

But Helen bit her tongue. 'Mr. Marchbank has informed me your share of the shop is legal. Have

207

you thought seriously about it?' Helen, filled with apprehension, hardly dared face him.

He nodded vigorously. 'I most certainly have. I've seen the stock list – not bad is it? If we can get the market price, we'll do well. Tell me, what's that stuff you've just sold, the Dresden? I know it's pottery but what's so special about it?'

'It's very delicate porcelain made in Meissen, East Germany, from the local kaolin. This is the set.' She pointed to the beautifully crafted statues near the back of the shop. 'It cost me less than half the price I've charged Mrs. Barclay. We've made over one hundred per cent profit. That must suit you!'

Donald appeared mystified but delighted at her words. He was about to reply when the shop bell rang. Helen looked up in surprise.

'What can we do for you my good fellow?' Donald was in there ready to serve, probably jumping to the challenge, thinking he could do just as well as Helen.

'It's not you I want, it's her.' It was Jack. He pointed across at Helen.

She moved towards him. 'Can I help you?' she asked crisply, taken aback that he should come to the shop, especially after she'd warned him off earlier in the week.

'Yes you can. That picture over there,' he said, pointing to a Monet print. 'How much is it?'

'I could give you a special price on that one,' she murmured. 'It's actually ten shillings and six-pence but I'll let you have it for nine shillings,' she offered with no hint of recognition.

'Nine bob?' he echoed. 'It's overpriced, if you

ask me.' He glared, and Helen was unable to weigh up his motive.

'Now look here, young man. We're not asking for your evaluation. We can do without your sort in the shop. This is a respectable establishment not a charity.' Donald believed he could deal with him man to man but, unfortunately, he'd no experience of the likes of Jack Bean, whose face told Helen he wasn't going to listen to a stuck-up prig like Valentine.

'Who the hell do you think you are? Don't give me that. I know what you're after.' Jack seemed to be touched by some sort of madness judging by the haunted look in his eyes. He stood and stared for several seconds, and then turned on his heel, leaving the shop as quickly as he had entered. Helen stared after him and felt a coldness touch her heart.

It was over two hours since Jack had left the house and Agnes couldn't for the life in her think what the devil he could be up to at this time on a Saturday. He usually called at the fish shop and had the order back by quarter past twelve – haddock and chips twice with scraps. The kettle had been on and off since ten past and the table was set. She hoped he wasn't stirring up trouble. Enough was enough!

Her heart was going nineteen to the dozen as she reflected on what had happened the day of the gas leak. She knew it was all her fault. If Jack hadn't given her that sleeping pill to slip into Mrs. D's coffee earlier in the morning, she'd have nothing on her conscience and Mrs. D would have been as right as rain. But Agnes couldn't forget it. It kept coming back. The problem was that, after she'd left, Billy Lockwood called in, mucking up the plan, just as Jack was about to pop round and collect the canteen of cutlery she'd hidden under the stairs months earlier. Mrs. D. seemed to have forgotten all about it. She'd not missed it and it was a tip-top set too.

Mrs. D must have felt groggy after drinking the coffee. That's why when Billy tried to take the money Mrs. D left the gas on. Agnes had half a mind to tell her and get it off her chest, ease her conscience. Jack had no idea how it had worried her and all the trouble she had having to lie to that P.C. Clarke. If Jack started his games again, she'd tell him straight. He'd not only get himself in trouble but her as well. But if he thought he could involve her, he could think again. And that was final!

She paced up and down the living room. *Was that a flutter she felt?* She put her hand to her chest. It wasn't surprising she had angina the way their Jack kept on upsetting her. She'd have a heart attack next. She could fair feel it coming on.

She pulled her thoughts together when she heard footsteps pounding through the passage. The door opened. It was Jack.

'My god,' she cried, still in a state of nervous anxiety. 'I thought you'd left the country.' The anger in her voice covered the guilt she felt.

'I'm a grown man, Ma. Surely I can go out without permission?' He plonked the parcel on the table and sat down. 'Come on. Dish 'em up,

Ma. I'm starving.'

Agnes was still fuming as she unwrapped the parcel, placed the fish on to the warmed plates and scraped the chips and scraps on top, carefully pulling away and eating the chips stuck to the paper.

'You'll know about it one of these days, Jack. I might not be here when you come home!' she said sorrowfully, sweeping her hand dramatically across her forehead, sitting down and tucking into the fish and chips as if it were the Last Supper.

Once she'd cleared the table and washed the plates she turned to him. 'You look as if you've lost a pound and found a penny our Jack. Summat wrong?'

'Summat wrong? It's bloody marvellous. She tells me to keep away and then I find another bloke in shop with her. A right stuck up devil he was. These toffee-nosed fellas get up my cuff,' he thundered, his tone scathing. He sat drumming his fingers on the table, his eyes full of anger whilst his ma picked up the teapot and poured another mug of tea.

'You might be going wrong way about it. He might have had summat to do with business.'

'She's taken him in as a partner more like, that's what I think. No wonder she wanted me out of the way,' he speculated through clenched teeth. 'I only went there to try and talk her back into seeing me. I fell soft, Ma. And I feel a right twerp now.' He took a deep swig of his tea and swallowed it noisily. 'When I saw him there in his blazer and slacks – a right dandy he looked – I saw red.'

'Drop it now Jack. You've gotten hold of wrong end of stick as usual.'

He shook his head and barked back at his ma.

'Why am I always in the wrong, Ma. Don't you ever see my side?'

Deciding not to answer him, she changed the subject. 'You know, I've been thinking. I can't get over feeling guilty about that sleeper I dished to Mrs. D. Shouldn't have done it you know. It came to nothing in end,' she admitted twisting her wedding ring around on her finger, clearly recalling exactly what had happened.

'There you go, Ma. As you say we got nothing. It was only a sleeping pill for God's sake. Forget it.' He drained his mug and pushed it across the table towards her.

'That's not the point, Jack. I feel bad about it. It's getting on me nerves. I feel like coming clean and telling her – ease me conscience like. I only expected her to nod off in the chair, didn't expect the kid to come calling, and then that damned complication with the gas stove. It's your fault, you and your bright ideas.' She looked down at her hands, toying with the whole business, and trying to shut out the guilt in her head.

'My fault? You didn't say no,' he said in defence. 'You must be barmy, Ma. Surely you don't want to drop us in it altogether, going and telling her, and having P. C. Clarke on your back. Forget it,' he said, sighing irritably. He banged his fist down on the table and pushed the chair back. 'Well, I'd better get that bit of digging done, Ma.'

She sensed he was trying to appease her. Had

212

his conscience got the better of him?

'No good waiting till it rains again,' he added.

But Agnes wasn't interested. She still hadn't sorted out her own problem. Did she confess all to Mrs. D or did she do as Jack suggested, keep quiet about it?

Chapter 16

After putting the finishing touches to her make-up, Laura took a final glance in the cheval glass. She was proud of the way the apple green crepe dress hugged her slender body and brought out the hazel glow of her eyes. Her fair hair, lifted in combs at the sides, fell loosely on her shoulders. Feeling glamorous and confident, she was ready to work on Donald, hoping to persuade him to sell the shop.

She knew she was not lacking when it came to the 'little woman' act, knowing that was very much in the style of her mother and, where Donald was concerned, she had a strong feeling she would come up to stereotype.

Donald arrived at seven fifteen and, as she opened the door, he leant forward and daringly kissed her on the cheek. 'Lovely to see you again, my dear,' he said, and his enthusiastic approach filled with caution, especially after the incident with Jack Bean and her recent problems with John. But she must try to relax and let the evening flow over her.

Donald drove the Jowett Javelin skilfully through the countryside and Laura smiled to herself. How would John have reacted had he seen her with another man? But she couldn't care less. What she needed was a little spark in her life; a little dalliance, even a brief affair would do no harm.

Their conversation during the drive was inconsequential. It was difficult to chat lightly to someone she barely knew and, aware he was concentrating on the road ahead, she was reluctant to distract him by making flippant comments.

When he pulled up at the Devonshire Hotel he stepped out of the Jowett, dashed to the passenger door and helped her out. 'That's the ticket,' he said as he held her hand and led her though to the bar.

'Dry martini?' He pulled out a bar stool for her.

'Please,' she replied thinking what fun it was. It had been some time since she'd been pampered, and her thoughts turned again to John. But she quickly cast him from her mind. Why dwell on the past?

When Donald flirted with the barmaid Laura studied him furtively. He was dark and rugged, not quite as handsome as she first thought but he was certainly attractive. But she was aware he could be so very dangerous, the sort of bounder to whom many women are inextricably drawn, the kind of man husbands disliked. But she would take care. Her only aim was to exert her power over him, make sure he did as she asked.

'Penny for them,' he offered, bringing her back into the conversation.

'Sorry, Donald. I was miles away, thinking

about Helen and the shop,' she confessed, needing to make a start. This was the perfect moment.

'Don't worry, darling. We'll sort it out together.' He handed her the martini, pulled out a second bar stool and sat facing her.

'By the way, I was at the shop today. I'm surprised you reckon she's no experience. She seems extremely au fait with everything about it.'

Laura interjected. 'She's brilliant at putting on an act. But what do you mean?' Laura felt a tinge of disappointment, but tried not to show it.

'She sold a set of Dresden figures to a friend of your mother's. She told me we'd made over a hundred per cent profit. How about that?'

'She'll tell you anything to string you along. I thought you'd have seen the light by now.' Why was he putting obstacles in her way?

'That's news to me, Laura. I must watch out. What did alarm me was a visit from someone called Jack, a low-life if ever I met one.'

'That's just about stitched it up. He is a low-life and more besides, but that's another story.' Casting aspersions at Jack and intimating Helen's vulnerability was Laura's ace card. Surely Donald would now realise Helen was more trouble than she was worth and, judging by the property he apparently owned, he was certainly not in need of the income. It was just another game to Donald.

'Your table, sir,' the waiter announced as he collected the drinks and took them across. Donald pulled out Laura's chair and, as she sat down, he squeezed her shoulders. 'Lighten up, old girl.' He sat down opposite and took hold of her hand. 'You know I find you very attractive. Where have you

215

been all my life?'

His lack of originality, churning out the old cliché, did nothing to impress Laura. He focused his eyes on her face, her shoulders, her breasts and he rubbed his thumb across the backs of her fingers, staring intensely into her eyes. And she realised she was attracted to him.

'Ready to order, my love?' Now he was getting into the mood calling her his 'love'.

'I'd like the prawn cocktail and the chicken please,' she murmured huskily and gazed back at him with equal intensity. Without becoming too involved, she would play him at his own game.

After dinner they sipped Napoleon brandies. Laura had to admit to herself that Donald's company, his attention, his suave approach and his gentle manner had given her back her confidence. A fierce determination swept through her. At all costs, she must persuade him to sell the shop.

When they left the restaurant he smiled an easy, radiant smile and, as he drove off quickly the atmosphere in the car was electric. A few miles on and he stopped the car at the side of a country lane, slid his arm around her waist and leant his head against hers. She felt comfortable and relaxed with a feeling of warmth towards him. His lips brushed hers, teasing and tormenting. His arms bound her tightly, and his hands stroked her body, exploring.

She had ached to love and to be loved since John had left. But not like this. Her confidence faded, and confusion clouded her face. This was sordid. She stopped him abruptly.

'Sorry, Donald, but this is not the time or the place.' She shook off the feelings.

'I'm so sorry darling. I couldn't resist. Come back and have a drink with me,' he begged, a bewildered expression in his eyes.

Sensing the genuine need in his tone, she knew she could have taken anything from him, the state he was in. But not now.

'I couldn't possibly. I must get back to the children.' She stroked his brow gently. 'Let's not rush it.' Her statement was filled with ambiguity but she knew she must keep her promise.

'Will I see you tomorrow?' His tone was optimistic. He smiled awkwardly.

'Why not?' she offered, a little ashamed she'd strung him along, but she knew she had to keep up the pressure now she had him firmly on the rein.

Helen thought of Charles and trickles of pure pleasure pervaded her body. The feeling was something different, something very deep and she wanted to savour every moment of that memory. He had made a lasting impression on her. But it would be four weeks before they met again.

The shop bell rang, bringing her sharply back to reality. She looked up. It was Donald.

'We need to talk business and get things sorted, my dear,' he said jovially.

Helen focused on his words. 'How do you mean?' she asked, covering a surge of irritation by straightening the pile of papers on the desk. The ominous way he had approached her was worrying.

'I've decided I'd like to sell. I'll give you first refusal to buy my share,' he proposed lightheartedly, joining her at the back of the shop.

Helen faced him squarely. 'Sell? I thought you were impressed with the profit margin.' She frowned. 'I don't have the money to buy you out, Donald. Can't we compromise? I'll run the shop and you could be a sleeping partner.'

'I don't mind being your sleeping partner, darling,' he said with emphasis on the 'sleeping', 'but not in the way you mean.' He chuckled, pleased at his own wit.

Annoyance swept through her. It was all a huge game to him. 'I'm very disappointed, Donald,' she confessed. 'What's brought this about?' She could try talking him round but she must curb her tongue, no icy comments or disparaging remarks.

'It's just not for me. I need rid of it. I thought you'd be glad to buy me out.' He laughed skittishly and the nonchalant way he talked about money infuriated her.

'Please reconsider, Donald,' she begged. 'I can't afford to give it up now. I have the girls to think about.' She was aware that should the shop be sold outright, she would have to ask Mary to leave, just as things had settled down.

'My mind's made up. I'll contact the agents. Get them to give us a price.' He shrugged in a lazy, familiar movement then he hesitated. 'The alternative is to get yourself a partner, buy me out.'

It was so easy for him. Her mouth was dry, making it difficult for her to speak. 'I can't think of anyone who could afford to buy you out,

Donald,' she said dejectedly. 'I suppose you'll just have to press on and get it over with.'

'I can't believe it,' Helen complained, her hands hugging the cup of hot tea. 'He's so cold-hearted. How will I manage?' she asked, looking to Mary for a solution.

'You're better rid of him if you ask me, even if it means losing the shop. You'd have been at his beck and call forever and a day, him having the lion's share so to speak. It's not like being with Vincent.'

'You can say that again.'

'The way I see it is to find yourself another little place, smaller premises.' Mary picked up her cup of tea and sipped it delicately. 'What about Moody's place down by the post office? That's been empty since Joe died.'

'But it was a cobbler's shop, Mary. Fitted out and everything. It'll need lots doing to it.' The idea was good, but facing all that work was another matter.

'We could do it between us. What are friends for? It'd be a challenge.' Mary's eyes lit up with optimism. 'We could go down there tomorrow, the two of us and have a look around. What do you think?'

Helen smiled bravely. 'I didn't realise I'd hired myself a business adviser as well as a nanny. I know our shop's not sold yet but I would imagine it'll go pretty quickly once it's on the market.' She breathed deeply and pulled herself upright. 'The stock will no doubt go with the business. I'd obviously start afresh and visit the salerooms.'

219

'That could be exciting, Helen, a fresh start with your very own business. No-one giving you orders.' Mary became animated as if it was going to be a fresh start for her too.

One thing was certain, even though Donald had put a damper on her plans Helen wasn't about to give in. She knew there would be no guarantees, but Mary's idea was sound.

Days later, a man, clipboard in hand, strode confidently into the shop. 'Granville Francis, Wright's,' he said stiffly. 'Mr. Valentine contacted me about his shop. I'd like complete access.'

'What are you talking about? Complete access? And why should I do that?'

He frowned. 'I'm from Wright's, estate agents,' he replied tersely, an impatient look masking his face.

'I see.' With an air of authority Helen stepped towards him. 'Let's get this straight, Mr. Francis. Donald Valentine is my business partner, not my employer,' she was quick to inform him. 'Do what is required and report back to me when you've finished,' she directed brusquely realising he was one of those men who assumed that property and assets could only belong to men, and that women were either stupid or incapable.

As she watched him disappear into the storeroom at the back of the shop, she latched on to her memories. Jim had been an exception to that particular rule. He'd never taken anything for granted. Their love had developed gradually; they had grown together as partners, friends too. With Charles things were different. There had been an instant magnetism, although she refused to admit to herself the fascination he held for her. After losing Jim she felt it an act of betrayal enjoying the company of another male. But she realised life must go on and Jim would have wanted it no other way.

'Any more rooms upstairs, Mrs. err... Sorry, you didn't give me your name?' Mr. Francis enquired, interrupting her thoughts.

'Riley, Mrs. Riley. Upstairs there's an office above the shop, and a kitchen and a lavatory above the storeroom. Do go up and check them out.'

The thought of selling the shop filled her with sadness. Vincent would have been appalled. He'd worked in the business for most of his life and it was sad to think that before he'd even given retirement a thought, he was gone. It was sacrilege the way Donald had decided so casually to dispose of it less than a month after his inheritance.

Mr. Francis broke into her thoughts. 'That's it, Mrs. Riley. I'll let you have the valuation as soon as I've worked on it. Good day to you.'

After he left Helen surveyed the shop. Just as she'd become used to the place, it was all change. But she must try to remain positive.

It was Wednesday and half day closing. She took her mackintosh from the coat stand and slipped it on. Donald had left everything to her yet again. He'd not been near the place all morning. It appeared he was the one making all the decisions, and she was the one doing all the work. But that would cease in the future. Mary was right. It would be much more rewarding running her own business with no-one to answer to, least of all Donald. A new challenge was waiting out there and she would give it her very best shot.

Storms with dark cloud formations had been threatening all morning, and as she closed the shop and stepped out, down came the rain. With the umbrella straining above her, she battled against the downpour.

'Hope you're enjoying your new fella,' a sarcastic voice barked.

She lifted the umbrella and peered ahead. It was Jack, his hair clinging damply to his cheeks.

'What on earth are you talking about?' she replied solemnly, wondering how he could possibly know about Charles.

'The fella you had in shop,' he blustered.

She listened with blank incomprehension. Puzzled at his accusation, she felt he had a dangerous aimlessness about him and it worried her.

'Who does he think he is? He rattled me.' His voice had turned as chilly as the rain.

When it dawned on Helen he was not referring to Charles she laughed, feeling her sanity had been saved and she breathed a sigh of relief.

'You mean Donald Valentine, my inherited partner.' She made direct eye contact and stared him in the face. 'He's nothing to me. But that's no concern of yours,' she said emphatically.

That seemed to be enough to lighten his mood and he grinned. But she hadn't finished with him.

'What are you doing here? Shouldn't you be at work?' The acrimonious edge to her voice reflected her resentment that Jack had been one of the lucky ones, whilst Jim had been laid off.

'We've knocked off for the day. It's only part-time now,' his voice droned on as he looked away sheepishly, obviously embarrassed at having drawn the wrong conclusions about the man.

'I must be off,' she said curtly. 'I would appreciate your keeping your comments to yourself in the future, Jack. I have enough on my mind without added complications.' Drawing her umbrella out in front of her, she continued on her way.

When she arrived at the post office, Mary was there looking down in the dumps. As Helen approached, Mary's eyes sprang to life. But something was troubling her. 'Come on, Mary. Out with it! What's the problem?'

'I called in at the agents. The shop's already taken, Helen. Another cobbler's renting it,' she explained.

Helen couldn't find it in her heart to reveal her disappointment, even though her hopes were gradually fading.

'It's not the end of the world, Mary. Goodness me, it's not a national priority,' she laughed. 'Come along. You're supposed to be the optimist, the one cheering me up.' Helen linked her arm through Mary's. She was proud of their companionable closeness and if Mother or Laura commented once more about Mary's familiarity, Helen would put them straight.

'It's just that I want it to work too. For my sake as well as yours,' Mary explained.

Helen fully understood. It would be a reciprocal arrangement. They were inter-dependent. But now her need was becoming desperate. They had a serious problem, but Helen refused to divulge

223

her fears to Mary.

'But Laura, darling, you promised to see me.' Donald urged.

'Donald, dear, it's become embarrassing for me,' Laura whispered. 'John's here to see the children. I really can't talk. You do understand, don't you?'

Donald was persistent. This was the third time he'd phoned and it seemed he was hooked. It was different at the beginning, it was exciting. Now, having tricked him into putting the shop on the market, she was reneging on her side of the bargain. John was calling regularly and she knew in her heart he was her priority.

Unfortunately, Donald was not used to being turned down. Time after time she'd escaped his dogged pursuit and he'd kept his temper on a taut leash, but now it seemed things were beginning to fray. She must break off the relationship. After all, it had been nothing more than a little dalliance.

After visiting Dora, Laura left Potters Moor and headed for Chatsbridge. Mid-afternoon was a quiet time of the day but when the driver behind her put on speed and overtook her, she realised it was Donald in his Jowett. He cut in front of her, forced her to stop, and drew the car to a shuddering halt.

She stared icily, her mouth pursed disapprovingly as she sat stiffly in her seat.

'Laura,' he called, 'why are you ignoring me? We had an agreement, so I thought.' He stepped from the car to talk to her, now appearing as charming and relaxed as ever.

Her frosty look melted. 'I've had so much on with John rolling up whenever he feels like it, it's been difficult.' With a look of guilt, she averted her eyes. There was little truth in what she said. It was merely an excuse to fob him off.

'All I'm asking is for you to see me. I could easily back out of the sale. I could even afford to give my share to Helen.' He paused and held it just long enough to see her physically squirm. He smiled. 'Either we do it my way, or the agreement is off. I'll pull out of selling the shop and let Helen run it. She'd be bloody good at it too,' he confessed, turning ready to leave.

Laura stared back at him, the panic already showing in her eyes. 'Don't do that, darling. I'll see you tonight. Promise. Pick me up at seven thirty.'

He took her hand and held it tight. 'You've seen sense at last.' He sighed and strode back to the car.

It was early evening and there was a loud knock at the front door. Phyllis answered it and let in the visitor as she'd been told to do.

'They're in the drawing room,' she said and gently pushed open the door.

His initial reaction seemed one of disbelief.

'Do come in, Donald. Allow me to introduce my husband, John.'

She smiled sweetly as John got up from the sofa and confronted Donald.

'So you're Donald. In the circumstances, can't say I'm pleased to meet you, especially after the way you've threatened my wife. What's it all about?'

Donald stared, a dazed, stupefied look on his face, whilst John remained calm, despite his obvious dislike of the man.

'What's all the fuss about, old boy? Laura agreed to come out with me, quite willingly. She told me you'd left her and gone off with another woman.'

John's face became flushed as Donald rubbed it in.

'It was tit for tat, a bit of a jaunt really,' Donald continued. 'As for threats, Laura's misconstrued my words entirely.'

Laura sat there looking vulnerable and she glanced up at John.

'Why did you stop her car, tell her she'd better see you again, or else? If you call that a bit of a jaunt, I'm glad she didn't have a firm contract.' John's serenity didn't budge.

Donald laughed. 'That was a ruse. Laura came to see me in the first place and asked me to get rid of the business to spite her sister. She's an attractive woman and I foolishly agreed. I put it up for sale, despite Helen's pleas for me not to sell. She knows nothing of Laura's devious trick,' he stuttered. And now although panic began to rise on his face, he kept his cool. 'But I can see you two are back together again. And I certainly don't want to play gooseberry.' He laughed nervously as, in a cowardly gesture, he backed away.

John followed Donald to the front door. 'I take it we've heard the end of this?'

There was no reply to the question as Donald stepped quickly into his Jowett and disappeared.

Chapter 17

Mary heard the letters drop to the floor and, once downstairs she collected them from the doormat. 'Post, Helen,' she called, turning over the two letters. The handwriting was not familiar.

Helen took the letters from the table and turned to Mary. 'Chilly morning, love.'

'I suppose it's what we should expect now. It is the first of December today.' The coals in the grate were still alight and Mary riddled the ashes, took fresh coal from the scuttle and placed it on top. Within seconds, the fire sprung to life.

'How time flies,' Helen replied vacantly checking the letters. One of them she knew was from Aunt Sybil. It was probably an early Christmas card. The other was a mystery to her. Looking tentatively at the envelope but unable to read the postmark clearly, she noticed the handwriting was rather untidy. But it was late and she slipped it into her handbag to read later.

After breakfast she was ready to leave. 'I must be off now cherubs,' she said, hugging the girls close. 'I'll see you this afternoon, Mary,' she added as she waved them goodbye and left.

The bus was late, and when she arrived Donald was already there, hanging around, getting in the way and achieving nothing in particular. After visits from two lots of prospective buyers sent by the agents to view, Helen felt a smidgen of irritation and hoped neither of them would put in an offer. The longer she held on to the shop, the more time she'd have to look for alternative premises.

She opened her handbag to take out a handkerchief and spotted the letter she'd received that morning. It had slipped her mind. She slit open the envelope and drew out a single sheet.

Dear Helen

I've missed you since we spent such an enjoyable evening together but hopefully I will see you again soon. There's an important seminar in York next week and I'm hoping we can meet when I'm up there. I intend ringing you at the shop on Friday to make arrangements. Sorry to be so brief but time is pressing. Please be there to talk to me. Much love, Charles

Her stomach flipped with a secret longing and she savoured those moments of pleasure.

Donald interrupted her thoughts. 'Something's pleasing you.' With a smug look on his face he pointed to the letter. 'Love letter is it?'

Helen looked up in surprise and felt hot blood rush to her face. 'It's nothing of the sort. Just good news.' She stuffed the letter back into her bag.

The morning seemed to drag and Donald annoyed her with his loud, garrulous attitude. All she wanted was peace and quiet to think and dream.

By mid-day the novelty of the shop seemed to have worn off for Donald. 'Mind if I get off, sweetie?' he asked, using his charm to no effect.

'I can manage fine, Donald. You go,' she replied, hoping he would leave before Charles telephoned.

But no sooner had the thought crossed her mind than the telephone rang. She jumped visibly.

'We are edgy today, aren't we?' he said, competing to grab the phone.

Helen picked it up and breathed deeply. 'Waxman's,' she announced stiffly.

'Helen, it's me, Charles.'

Her heart leapt. By now she was oblivious to Donald who stood before her, a puzzled look on his face. But suddenly she was aware of his presence.

'Would you hold the line please,' she said formally and placed her hand over the receiver. 'It's for me, Donald. I'll see you tomorrow,' she said with a weak smile on her lips.

He sighed his displeasure at being shooed away, waved his hand dismissively and left.

'Charles. Sorry about that. It was Donald.' The words seemed to tumble out of her mouth. 'When are you coming up?' she asked, laughing with excitement, a blaze of desire tingling inside.

'Thursday for a Friday seminar. Are you free Thursday evening?'

'I'll make sure I am, Charles. There's so much I want to talk to you about.'

'Me too, darling. But I must go now. I'll collect you at seven.'

When she replaced the receiver all her troubles seemed to dissipate and, after locking up, she left for home, having arranged for Veronica to come to the house and give her opinion on the landscape picture. Mary was there baking bread when she entered the kitchen.

'I'm glad Veronica isn't here yet. I've something

229

to tell you.'

Mary took her hands from the baking bowl and turned quickly. 'Don't keep me in suspense then,' she replied, smiling.

'The letter I received this morning was from Charles. He rang the shop and asked if I'd be free Thursday evening.' She rubbed her hands together gleefully. 'Do you mind if I go, Mary?'

'Do I mind? Not at all, dear. You go out and enjoy the evening.'

'Thank you so much,' Helen concluded and minutes later Veronica arrived.

Helen took down the picture and Veronica looked at it carefully, standing back and viewing the scene from a distance before moving closer, lifting a magnifying glass to her eye and scrutinized the signature. She flicked through the pages of the reference book she'd brought with her.

'In my opinion, it's certainly a Pissarro but it may be an idea to get a second opinion.' She clapped her hands with pleasure. 'If I'm right, its value runs into the thousands. But I'd like to confer on that one. I hope it's insured.' She faced Helen sternly.

'Not here, it isn't,' Helen responded, dazed at the news. 'I hadn't thought about that.'

'Then it needs to be covered immediately,' Veronica suggested seriously.

'That might pose a problem. The picture belongs to Mother. She's insured but I'm not sure about cover for single items.'

'I suggest you return it and ask her to check it out once we have an official valuation,' Veronica continued.

'After that of course, it's all a case of affording the premium before I can take it back.' Helen turned to Veronica. 'I'm really grateful to you. Are you sure I can't pay you for the consultation?'

Veronica laughed. 'Don't even mention it.' She turned to leave. 'By the way, how's that rude man doing, the one who's inherited Vincent's share of the business?' she asked, frowning.

'Oh, Donald. Believe it or not, he's put the shop on the market. He doesn't want it, and mine's the minority share. No-one in the trade knows about it yet. It was only valued a few days ago. We've had a couple of interested parties,' she said lightly, not wanting Veronica to become any further involved.

'But, Helen. How will you cope?' Veronica's frown deepened.

'Don't worry. I have one or two ideas. We'll get by,' she replied bravely, digesting her own words and wondering if they spelt the truth.

At the sound of footsteps, Sarah tweaked the velvet curtain and looked out. To her surprise Helen was standing there. Sarah unlocked the door, stretching out her arms in a fond welcome. 'Darling, it's lovely to see you,' she said as she stepped back and opened the door wider.

'You're looking well, Mother,' Helen said.

'Yes, I'm feeling much better,' Sarah replied.

'A quick visit, Mother about the landscape you gave me. Veronica Brightwell has checked it out and she's fairly certain it's a genuine Pissarro.'

'I see,' Sarah replied. 'But what does it matter?'

'If that's the case and it is genuine it's worth a

231

lot of money.'

'What difference does that make? Don't say you're refusing it,' Sarah interjected.

'Mother, do bear me out. Veronica stressed the need for insurance cover. I don't have any, but you do. In view of its value, I propose bringing the picture back to you until we have it valued.' She sank down on the Chesterfield.

'That's fair enough, Helen. But I don't understand. It's yours. I've given it to you.' Sarah was adamant.

'I'll need to insure it before I take it back,' Helen explained. 'And another thing. Laura was none too pleased.'

'It doesn't belong to Laura. She's well set up. She needs to sort herself out with John.' Sarah was sometimes over-indulgent, especially to Laura's whims. But she had her principles, and on this occasion she was sticking to them. 'You hang on to your man through hell and high water,' she said, trotting out her familiar cliché.

'I think there are moves towards a reconciliation, Mother, but don't quote me. The last time I saw Laura, John had stayed the night.'

Sarah clapped her hands. 'And not before time.'

'I can't stay long, Mother. But I've something to tell you.'

'Do have a cup of tea before you leave, darling,' Sarah begged persuasively. 'I'm delighted at the news. And that's all the more reason why you should keep the picture.' She went through to the kitchen, and Helen followed her. 'And what is it you have to tell me?'

'I have a friend coming up from London. We're

going out to dinner tomorrow night. I wanted you to know in case we're seen.'

'A friend? I wasn't aware you had friends in London. Who is she?'

'His name is Charles. I met him when I was in London with Vincent. He's coming north to a meeting.' She searched her mother's face for a response.

'That's wonderful news,' Sarah replied but by the tone of her voice and the look on her face Helen could tell she was wary about the background of this mystery man. 'Tell me more,' she added.

'Charles is a consultant surgeon, orthopaedics.'

A smile touched Sarah's lips and she sighed with relief. It was the best news she'd received for some time. What an achievement, what a catch. It would prove to be a shrewd move if she ended up with a surgeon.

'Don't worry about what people might say. It's over two years since you lost Jim. You have to pick up the pieces some time, darling and get on with your life.' Sarah took the news with relish, speculating on the future. It would be something to brag about. After Helen's marriage to Jim, she had always felt her reputation had been besmirched.

'Don't jump to any conclusions, Mother, it's a friendship, nothing more,' Helen said reprovingly. 'But back to the picture. I'd like to bring it here until the insurance is sorted. Is that all right?' Helen crossed over to the door and opened it.

'That's fine, darling. But I'll not keep the picture. I'm determined. It's yours.' And those were her final words on the subject.

Charles travelled from Oswestry by car. He told himself he mustn't rush things. He must be cautious especially after his experience with Rita.

Rita was his first love. They met shortly after his appointment at Harlington Royal as junior houseman. Rita worked there as a probationary nurse and, during his second year after she qualified they married. But Rita easily succumbed to flattery and she became embroiled with consultant gynaecologist, James McCann who was twenty years her senior. But, within months, he grew tired of her and, filled with remorse, Rita begged Charles to take her back. But by then his love for her had faded. He refused and the marriage ended.

That was nine years ago. Since that time he'd been careful. He'd certainly not let down his guard. But now it was different. No matter how he tried to reason with himself, he knew he was drawn to Helen. And whilst he knew Helen was a widow, she knew nothing of Rita. It was early days and he was unsure how she might react to the stigma 'divorce' seemed to incite.

He drove for almost three hours and when he drew up at the next road junction the sign indicated five miles to Leeds. It was coming up to five o'clock which gave him time to book in at The Queens and relax before meeting Helen.

It was almost seven when he climbed the steps to the house in Emley Street and Helen was ready to greet him. As she moved to pick up her coat, his eyes settled on her lithesome body. He felt himself flush with pleasure, his attraction for her intense.

234

'You look wonderful, darling,' he breathed as he took her arm. The pale blue satin dress brought out the rich chocolate brown of her eyes and the light danced in her hair like a glowing torch of gold and copper. They reached the pavement and as she turned to get into the car, he took her hands in his and pulled her towards him, kissing her gently.

'I've missed you,' he purred, his eyes reflecting his passion.

'It's seemed an eternity hasn't it?' she confessed.

'I'll say,' he agreed. 'I've booked a table at The Queens. Is that all right?' He squeezed her hand.

'That's fine, Charles. You know I don't mind where we go.'

They sat in silence as he drove into the city, and from time to time he clasped her hand in his, unable to resist the soft touch of her skin.

It was the early start to the Christmas season, and the atmosphere was festive as they entered the restaurant where there was a noisy buzz amongst the diners. They were shown to a table in a small alcove by the window, where Charles reached out and took Helen's hand in his. When he felt the warm tingle of her fingers, ripples of excitement flashed through him at the intensity of her gaze.

The waiter broke into his thoughts, offering menus and, when Helen gazed at hers absently, Charles grinned. 'I think he expects us to take a serious look,' he volunteered, holding up the menu. He winked and Helen blushed.

During the meal she told him of Donald's

235

intention to sell the shop, and Charles was disappointed for her, although he sensed she'd tried to inject an air of optimism into her voice as she related her plans for the future.

'Don't let that fellow bamboozle you into selling the shop to the first people making an offer. Be firm.' His face became serious with concern.

'Don't worry. I'm keeping a careful check,' she replied.

They sipped Gaelic coffees after the meal, and he related stories of his student days. She told him she'd not laughed so much in a long time.

But he knew he was stalling and, eventually, he drained his cup. 'There's something I need to tell you, something confidential. Do you mind if we go up to my room. It's rather public here. We can talk there without being disturbed?' His face searched hers for any sign of discomfort at his suggestion.

'If it's important, perhaps it's the best place to talk.' Her voice faltered slightly.

Once inside his room he steered her towards the armchair whilst he perched on the edge of the bed. Starting at the beginning, he told her about his unhappy marriage to Rita.

'After my promotion to senior houseman, Rita finally accepted the marriage was irreconcilable. Shortly afterwards I moved to Oswestry as registrar to Sir Henry Moat, the consultant orthopaedic surgeon there, who subsequently became my mentor. When he retired, I replaced him.' He paused. 'Rita contacted me at regular intervals hoping for a reconciliation, but I'd made my decision.' He looked for a reaction from Helen, and sensed disappointment, but she smiled reassuringly.

'We all have skeletons in our cupboards, Charles. Are you still married?' she asked.

'Goodness, no. The last I heard she was planning to re-marry an architect.'

With a sense of relief he moved towards her and sat on the arm of the chair. Unable to resist her, his pulses started to pound and he felt a surge of blood in his veins. He leant over and kissed her forehead, trailing his lips over her cheeks, her ears and neck, and he noticed the dark pupils in her eyes had widened and softened. His feeling for her was a driving force, and he searched her face for some sign of acquiescence.

For Helen this was verging on ecstasy and she felt guilty admitting that to herself. Having earlier tried to avoid this situation, she knew now it was impossible. Desire seemed to throb through every inch of her body and she lifted her hand, touching the line of his cheekbone, tracing his jaw and directing her fingertips to his mouth.

Charles circled his arms around her waist, gently pulled her up beside him and drew her to the length of his body. Her response felt natural and she had no alternative but to give in to her passion. Her defences were gone, and she slid her arms tighter around his neck. Although she told herself it was too early in the relationship for her to feel this way, it was a strain to resist. Her head was spinning, her body pulsing and she refused to admit to herself that she might be in love with him.

Charles looked into her eyes. 'Don't fight it, darling,' he implored, his voice shaking with desire.

He was gentle in his caresses and she dug her fingers into his thick hair and pulled him closer. Slowly he lifted her up and set her on the bed, his hands trailing over her skin. He followed her down with his body and, caught up in the heat, she cast all responsibility from her mind. She stopped thinking, and allowed herself to belong to him completely.

His lovemaking was tender. Pleasure came from deep inside her in a storm of sensations flowing over and over her until eventually all the passion was spent. Encapsulated in his arms, she reflected on the thrill and intensity, and she savoured the comfort of his warm body against hers.

'I didn't expect that to happen,' she murmured coyly.

'I can't apologise Helen,' he whispered. 'I couldn't resist.'

She giggled. 'It takes two to tango.'

Charles drew his arms around her from behind, slowly lifting her hair and kissing the nape of her neck. He turned her around to face him, studying her at arm's length and obviously feeling confident after the exhilaration of their love-making.

'I've something to ask you,' he said.

Helen smiled. 'Go ahead,' she replied.

'How about an introduction to your girls?' His eyes sparkled. 'I'd love to meet them.'

His suggestion came unexpectedly. She wasn't sure how to react and she felt claustrophobia pressing in on her. That spark of guilt was back. Was she denying Jim and cheating on his memory? Although Mother had urged her to let go, it wasn't as easy as that. What if the girls didn't like Charles?

What if they resented him? She'd already had her problems with Jack – not that there was any comparison.

'Maybe I could call tomorrow evening,' he offered, 'on my way back from York.'

'Let me think about it, Charles. I need to talk to them first.' She was reluctant to make empty promises she couldn't fulfil.

After the euphoria of their love-making, Charles seemed deflated and his smile faded. 'I'm sorry you need to think about it, Helen,' he said coolly, obviously not understanding her dilemma.

'Charles. Please don't pressurise me,' she urged. She sighed heavily. 'I must leave now. I don't like to take Mary for granted.' There was silence for a long moment before they left the hotel.

The steely atmosphere continued as they travelled to Kidsworth. Charles drew up outside the house and he spoke with heavy sarcasm.

'What's it all about, Helen? Surely you know my intentions are completely honourable.' he stressed, having let his defences down.

Opening the driver's door, he stepped out on to the pavement and his stomach gave an almighty lurch as he realised she was out too, walking towards him.

'I'm sorry you've taken it the wrong way, Charles. It's been a lovely evening.' Her eyes were moist as she faced him. 'I hope this is not the end.'

He averted his gaze. 'I wasn't asking for a full commitment. All I wanted was to meet the girls.' He leant forward and the touch of his lips on her cheek was fleeting. His eyes were bleak as he returned to the car and quickly drove away.

Chapter 18

'Double top. That's all you need,' Jack called to Walt as he lifted his gill of bitter and took a hefty swig.

Walter drew back his arm and threw the dart.

'Done,' Jack added and finished off his beer. 'I must get back to work, Walt. Don't want bosses after me.' He gave his pal a knowing smile.

'I'll walk back with you, Jack,' he said as he drained the last drops of beer from his pint glass and placed it on the cluttered table.

'I was in Leeds last night picking Auntie Nellie up. I was stunned when I saw that corker, Helen Riley coming out of Queens with a posh-looking bloke. Didn't take her long to get fixed up,' he snorted derisively.

'Did he have a moustache, blazer and slacks?' Jack challenged.

'No. Just the opposite. Posh black overcoat, velvet collar. A right nob.' Walt gave a muffled laugh. 'Don't know what they'd been up to in the Queens.'

'Stop your mucky thoughts, Walt. She's not that type,' Jack responded defensively, a streak of jealousy shooting through him. All the same it was strange. They all wanted her; but he didn't get a look in. She'd changed her tune since Jim died. Become a proper snob like rest of 'em...

'I've tipped her the wink a couple of times but

she won't have it,' Jack said churlishly.

'She's not your type, Jack. You'd be better off with Maureen from the office,' Walt added noisily. 'See you tonight,' he called.

Jack set out in the opposite direction, at a loss to understand who the new chap was. She'd more or less told him there was nobody else when he challenged her about the other one. Maybe he was a relative. He'd find out if it was the last thing he did. If new bloke thought he could muscle him out of the picture, he had another think coming.

He continued to mull things over once he was back at work and when he arrived home his mother confronted him.

'Picture's back at Mrs. D's,' Agnes couldn't resist telling Jack, although she realised it might spell trouble. 'I saw it today. She didn't mention it and neither did I.'

'That's funny,' Jack replied. 'Have they had a row? Surely her ma hasn't asked for it back.' He paused. 'Helen's acting funny these days. Walt saw her at Queens in Leeds with a right nob – not the one working in the shop neither,' he said, his voice heavy with resentment. 'Shoves me out but she's alright with others.'

Agnes could see by the look on his face he was puzzled, but after overhearing Helen telling him not to call at the house again, she was determined to discourage him from any more involvement with her. 'Well, picture's back now so it could still be in her will for me,' she speculated and when Jack didn't respond she dreaded any more scheming.

They ate their meal in silence. It wasn't the

picture he was thinking about, it was Helen. The whole issue had upset him. Just as things seemed to be going his way, she'd told him not to call again. And what he couldn't understand was what she was doing with this other bloke in Leeds.

He must do a bit of sniffing around to get to the bottom of it. It was the same when Jim Riley took her away from him. Granted they were only sixteen at the time.

Pulling his thoughts together, he took his muffler and cap from the back of the door and called out to his ma who was lighting the front room fire ready for his Auntie Cissy's visit. 'I'm off down to Cock and Bottle, Ma. Won't be long,' he promised, knowing that the pair would need time to catch up on the gossip before he returned.

There was a noticeable change in Helen, she'd become withdrawn and was short-tempered with the children. Her face looked pinched and her eyes were puffy. After she'd returned that night, she'd excused herself and gone straight to bed. Usually she talked things through with Mary first. But now she was walking around like a zombie.

She returned from the shop and flopped in the chair beside the fire, slouching moodily, staring vacantly into the fire, her face revealing little spirited emotion. Mary was silent, brewing the tea as usual. She handed a cup to Helen and sat down in the chair opposite. There was complete silence between them except for the coals settling in the grate and sending up a shower of sparks.

'Come on, love. I know there's something

242

wrong. Do you want to talk?' Mary coaxed her gently.

Helen, unaware that Mary had noticed anything wrong dismissed her abruptly. 'I don't know what you're talking about, Mary. I'm tired, nothing more,' she lied unconvincingly.

'If you won't tell me, I can't help you.'

'I've nothing to discuss. I've just told you.' Helen jumped up from her chair and dashed out of the room.

Mary stared after her. Helen was aware she might have put two and two together and guessed she and Charles had argued, especially since they'd been so close earlier. But she was adamant. She didn't need anyone to analyse her feelings. She was perfectly capable of doing that for herself.

The birthday party the girls had attended was due to finish at six, and Mary had arranged to collect them. It was half past five and a fair walk down to Roundwood Row.

'I'm going for the girls,' Mary's voice echoed.

'Wait a minute, Mary,' Helen called out and came downstairs. 'Sorry, I'm so prickly. I do need to talk. Tonight, when we're alone,' she suggested, her face tear-stained.

'That's fine, love. I only wanted to help. I won't be long,' she promised, fastening her coat and opening the door. 'My goodness,' she said. 'This is a surprise. It's snowing. I must put my galoshes on,' she said and she drew herself back. 'Now where are the girls' Wellington boots?'

Helen went to the cupboard under the stairs. Taking out the two pairs of boots, she added,

243

'Here they are, Mary. Shall I come with you?'

'You stay here, love and put your feet up. Try to pull yourself together before the girls come back. We don't want them worrying, do we?' she said in her own comforting way.

Later that evening when the girls were tucked up in bed, Mary sat in a fireside chair. She usually went home on Fridays but tonight she'd agreed to stay and talk things through with Helen.

'Charles and I had a misunderstanding last night,' Helen confessed.

'A misunderstanding? It seems a bit more serious than that the way you're moping. Do you want to tell me what it's all about?' Mary asked, gently coaxing Helen to explain.

'He wanted to come and be introduced to the girls tonight but I said I wasn't sure it was the right time. It's a bit early to expose them to someone else. It's only two years since I lost Jim.' She broke off and swallowed. 'I feel awfully guilty even going out with Charles. I suppose I got cold feet.' She felt confused yet she knew she was desperate for his affection.

'I understand, Helen, but did Charles understand? Did you explain how guilty you feel and how you need to protect the girls?' Mary asked.

'In a way, but he seemed to take the huff before I had the chance to explain.'

'There's nothing to be gained by wearing yourself out. What exactly did he say?' Mary began to probe.

'He inferred I was being casual. He admitted he wasn't expecting a commitment. It's just that I wanted to establish some independence before

244

things became too serious. I want to get the shop sorted and hopefully find other premises. I can't go through life being dependent on other people,' she stressed, fingering her wedding ring nervously.

'Why don't you talk it through with him, sensibly, rationally? It seems to me you were both a bit fraught.'

Maybe Mary was right. Maybe after what had happened they'd both felt vulnerable. She hadn't considered his plight. Maybe he felt insecure too. Perhaps she had been rather hasty with her negative reaction.

'You may be right, Mary. He's already had a failed marriage. I probably hurt his feelings.' She paused and shook her head. 'Why am I being so selfish?' she said, questioning herself in a reprimanding tone.

'You could put it all to rights, love. It's half past seven,' Mary said as she looked up at the clock on the mantelpiece. 'If you think so much about him, you need to eat humble pie. Slip down to the telephone box at the corner and ring him at the Queens? You've got to make amends Helen. You can't go on wrecking your life with these unnecessary misunderstandings.'

'Oh, I couldn't ring him. What would he think of me?' The colour drained from Helen's face.

'If he thinks enough about you he'll be over the moon,' Mary replied, her wise words ringing true.

Helen knew Mary was right. She must talk to Charles before he left Leeds or she would never forgive herself. 'You're right, Mary. I'll go straight away.'

'Good for you, love,' Mary said, praising her as though she was one of the children. Helen grinned and left the house.

But things didn't go to plan. 'He's left. He told me he intended to stay. What a fool I've been,' she admitted. 'Now I'm not going to be able to contact him. It's over.'

'Don't give up hope, Helen. If he wants you so much, you can be sure he'll be in touch again.'

Mary draped an arm around Helen's shoulders and patted her back gently. 'Mark my words.'

Laura set out for Kirk Grange. Dora's perpetual cheerfulness was inclined to irritate, but the renovations at the house were now almost complete. It wasn't very far to Mother's and Laura decided to make a quick visit. Now that John was back she would need to help Phyllis prepare the meal and, of course, the boys would be home soon. They'd been delighted at John's return. Thomas in particular had clung to him every time he entered the house.

The jaunt with Donald had brought her to her senses. He was handsome, witty and dashing, but he had become a bore. And now the guilt at having lied so smoothly about Helen weighed heavily on her. A sense of her own failure with John and resentment at Helen's success with the business had triggered the panic. She had been desperate to become established in her own right and prove her independence. Unfortunately the bitterness manifested itself in empty revenge but, in the end, she had gained neither pleasure nor comfort from the victory.

She had forgiven John and he seemed untroubled by her recent infatuation with Donald. Clarissa was now non-existent in Laura's mind. And thinking about it, had it not been for John's affair, things might have continued in pretty much the same mundane way. He had always provided a broad shoulder for her but what had she provided for him? She'd been a self-centred, egocentric prig. And Mother was right. You needed to keep hold of your man and provide him with the comforts he expected, or suffer the consequences.

Her biggest problem was how to resolve the situation she'd caused Helen. The damage she'd done was unforgivable. She must try to salvage whatever remained of a deteriorating relationship, but how? She'd have to leave things be and hope for some positive solution.

The rift between her and John and the subsequent reconciliation had brought them closer. Laura enjoyed her independence with her design business but it didn't compare with the warmth and the love she felt when John was close. And now she had both. Of course, Mother had been delighted, everything neat and tidy with no loose ends.

'It's me, Mother,' she called brightly as she entered the hall. She noticed the landscape picture was back on the wall and her mouth felt dry, her heart thudding heavily. She hadn't wanted the picture, but Helen had, for its aesthetic quality not its value. She'd been mean, and it was probably her fault that Helen had returned it.

'She's just upstairs, Mrs. Conway. I'll tell her you're here.'

Laura looked up and saw Mrs. Bean on the landing. Her stomach always knotted at the sight of her. Poor woman. It wasn't her fault; it was the reminder of Jack that hurt.

'Laura, darling,' Mother called from the top of the stairs. 'Glad you've called.' She negotiated the stairs nimbly and ushered Laura into the drawing room. 'I can't wait to tell you. I think Helen's got herself a man,' she divulged.

'Oh, Mother. That's wonderful.' Laura felt the release of some of her guilt at the possibility of Helen being supported again.

'What do you think? A consultant surgeon. He came up to see her last week. They went out for dinner. She met him at the exhibition in London,' she revealed, bunching her shoulders and squeezing her hands together with delight. 'I'm sworn to secrecy, so do wait until she tells you herself,' she said, flopping down on the Chesterfield.

'That's wonderful news.' She turned and pointed to the picture. 'I see you have it back. Why hasn't Helen kept it?' She was anxious to make sure it wasn't her fault.

'It's the insurance. Apparently she's had it valued. It's an original, not a copy as I'd thought. Veronica Brightwell checked its authenticity – apparently it's worth thousands. Unfortunately, Helen hasn't insured the picture and Veronica recommended she brought it back here until things were sorted.' With the poise of the mannequin she once was, Mother stood up and walked sedately across to the hall door. Laura observed with pride how graceful she still was, not a great deal different from when they were children. As she opened the door, Mrs. Bean was standing there.

'Just coming to make a cup o' tea, Mrs. Dorrington,' she said, through guilty tones.

'You've read my mind Agnes. That's exactly what I'd like.'

Agnes finished the cleaning at Kirk Grange and set out for home. She trudged through the fine sprinkling of snow afraid she might slip. It was right what they said. You did lose your confidence as you got older. Jack was always telling her to put her feet down properly instead of pussyfooting around.

He'd know about it himself one of these days when he was her age!

Her mind drifted. Fancy, Helen bringing that picture back because it was so valuable. It must be worth a packet. Mrs. D's promise was easily broken. But that was what you got when you worked for the toffs – no sense of loyalty. Of course, Mrs. D would have had to pop her clogs before Agnes got her hands on it, but that was all in the past now. And she'd keep it from Jack. It didn't pay for him to know too much.

By the time she reached the front of the house her back was giving her gyp. She took a deep breath. She'd be relieved to undo her corsets. They were digging in like nobody's business. And she needed to get her shoes off. Galoshes always drew her feet and they were bad for her bunions.

She unlocked the door and felt a sense of pride as she entered. At least no-one could accuse her of being bone idle like some she knew. The place was fair sparkling. At least it would be until Jack walked in. It was either his bike propped up against the wall, or his overalls and toolkit thrown down. It was no use trying to train him like she had Godfrey.

Now there was a man who knew how to please. He never looked at another woman. He had no reason to. She kept him happy enough. Lovely chap he was and she missed him when he'd passed away. But they say time is a good healer.

But, never mind, Jack was good enough company, if he was the right way out. She could never understand why he'd not married. He got on famously with Freda Beckwith but he always said she wasn't good enough. He never got over Helen Dorrington. Jealous to death he was when Jim took her on. Well he'd mucked his ticket now. Helen had told him not to call again so that was that.

If she'd still been in Mrs. D's will and that picture had come to her, she'd have been well off when she sold it. She could have afforded a rib of beef instead of the brisket she was cooking. But she'd never move house. She liked it where they were, good neighbours and all that, except for Mavis. But better the devil you know.

She lifted a pile of newspapers and started to fold the sheets and tear them into squares for the lav. If they came into money she'd buy proper toilet rolls like Mrs. D. She gazed vacantly at the fire crackling in the grate wondering how much the picture would fetch. She'd have been on to a good number there – thousands Mrs. D had said. 'It's not right,' she mumbled out loud.

'What's not right, Ma?' Jack barked as he flung open the door.

Agnes was startled. He'd taken her unawares.

'That picture. They say it's worth a fortune.' It should have been a moment for caution but it wasn't always easy to separate thoughts from speech. 'But it still belongs to Helen, Mrs. D told Laura.'

Jack showed little emotion. 'Well that's that,' he said in a less than defiant tone.

Agnes felt confident he wouldn't be spoiling for trouble. He was in a good mood. 'Helen's got herself a chap. A surgeon by all accounts,' Agnes boasted, her face showing her eagerness to be first with the news.

'Is that so?' Jack continued calmly. 'Well I never.'

Without Mary to confide in, Helen spent the weekend completely immersed in entertaining the children. It was when they were in bed she felt at her loneliest. But this foolishness must stop. The whole sorry mess was down to inexperience. She'd been tactless, and it was probably too late to reconcile things, but she knew she must try.

Longing to contact him but constantly screwing up the courage, she finally took the telephone number of the hospital from her bag and stared at his handwriting, touching it gently with her fingertips. It would be a long shot and he may refuse to speak with her, but she supposed she could ring him from the shop tomorrow. There was nothing to lose except her pride.

On Monday morning she felt a tinge of anxiety and it triggered an irregular beat in her chest. She dithered, but what was stopping her from 'phoning? Her excuse was he may have a theatre list and starting around nine o'clock. Better to try at lunchtime.

Donald arrived looking smug. 'I think I've done it,' he bragged, 'I think I've got a buyer.' He licked his lips with anticipation.

Helen's heart came to a standstill. She tried to smile but her lips were paralysed. Her mind switched elsewhere as she gazed into space, thinking about Charles. She'd been a fool. Not only would she end up without Charles, she'd end up without a business too. Maybe this was her punishment.

'Did you hear me, Helen?' Donald asked.

'Of course,' she replied vacantly as she leant against the desk at the back of the shop. A dizzy feeling came over her and her legs seemed to lose strength. The room started to spin, making her feel nauseous. She couldn't stop herself. Her legs buckled and she fell to the floor.

She felt someone tapping her face gently and when she looked up, it was Donald.

'Come on old girl. Let me get you on the chair.' He held a glass of water to her lips and she sipped it. 'Don't go upsetting yourself. I'll see to everything. I'll close the shop and take you home. It's a rest you need.'

She tried to plead with him but he resolutely turned his head away. The car was out front and he helped her into it. She couldn't understand what had come over her but she felt exhausted.

They reached Emley Street and as Donald helped her out of the car, Mary dashed outside. 'What is it?' she asked him. 'She's looking ever so pale.'

'Passed out in the shop. I think the best place for her is bed.'

'Come on, love. Let me get you inside.' She hooked her arm through Helen's and gently led her up the steps. She turned to Donald. 'Thank you so much.'

When Helen arrived at the shop the next day, Donald was obviously brimming with enthusiasm to spill his news, disregarding the fact that she'd been off-colour.

'You're early, Donald. Couldn't you sleep?' she asked, laughing frivolously, not wanting him thinking she was a sickly, weak woman.

'It's sold! We're going to be in the money sooner than we thought,' he said tactlessly, totally insensitive to her feelings and with scant regard for her financial needs. Picking up a letter from the desk he tossed it towards her.

There was nothing to be gained by falling to pieces and nothing she could do to change matters now the shop was sold. She told herself to ignore his tone and dispassionate emotional display. She must stay calm.

'Who are the buyers?' she enquired, feeling they had betrayed Vincent.

'Mr. and Mrs. Worsnop. Sold a pawnbrokers shop, but it was no more than a junk shop according to Granville. They're keen to move into antiques now,' he said in a noisily adamant manner.

Helen quietly resigned herself to the fact that it was over, cut and dried. Donald might think he was perfection, but he was cold-hearted.

'When do they want to take over?' she asked,

despair spiralling through her.

'As soon as possible. They've sold their place. Been looking round for a while. They reckon it's a good spot and just what they wanted.'

Inwardly Helen was furious. He'd assumed he was entitled to take on an exaggerated importance over the sale of the business.

'I take it all the stock's gone with the sale, at the valuation price,' she added, needing confirmation that decisions had not been made behind her back.

'Lock, stock and barrel. Exactly what we asked, poppet,' he replied jovially. 'I take it you're back to normal and feeling better after yesterday,' he added.

'I'm fine, Donald,' she said, but her tension was increasing. She needed time to think objectively, away from him. 'Since you've obviously taken over, Donald, I'm sure you won't mind running the shop whilst I slip out. I've quite a number of things to do, like looking for another job. That's an absolute priority.' She tried not to sound bitter.

'Sorry, sweetie, but business is business.' A devious smile spread across his face. 'Go ahead. I can cope. We need to start preparing to move as soon as possible.'

Helen left and headed in the direction of the bus stop for Leeds. Now that the shop was sold, getting another job had become an overwhelming preoccupation, otherwise how would she be in a position to pay the bills and the small pittance she gave Mary?

But Mary had decided to stay on, whatever the outcome. Her only income was a very small

254

annuity her father had left and she'd managed fine before she took up the job, so she saw no reason to change the arrangements. She was thrifty when it came to housekeeping and, like all working-class families, she was able to manage.

Helen joined the queue at the bus stop. The sun cast its golden rays through the washed blue sky, penetrating the shimmering frost covering the paths. She looked up, and despite her anger towards Donald who had a sliver of ice in his heart, she felt the warmth of the comforting rays on her face.

'Sorry shop's sold, Mrs. Riley.' Gertie Brumfitt broke into her thoughts.

'Hello, Gertie. I'm sorry it's going, too, but you realise the decision wasn't mine.'

'I know. I'll be lucky to find another job,' she said, hunching her shoulders and shaking her head.

The bus drew up and several people stepped off. Helen sat near the front on the lower deck. Gertie plonked herself heavily beside her.

'Pity about Mr. Waxman,' she said. 'He'd turn in his grave if he knew.'

'Absolutely,' Helen replied. 'It's been done in such a rush. Apparently it's a couple who've had a similar shop before.'

'I don't suppose they'll need me if there's two of them,' she declared in a half-anticipatory way.

'Well, there's no harm in asking,' Helen proposed.

Gertie perked up. 'I'll do that, love.' Her voice had an air of determination to it.

'When I see them I'll put in a good word for

255

you, Gertie.'

'Thanks for that,' she called as she stepped off the bus.

City Square, clamorous with traffic, was Helen's destination. Across the road was a tram bound for Guisborough, the vivid lettering down the length of it promoting *Wright's Coal Tar Soap*. Dodging nimbly in between the traffic, she managed to step on to the tram before it lurched forward and set off. It was full and she clung to the overhead strap and handed sixpence to the conductor who pulled a pink ticket from one of the coloured bundles on his belt and punched it with his clipping machine.

She gazed out of the window across Plumpton Park where some of the children were playing hopscotch, flinging their coloured pebbles and bits of glass over the concrete. Others were patterning their spinning tops with coloured chalk, watching the lovely displays as they whirled around.

Helen's mood lightened. She felt more refreshed and alert when she eventually reached her stop and climbed down from the tram. She stood on the pavement outside Brightwell's Antique Shop, hoping Veronica would be able to help.

'Darling, how lovely to see you,' cried Veronica. She was polishing a bronze statue which she replaced on the counter in front of them.

'I'm so glad you're in, Veronica,' Helen replied timidly. 'I've come to ask a favour.'

'Fire away,' she said. 'Whatever it is, I'll try my best.'

'Remember Donald Valentine? He decided to sell the shop but I couldn't buy him out. Now the

256

worst has happened and it's sold. I'm out of a job and wondered if you had any contacts, anyone at all who needs a hand, provided it's not too far to travel.'

'Gosh, that's a difficult one, Helen. Off the top of my head, I've no idea. But give me time to think about it,' she offered. Leading Helen into the back of the shop she continued pleasantly. 'Do have a cup of tea with me and we'll try to work something out temporarily.' Placing the kettle on the gas ring, Veronica paused and, as though she had struck a notion, she turned to Helen. 'I could offer you four mornings in the shop here but obviously it's quite a distance for you to travel. I'd pay your fares, of course. It might just keep the wolf from the door.'

'Oh that's wonderful if you're sure, Veronica. I'd be extremely grateful. It would be a good start, and give me time to find something nearer.'

'Then that's settled.' Veronica poured water into the teapot. 'It's a pity about the shop just when you were making a go of it.' Taking two cups from a cupboard, she continued. 'Don't forget, you always have the picture to fall back on. There are buyers out there, in fact I could think of a couple.'

'It's of sentimental value to me, one my father bought for Mother just before he died. I wouldn't like to part with it,' she admitted, sipping her tea.

'Well, it's a thought if you become absolutely desperate,' she prompted.

The word 'desperate' brought Charles to mind again. Her stomach churned. She'd not contacted him. Donald had spoilt that by being in the shop early. At all costs, she must phone him before the

257

end of the day and that meant setting off back pretty quickly.

'Are you all right, darling?' Veronica asked, looking searchingly at Helen.

'I'm fine, but I must get back soon. I must call back at the shop on my way home. Thank you so much for offering me the job. I'll repay you one of these days.' She took Veronica's hands and gave them a squeeze.

'Don't mention it, dear. That's what friends are for. I take it you'll start as soon the shop is out of your hands. Is that all right?' she asked.

'Fine. I'll keep in touch,' she concluded.

The raw cold had dispersed the crowds and her breath sent white clouds into the frosty air as she arrived back in Leeds City centre and made her way to the bus station. At least it was too cold for the rain that had threatened earlier. If it came, it would more likely turn to snow.

Her thoughts returned to Charles. She must phone the hospital the minute she arrived at the shop and make arrangements to talk to him again.

Chapter 19

The sun in flames of crimson glory shone low in the sky and the breeze managed to stave off the threatened snow. Night was rapidly approaching and the bus seemed to take forever to travel back to Kidsworth. Helen felt weary but the sharp bite of the cold air cleared her brain. The main priority now was to call in at the shop and make that all-important telephone call to Charles. She rifled through her handbag for the key, switched on the lights and walked slowly over to the telephone, not relishing the task and reluctant to dial. But her decision had been made.

The silence around her was absolute and, when her elbow touched upon a potted palm she knocked it, causing it to wobble precariously. Still on edge, she steadied it with shaking hands. Her stomach wavered at the thought of a negative reaction from Charles, but she told herself to be brave and stop procrastinating. She desperately needed reassurance that his feelings towards her had not changed. But she was unlikely to achieve either until she made a move. The telephone number was scribbled on the piece of paper spread out in front of her and she dialled. Her heart was thumping noisily in her chest as she waited.

'Is Mr. Charles Ravel available?' she enquired anxiously. The operator transferred her to his office and the woman who answered identified herself as Mr. Ravel's secretary. After an enquiry akin to a third degree, she eventually informed Helen he was going to be away for a few days and would not be returning until sometime later in the week. Helen was bitterly disappointed as she stood clutching the phone, her hopes were completely shattered by the news. Now she must work out her salvation plan.

The chill outside reminded her that Christmas was fast approaching, and she wrapped her coat tightly around her. As she locked the shop door another worry loomed. How would she afford to buy the girls decent Christmas presents on the money she'd earn from Veronica? She had hoped to save her share of the proceeds from the sale of the shop specifically to re-invest if suitable premises became available, but she knew she would have to take some of the money to tide her over until something permanent came along.

Her thoughts preoccupied with what lay ahead, she almost stepped in front of a car. The sound of a blaring horn jerking her back to reality and, as she thought of the girls, the knot of frustration inside eased. It was time to take positive steps to remain sane and alert. It was no use looking in retrospect at what might have been. She must forget Charles for now, concentrate on the girls and give her best shot to the job at Veronica's shop.

There were no signs of life from within as she climbed the steps to the house. As she looked up at the stars strewn across the sky, she was puzzled as to where Mary and the girls might be. Beams of moonlight filtered into the room when she opened the door to Nell's noisy greeting. She stroked the little dog's coarse hair, patting her gently on the back. 'I'm home, Nell. At least you're here to greet me,' she murmured.

The fire was getting low. She removed the guard, riddled the ashes and strategically placing several pieces of coal on top, she turned off the damper.

Within seconds, flames leapt up and the fire came to life again. Helen held her hands in front anticipating the warmth and its glow fell around her.

She was alerted to Mary's return by the laughing and giggling outside. The door flew open, cold air rushing in as Jessie and Sylvia held out their arms to her. 'We're back, Mummy,' they chorused.

Helen gathered them up as Mary took off her coat and quickly placed the kettle on the hob. 'Sorry we're late back, Helen. I had to call at Danby Place to check my post. I'm expecting a letter from the bank. I made a meal before we went.'

'Don't worry, Mary. I've only been back five minutes myself. I called on Veronica Brightwell. But I'll tell you all about it later.'

'Come along girls,' Mary said as she looked at the clock on the mantelpiece. 'Let's get you both off to bed.' At Mary's calling, the girls rushed upstairs and five minutes later Helen followed to tuck them in and tell them a story.

Jessie's eyes were closing but she fought to keep them open as Helen finished the story. Sylvia was already fast asleep.

'I'll see you in the morning, darling,' Helen said, kissing Jessie on the forehead.

'Mummy, what will happen when you leave the shop? You won't let Aunt Mary leave us, will you?' she asked, a worried frown on her face.

'Not at all, treasure,' she stressed but it was a worry to her too. She could just about manage but without complications, and she desperately needed Mary to stay now that she had the new job to go to.

Sarah placed the bolts firmly into place locking

261

the front door. It was only half past nine but she felt weary. After checking all was secure, she went into the kitchen to make herself a cup of Ovaltine. It was her nightly ritual and helped her swallow the pills her doctor had prescribed and settled her ready for a good night's sleep.

Absently she watched the blue flames licking the sides of the pan and her mind reverted to the gas leak. The problem was she had been distracted by Billy and she'd seen nothing of him since that day.

The milk spluttered up the sides of the pan, rising to the surface. Startled she quickly unfolded her arms and switched off the gas, vigorously stirring the milk into the powder. Taking a sip, she switched off the light, went through to the hall and climbed the stairs.

The news that Laura and John were back together delighted her. It had been a major concern when John left. She'd been so confident of their relationship that she could have guaranteed a secure future for Laura. But there were no guarantees in life. It would have been wonderful had William lived longer, but that was the way of things.

The idea of Helen's involvement with a surgeon impressed Sarah immensely, and she secretly relished the thought of meeting him. Helen deserved some happiness. Goodness knows how she'd coped in the past with the lack of money and Jim losing his job. It was a stroke of luck her meeting up with the surgeon. When things were official, she could wallow in front of her bridge friends. That would cancel the embarrassment she'd encountered when they learnt about Helen's marriage to Jim.

The grandfather clock in the hall struck ten. How time flies, she mused. It had seemed to pass more quickly since she turned sixty. She hoped senility was not setting in, but who was she to judge. She took a ball of cotton wool to cleanse her face. Provided she kept up her daily regimen she could still pass for fifty. Her figure was slim and no-one could accuse her of slipping into neglectful ways. She looked in the mirror. Her reflection was cruelly accurate. Deciding more effort was needed, she plastered night cream thickly over her face. That should do the trick. Drawing out her hairnet, she carefully placed it over her hair and clipped a couple of bobby pins in the front to hold it.

The brass and iron bedstead, a family heirloom highly cherished by Sarah, stood majestically in the centre of the long wall. It had been a wedding present from William's parents. She pulled back the eiderdown and covers, and climbed in. The pills were already taking effect. As she thought of her girls, both now safe and secure, a smile lifted the corners of her mouth and relief surged through her.

Apprehensive about his visit but, knowing he had to face the situation to win Helen back, Charles drew the car to a halt and stepped out. He opened the passenger door and took hold of a bouquet of red roses. Brushing the front of his jacket with the palm of his hand, he headed for the house.

He started up the steps and fleetingly a shadow

263

loomed before him. He looked to his right anticipating its source but a heavy weight came down on his head and he fell to the ground. A second blow smashed into his temple rendering him unconscious. The roses fell from his grip and scattered down the steps. All went quiet and within seconds the shadow vanished.

Inside the house Nell started to yap and she wouldn't stop. Helen went to the back door and peered out but there was no-one there. Nell shot through her legs and disappeared down the front steps. Normally she was an obedient little dog, but despite Helen's repeated calls, Nell began to whine and refused to return.

'I'll have to go out and fetch her back, Mary,' Helen said rubbing the backs of her arms. 'It's really cold and frosty out there.'

'Take care, love,' Mary called after her, her face puckered in concern.

The visibility was poor and the side path was white and slippery. Helen was puzzled as she made her way to the front steps where she spotted Nell. It was uncharacteristic of her to linger outside in the cold weather.

Helen called out again. 'Nell!' She gave a whistle but her heart began to beat rapidly as she heard a cry from the steps. Turning quickly and dashing back towards the house, she called out again for the little dog. But Nell stood there, still whining.

'There's someone down there, Mary,' she said, her lips trembling with the cold. 'Come with me. I can't get Nell back. Something's upsetting her.'

Mary grabbed her coat and slipped it on, taking

hold of Helen's arm and linking her. 'Sounds to me as if someone's hurt,' she said as the moans started again.

'Helen!' The call was faint.

At the sound of the cry, Helen was startled. Surely it couldn't be Charles. But the voice sounded familiar and she ran towards the steps, almost slipping. When she saw Charles lying there breathing heavily, she leant over, peering into his face. 'Darling, what's happened?' she asked urgently, her heart palpitating, her hands touching his face lovingly.

'Bring the torch, Mary,' she called out realising the blood in his hair was sticky.

'I was hit over the head. That's all I know.' He tried to struggle to his feet.

'Let's get you inside,' she said, a guilty edge to her voice, aware that, had she not dismissed him so hurriedly, he would not have been visiting unannounced.

Mary arrived with the torch and together they managed to help Charles to his feet. As she flashed the torch ahead of her, Helen noticed the roses strewn down the steps. But she had to ignore them. It was more pressing they helped Charles into the house and, although it was a struggle, they managed to get him on to the sofa.

Helen filled an enamel bowl with water and started to dab away the blood from around the injury, her tiredness now miraculously concealed. 'I think you need stitches,' she said, having swiftly noticed that the cut was deeper than she'd first realised. 'Mary, will you call the doctor, love?' she asked.

Charles interjected. 'There's no need, Helen. I'll be fine once you've stemmed the bleeding,' he said optimistically but, by that time, Mary had set off for the telephone kiosk down the road.

'Mary's left already, and it's not stopping,' she insisted as she carefully examined the cut.

He caught her hands and whispered into her hair. 'I'm desperately sorry, darling.' His voice was husky with emotion. 'I came to apologise, to sort things out.' He spoke in jerky phrases, obviously still drifting in and out of consciousness.

When Doctor Jacobs arrived he was carrying a bunch of roses which he plonked down on the kitchen table. 'I take it these were intended for someone,' he said and he gave Helen a wink. She smiled, although her tension remained.

'Let's have a look at that head of yours,' the doctor said, scrutinising it carefully and gently touching it to ascertain the severity of the cut.

'It's pretty nasty. I know we professionals don't like to admit it, but I'm afraid the lady's right. You do need stitches,' he said lightly. 'We must get you to hospital.' He turned to Helen. 'It might be an idea if you come too.'

'Will you be nervous staying here alone, Mary, after what's happened?' Helen asked.

'I'll be fine, love,' Mary replied bravely. 'I'll lock the door as soon as you've gone.'

'This needs to be reported to the police,' the doctor added. 'Someone else might get hurt. Is there anything missing?'

'I haven't checked but I don't think so. Goodness knows why he picked on me. The only person I know around these parts is Helen.'

She clung tightly to his hand, hoping the culprit was nobody wishing to punish her. As far as she knew, she had no enemies and she was at a loss to understand why it had happened, unless of course the motive was robbery. But she would have to leave the police to puzzle that one out.

The clock struck a quarter past midnight and, making his way up the drive to Kirk Grange, he glanced around him, checking that no-one was watching. The balaclava he wore to carry out the job gave him the anonymity he needed.

The front path beneath the window was slippery with moss. He leant over and used the jemmy to prise open the window. It came cleanly and without sound. With quick and well-coordinated movements, he pulled himself inside and flashed the torch. He turned around to check outside. Still nobody around. The house was clad in darkness.

From the light of his torch, he spotted the French ormolu clock, an intricately engraved silver bowl and a pair of heavy brass candlesticks. Lifting them gently from the mantelpiece, he placed them inside the bag. Carefully handling the porcelain figures, the pair of Dresden vases and the Coalport china, he wrapped them in rags and packed them into a second bag he'd left beneath the open window.

Flashing the torchlight on the pictures as he stepped nimbly into the hall, he studied them intensely. He selected two and leant them against the wall. Eying the cupboard under the stairs, he noticed the door was slightly ajar. He walked stealthily towards it, pulled it open and rummaged quietly amongst its contents, finally bringing out a large box. He lifted the lid to check its contents and, turning quickly he placed the box in the bag, collected the pictures and slipped them under his arm, taking care as he passed through the sitting room. He approached the window and, struggling with the weight of the bag, he lifted it. Without a sound he leant over and carefully placed it outside on the front path. Finally he made a quick exit, silently closing the window. He looked around and was soon on his way.

'Where the devil have you been till this time?' Agnes was at the end of her tether. Jack had left the house at seven o'clock and here he was returning at one o'clock in the morning. He needed to be up for work by a quarter past six. What did he think he was playing at? She was usually in bed by this time but she knew she'd have to wait up for him. He'd left his key on the sideboard.

'Walt called in for you at half past seven, but as usual, I didn't know where you were, so I couldn't make him any the wiser. You never tell me where you're going these days,' she moaned.

'How many times do I have to tell you, Ma? I'm not a kid anymore. I don't need your permission,' he stressed cuttingly, his hair falling in untidy wisps over his forehead.

'Lord knows where you've been, looking as if you've been dragged through an 'edge.' She paused. 'Permission you say? I'm your Ma. I'm entitled to know what's going on!'

Jack shrugged his shoulders, ignoring her. 'I'm off to bed.'

'What about your supper? I've made cheese and onion sandwiches,' she said, sulking. 'They'll go to waste. Money doesn't grow on trees, you know.'

'I don't want any.' He yawned and stretched his arms. 'And there's no need for you to wait up for me. As I said, Ma, I'm off to bed.'

'You left your key. You didn't expect me to leave the door open did you? You don't know who's knocking about these days.' Agnes was livid. It was too late for her to eat the sandwiches. In any case, cheese always made her dream. There was nothing for it but to get off to bed. The fire was dying down but it would need riddling in the morning ready for a good clear out.

She switched off the light and, as if on impulse, pulled the curtain aside and took a surreptitious look outside. There at the roadside was the factory van, the name blazoned on its side. Her curiosity aroused, she stood gawping, and then she dropped the curtain. Her heart started to palpitate. Goodness knows what Jack had been up to, but she hoped he'd not been on one of his moonlighting jobs again. She was choked up with it all and she'd not tell him again. If they found out what he was up to with the factory van he'd have to suffer the consequences and that was that.

After conferring with Casualty, the police confirmed that Charles had been hit on the head by a heavy metal object, but they had no clues as to what it was, or who the culprit might be.

'We need you to check your pockets, sir. If the

motive was robbery, then we know what we're up against,' the constable explained.

'Shall I check, Charles?' Helen offered.

'Please.' Still dazed, he pointed to his jacket. 'My wallet's in the top pocket.'

Helen slipped her hand inside, quickly realising it was empty. 'It's not here.' Her body stiffened. 'Shall I check your other pockets?'

'I can't see it being anywhere else, but do,' he returned.

After checking she retrieved only a neatly folded handkerchief.

'Nothing, not even the car keys,' she confirmed indignantly. 'It looks as though he was after your money and your car.'

'We need your registration number to chase up the car,' the constable said, pencil poised.

'It's an olive green Jaguar saloon, MCS 420. I shouldn't imagine there are many around,' Charles replied smoothly.

'Maybe not, sir, but these fellows are quick at passing on stolen goods. It could be in a garage somewhere at this very moment being sprayed a different colour,' he reflected bleakly.

The clock struck a quarter past one as they left the hospital. The gash had been deep and Charles had lost a lot of blood. Casualty Sister reluctantly gave her consent for his discharge, stressing vigilance was needed in case he lost consciousness again.

'You know,' she'd cut in philosophically, 'when it comes to following medical instructions you doctors are the worst type.' Darting a quick glance at Charles, she flashed him a thin smile and pointedly nodded her mousy brown head towards him.

They took a taxi back to the hotel. 'You need a good night's sleep, Charles,' Helen murmured sympathetically, making an effort to lighten her tone. 'Let's get you into bed and comfortable,' she said, her mind still not taking in fully what had happened.

Charles cleared his throat. 'I must talk to you.' He hesitated, his face strained after the ordeal he'd been through. 'Sorry I went off like that last week. Tell me you forgive me.'

'Of course I forgive you and I must admit I couldn't come to terms with my own stupidity,' she began hastily, remembering uncomfortably the past events. 'Let's give it another try.' The earlier doubts flickering through her mind had now completely faded.

'It was worth suffering the attack to get you back,' he grinned, obviously relieved at her re-action.

Helen read the intensity of his feelings as she lay beside him sensing his body close to hers. She felt both relief and contentment that the situation was resolved, and that they were back together.

'I'm determined not to let the business of the robbery drop. Let's hope the police can get to the bottom of it. It's a complete mystery to me,' she said pensively, a hint of irritation in her voice.

Chapter 20

It was later than usual when Sarah opened her eyes. A shaft of sunlight beamed through a chink in the curtain as she dressed in her pale blue crepe-de-chine blouse and navy-blue woollen skirt. But she was haunted by a vague recollection of her dreams. She went to the window, opened the curtains and looked across the valley. There was still a glistening of dew on the grass. The sun had lifted and a fine mist was rising from the verges. She stared at the unmade bed and decided to leave it until Agnes arrived. It was her day for the bedrooms and she may as well make the bed at the same time.

There was a letter on the doormat as she passed through the hall, and she stared vacantly at the envelope. She slid her thumb inside and ripped it open. It was from her accountant. William had left her well-placed with a private income. She stood poised ready to open the sitting room door but, as if possessed of a sixth sense, a strange feeling came over her, a feeling that all was not well. There was a muffled stillness about the house.

Seconds later, she pushed open the door and stared in horror at the bare mantelpiece. Paralysed with fear, she stood rigid as an unpleasant sensation took over. Her mouth went dry, and the sudden feeling of panic made her heart race.

Anxiously she scanned the room for further signs of intrusion. Her whole being was suffused with shock and she was unable to focus her mind adequately.

But Sarah was made of strong stuff and she took a deep breath, pulling her thoughts together sharply. Before doing anything she needed to sit down for a minute or two to compose herself. Only then would she be able to decide the next step. She should, of course, telephone the police, but would it be better to ring Laura first?

She dialled and the telephone rang constantly but there was no reply. Had Laura left for Dora Bristow's? But there was no reply from Dora's either. Sarah was adamant she'd prefer Laura to deal with the robbery. Having decided to walk to Dora's and, hopefully, speak with Laura there she made to go into the hall for her camel coat. It would take about fifteen minutes, far more than she was used to these days, but she could surely manage it if she took it gently.

A knock at the back door gave Sarah a start. It was Mrs. Bean. She'd let herself in with her own key and was shuffling her feet noisily on the doormat.

'Is that you, Agnes?' Sarah called gloomily.

'It is, Mrs. Dorrington,' she cut in cheerfully.

'Something terrible has happened, Agnes.'

Agnes gave a startled cry on hearing the word 'terrible', and she raced into the sitting room. The smile faded from her lips as she looked around in evident dismay.

'What's happened Mrs. Dorrington?' she asked, looking flustered. 'I can't believe my eyes.'

273

'Goodness knows what I've done to deserve this,' Sarah moaned, waving her hands airily around the room, waiting for sympathy. Hot tears flooded her eyes as she continued. 'I've tried getting in touch with Laura but she seems to be out,' she wailed. 'What am I going to do?'

'Come on Mrs. Dorrington, sit yourself down. I'll make a cup of tea before we do anything. It's no good getting yourself all worked up; it won't do your health any good,' she advised, settling Sarah in an armchair and heading for the kitchen.

Agnes's face was scarlet as she picked up a box of Swan Vestas and lit the gas, placing the kettle on the hob. She was finding it hard to concentrate and she swore under her breath she'd swing for her Jack if this business was his doing. If he thought she was going to let him off the hook this time, he could think again. But she knew she was getting herself into a right old lather again and she tried to compose herself before taking in the tea. She blew her nose and washed her hands under the running water, dabbing her face to try to calm down the flushes and stop the perspiration.

'What exactly is missing?' she enquired, trying to appear casual as she placed the tray on the occasional table and started to pour the tea.

'I'm not sure yet, but everything from the mantelpiece for a start.' She indicated its bareness with the palm of her hand. 'My lovely French clock, a genuine antique,' she continued, 'the brass candlesticks and, my pride and joy, the beautiful silver rose bowl. They were all wedding presents, expensive ones at that.' She sniffed and gently

274

patted her nose with a white lace handkerchief. 'Goodness knows what else. I haven't had time to check,' she complained. 'But I've decided to go to Mrs. Bristow's and see if Laura's there. I'll finish my tea first and give Laura a chance to arrive.'

Agnes thought this a good idea and told her so, not offering to go herself. Her bunions were playing up this morning. And she'd decided to do her own snooping, casually of course. She knew more or less where everything should be and would surely recognise empty spaces. 'There's no-one better to sort it out than Mrs. Conway,' she said dryly, hoping Mrs. D would be quick and finish her tea. Then she could start checking. 'You'll need to wrap up well. It's cold out this morning and a little damp,' Agnes warned. 'What about your camel coat and fox fur. Will that suit?' she prompted, hoping Mrs. D would take the hint and go.

'Admirably!' Sarah was like a spoilt child. It was in her nature to be waited upon.

It's all right for some, Agnes thought to herself as she clomped up the stairs and into the main bedroom, noticing the bed had been left for her to make, yet again. It was getting to be a habit. She took the fox fur from the walnut wardrobe and slung it over her arm before collecting the camel coat from the hall stand. She opened the coat and Mrs. Dorrington slipped it on, buttoned it and draped the fox fur casually around her shoulders. 'There you are. You'll be as warm as toast now,' Agnes told her.

'Thank you, Agnes. I don't know what I'd do without you. I won't be long, dear,' Sarah pro-

275

mised, pulling the fox fur snugly around her neck and fastening the clasp. 'I'll get Laura to telephone the police when we get back.'

'Take as long as you need. Don't be rushing, Mrs. Dorrington,' she said, knowing this was the ideal opportunity to look around before she came back with Laura. 'I won't touch anything downstairs.' Agnes gave her a wry smile but inside she felt cheated. If the woman didn't know how she'd cope without her, why hadn't she kept her promise about the picture? Why had she given it to Helen?

Agnes listened for her footsteps on the drive before she went back into the living room. Despite the problems with her bunions, she managed to scurry around and give it the full inspection. There appeared to be little else missing, except the china which Mrs. D had already detected.

Advancing into the hall, she looked at the hat stand in the corner – nothing missing there either. But as she turned, she spotted the yawning gap on the wall where the landscape picture had been, and another gap opposite. It dawned on her very clearly that this definitely had the hallmark of her Jack.

'What a bugger!' she breathed to herself and turning swiftly, she made her way to the cupboard under the stairs with a deliberate purpose. Just as she thought! The cutlery had gone too. That irritated her unbearably. That proved it was Jack. 'Wait until I get my hands on him!' she muttered. The cutlery must have been in the van when she looked out last night. 'It needs stamping out right sharp,' she added, anger rising within her. She'd tell him when she got home. If this continued he could leave, find his own place. He'd soon change his tune then.

If Mrs. D and Laura wanted to know what was missing, they'd have to check for themselves. The best thing Agnes could do was to clear off upstairs and get cracking with the bedrooms. She closed the door to the cupboard under the stairs. With luck, Mrs. D probably wouldn't miss the canteen of cutlery. It hadn't been in its usual place for some time. But the picture was a different kettle of fish.

Agnes was running the Ewbank sweeper over the bedroom carpet when she heard the muffled sound of the door closing. 'Is that you, Mrs. Dorrington?' she called, advancing from the bedroom to the top of the stairs. 'Would you like me to make some coffee?' she asked pleasantly, knowing she'd have a cup too and one or two of Mrs. D's choice biscuits.

'Just the ticket, Agnes. I'm so tired after walking all the way to Mrs. Bristow's, but at least I came back in the car with Laura,' she said proudly.

Laura stifled a gasp as she stared at the blank wall. 'The Pissarro's gone! It can never be replaced,' she said emphatically, 'and it's worth a fortune.'

Agnes caught the words and struggled to calm herself, deciding to stay upstairs until they were both safely installed in the sitting room. And once she was in the kitchen she could hear their urgent discussions as she prepared the coffee, but she didn't catch exactly what was being said. Best keep out of it and, trying to cast it from her mind, she took the coffee percolator from the cupboard. It was a bit of a job having to mess around with that thing! What was wrong with a cup of Camp coffee? It was as good as that grained stuff any day. And it would have to be the best china seeing Mrs. Conway was here. Proper snob she was. It wasn't surprising Jack disliked her. He could get on his high-horse at times. But sometimes you had to learn to like people, or pretend you did.

'There we are Mrs. Dorrington. Nice to see you again Mrs. Conway,' she said obsequiously. 'Nasty business,' she added.

'I'll say, Mrs. Bean. As if Mother hasn't had enough, now this!'

'Get yourself a cup, Agnes,' Sarah insisted, her face brightening a little now.'

'Oh, thanks Mrs. Dorrington,' she replied, moving back into the kitchen where she'd already prepared a beaker for herself.

Helen tossed and turned, worrying about the attack on Charles. Who could have carried out such a malicious act? With mingled feelings of anger and guilt, and overcome by restlessness, she decided to get up. Despite her broken sleep, surprisingly she felt refreshed but her head was still buzzing with the events of the previous evening.

'Charles, I think I ought to check with the police, see if the car's turned up,' she suggested.

Charles leant on one elbow, kissed her and then eased his weight back into the bed, wincing as he lowered his head on to the pillow.

'I agree, but your first priority must be to get back to the girls and Mary. Arrange a taxi and put it on my bill.'

278

'Don't you think it's a little early for you to be left alone, Charles?'

'Not at all. The worst is over now. I'll be perfectly all right. Don't fret,' he insisted, but Helen had a feeling he was putting on a false front.

'Are you sure, darling?'

'Helen, please go,' he insisted. She left the room reluctantly.

The minute Helen arrived home, Mary asked about Charles.

'Much better, Mary. Whoever attacked him used a metal object; the police don't know exactly what. The thief took his wallet and his car keys. It never occurred to me to check on the car when we left for the hospital. I wouldn't have recognised it anyway but, let's face it, there aren't many cars on the roadside around here.'

'I agree but I'm surprised at the robbery. Most folk around here are honest, even if they're poor,' Mary said with a sense of pride. 'You can leave your door open at night and nobody will bother you. But we'll need to think twice now,' she conceded.

'I agree.' Helen fought against the frustration welling up inside her. 'Where are the girls?'

'They're upstairs. Just changing ready for a walk on the moors. Why not come with us, unless you need to get straight back.'

'I think Charles will be fine for an hour or so. I feel so tense, a bit of fresh air might just pull me round,' she said, her tone placatory.

Her anger faded completely as she spotted the vase of roses and reflected on her good fortune at being reunited with Charles. The circumstances had not been ideal but she had a gut feeling that things would turn out right this time.

The girls came downstairs, togged up in knitted hats and mittens. 'Is Mr. Ravel better now?' Jessie enquired.

'He's much improved, cherub,' Helen said, unsure as to how much they knew.

'Will he come to see us, Mummy?' Sylvia chipped in. 'We'd like that wouldn't we Jess?' she said, her liquid blue eyes staring in innocence.

The comment brought a smile to Helen's face as she realised how adaptable children were. The possibility of their meeting had been the reason she and Charles disagreed, and yet here the girls were suggesting just that. Mary gave her a knowing glance.

'We'll see, Sylvia,' Helen replied, trying to answer their tentative questions as smoothly as possible.

The winter sunshine danced across the fields as they set out for the moors. The girls held hands and skipped along as Helen and Mary linked arms and followed.

'I can't think who would want to attack Charles, unless it was some opportunist who spotted the Jaguar. But it all seems too pre-meditated for that. And what sort of person carries a metal object around, anyway?' Helen was mystified.

'It's no good racking your brain, love. That's a job for the police. They'll check it out. When they find the car there'll be fingerprints. It's amazing what they can come up with,' Mary replied positively.

The piercing winds swept across the moors and

over the hills as the sheep huddled together beside the reservoir, sheltering from the chill. It was quiet and fresh as the two women leant against the wind, Mary's nut brown hair in fine wisps escaping from the sides of her headscarf. The girls laughed as they enjoyed the spongy feel of the grass and developed a fascination for jumping up and down, listening to the squelching under their Wellington boots.

Helen turned against the wind to face Mary. 'What did you think when Sylvia asked when Charles was coming to see them?' She mouthed the words and stifled a chuckle.

'It just goes to show how kiddies can ride it all.'

'That's exactly what I thought,' Helen confessed, and they both laughed.

The wind dropped suddenly and the sun was obscured by a thick wadding of dark clouds amassing over the hills. 'Looks like we're in for a storm,' Mary said. 'Perhaps we'd better head back.'

'Come along girls,' Helen called. 'It's going to rain. We need to get back.'

'Oh no, Mummy,' wailed Jessie. 'We're really enjoying it.'

'Sorry, sweetheart but we're going to get drenched if we don't put a spurt on.'

The natural light began to fade as the first chilly drops plopped onto their heads like tiny pebbles. It grew darker still and the air became chillier, the rain heavier. The unmade road deteriorated into a rutted track and the water raced along it. The girls became excited as they lingered behind, dipping their boots in the puddles.

Helen became restless as they neared the house. Checking her watch, she noticed it was almost half past two and time she was making tracks to the hotel. The edgy feeling persisted as she approached the telephone box at the corner of the road. She dialled the number and braced herself. 'Mrs. Riley speaking. Mr. Ravel's room please.'

'I'm sorry, Miss but he's back in hospital.'

Chapter 21

Agnes called at the post office and spotted Maisie Blenkinsop with curling pins poking brazenly through her turban. She gave a slow blink. Common as muck she thought and she tried to avoid the woman. But Maisie sidled up. 'I've seen your Jack next door a couple of times,' she chirped. 'Is there summat going on?'

'How do you mean summat going on? He's offered to help her out. What's wrong with that?' Agnes complained tartly.

'She's with a lovely fella now, a bit of a toff,' Maisie continued, completely ignoring the other woman's resentment. 'But there was a commotion outside last night,' she said furtively, leaning closer. 'Someone hit him on his head and knocked him out,' she added, a suspicious edge to her voice. 'I was sweeping my steps and heard the racket.'

Sweeping her steps? Busy bodying more like! 'Well I never,' Agnes replied, now taken aback.

'There's no smoke without fire. Someone's got it in for him,' she offered, pointing a finger.

What was Maisie insinuating? Agnes hoped she wasn't suggesting it was Jack, although it was a puzzle right enough. First of all Mrs. D's place is burgled, picture and cutlery stolen, then this business at Helen's. Fair enough Jack was cut up about Helen giving him the push and she'd over- heard Walt mentioning the new man. But surely Jack couldn't have done the all that? Not that she was excusing him. He must have been up to no good leaving the works van outside. Even think- ing about it gave her a headache. The sooner she got to the bottom of it, the better. Although as usual he would only tell her what he wanted her to know.

She was mending the fire when she heard his bike clatter against the wall. As the door opened, she turned to look at him, her face beetroot red. 'I have a bone to pick with you lad,' she snapped through tight lips, her voice wavering.

'What's up now, Ma?' Jack sighed, took off his bicycle clips and placed them on the sideboard. He supposed she had another bee in her bonnet and, as usual, whatever it was a pound to a pinch of salt it would be his fault.

'You can get them off sideboard for a start,' she shouted, pointing a finger towards the offending clips, her scarlet face taking on a deeper purple hue. She finished mending the fire and pushed herself up from her knees, sighing heavily.

'Now then, what d'you know about robbery at Mrs. Dorrington's, first of all?'

Bloody hell. He was in for the third degree!

'Robbery, Ma? Don't be blaming me for summat I know nowt about.' He could be a secretive bugger at times, but for God's sake, why him this time? 'What makes you think it was me?' he asked sourly, a trace of exasperation in his voice.

She was in one of her bossy moods, and it was useless arguing with her.

'I'll tell you why. The canteen of cutlery I hid, and the picture Mrs. D promised me have disappeared. If that doesn't strike you as suspicious, I don't know what does. The two things you were after.' She folded her arms under her now heaving bosom.

'Honest Ma, it wasn't me.' He paused momentarily. 'But I can see why you thought it was.' He frowned, at a complete loss himself to understand who could have taken them.

'And another thing,' she continued, her chubby face contorted into a scowl. 'That new gentleman friend of Helen's has been attacked.'

Jack started to laugh loudly, mockingly but it was obviously too hearty for her liking.

'Stop that now, Jack. It's a serious business.' Her temper started to run wild. 'If anything happens to him, it'd be murder.'

The minute she uttered the word, his laughing stopped and an awkward silence followed.

'Innocent again, Ma,' he insisted, having digested what she said. 'I was only laughing 'cos Walt says fella's a bit of a ponce. Probably couldn't defend himself anyway. Are you satisfied now, woman? I've nowt to do with any of this, and that's a fact,' he said icily. With that, he pulled open the door to the stairs and went quietly up, leaving

Agnes openmouthed and no doubt in something of a flat spin.

He knew he could show a bit of a paddy in front of her, but most of the time it was bravado, especially if she annoyed him. He just couldn't weigh up who could have pinched that picture and the cutlery. He racked his brain to try and recall if he'd told anyone about it, but nothing came to mind. He decided to have a wash, spruce himself up and nip round to Walt's. If all she could think about was blaming him for everything that went wrong, then she could shove his bloody tea where the sun don't shine.

Giving his face a quick rinse, he dragged a wet comb through his tousled hair. He'd talk it over with Walt. Bloody hell, if anyone got wind he knew about the stuff taken from old Ma D's, he'd definitely be in the frame. That business about Helen's bloke was a funny going on as well. Why should anybody go around clobbering folk on the head? He enjoyed stirring up a bit of trouble, but he never stayed around to get involved.

Once at Walt's, he waited at the door whilst Walt grabbed his cap and muffler.

'This is a bit sudden, Jack. You didn't mention it last night.'

'Summat serious has cropped up. Well, a couple of things. Ma Dorrington's place has been broken into. You know that picture I was telling you about. It's been nicked and so has canteen of cutlery, one me ma had squat under stairs,' he said as they set off to the Cock and Bottle. 'Have you told anyone about that picture Walt?'

'I haven't, Jack,' he said emphatically, 'but you

have. Remember that night we went to Mucky Duck, that night Maureen's fella gave you the big heave-ho, and you had a drop too much to drink?'

'What about it?'

'There was one or two in tap room when you started shooting your mouth off about your ma and picture.' He pushed open the door of the pub and walked over to the bar. 'Two pints of bitter, love.'

'I was dreading I'd opened my big trap.' He followed Walt into the tap room. 'Who was there? Usual lot?' he asked tentatively.

'There was George Bradshaw and Maureen over at bar. Wilf Lockwood was throwing arrows with Norman Preston. And then there was usual lot, Harry, Eric and Ron,' he recalled. 'I remember it clearly, because Wilf and Norman had a row over darts game. Norm called Wilf a bloody cheat, and Wilf didn't like it. Threatened to clock him one.'

'Did I say owt about cutlery?' he asked, his face becoming taut as he racked his brain, trying to recollect exactly what had happened on the night.

'I can't remember, Jack.' Walt pulled the darts from the board and handed a set to Jack. 'Forget it now. Let's have a game. Don't get riled. As long as you're not involved, you've nowt to worry about.'

Jack threw a double twenty, pulled his darts from the board and chalked up his score.

'I thought you said a couple of things had cropped up. What's other then?' Walt stood purposefully, ready to throw.

'You know that new fella Helen Riley's knocking about with?' Jack started.

'The one I saw her with at station?' Walt chipped in.

'That's right. He's only got his head bashed in other night. Course, me ma thinks I did it, just 'cos Helen gave me the push,' he said sulkily.

'And, did you?' Walt asked, keeping his face straight.

'Bloody hell, Walt. I wasn't born yesterday. I'm not altogether stupid, even though me ma sometimes thinks I am,' he said defensively.

'I'm only kidding,' he said, patting Jack's back. 'Strange though. Who'd do summat like that?' he asked, puzzled.

'It's a bloody mystery.' Jack stared ahead, vacantly contemplating the dart board.

Casualty was buzzing with activity when Helen arrived. 'I need to check on Charles Ravel,' she said. 'I believe he's been admitted from the Queens Hotel in Leeds.'

'Are you a relative?' the reception nurse enquired.

'A very close friend,' Helen replied.

'Not a relative, then?' the nurse continued.

'No, as I said, a very close friend,' she reiterated sharply.

'We're not supposed to reveal confidential information to people other than relatives,' the nurse said, extending Helen's suspense.

'Please, nurse. I was here with him last night. He was hit on the head by a metal object. The

287

sister knows me. Please check and tell me what's happening.'

The nurse disappeared down the corridor, and re-appeared with the casualty sister.

'Yes,' sister said pointedly, a heavy scowl on her face, 'this is the lady I entrusted him with.' The withering look she gave Helen was intended to put her in her place. 'But what happened?' she said, a sardonic edge to her voice. 'You promised to stay with him. I warned you of the possible dangers.' There was an awkward silence. Her hard stare remained fixed on Helen.

'Mr. Ravel has a mind of his own, Sister. He assured me he would be perfectly safe to be left after a good night's sleep. He insisted I go and check on my family. Now please, tell me why he's back in here.'

'I'm afraid he's been foolish.' The sister's voice softened. 'He got up out of bed and must have had a dizzy spell. You should have been there to help him. He fell against the corner of the wardrobe and two of the sutures split apart. We've had to re-suture and re-dress the wound,' she explained.

'I'm really sorry I left him, Sister, but he did insist. When may I see him?' She sighed in relief that it was nothing more serious.

'It's for certain he's not leaving again, not until we're absolutely sure there's no further danger. We've just sent for the orderly to take him up to ward five. Give him a quarter of an hour before you go up to visit,' she said finally and, shrugging amiably she swept off down the corridor.

The ward sister was caring and concerned as

288

she pointed to the bed Charles was occupying. Helen raised her eyebrows and shook her head as she approached. The minute he saw her, his face puckered into a sheepish grin. Helen remained straight-faced.

'Charles, I'm very cross with you.' She kissed him gently on the cheek. 'You promised faithfully you'd behave and what happens? I should have been there. I'm beginning to think the casualty sister was right when she said you doctors are the worst patients of all.' She laughed, holding both his hands and squeezing them tightly. 'And apparently it's all my fault for leaving you!'

'I'll put her straight. But I'm here overnight so they say. I 'phoned Miriam. The problem is they've had to put all my major ops on hold.' He frowned.

'Stop worrying, Charles. There's nothing you can do. I'm sure Miriam is a very capable lady. She'll organise things in your absence.' She smoothed his brow. 'On a lighter note, the girls have asked to see you, but the ward sister won't allow children in here. So I expect you to pull yourself together pretty quickly and then they can meet you officially.' Her voice was light and a warm glow shone in her eyes.

His face became serious. 'Helen, I hope you're not making these suggestions flippantly. I'd love to see them but not without your wholehearted agreement, especially after our differences.' He freed his hands and pushed himself up on his pillow.

They had to get it right this time. There was no room for blunders. 'Charles, I can assure you the

289

girls have asked to see you. But I'd made my mind up before they asked. I know I was wrong in denying you. I'm so sorry.'

His face softened. 'I needed to be sure you weren't arranging it just to appease me,' he stressed, taking hold of her hand once more.

She sat on the chair beside the bed. 'I've heard nothing from the police about the car. I thought they might have been back by now but I suppose these things take time.'

'Let's not think about that, darling. It's the least of my worries. All that matters is that you weren't attacked.' His tone was endearing. Changing the subject, he continued. 'Tell me about the shop. Have you sorted things with the new partner?'

'It's a long story,' she started. 'Things developed rapidly after I last saw you,' she murmured sadly. 'The shop is sold. It's over. But I'll tell you all about it when I come back tonight.'

Constable Clarke smiled to himself. He was the man for the job after his previous success at catching Billy Lockwood. The lad must have tried his luck again.

'Come in, constable.' Mrs. Dorrington opened the door. 'I can't believe it,' she added dramatically.

'The number one suspect is young Lockwood,' he reasoned. 'He got off Scott-free last time.'

'Just a minute, constable, we can't go accusing young Billy without evidence. To me, it was someone with far more about him than poor Billy. Whoever did it, knew which pictures to take. I tell you, they were hand-picked,' she stressed.

'What do you mean hand-picked?'

'Did my daughter not tell you?' She stared at him in genuine puzzlement. 'One of the pictures he took was very valuable indeed. We're not quite sure exactly how much it was worth, but it was considerable.' She looked him straight in the eye, emphatic in her conclusion. 'Now that's not the sort of trick a young boy pulls.'

Clarke realised it was not quite as straightforward as he'd hoped, the picture being very valuable threw a different light on the case. 'I'm inclined to agree with you there, but still I must ask the lad for his whereabouts last night.' His tone was now less than positive.

Clarke left the house heading for the Lockwood's and when he arrived the gang of ruffians running wild around the garden ignored him as he stepped over the broken gate and kicked a bottle out of the way. How could they live in such squalor? He knocked on the door which was already half open and began to swing as he put on the pressure. From inside, a mongrel came sniffing through the gap before the door was slammed in his face.

'Who is it?' a voice called out.

'It's me, P.C. Clarke,' he replied as formally as he could. He bent down, pushed open the letter box and peered through, 'Is your Billy in?'

Two warm brown eyes, sad but honest, appeared at the other side of the letter box. 'What you want him for?' The eyes turned cold. 'I'll break his bloody neck if he's been up to his tricks again.'

'We're not sure, Nora, but we need to know his

291

whereabouts,' Clarke confirmed, 'even if it's just to eliminate him.'

'I think he's down at Jimmy Clinkard's sorting ferrets out,' she said more calmly.

'Thanks. I'll catch up with him there.'

Billy had a cast-iron alibi. 'Me and Jimmy went to flicks.' He started to relate the story of the 'Lassie' film, and pulled out two crumpled tickets from his trouser pocket. 'Here you are. Now do you believe me?' His woeful eyes peered out of his grubby, pinched face.

Clarke felt guilty and mean. 'Sorry lad. After last time, you can't blame me for checking up can you?'

The Jaguar was still missing and Charles had no alternative but to book a train ticket to travel back home after his discharge from hospital. Before he left he met the girls and they clapped their hands with delight when he surprised Helen with his invitation. 'I'd like you and the girls to come down to Llanypen for Christmas and stay with me at Willow House, Mary too. Is that feasible?'

'It certainly is,' she replied, her spirits soaring. 'I'd love to come.'

But Christmas was only two weeks away and the proceeds of the shop sale had still not been released. Unless this happened quickly, she would be short of money to pay for rail tickets. The only solution was to ask Mr. Marchbank for a loan on account even though that was degrading. But she'd not bought Christmas presents for the girls either and her only solution was to look

292

for a couple of cheap dolls and run up a set of clothes each for them on the Singer.

She was twenty minutes early when she arrived at Veronica's shop the following Monday morning. Travelling to the other side of the city was another obstacle, but she tried to remain bright and fresh. Veronica was in the little kitchen at the back of the shop. 'You're early Helen. Let's get our priorities. Cup of tea before we start?' she suggested.

'That would go down well,' she enthused. 'But I must tell you the bad news. Mother's Pissarro has been stolen.'

'Yes I know and what a disaster here at the shop! The police said they arrived too late to catch the culprit.'

'I think we're talking at cross purposes, Veronica. I'm not sure what you mean by catching the culprit at the shop.'

'Didn't they inform you?' she asked. 'I couldn't believe my eyes when the customer showed me the Pissarro and asked for a price. We tried to stall him but by the time the sergeant arrived he'd scarpered.' She poured water into the teapot.

'Goodness, I can't believe the picture was here on the premises. It must have been galling when you knew exactly where the picture belonged and you couldn't hang on to it.' Helen gasped. 'I'm surprised he came so close to home.'

'My thoughts too but he obviously wanted to offload it quickly before it became common knowledge.'

'Let's hope the thief is caught soon. The picture's insured but that's not the point. It means a lot to us.' Helen gripped her mug of tea firmly with both hands, warming her cold fingers. 'Yes it was frustrating especially knowing the picture belonged to your family,' Veronica continued. 'But on to other business. Mondays are usually quiet, Helen, but I asked you in today to help me check the stock and decide what we need from the salerooms. I'd like to offer more porcelain and china and I know that's your specialist area.'

Helen's face became flushed. 'I'd like that.'

'You're a jolly sight more up to date than I am on that score.'

It was not long before the shop bell rang and Helen looked up. A well-dressed young woman entered. 'I'd like to look at the pair of dogs in the window, please,' she said. She had a slightly foreign accent, one Helen couldn't quite detect.

'The Staffordshires? They're lovely aren't they, and in pristine condition. They've been in the same family since they were bought. Their owner died recently.' Helen crossed over to the window, picked them out and continued to elaborate. The young woman, obviously intrigued by what Helen told her, not only about their history but also about their manufacture, decided on the spot to buy them.

After they'd indulged in a long, leisurely discussion about porcelain and china, the woman described to Helen a particular Georgian teapot she admired, one in the style made popular by Daniel Marot. 'My good friend Bridget Carter-Swann has one. I was positively entranced by the delicacy of its patterning. Apparently there are several in a variety of different patterns. Do you have anything of the same style and period?'

'I know exactly what you're describing but we don't have one just now.'

'Maybe you'd keep a lookout for me. If you do come across one, perhaps we could view it together before any decision is made.' She handed Helen her card, thanked her and left the shop. Helen glanced down at it as the woman closed the shop door. It read, Baroness Cranviers de Villeneuve.

Veronica came out from the storeroom. 'That was wonderful, Helen. Did you realise that Bridget Carter-Swann is Lady Swann of Silverdale Hall? Working with a close friend of hers, Baroness Cranviers is such a coup. Her husband is a very well-known French jeweller. What can I say? And you knew everything about the Staffordshires.'

Veronica was wildly impressed. Within one morning, Helen had acquired a sound knowledge of many of the items in the shop, and it was obvious she was used to the sophisticated ways of the middle and upper classes.

Chapter 22

Clarke quickened his pace as he approached Kirk Grange and knocked sharply on the front door.

'That valuable picture of yours has been spotted at an antique shop in Guisborough,' he told Sarah.

'That's good news,' Sarah replied, smiling.

'Not as good as you think, Mrs. Dorrington. Someone took it in to be valued. I think he wanted to sell it as quick as he could. But it didn't work out.'

'How do you mean?' Her smile turned to a frown.

'The owner tried to stall him but, unfortunately, Richards, that's the name the thief called himself, left before the sergeant could arrest him. Ever heard of him, Mrs. Dorrington?'

'Not at all, constable,' she said positively.

'Of course, the name is probably an alias,' Clarke said brightly. 'The Jaguar car he used we think was the one stolen from the surrounding area the same evening as the robbery at your place. It could be that there's a go-between involved here, a Mr. Big so to speak.' He paused. 'How many people exactly knew about the picture?'

'I can give you the answer right now, my daughter Mrs. Riley, her friend Miss Brightwell who checked the picture out, my other daughter, Mrs. Conway and me. That's it,' she said with finality.

'Are you sure you had no callers, workmen or anyone else who saw it? Take your time. I don't want to rush you but it would be useful if I had something to go on.' He ran his finger round the rim of the helmet tucked under his arm.

'Mrs. Bean, my daily help, obviously knew the picture was missing but she didn't know its potential value. I certainly never told her.'

'Ah, the famous Mrs. Bean keeps cropping up doesn't she? I could pay her a visit.'

'That's fine, constable, but don't you upset her.'

Agnes heard the footsteps and lifted the lace curtain to peer through the window, wondering who it was at this hour. Then she spotted him, the dreaded P.C. Clarke. She heard the knock but decided to make him wait. Why dance to his tune?

Her stomach lurched like it always did when there was trouble in the air. And she was furious. Jack would definitely get it in the neck when he was back home, leaving her to face things on her own. He'd no business flying off the handle like that.

Why had he gone off in such a huff without tucking into his tea first? He knew she was getting him a bit of Finnan haddock. It always went down well with a few slices of brown bread and butter. It was quite dear this week. She'd asked Dodsworth for half a pound, and he'd given her three quarters, crafty devil. Jack would have to eat the fish for his supper.

She opened the door. 'Oh it's you,' she said, putting on a smile. 'Nothing wrong is there?'

'Glad you're in, love. It's you I wanted to have a word with,' he replied pleasantly.

The supercilious smile left her mouth. This was the thin edge of the wedge. It was always the same. She always had to do the explaining; it was never Jack. This must be her just reward for putting those pills in Mrs. D's drink.

'You'd better come in,' she said sullenly. 'I suppose it's about robbery at Mrs. Dorrington's. I know nothing about it.' She looked at him defiantly. He could question her until the cows came home but she couldn't help.

'I know that well enough. Just wondered how much you knew about the things that were taken. Apparently the picture was quite valuable.' He paused momentarily, and then he continued. 'Now I have a vague recollection of Mrs. Dorrington telling me some time ago that she'd left you a picture in her will, one you'd admired apparently, a landscape. Sounds like the one that was stolen. Did you know its value, Mrs. Bean?' He held her gaze unwavering until she replied.

'She's changed it,' she assured him, looking away, a pink flush spreading rapidly from her neck to her cheeks. 'She gave it to Helen and offered me a water-lilies picture, a lot nicer than the other one,' she lied craftily.

He seemed to take in every nuance of expression on her face. 'I see,' he said, taking his notebook from his top pocket. 'Water-lilies, you say?'

'That's right,' she added and, in complete contrast to the agitated state she'd been in a few minutes ago, she became quite calm. Perhaps she could kid him on a bit. He might back off if she made out she preferred the other picture. She needed to make sure he stayed a while to digest what she'd said, but it was time grudgingly given. 'Cup of tea?'

'That's right decent of you, Mrs. Bean.'

He took his place on the wicker chair next to the dresser whilst she slipped the kettle on to the hob over the glow of the coals. Within seconds it was hissing, hardly giving her time to take the beakers from the hooks and the cake tin from the cupboard.

'Fancy a nice piece o' parkin?' she asked, her

298

voice now light.

'If it's as good as your butterfly buns, I can't resist.' He rubbed his hands together in anticipation.

She'd fooled him. He hadn't suspected a thing. Not that she'd done anything wrong. But Jack caused no end of trouble for her. Clarke devoured the parkin and swigged back the tea, scribbling a few words in his notebook and putting it back in his top pocket with the pencil. He dashed the crumbs from around his mouth onto the floor and left.

Agnes smiled to herself, hoping she'd thrown him off scent. She must make sure she didn't drop either herself or Jack in the frame, not that he deserved her protection.

He was late back again and she was livid. He had no regard for anyone but himself.

When he did return, Agnes was on to him immediately. 'I've had police here. You left me with Clarke again. It's always me,' she complained, dabbing her forehead with her handkerchief.

'It's nowt to do with me Ma,' he said tetchily. 'And it's time you stopped accusing me. I'm just about up to the gills with it. For the last time. I've done nowt wrong.'

'If it carries on, you'll pack your bags. I've had enough,' she said, ignoring his pleas. But she jumped visibly when she heard a loud rapping on the door. She was a bag of nerves these days.

'I'll get it.' Jack turned the key and opened up.

'Jack Bean,' Clarke chanted in formal voice. 'I have reason to believe you broke into the house of Mrs. Dorrington on the night of the twelfth of

December 1949. Anything you say will be taken down and used in evidence...' he droned on.

'You what?' Jack answered, badly shaken by the accusation.

'You heard me.' Clarke stepped forward and slipped on the handcuffs. 'It's down to the station for you. You've a lot to answer to,' he warned.

'Dammit all. What's our Jack done to deserve this?' Agnes pursed her trembling lips. And after she'd given Clarke the tea and parkin! Talk about two-faced.

'He's the one who broke into Mrs. Dorrington's, that's what, Mrs. Bean. I'm sorry to have to do this. But I'm sure you'll realise I have my job to do.'

'It's not our Jack. I know when he's done summat wrong, always did. And this time he hasn't. It's not him. It's someone else, constable, believe you me.'

It was two days later when P. C. Clarke swore he'd seen a green Jaguar down Coppice Lane, but he had no chance of following on his bike. He reckoned it was being driven by Richards, the man who had approached Miss Brightwell at the shop. But he could be anywhere by this time, out of the district or even the county for all he knew. He dashed to the nearest telephone box and rang the sergeant.

'I'll get in touch with the county lot,' the sergeant replied. 'If there's a car as distinctive as that in the vicinity they'll track him down.'

Clarke felt triumphant when he discovered later that Richards had been caught speeding down the A1. As the sergeant had suggested, the

300

car was unusual for those parts, and the county lot had been observant.

Richards, whose real name was Dawson, denied all charges, but his fingerprints and background led the police to his previous convictions and his time in Armley Prison. His accomplice, whom Dawson named as Rington, had been in Armley at the same time and the two had formed a partnership. If a 'job' presented itself, the accomplice would do the legwork, and Dawson would be the brains behind it. But between them they'd slipped up, especially when Dawson tried to pass the stolen picture on to a fairly local shop. He was locked away again only weeks after he'd been freed. But the accomplice was yet to be identified.

The car was returned to Charles but Jack still remained locked up accused of the robbery at Mrs. Dorrington's house.

'Come on young man.' The sergeant swung open the cell door. 'I'm afraid there's been a mistake.'

'Mistake,' Jack repeated, 'a bloody mistake? I should think there has. I should get compensation for this.' He was well cut up, but his relief seemed to counter it.

'Keep your shirt on. We only did what we thought right. You were set up. Everything pointed to you. But P. C. Clarke's pulled in George Bradshaw. Girlfriend dropped him in it apparently and police checked his prison record. He fitted the bill.' He stroked his chin pensively and smirked. 'What's his girlfriend to you anyway, sticking up for you?'

This annoyed Jack. 'Nothing. But I'll swing for Bradshaw.' Jack spat out the words. 'Trouble causer! Anyway I'm glad Maureen saw the light.'

'I wouldn't get too cocky if I were you. Bradshaw tells us the factory's not too happy about the way the works vans keep disappearing.' The sergeant's words implied major problems for Jack, especially with his job. There was an ominous silence. Jack's face turned milky white and his stomach flipped. What with the boss to face, and then his ma, he'd definitely cop it when he got back.

Walt was crossing the road to meet him as he stepped outside the police station. 'There's been a right palaver,' he said. 'But Maureen got it out of Bradshaw.'

'So I hear. But how did you find out?'

'She told me. She knew he'd done a stretch and that he did a bit of moonlighting on the side. It pays for luxuries. He's bought her scent and black underwear regularly, so she said.' He laughed. 'She told me he likes a bit of black, gets him going.' Walt rolled his eyes. 'He bought her chocolates and a pair of silk stockings the day after Ma Dorrington was burgled. Maureen put two and two together and tumbled to it after the rumours started.'

'Rumours? What rumours?' Jack was curious to hear the rest of the story.

'George tried to get his revenge after that night you tried it on with Maureen. He's jealous to death. When he heard you spouting your mouth off about that stuff at Ma Dorrington's, he couldn't resist. You put it on a plate for him.

heard he got in touch with a friend, someone he'd met in prison. They cooked up the plan between them.'

'Now it all fits, Walt. I'm not surprised.'

'He knew they'd trace the burglary to you if he spread a few lies around. He wanted to show you who was top dog.'

'Top dog? I'll show him who is bloody top dog!'

'You know Maureen's always fancied you. You've a lot to thank her for, and don't forget it.'

'Thank her. I'll thank her right enough. I'll give her summat special,' Jack cut in, now winking back at Walt.

When he let himself into the house he could see his ma was aggrieved.

'Are you wrong in your head, Jack, messing about with firm's van? I knew it spelt trouble as soon as I looked out of window other night,' she said piously. She took a deep breath. Her palpitations were back again. What would they do for money now Jack had lost his job? Charlesworth had sacked him straight off without a chance to explain.

She sat down in one of the fireside chairs, her heart racing fifty to the dozen. She'd have to cut back if Jack left. There'd be a bit of pension to come soon and there was always her job at Mrs. D's, but a few bob a week didn't get you far. Might as well say goodbye to that new gas cooker she'd promised herself.

'You're right, Ma, I've learnt me lesson hard way,' he continued, trying to appear casual but obviously in a state of remorse. 'I'll tell you what! You wouldn't have got that new carpet square for front room but for my extra money.' He paused. 'I'm thinking of going across to Oldham. Seems there's one or two places I could try for a job.'

'Oldham? You can't be going all that way.'

'I've thought about it careful like and if owt crops up there, I'll have to find a place to live. Can't be helped. I've a living to make,' he stressed, apparently trying to come to terms with the full situation. But he fell into a morose silence again.

With George Bradshaw behind bars, Jack felt free to pursue his job search. He was restless and un-settled as he stood at the bar of The Cock and Bottle, feeling bitter against George after the cheap trick he'd pulled. The body beside him felt unusually warm and cosy, and he could smell the sweetness as he turned to face Maureen who'd sidled up to him. He felt the flush of her cheeks and the warmth of her breath as she leant over. 'How are things, Jack?' she asked, her eyes narrow-ing suggestively.

'I don't know what I'll do, Maureen. I've put a word in here and there but I'll have to give Oldham a try, see if there's owt doing there,' he answered gloomily. 'By the way, never got chance to thank you for getting me out of mire,' he said self-consciously, not used to offering his thanks. 'Fancy fish and chips on way home?' he asked. 'You could tell me the tale then, without this lot listening in,' he said more brightly, looking directly at Walt.

Walt smirked back. 'Bloody hell,' he called out. 'Doesn't take you long to get your feet under table.'

'It's business, Walt, that's all,' Jack said, smiling wickedly. Giving Maureen a sidelong glance he acknowledged she wasn't a woman men would die for, and not the beauty Helen was. She lacked something indefinable, something Helen possessed. But Walt was right. Maureen was more Jack's cup of tea. She had the bluest of blue eyes which sparkled wickedly. She was good-hearted, well-spirited and, according to George, she liked a bit of fondling. That was more his style. After being cooped up in the station, coupled with the sheer humiliation of being arrested, he felt defiant. He needed to be the hunting male again. And he felt it in his water that she was the one who could reciprocate and give him that pleasure. The more he thought about her, he was overcome with excitement. He took in the sight of her, the ruby bow lips he could kiss and that almost luminous cloud of gold hair he could run his hands through.

Apparently aware of his thoughts, she smiled her consent, her voice light, almost musical. 'I thought you'd never ask,' she replied, her eyes soft with feeling.

What a reaction! 'Come on then,' he said triumphantly. 'Drink up.'

The queue at Entwhistle's fish and chip shop stretched right to the door and outside across the front of the window. Holding Maureen close, he gently fondled her, sliding his hand round to her soft but firm breast. He would willingly have gone without the fish and chips for half an hour with her right now, but he'd made a promise and couldn't fashion to break it. How he managed to get through his fish and chips without devouring her as well, he didn't know. The urge became stronger as they walked along Chapel Street and he watched her as a whiff of breeze brushed a strand of hair across her face. After a few pints of bitter, his desire was becoming more and more urgent. But where could he take her?

She must have read his thoughts. 'Want to come back to our place, Jack?' The light of the gas lamp danced in her eyes. 'Me ma's gone off to me Auntie Florrie's for the weekend. She's got a touch of bronchitis and Mam always looks after her when she's poorly.'

Bloody hell. An empty house was exactly what he could do with. He hadn't had a woman since he tried it on with that Conway bitch. A bit of excitement that. Always better when they reckoned they didn't want it. He enjoyed a good struggle but it ended in nowt.

'If you're sure it's all right,' he babbled, unable to get the words out, his excitement rising to such a pitch.

'Course it is,' she confirmed. 'Would you like that?' she said teasingly.

Would he like it? He'd bloody love it. He suppressed a smile. His passion now unabated. He couldn't wait to get into the place and strip her down. He shuddered. Better control himself. Didn't want her to think he was too eager, even though he knew he held a sort of magnetism over her.

The door stuck as she jiggled with the key. Jack took it, twisted it viciously and forced it open. The way he felt, he couldn't be hanging about.

'I think you've bent key, Jack,' she said, giggling. 'Come in. Don't stand on ceremony.'

The minute he entered the house, he took hold of her wrists, pushed her body against the wall and pressed his hot, moist lips on hers, his tongue searching her mouth. She pushed him away playfully, her blue eyes soft and luminous, her ruby lips parted.

'You rogue, Jack Bean,' she laughed. 'I knew you fancied me.'

'But you've always had George Bradshaw sniffing round,' he complained, reminding himself of the strong mixture of dislike and contempt he now had for the man.

Taking off her cardigan and tossing it on a chair, she put her arms around him, consoling him. 'Well he's not here any longer, love. Just you and me. Is that what you want?' she coaxed, pushing him to the sofa and bending over him, her firm, rounded breasts heaving an enticement that dazzled his eyes.

'Good God, Maureen. Look at them bloody tits staring me in the face. What do you expect?' She straddled him as he lifted her dress and drew it over her head. 'Let's get this lot off,' he said, his hands trembling with excitement.

Stretching up and, without taking her eyes off him, she slowly stripped off her slip, leaving the rest for him. But he couldn't wait. He felt a deeper stimulation seep through his body and a feeling of disbelief at his luck. He ripped off his shirt and trousers and slung them on to the floor. This was what he'd been missing. Maureen had more about her than the Dorrington lass would ever have.

She straddled him again proudly, her fingers tantalising, teasing him. He ran his hands over her silky breasts and taut nipples. Her mouth was soft and damp as she brushed her lips over his chin, his cheeks, his neck and she then pressed them gently on his mouth. She quivered and uttered a low moan. And now Jack was completely out of control and took her emotion as his signal. Turning her over, he pressed his body on top of her, thrusting himself hungrily, urgently.

She sighed, she moaned, she cried out. 'Oh, Jack. That was wonderful,' she screamed, having surpassed herself. Her perfume wafted heavily over him and a wry, devastating smile danced around her mouth and lit her eyes.

He felt his eyes closing. This was bliss. This was what a man was entitled to. He was gone to the world.

Maureen slipped from the sofa and, as he snored loudly, her eyes twinkled with apparent victory.

Chapter 23

The office was conservatively trimmed for Christmas with little bunches of holly here and there and mistletoe hanging over the typing-pool doorway. In the corner was a small Christmas tree trimmed discreetly with one or two choice baubles and a few pieces of tinsel. The receptionist peered through the hatch. 'Can I help you?'

'Is Mr. Marchbank in today?'

'He's engaged at the moment,' she replied. 'I'll ring through and ask if he can fit you in when he's finished with his client.'

Helen sat on the edge of a high-backed chair and her mind began to wander. Donald Valentine had caused so many problems when he stepped into her life. He made decisions without consulting her and, for the last three weeks, when things had become stagnant, she had received no income from the shop takings. And now she was stony broke.

The receptionist returned. 'He'll be with you in ten minutes. Will you wait, Mrs. Riley? He says for me to make you a cup of tea.'

'That's very kind of you.' Helen picked up a copy of Punch from the magazine rack but her mind wasn't on its content.

Eventually Mr. Marchbank greeted her in his usual genial way obviously unaware of her discomfort. 'You're looking well my dear. Now what can I do for you?'

'This is all rather embarrassing I'm afraid. The thing is I'm in a bit of a fix. Donald Valentine made a number of unilateral decisions, first of all with the sale of the shop and then he suggested we take no income until everything was finalised. Initially, I agreed. I thought I could manage for two weeks, but now it's almost four and, quite frankly, I need the money.' Having off-loaded her problem, she felt relief surge through her.

'We must contact Valentine,' Marchbank insisted.

'I've tried but he seems to have gone away. There's no reply from his telephone.'

'Oh dear,' he said, 'that puts me on the spot. Unfortunately I can't offer you anything without his signature. It's awfully selfish of him to have done such a thing, but he probably doesn't realise that the business means more to you than mere pin money.' He sighed and shook his head. 'Perhaps if you went over to the bank they could let you have something to tide you over, but it would cost you the interest.' He frowned. 'I'm sorry, my dear, there's very little I can do until we make an arrangement for you both to come in and complete the sale.'

Helen's heart sank. She certainly couldn't afford to pay bank interest.

Laura deeply regretted her actions. They had led to such a devastating situation for Helen, and now she was desperate to appease the situation. But she couldn't apologise for something Helen knew nothing about and, since she wasn't in the habit of visiting, she needed an excuse to do so. The ideal opportunity arose as Christmas was drawing near.

With a surge of apprehension and a flicker of guilt she knocked on Helen's front door. There was no reason to suspect that Helen would spurn her, but somehow Laura's conscience took over and, as the key turned in the lock, she felt her courage flag. But her confidence was momentarily reinstated when Mary opened the door.

'Hello, Mrs. Conway,' Mary said courteously. 'Come in. I'll tell Helen you're here.'

Laura stepped over the threshold and a gut feeling told her she owed Mary an apology.

'Mary dear, before you go through, I'm sorry if I appeared a little frosty the last time I called. I know it's no excuse, but we'd had a spot of trouble at home and I was rather tetchy. I do hope you understand,' she said with genuine regret.

'Don't give it a second thought, Mrs. Conway. It's forgotten already.' Mary shrugged her bony shoulders and called Helen.

'It's so good to see you, Helen. Did you know John and I are back together again?' Laura gave her brightest smile, feeling more relaxed, sensing that Helen was unaware of the collusion with Donald.

'Yes. I'm delighted you've sorted out your differences.'

'I promised Mother I'd pop in and give you this. It's her Christmas present to you.' Laura handed over an envelope. 'It's money, and Mother apologises for that, but you know she's been out of sorts recently. I think she lost her confidence again after the burglary. She'd like you to choose your own present.'

'This is such a relief to me,' Helen replied as she opened the envelope. 'But I did say I wouldn't accept charity.' Her eyes became as dull and empty as her voice.

'Charity, Helen? You can hardly call a Christmas present from your mother charity. If it's any consolation Mother's given me exactly the same and I don't regard it as charity,' she explained. 'She would have made the journey herself but she's still feeling a little off colour. It might be an

311

idea for you to call in and see her when you get a chance.' Laura's interruption and her firm response appeared to stave off any further doubts in Helen's mind that Mother was being charitable.

'Of course, Laura. I did intend taking the girls to see her once I had a minute to spare.' She stared at the envelope. 'I'm actually waiting for the proceeds of the business to come through. I'm stony broke. And the thing is that Charles has invited us all down to Llanypen. I hadn't even the price of the train fares,' she said, 'until this,' she added waving the envelope in the air.

'Well then you must take it. At least it'll give Mother some satisfaction,' Laura reasoned, and then added in gentler tones, 'Let's hope 1950 turns out to be more a positive year for us all.'

'I couldn't agree more.' Helen took a deep breath. 'I promise I'll buy myself something with the money, but until I'm paid out, I'll need it to buy rail tickets. Please don't mention the situation to Mother,' she begged.

'Helen, darling, Mummy and I are family. We're here for you. But, don't worry, I won't breathe a word. And another thing, when are we going to meet your Charles? Mother and I are awfully keen to be introduced.' Laura took hold of Helen's shoulders and hugged her.

'Very soon, I hope. But so many things have happened recently, we've barely had time for each other. You heard about the attack, the theft of his car,' she said. 'But I haven't seen you to tell you, have I?' Helen related the story, adding that the car had since been returned to Charles.

312

Laura was amazed it all tied in with the burglary at Mother's. 'You know Mother has the picture back and she's adamant it belongs to you. And I agree. You must get the insurance sorted and take it back. I know how much you love it,' she stressed.

'I've been thinking seriously about it. It would be better left at Mother's until I move away. The insurance is likely to be very expensive and it's not a priority just now.'

'Provided you bear in mind it belongs to you, darling, that's all that matters.'

They looked at each other in the old familiar way. The sibling relationship was just about back to normal and, having eased away some of the guilt, Laura found herself beginning to smile.

The cases were heavy with Christmas presents and there was wild excitement as Helen, Mary and the girls reached the platform. It was the first time the girls had been on a train and such a novelty for them. The guard chucked them under the chin, pulled open the compartment door and lifted them over the deep step.

They settled themselves in a carriage and Helen recalled the meeting with Donald and Mr. Marchbank when her share of the proceeds had been established. She turned to Mary.

'Now more than ever, I'm determined to save as much as possible in the hope that something promising will turn up.'

'It will, Helen. But we need to be patient.'

Helen smiled to herself. She was delighted that Mary included herself in all the planning. She

313

was part of the family now.

One thought led to another and she reflected on her first ten days with Veronica, concluding that, despite the monotonous journey to the shop, her time there had been far more enjoyable than she'd ever expected.

As they neared their destination, the girls became more and more animated.

'I can't wait to see Uncle Charles,' Sylvia said laughingly.

'We haven't seen him for ages,' echoed Jessie, wide-eyed with excitement.

The train drew into the station and Helen searched the platform for Charles. When she spotted him standing on the platform, her heart beat a rapid tattoo. The girls waved and he came towards them, kissing each of them on the forehead before approaching Helen. When he put his arms around her all her worries and fears seemed to vanish. She looked into his eyes and they conveyed his soft, secret smile of love.

'Helen, darling. I've missed you so much. I'm delighted you've made it,' he whispered, holding her at arm's length and gazing lovingly.

He picked up the cases with ease and carried them to the waiting car. Turning to Mary he said, 'I'm so pleased you've come, Mary dear.'

The journey to Llanypen was swift and smooth. The sky was painted gold and layered in shades of soft grey, and the pale winter sun, now dipping low in the sky, gave the clouds their silver lining.

Willow House, on the outskirts of the village, was perched high on the road above and, as they started to climb the hill, Charles pointed it out in the distance, a large, stone-built Victorian house with a grey slate roof. The windows faced the valley overlooking the picture-book village nestled below. The vista was idyllic.

As they swung into the drive, the completely bare trees formed an archway as if in salute. Charles stopped the car and the huge front door opened. A middle-aged woman dressed in navy blue stepped out on to the drive followed by a man of a similar age.

'Meet Gladys, my housekeeper and Joseph, my gardener,' Charles announced placing his arm around the woman's shoulder. The two smiled warmly. He turned to Helen. 'Helen Riley and Mary Grant, my guests,' he announced, 'and of course, Jessie and Sylvia.' Both Helen and Mary stepped forward and shook their hands.

The girls were happy to investigate the house and the garden and, for the first time since they arrived, Charles had Helen to himself. He looked into her eyes. Would she approve of his plans? Would she feel he had been premature in his arrangements?

'I've put you in a room opposite the girls, Helen. Yours is adjoining mine on the other side. I do hope that's appropriate, darling. I couldn't possibly spend all night without you,' he whispered.

'I've missed you Charles, especially since your last visit was ruined by that evil man,' she said, her voice husky with emotion. Ripples of sheer pleasure danced along her nerve endings and her heartbeat began to accelerate.

Charles felt an urgent need to be close, and he

315

ached for a little excitement with her. But he reprimanded himself and took control of his senses.

'Where's Mary's room?' Helen asked.

'We've put her next to the girls. Gladys thought that might be best, just in case either of them woke up in the night,' he said, pausing for a few seconds. 'Does she know about us, our closeness?' He hesitated and looked a little embarrassed. 'I think Joseph and Gladys suspect.'

'Mary knows everything. She's a wonderful confidante. I wouldn't have it any other way.'

'At least that helps our cause,' he said as Jessie and Sylvia ran through into the sitting room.

It was Christmas Eve and, after dinner, there was a frenzy of activity when the girls played games with Helen and Charles. Mary had earlier taken herself off to the kitchen to help Gladys, despite everyone's insistence that she was a guest. But that was her way and nobody could budge her.

The girls were allowed to stay up until eight o'clock when Mary came back into the sitting room. 'Come along, girls. Time for bed,' she said. 'You don't want to be up when Santa Claus visits, or he won't leave you anything.'

After such an announcement, it was an easy task to get them upstairs and they were soon tucked up and asleep. By nine-thirty Mary excused herself.

'It's been a tiring day what with the early rise this morning and the journey. I'll see you tomorrow.'

Gladys declared that she and Joseph must be away to bed too, since they would need to be up very early the following morning. 'There's the tur-

316

key to prepare and the rest of the food to organise.'

Alone at last, Charles took Helen's hand and, breathing in the sweet, flowery fragrance of her, led her to the door. He turned off the light and before she knew it he was kissing her. The moment his mouth touched hers, he was lost, and he carried her up the stairs into his warm, dark bedroom, setting her on her feet again.

'Charles,' she whispered urgently.

'Yes my darling?' He framed her face with his hands, kissing her gently.

'I thought this moment would never come,' she confessed.

When he heard the words, he was in such a state of ecstasy that he kissed her again and again with such intensity and tenderness that she was breathless. He held her at arms' length. 'You know it's seemed like an eternity since I last saw you.'

He unbuttoned her dress and it fell to the floor and she slipped off the rest of her clothes. He caressed the glistening beauty of her and threw back the blankets, lifting her to the middle of his bed.

He tried to remove his own shirt and trousers but she clung to him desperately, refusing to let go. To his surprise her boldness delighted him as she pulled him down beside her, slipped off his clothes and tossed them to the floor. She gasped with pleasure as he stroked every line of her and explored every curve and hollow. He had intended to continue but she took over, kissing his chin, his neck and the length of his throat, and he remained coherent until she reached his waist. He fought gently for control and eventually won

317

as he felt her arch against him. Then his mind went blank as he went over the edge into complete ecstasy.

He gradually focused his mind and he knew as he watched her, dazed, sated and exhausted, that she was asleep. All the tension within her seemed to have ebbed away as she breathed easily and steadily again. The way she enveloped him, trapped him with her body told him she would be his forever. Anything less was unthinkable. He fell asleep.

When Helen opened her eyes to see the glow of the garden lamp stippled in the shadows of the room, she panicked. The children! She'd slept through most of the night and never even checked on them. She turned to look at Charles and, gently pulling her arm from underneath his neck, she slid quietly out of the bed and stepped on his shirt. She picked it up and slipped it over her nakedness and crossed over to the girls' room. They were fast asleep, Sylvia sucking her thumb. Helen peered at the clock on the bedside table and realised it was only four thirty.

Slipping back into bed with Charles, she kissed him on the shoulder, on the neck and then gently turned him over to face her. He responded to her touch as though conditioned by her. She needed him again before she settled back into her own bed and he opened his eyes, realising her intentions. The combination of his words, his husky voice and the closeness of his body all conspired to weaken her. She kissed him hard on the lips and the pleasure came from deep inside her, flowing over her.

It was seven o'clock next morning when the girls stood before the Christmas tree, marvelling at all the presents piled there. Helen watched from the top of the stairs.

'We must wait for Mummy and Uncle Charles,' Mary insisted as the girls danced about frantically, unable to resist touching the presents.

Helen came down the stairs and into the hall. 'How long have you little monkeys been out of bed?' she asked. 'I hope you didn't wake up Aunt Mary,' she joked.

'Mummy. When is Uncle Charles getting up? We need him now,' Jessie demanded. 'Aunt Mary says we can't open the presents until everyone is here.'

'That's right, treasure,' Helen confirmed, knowing Charles would soon be up. She needed him too.

'What a bevy of beauties!' he exclaimed and he caught Helen's gaze as she took in his fresh appearance. His eyes held a new intensity and told her he wanted her again, quite desperately too.

The girls spent most of the morning playing with their presents and needed no supervision, which meant Helen and Charles could spend a leisurely time together catching up on each other's lives.

After a light lunch, Helen wrapped the girls in their blue woollen coats and matching bonnets. The cream fur muffs, given to them by Charles as Christmas presents were just another novelty to add to their Christmas highlights. They set off down the hill to the village where there was com-

319

munal singing in the square. The shops were bedecked with tiny fairy lights, the first the girls had seen and probably the first the shops had provided since the war years. In the evening, Gladys excelled herself with a turkey meal cooked to perfection.

All too soon, the Christmas holiday at Llanypen was over. Veronica's shop would open again the day after Boxing Day but Helen was not due back at work until the twenty-eighth. They set off to the station and a cloak of sadness settled over them. Sylvia's tears trickled down her rosy cheeks and plummeted onto the station platform.

'Why do we have to go, Mummy?' Jessie wailed, her eyes pleading.

'All good things come to an end, treasure. We'll come again,' Helen said hopefully, her heart lurching against her ribs.

Charles lifted Sylvia on to his shoulders. 'What if I come up to see you in a couple of weeks' time? Would you like that?' he asked, trying to humour the girls into a more cheerful mood.

'Yes, yes, Uncle Charles,' Jessie cried.

The train arrived and the guard ushered them towards a compartment. Charles kissed the girls fondly and Mary lifted them on to the train. Helen stepped towards him and he brushed his lips against her damp eyelids and her trembling mouth.

'It's been wonderful, darling,' she told him fondly. 'I never wanted it to end.'

'I'll be with you very soon. It won't be long my love,' he promised, giving her a final squeeze before she stepped into the compartment.

320

Chapter 24

Towards the end of January Helen was surprised when Veronica broached the subject of premises at Potters Moor.

'I've been toying with the idea for some time. The shop is quite large and it's certainly the right sort of area for antiques. I'd like you to view the premises with me, Helen. I think you'll agree it's a favourable area.'

'There's no doubt about it. I know Potters Moor well. The shop you mention is not far from Mother's. It is the perfect area.'

'A business venture there appeals to me, but neither the shop at Guisborough nor the one my brother runs at Thornbridge is taking enough for me to make a confident investment.' She rubbed her hands together. 'I thought maybe we could set up a lucrative business together. How would a joint project interest you? With your knowledge of china and porcelain, and my background in pictures, I have a gut feeling we could make a success of it. What do you think?'

Helen stared blankly. Veronica's suggestion had come out of the blue.

'My prime concern is the cost, Veronica. I've nowhere near enough capital to partner you in a shop of that size and in such a class area. The cost of the overheads and stock needed are completely beyond my means financially. My share of the business with Vincent was only a third.'

'Don't worry, I'm happy for you to invest the rest of your capital as we progress. Let's talk money later.' Veronica insisted. 'My brother is not interested in a further investment which means you and I could split the business equally,' she added, pausing to take in Helen's reaction. 'That doesn't mean you need to raise all the capital now. We can sort that out amicably. Shall we go take a look?'

'I'd love to. But I don't know what I've done to deserve such luck.' She reflected on the positive trends in her life since the start of 1950.

'It's certainly not luck, Helen. I can't afford to let you go especially when you can bring in clients like the Baroness.' Veronica smiled. 'My motive is rather a selfish one.' She went into the back room and brought out their coats. 'Let's go. There's no time like the present.'

'The shop belonged to a jeweller,' the agent told them. 'Unfortunately he was caught 'receiving'. The business folded when he was sent to prison.'

'We'll need to renovate the place but nothing too drastic,' Veronica announced.

'I think a few changes to the shelving, a little plastering here and there, and a lick of paint to brighten it up would make a tremendous differ-ence,' Helen replied. 'The general fabric of the building seems to be sound.'

'That's right. I have a report here,' the agent told them offering a document to Veronica. She took it and glanced at its contents.

'The frontage is quite broad. We could use the back room for storage, cleaning and renovating,'

Helen added, excitement now taking hold.

A decision was made and the deal was done. And when Helen later collected the key she met up with a builder Laura had recommended. He agreed to start the work immediately.

To Helen's delight Laura offered to design the interior and choose the colour scheme at her own expense. The work was completed earlier than expected and, by the second week in February, Laura helped Helen move in the stock she'd bought at the salerooms, ready to start business.

'This is amazing,' Veronica acknowledged. 'You're so lucky to have a sister like Laura, someone who gives you her willing support. She must be very special to you.'

Helen nodded. 'We've always been close.' Laura linked her arm through Helen's. This was payback. She'd achieved what she'd set out to do and Helen had never suspected her liaison with Donald.

During her visits to the salerooms, Helen came across a Marot style Georgian teapot due to be auctioned in Manchester with many other lots from a stately home in Lancashire. She contacted the baroness.

'I'd be delighted to check it out Helen. I could pick you up from the shop and we could view it together at the saleroom.'

'The sale is Thursday; it starts at eleven in the morning. Could you manage to be here for say, nine, to give us time to view?'

The teapot was exactly what the baroness had been looking for and they agreed a bidding price with a handsome commission for Helen. And she

323

was elated when she managed to secure the item for less than the ceiling price, which reduced the amount of her commission. But she was taken aback when the baroness offered her a cheque for the agreed percentage plus the short-fall. At first, Helen refused the extra commission.

'You deserve it, my dear. Veronica Brightwell is jolly lucky to have someone as talented as you choosing the porcelain.'

Veronica was equally insistent. 'Let's say the normal percentage goes into the takings but the extra can be ploughed back into our joint business as part of your investment.'

For the first few days of opening business was quiet but as word went round that Helen was a partner at the shop, the Potters Moor residents were curious. Many of them called in to check things out. And Helen knew she would only need to get them inside the shop to secure their interest in the lovely pieces they had in stock. Dora and Gordon Bristow turned up, having been tipped off by Laura, as did Winifred and Bernard Wallace.

'It's becoming an even bigger success than I'd ever have anticipated,' Veronica said as she marvelled at the response. 'The people around here trust you Helen and that certainly is a bonus.'

Helen worked to exhaustion, each night returning home with the satisfaction that she was now earning enough to cover her own expenses, pay Mary's wages and plough a little into the business too.

Mother's Christmas present, now rather belated, was to pay for driving lessons. Having earlier replaced the amount she'd borrowed to pay for the rail tickets, Helen decided driving was more important than ever. It made sense to save time on travel and see more of the girls.

After several lessons, the instructor was impressed. 'You're the second lady I've taught, Mrs. Riley. It's such a change for me to have someone who'll listen to what I say.'

'But I've no alternative, Mr. Smithers,' she said laughingly. 'I hadn't the faintest idea how or where to begin before I started the lessons.'

'A couple of weeks now,' he said optimistically, 'and you should be ready.'

After her final driving lesson Helen went along to the cemetery with fresh flowers for Jim's grave. Ben Lawler from the factory was there, filling a water jug for the spray he'd brought for his mother's grave.

'You're looking better, Helen. You must have had a hard time making ends meet,' he said with genuine concern.

'It's been quite a struggle, Ben but, hopefully, the worst is over. We seem to have turned the corner now that 1950's here. I'm working in a shop in Potters Moor. Mary Grant's helping me with the girls, and I'm taking driving lessons in the hope I can pick up a little car to make life easier for me.'

'Now, that's worth knowing,' he said, perking up. 'My pal Dave Gibbins has a grand little runner for sale, a Morris Minor. You weren't wanting new were you? There's a devil of a long waiting list. It could take a year or more. If you're interested in Dave's car, I'll put in a word for you. I believe he's one or two interested though. Second-hand cars go like hot cakes, especially if they're in good nick.'

'It depends on the price, Ben,' she confessed.

'Don't worry, love. As I say, he's a pal of mine. If you're interested, I'm sure he'd work something out,' he stressed. 'What d'you think? Want me to mention it?'

'If you don't mind and of course if you think it would suit,' she said.

'I'll have a word with him and then I'll come over and see you.'

'I look forward to that, Ben,' she concluded as she walked off towards Jim's grave.

A few days later Ben arrived with his pal, Dave. 'What do you think then?' He enquired as Helen looked at the shiny, black Morris Minor.

'It's only done five thousand miles, Mrs. Riley,' Dave explained. 'I think the price is reasonable for a good runner like this.' He beamed at the car lovingly, his voice throbbing with pride. 'I don't really want to sell but it's 'cos I'm getting married.'

'Well, which would you prefer, to keep the car or to have a new bride?' Helen joked, her bright eyes sparkling with laughter.

'Seeing you've put it that way, it's Brenda I want more than anything, even before this little beauty,' he said, patting the bonnet of the car affectionately.

'Joking apart. You're right. It looks in very good condition. You've obviously taken good care of it, and it certainly runs well,' she had to agree. 'I would like it,' she hesitated, 'but I wonder if I could possibly pay you in two instalments, one this month and one next. I could manage that,' she offered, her embarrassment causing a deep pink flush to spread from her chin to her cheeks.

'That's fine, Mrs. Riley. Don't worry. Ben's explained. I'm not getting married till end of March at any rate,' Dave said, 'so any time before then will do.'

They shook hands and she watched the two men disappear. The deal was done and by the end of the week Helen was mobile. The girls were filled with pride that Mummy could drive now, and Jessie broadcast the news to all the children in her class at school. Mother was happy too. Now that Helen was working permanently at Potters Moor, she could call in any time.

'But, Jack,' Maureen sobbed. 'I haven't been with anyone else, just you. Me ma is going to kill me when she finds out. And you'll be in for it as well if you don't do right by me,' she ventured, her blue eyes velvety with tears, her mouth tight with strain.

'Don't bloody threaten me Maureen,' he retorted acidly. 'Can you prove it?'

'You know it's yours, Jack,' she wailed. 'I'll be sent away to one of them convents if you don't admit it. Me ma won't have it. How do you expect us to manage? You know me Dad's left us,' she blubbered.

But the words washed over Jack. 'How do you expect me to look after you with no job? I've all on scrounging money to help me ma, never mind you as well,' he complained bitterly.

'You should have thought about that when you put this in me belly,' she said pointedly.

'Could be Bradshaw's for all I know,' he insinuated.

'It could not, Jack. Reckon it up! I'd finished with him a month before this happened. He was in prison,' she informed him positively.

Jack needed time to think. For starters he had a job to find, and there was nothing locally or in Oldham. Fair enough, he'd been with Maureen once or twice; she was easy. But what was to say the kid wasn't someone else's? She'd no proof it was his. Telling him she was up the spout didn't force him into any responsibility. That was his excuse and he was sticking to it. But at the back of his mind he knew bairn probably was his.

He might have to try Huddersfield for a job. It was a bit nearer than Oldham but too far to travel every day. It was his only chance. If anything turned up he'd have to move over there. He couldn't expect his ma to slave away, day after day at Ma Dorrington's house. Anyway, he'd gone right off that lot. What with the break-in and him being blamed, and then that business with Helen fobbing him off. He'd had enough.

'Don't you be telling your ma. I can't do with any more problems. Keep it to yourself for now. You're flapping over nowt, Maureen. I'm sure we can sort it out somehow,' he raged through clenched teeth, hoping to string Maureen along in his own cunning way, at least until he'd been to Huddersfield and checked the place out. If anything turned up there, he'd move sharpish, do a bunk. She'd have a job getting at him then.

'You've no idea what a worry it's been Dolly, especially after shindig at mill, our Jack being picked on,' Agnes told Mrs. Platts as they queued in the Co-op to collect their 'divi'. 'He's been over to Oldham but there was nothing doing there. But he's got fixed up in Huddersfield. Good job by all accounts. Seems they needed an overlooker and he stepped in just at right time. I'm fair proud of him.'

'I am pleased for you, Aggie love. Will he be moving then?' she asked.

Agnes hated the name 'Aggie'. It was common and not her style at all. She supposed 'Dolly' was common as well. 'Dorothy' was much better. But it wouldn't do to be ticking folk off over a name.

She'd enough on covering up Jack's dismissal from the mill.

'That's trouble, Dolly. He can't find anywhere to live, not for one. They say if he was married, he'd qualify to rent a corporation house.' She shook her head. 'He'll just have to keep on looking.' She moved a few steps forward, fingering her Co-op share book. 'How's your Maureen anyway. Still working in office?'

'She's still there. She's all right I suppose, but she's been a bit peaky lately, bit moody an all,' Dolly confessed. 'I don't know what's up with her. It's her birthday next week, nineteen, you know. Pity her dad didn't stay around to see her. Even though I say it myself, she's turned out a bonny lass. She'd be a good catch for any fella.'

'Nineteen?' Agnes repeated. 'She was a bit of a kid last time I saw her playing out with a skipping

329

rope. They're only bairns for two minutes and then they're grown up.' She thought about it. Jack could do worse. Nice lass, Maureen and she'd always had her eye on Jack.

The woman in front of her counted out the pound notes and coins in her hand, smiling as she did so. The queue moved more quickly and Agnes presented her share book.

'Do you want paying out, love or do you want to bank it?' asked the clerk.

'I'll have to take it,' she whispered. 'I'm a bit hard up,' she added furtively, taking the money from him and tucking it into her purse. She waited for Dolly and they walked back together.

'Have you heard about your neighbour, Mavis?' Dolly said through tight lips.

'No, I haven't.'

'In family way again,' she related, relishing the words as she spoke them.

Agnes shook her head. 'Left in lurch again. Our Jack reckons she's slovenly. He's got his standards; reckons men should take responsibility.'

'I know what you mean,' Dolly returned. 'He's always been fair has your Jack.'

They came to a deflection in the road where Dolly turned off to Cob Row. 'Hope your Jack finds somewhere to live,' Dolly called as she left Agnes struggling through the passage with the shopping.

'Thanks,' she said, puffing and panting, making it to the door as Jack opened it.

'Give us them bags, Ma and get yourself inside,' he said, noticing the puce bloom on her face, but trying not to sound too perturbed. 'You should let me know when you need a bit of carrying doing. These are too heavy for you,' he observed. 'Who were you talking to anyway?' he asked, purely out of interest.

Agnes dragged off her shoes and lowered her heavy frame into the fireside chair. 'Dolly Platts, you know, Maureen's ma.'

Jack's blood began to surge through his body. That was all he needed, for his ma to be gossiping to Ma Platts. She was a right domineering old witch and just like the rest of them. Can't keep her mouth shut.

There was a sharp knock at the door and Jack could hear loud mutterings from outside. That was ominous. Suddenly a bout of nausea came over him.

'Who can that be at this time of night?' his ma said. She called out, 'Who is it?'

'It's me, Aggie, Dolly Platts with our Maureen,' she said, a peevish ring to her voice.

His ma pulled back the bolts and turned the key. Jack's heart sank to his boots. Bloody hell, this could be curtains for him.

'It's late to be calling Dolly. I hope nothing's wrong,' Agnes said gently.

Brushing her aside, Dolly stepped heavily over the threshold, followed by Maureen.

'Nothing's wrong? Wait till I tell you what we've come about,' she insisted tartly, her face falling into sullen lines.

Jack braced himself and glanced at Maureen's swollen, red-rimmed eyes, her face twisted with hurt. He was in for the high jump. There was no

331

stopping Ma Platts, who had a grim look on her face as though the world were coming to an end. Then there was his ma. Bloody hell he'd cop it when all this was over. He'd have to take a mouthful from her, notwithstanding Ma Platts. He felt like shrivelling up in a corner and escaping, anywhere to get out of the way of these cronies. If Maureen had given him time, he'd have tried to help her. He pondered. He was kidding himself of course. He sighed. Why spring it on him like this?

'What's up, Dolly? We haven't done anything wrong,' his ma said blandly, obviously hurt by the way Dolly had bombarded her way into the house and started bad-mouthing.

'Done wrong?' Her voice was like the lash of a whip as she clutched Maureen's hand and dragged her forward. 'Your lad has,' she accused, her face now contorted with rage as she turned her icy gaze on Jack. 'I'll tell you, Aggie, he's only put her in family way,' she said, stressing the word 'family' and patting Maureen's belly.

'That can't be right,' his ma replied naively. 'What have you to say, Jack?' she asked, and he sensed she wasn't expecting confirmation of the issue.

'It's all a load of boloney, Ma,' he remonstrated hotly, his face a mask of anger. 'I don't know owt about it.'

'You lying devil,' Dolly shouted, flashing hateful glances at him. 'He's a grown man and my lass is only eighteen. He's had it off with her, and in my house! Our Maureen says it was when I went to see Florrie just before Christmas,' she said with finality, her temper now seeming to reach breaking point.

Jack swallowed, not quite sure what his next move would be. Maureen continued to look him straight in the eye, and he didn't like it. It made him feel worse.

'Why don't you have a go at George Bradshaw? It's all right blaming me when he's banged up,' he moaned, fighting to control his temper. If he wanted to take on Maureen, he'd do it in his own time, not when her ma demanded.

'It's nothing to do with George Bradshaw. Our Maureen's not been with him, have you?' She poked a finger into Maureen's chest.

'No, Ma,' Maureen stuttered in confusion, a shifty expression fluttering across her face as she looked sheepishly at Jack, who turned a cold glance to her.

'It was George who told me how you liked a bit of that,' he confessed, having heard that from the horse's mouth. 'Why do you think I took her on?' he said, realising immediately he'd dropped himself in it.

'Don't be blackening our Maureen, or else,' she threatened, avoiding his angry stare.

'Or else what, Mrs. Platts?' he asked directly, feeling a tightening in his throat, his face dark with rage now that he'd made such a stupid mistake.

'Or else I'll get our Derek to sort you out if you don't do right by her.' She banged her tightly clenched fist on the table.

'Now then, Dolly,' his ma chipped in, her calmness in complete contrast to Dolly's fury. 'Don't be getting yourself worked up. Let's try sort it out fair like. Come on, Jack. Let's have truth,' she said giving him the sort of look she'd given him when he was a boy and in trouble for breaking someone's window.

'I might have messed about a bit Ma, but so has George. Why me and not him?' he sneered but he had pushed his luck as far as he could.

'Now Jack,' his ma said firmly. 'Is it you or isn't it? That's what we want to know, one way or other?' she asked, biting off each word sharply as she looked up at him, pointing her finger and making such a demand on him that he knew he would have to answer fairly and squarely.

'All right, Ma. It could be me. But it doesn't mean to say kid's mine, does it?' he said, his admission grudging, a scowl furrowing his face and a knot of guilt forming in his chest. Listening to Maureen's agonising sobs made the palms of his hands feel slippery as he held on to the wooden chair arms.

His ma sucked in a long breath, a look of determination settling round her mouth. 'You want a kick up the arse, you great stupid bugger. I thought you'd have had more sense. Couldn't you have taken caution,' she said euphemistically. 'That's it as far as I'm concerned. You've made your bed, now you can lie in it,' she preached, her tone mutinous. 'If that bairn's my grandchild, you can do right thing and wed Maureen,' she added, her voice low with resignation. 'And if you don't, you'll have me to answer to,' she said with finality, her words carrying their own veiled warning. And Jack knew what lay behind those words.

Chapter 25

Helen made a discerning estimate of her clients' preferences, improving the quality of the items and increasing the stock. The small Italian figurines were popular, soon becoming collectors' items, as were the pictures, especially the new range Veronica had discovered.

Her income increased and she decided one of her future priorities would be a house in Potters Moor. It would give the girls a fresh start and, with an extra room for Charles, he would not need to stay at The Queens. But she had her reputation to guard, and, although it was now some time since she'd lost Jim, the guilt still plagued her.

But her first priority was to contribute her full half share of capital in the business, so as to equate with Veronica's investment. Once that was settled she could consider buying a house, although the big question was obtaining a mortgage. As a widow with two young children, she'd obviously face problems.

Easter passed. It was the middle of April and Pamela, a new and promising assistant, agreed to cover at the shop on Saturday giving Helen free time. The weather was unusually mild and a shaft of spring sunlight came through the gap of the open door. Helen was catching up with her bookkeeping and as she looked up she could see glimpses of the girls outside flashing past the doorway as they chased each other around the garden.

Tentatively she looked at the clock on the mantelpiece. It was twenty past twelve. A warm surge raced through her. Charles would be arriving shortly. It was three weeks since they'd visited Llanypen for a second time, and the withdrawal symptoms had been with her since the minute she'd left him.

Mary interrupted her thoughts. 'Would you like me to stay for the rest of the weekend? I could take the girls to Broughton Park. They'll be in their element in the playground and exert lots of energy.'

'Thank you, Mary. That would be lovely and the girls will think it a real treat.'

When she heard the Jaguar draw up outside the house, Helen went through into the front room and opened the front door for Charles. She felt a glow of pleasure when he took her in his arms. He brushed a strand of hair from her forehead and kissed her gently. The girls ran towards him excitedly, and he scooped them up, one at a time.

'Lunch first, and then to the park, lucky girls,' Helen said, and Charles watched as her smile lit her lovely face. Her rich brown eyes drew him into their depths, eyes that dispelled any doubts.

When Mary and the children left for the park, he gathered her close, smoothing his mouth on hers, caressing her enticing lips. He released her and held her at arm's length. 'Any regrets,' he asked, 'about us?'

She kept her eyes on his for a long moment, as though searching for a message. Wrinkling her nose and with a mischievous smile lurking behind

336

those luminous eyes, she asked, 'What about you?' her voice a throaty shimmer of sound.

'None at all, my darling,' he replied, kissing her again, soundly and thoroughly.

She shook her head and whispered, 'Me, neither,' as she slipped on her coat ready for a stroll over the hills outside Chatsbridge.

On the way out Charles looked carefully over the Morris Minor, scanning every inch of it before giving Helen a nod of approval. 'You have a sound little motor there, darling. This model has a good record for reliability,' he remarked positively. 'Is it running well?'

'It's simply wonderful. No trouble at all,' she replied as he ushered her into the Jaguar and closed the passenger door behind her.

'How would you feel about coming down in the car next weekend? If you set off early Saturday morning, you could be with me by mid-afternoon,' he suggested. 'Of course you'll need to feel confident enough to drive such a distance, but I could plan the route out for you if you'd like to give it a try.'

'Sorry, darling but I'll be in the shop. Pam covered for me this week. Maybe the following week. Whether or not I could cope with such a long journey is another matter, but I'll give it some thought,' she promised.

Chatsbridge was buzzing with life. The women had ventured out in twin-sets and light skirts, some in summer swaggers, the men in sports jackets and flannels. The earlier clouds had dissolved, the sunlight now emitting its brightness on the pink cherry blossoms festooning the trees lining the park. Helen surveyed the acres of velvet lawns and the flowers in a blaze of delicate colours. The spring buds were thick and fat, and the hedgerows were bursting out in their finery. The birds sang joyfully, swooping and chasing each other in their courtship rituals.

Charles took her hand and they set out towards the hills. Beneath them the spongy grass was bright and mossy on the lush, verdant hills, patched here and there with swathes of waning daffodils and narcissi, their trumpets still ablaze in yellows, golds and tints of orange. Higher up, bluebells carpeted the grassy slopes, their fresh and delicate scent drenching the air.

Content to walk in companionable silence, occasionally stopping on the deserted hills to embrace, they reached the peak of the lowest hill. There before them was an artist's dream, a huddle of houses standing forlornly in the hollow down below with a stretch of water and a small spinney some distance away.

'This is rather remote,' Charles said, his words dropping into the silence. 'But it would be an absolute luxury for anyone wishing to get away from the bustle of the city.'

'The peace of it,' she murmured, a hint of envy in her tone. 'My next priority is a house of my own, that's when I've saved up enough money. I'd like something nearer the shop where everything's greener and healthier for the girls. And somewhere for you to stay, instead of booking in at The Queens each time you're here.'

'Don't rush into anything, darling. You need to give it a great deal of thought before you make such a major decision,' he offered, a slightly puzzled expression on his face. A knot of tension started to build up inside him, but he couldn't understand why.

Had she hit on a sore point? He knew the pull between them was powerful, but he realised any commitment he made involving their future together could jeopardise his self-contained life-style. Was he ready for that? And could he afford to let down his defences completely after his experience with Rita? Despite the time lapse and his outward confidence, inside there was still a fragile shell around his heart which could easily be shattered.

That was something with which he needed to come to terms.

'You're perfectly right there, darling,' she replied, looking up at him coolly. 'But it's going to be some considerable time before I reach that stage.'

A breeze sprung up, ruffling the waters of the lake far below and already it was cooler. 'Maybe we should head back to the car now,' he suggested, and for some reason he felt a trickle of disappointment inside. 'It's not as warm as earlier. There's a chill in the wind and we need to be ready in time for the dinner dance at the Queens.'

Helen nodded her agreement, but the air of frivolity seemed to be lost as, without another word, they quickened their pace and left the hills behind.

Despite her initial doubts, Sarah was delighted at the comments in praise of her two girls, now both successful businesswomen. The popularity of the Potters Moor shop continued as news spread and business boomed. Within two months of opening, Veronica had returned to the Guisborough shop and Helen was in sole charge. She relished the challenge and by the beginning of July she had employed two assistants. It soon became prestigious to shop at Potters Moor Antiques as a mark of one's standing in the community.

Laura's business continued to develop too especially now that she and John had a renewed understanding. The break-up between them had been nothing but a hiccup, so Sarah always preached. The separation had strengthened the bonds between them. And she congratulated herself on their reunion, believing she was partly responsible. Hopefully she could soon gloat about Charles too but, for now, she'd promised to keep it to herself. But wasn't it about time she met him? She'd hinted at an introduction on several occasions but so far nothing had been forthcoming. It would be reassuring if Helen settled down with someone of their standing.

To her joy, Helen called later that day and came up with the invitation. 'I'll bring Charles along at the weekend, just an informal visit of course. I don't want to give him the wrong impression and spoil things.'

'How do you mean, spoil things?' Sarah asked, wanting to get this whole business cut and dried.

'You know what I mean, Mother. If you start meddling,' she said, pointing a finger, 'we'll walk out. I don't want any pressure on either of us. Is that clear?' There was a stern edge to her voice.

340

'Stop worrying, darling. I'll not say anything out of place. Promise,' she vowed, knowing the definition 'out of place' could be flexible. 'You will have afternoon tea with me, won't you?' she asked, already putting on the pressure in her own persuasive way.

'Take it as it comes, Mother,' Helen told her. 'I can't stick rigidly to any firm arrangements. There are too many other people to consider.'

'I know what you mean, darling, but it will be lovely to meet Charles.'

When Helen left, Agnes arrived earlier than usual. 'I hope you don't mind, Mrs. Dorrington but I've a bit of important shopping to do and I wondered if you'd mind if I left a bit earlier today?' she asked apprehensively.

'That's fine Agnes,' Sarah replied, still dwelling on the fortunes of her two girls and not particularly bothered whether Mrs. Bean came or went.

'Well it's like this. Jack's marrying Maureen Platts Saturday. I know it's a bit of a rush but he's moving to Huddersfield. He's managed to get a corporation house there,' she babbled on. 'I've seen a nice navy costume in Wigglesworth's, and I'd like to pop in and try it on,' she added, but Sarah was still not taking it in.

'I see,' she replied vaguely. 'Lovely. How about a cup of tea?' Perhaps she could tell Agnes about Helen's surgeon. William had always said how discreet Agnes was.

The breeze was soft and warm on his skin, and with the long, confident stride of an athlete, he crossed over to the Jaguar. It was Friday evening

341

and, except for his visit to Merthlyn, it was the end of his working week until the following Tuesday. The sun, now low in the sky and almost ready to dip behind the distant hills, gleamed horizontally. He looked up. The sky, filled with a pale yellow glow was tinged with pinks and reds. It was going to be fine tomorrow for his drive to Kidsworth.

The thought of Helen awoke in him a hunger that consumed him day and night and triggered a multitude of intimate and secret thoughts. But he steered his mind back to the purpose of his visit to Merthlyn, a small, private hospital where he needed to check out two of his patients. He should have visited the previous day, but a serious road accident had caused his schedule of complex surgery to be far more extensive than usual.

He parked his car in the private car park and surveyed the gardens to the front of Merthlyn. French marigolds and pansies searched skyward, their bright faces stretching out to the sun. Lobelia, in patches of vivid blue and white, stood sentinel over the colourful beds. And roses, separately bedded, proudly displayed their superiority.

A man in his mid-fifties strode briskly from the front entrance, prodding the ground before him with a rolled up umbrella.

'Good evening, Sir Michael,' Charles said as he swung his long legs from the Jaguar.

'Charles, my good man. How are you?' Sir Michael replied jovially. 'Still getting plenty of practice, I gather.'

'It's never ending.' He smiled but he had a weary edge to his voice.

'You should take a break over the weekend, laddie,' he suggested, his Scottish brogue prominent as he opened the door to his Rolls Royce.

The rose-scented air from the garden outside drifted in through the open windows of the long corridor, but the heavy smell of Dettol and carbolic soap, the hospital's stamp of hygiene, was a strong contender as he neared the ward. Sister was waiting when he arrived, and she accompanied him into the ward.

'Mrs. Gascoigne. How are you, my dear?' he asked, gently taking the hand of the elderly lady whose hip and leg were solid with plaster of Paris.

'Much better,' she replied, her voice threadlike.

He made a decision as he lifted her X-rays to the light and examined them. 'The hip has healed after the pin and plate I inserted. The plaster cast can come off tomorrow,' he reassured her.

'What a relief,' she said. 'It won't hurt removing the plaster, will it?'

'Don't worry, dear. I'll get the experts on the case,' he said, smiling.

'Now, Sister, Mr. Goodman's fingers. Everything satisfactory there?'

'Excellent,' she said, removing the dressing and gently lifting the patient's hand. Charles looked carefully, checking that the skin had healed satisfactorily.

'These look fine, Mr. Goodman,' he said, turning the hand over. 'You've been lucky this time. Let's hope it doesn't happen again,' he said lightly. 'Take these out, Sister and discharge the patient.

343

He'll need a four week appointment.'

Charles strolled off towards sister's office. 'What's the list for Thursday?' he asked, turning the pages of the diary.

'Just a knee; a meniscectomy. The footballer,' she prompted.

'Thank you Sister, I'll see you Thursday,' he concluded, leaving the ward and setting out for home.

He'd given the Jenkinsons the weekend off to visit their daughter in Cardiff and, as he entered the lofty hall, the house echoed with emptiness. He closed the heavy oak door behind him, placing his briefcase next to the coat stand and carelessly slinging his jacket over the banister, completely forgetting that Gladys would not be around to organise him. He picked up the *Llanypen Echo* from the doormat, glancing idly at the headlines. As he reached for the handle of the sitting room door the doorbell rang. Uttering a sigh of exasperation, he wheeled around and swung open the door impatiently.

He did a double take. Rita was standing there, her dark hair limp and her face pallid. Her eyes were swollen and red-rimmed. His stomach turned. It was years since he'd set eyes on her and she meant nothing to him now. Her visit spelled trouble.

'Charles, I'm really sorry to trouble you,' she said, 'but I've no-one else to turn to.'

'How did you find me?' he asked, his face hardening uncharacteristically.

'I rang the hospital and said I was your sister from Canada, ringing from the airport,' she admitted. 'I had to do something, Charles. I was desperate.'

'You'd better come in,' he said resentfully. Whatever she was up to, she couldn't fool him. She'd cried wolf once too often. He went through into the sitting room, shrugging his shoulders dismissively. Rita followed him. He placed the newspaper on the heavy oak writing desk and sat in one of the leather arm chairs. She looked around cursorily and sat down opposite.

'What's it all about?' he asked brusquely, turning on a cool stare.

An expression of vacant bewilderment covered her face. 'I don't know how to start,' she whispered, her voice shaking with emotion.

'Well you'd better start somewhere, Rita. I've no time for beating about the bush,' he said, irritation spreading across his face.

'It's Hugh,' she said, staring vacantly ahead. 'He's become violent.' She shuddered, tears welling up in her eyes as she pulled back the top of her dress to reveal a bruised area on her neck. 'I don't know what's come over him,' she said, looking down at her feet.

'I don't suppose you've been two-timing again,' he hissed through gritted teeth.

'You've got it all wrong, Charles. Don't trot out the old maxim. That was in the past. It doesn't happen anymore,' she whimpered. 'I'm at the end of my tether with him. I wondered if you'd let me stay here for a while.'

'Stay here? You must be off your head!' An even fiercer anger broke out inside him. How dare she? The past was the past. It was over. 'The

345

answer is no,' he thundered. 'Sorry about your injury. It's only superficial. I have my own life to lead and I won't be available. Why not consult one of your boyfriends? You must have several in the medical profession,' his voice rang out sarcastically as he stood up and ushered her to the door. He wanted her out of his life for good.

John called at nine to collect Sylvia and Jessie, leaving Helen valuable time to spend with Charles. Since Laura's business had developed, they'd bought a holiday bungalow at Lytham St Anne's, a clever investment and a means of saving on income tax. They were to spend the weekend away there with the four children.

It was already half past one and Charles was usually here by now. Helen had arranged the afternoon visit to Mother's and Charles had asked to visit the shop afterwards. As the minutes ticked by, Helen became concerned and she felt a persistent gnawing sensation in her stomach. A multitude of thoughts bombarded her mind. Had he been involved in an accident? Had he been called back to the hospital urgently? Maybe the car had broken down. These things happen when you least expect them. But surely he would have been able to get someone on the job pretty quickly.

She must stop this foolishness. It was getting her nowhere. She consulted her watch for the umpteenth time. It was a quarter past two and still there was no sign of him. The frustrating part was that in a few days' time arrangements had been made for a telephone to be installed. But, until then, Charles had no way of contacting her at home.

She switched on the Phillips wireless set and it crackled into life and she tuned it into the station. Geraldo and his band were playing a familiar tune. Normally she would have been tapping her foot, but she couldn't concentrate. She picked up her knitting bag and gazed vacantly at the partly completed sleeve of a cardigan she was making. But her mind was full of other things and she stuck the needles back in the ball of wool. The best idea would be to telephone his house in Llanypen. In his recent letter, Charles had told her the Jenkinsons would be away for the weekend. He planned to set off at around nine o'clock on Saturday morning. She stuck a note to the back door in case he turned up whilst she was out.

There was already someone in the telephone booth when she arrived and she waited anxiously, hoping the man would move out soon. Eventually, he pushed the heavy door open and stepped out. 'Sorry I've kept you waiting, love,' he said sadly. 'Death in the family.'

'Sorry to hear it,' she said, her heartbeat increasing rapidly as she lifted the receiver to dial the number. As she'd anticipated the telephone rang and rang but there was no reply. That meant he had to be on his way. But where was he now? She became more and more disturbed. Then it all came back to her, the worry and the ordeal of losing Jim. Not again, surely.

Chapter 26

A light, hazy mist hung over the garden as Charles looked out early Saturday morning, but there was a break in the woolly clouds where the sun was pushing its way through. He turned to go downstairs, a nasty stirring in his stomach reminding him of the previous evening when he'd sent Rita packing. His night's sleep had been fitful. Perhaps he had been overly-hasty insisting she leave. But she wasn't worth the anxiety she was causing him. She was gone and he'd washed his hands of her. The frown on his face eased and his spirits lifted as his thoughts turned to Helen. He'd packed a small weekend case the previous evening ready to leave after breakfast.

A stab of doubt speared his heart at the prospect of meeting Helen's mother. He hadn't rid himself of the disappointment he'd felt when Helen mentioned buying a house. But he hadn't made any commitment either and yet in his heart he knew exactly what he wanted. He needed Helen as much as the air he breathed.

His thoughts were broken by the sound of heavy knocking on the door. Surely it couldn't be Rita again? He snatched at the handle and opened up. Two police officers were standing on the doorsteps. 'Mr. Ravel?' one of them asked.

'Yes,' he replied, feeling unusually apprehensive, his voice sticking in his throat.

'May we come in, sir? This is confidential,' the officer continued.

'By all means.' Charles opened the door wider to allow them access.

The second officer produced a crumpled piece of paper from his uniform pocket and held it out to Charles. 'Do you recognise this handwriting, sir?'

Charles scrutinized it carefully. His address was written on the paper, nothing else.

'It looks like Rita's,' he maintained, 'my ex-wife. She was here last night.'

'What was the purpose of her visit Mr. Ravel if, as you say, she is your ex-wife?'

'But why are you asking me that?'

'We have bad news I'm afraid, sir. She has been found dead. She's been murdered.'

'I don't believe it. She was with me only last night.' Charles shook his head and his stomach churned. He shouldn't have sent her away.

He explained the reason for her visit and exactly what had happened.

'She was found dead by a milkman on his rounds early this morning, two hundred yards from your house. It seems you were the last person to see her. In the circumstances, we'll need you to come to the station for questioning, sir.'

His heart sank. His intuition had told him there was something wrong. He should have known it was foolish to send Rita away. But that's how the mood had taken him.

'I just can't believe it,' he muttered, closing his eyes and lifting his hands to his face. 'She was perfectly all right when she left me last night.'

'Was she? But it's strange it happened so soon after she left you. We must start our enquiries immediately, sir. Are you ready?' the officer asked, his voice lacking either comfort or understanding.

'I've told you everything I know. I can't spend any more time this morning. I've made arrangements to travel to Yorkshire,' he explained.

'Sorry about that, sir, but in view of the fact you were the last person to see her, and after all you are her ex-husband with an estranged relationship, I'm afraid we've no alternative.'

'But she married again after we divorced and I've told you the name of the man she was living with.'

'That's nothing to go on, sir, a Christian name.'

Charles shrugged, slipped his Crombie over his shoulders and took the key from the lock. He followed them out. He desperately needed to contact Helen and let her know he would be late. Surely the questioning wouldn't take long.

Helen spent the weekend locked inside the house, not disclosing to a soul that Charles hadn't turned up. The whole of her body felt numb. Her only solution was to wait until Monday and ring from the shop. Of course she knew she'd be answerable to Mother but a feeble excuse would suffice.

When the children returned on Sunday evening she tried to keep up her spirits, not give way to her genuine emotions. Laura came with the girls, but she was wrapped up in her own success, and she barely touched on Helen's weekend, apart from a few pleasantries. It was a relief when she left.

Mary was the perceptive one, but luckily Monday was wash day and if Helen could concentrate on discussing what was needed, like a new packet of Sylvan Flakes for the woollies, and a drop of bleach for Jessie's school blouse to get rid of the ink stains, perhaps she could avoid any direct questioning. That should keep Mary off the subject of Charles and their weekend together.

The inspection by Mary passed muster and Helen was grateful to be alone with her thoughts. She drove towards Potters Moor, hoping to arrive before any of the staff. But part way there, a Clydesdale horse pulling a cartload of furniture stood in her way as the harassed driver, red-necked and red-faced, tried to retrieve the items that had toppled on to the road. By the time he'd started to collect them, there were four vehicles queuing up behind him.

More than ever anxious to get to the shop and take her mind off the disastrous weekend, Helen sat there impatiently and, turning to look at the shops on the little parade she noticed a van pull up at the side of the road. The driver got out, carried two huge bundles of newspapers into the shop and returned to place the daily news placard outside. It read: HOSPITAL CONSULTANT ARRESTED ON MURDER CHARGE. Helen's heart turned over in her chest, but she reprimanded herself for having foolish thoughts.

By the time she arrived at the shop it was half past eight. She picked up the mail from the

351

doormat and hung up her coat. Her first priority was to try the Llanypen number but the telephone rang incessantly. It seemed neither Charles nor the Jenkinsons were at home. Disappointment mingled with dejection shot through her. She'd allowed herself to hope, to believe he'd be there, but now she felt that hope slipping away. There was nothing more to be done other than throw herself wholeheartedly into the job.

Changes needed to be made in the window. There were yawning gaps where she'd sold some of the pieces during the previous week.

The telephone rang, but Helen was poised awkwardly in the window, unable to reach it until she'd carefully positioned the delicate Victorian vase next to the two green lustres. As she grasped the receiver, it rang off. Disappointed, she replaced it and went back to the task of setting out the window. But it started to ring again as she stepped back. Whoever was at the other end was persistent.

'Potters Moor Antiques,' she replied, business-like in her manner. 'Can I help you?'

'Helen?' a woman's voice echoed in her ear.

'Yes,' she replied, her heart beginning to pulsate rapidly. 'Who's speaking?'

'It's Miriam and it's bad news, I'm afraid.' There was an ominous pause as Helen heard her take in breath. 'Brace yourself, darling. I know this will sound preposterous, but Charles has been taken into custody. His ex-wife was murdered on Friday night. I know it wasn't Charles,' she stressed. 'But, sorry I don't have any more details.'

Miriam's words fell into a vacuum. Helen was

stunned and silence surrounded her. She felt the blood in her veins turn to ice.

'Are you there, Helen?' Miriam asked hesitantly.

'I can't believe it,' Helen replied, panic-stricken now. 'I've got to see him,' she garbled, not meaning to snap, but the news had knocked her off balance.

'The police took him in for questioning on Saturday morning. He was about to set off for Yorkshire. He's been beside himself not being able to contact you.' She paused. 'But is it wise to travel all this way on your own, Helen?'

'I must. Don't you understand?'

'Then take your time, and get here safely.' Miriam's tone was gentle and supportive.

'I'll ring you back before I leave, Miriam,' she stuttered, replacing the receiver and clamping her hand over her mouth in horror. Her heart pumped furiously in her chest, her mouth was dry, and she had the urge to scream in frustration that she was not there with him right now. As if riveted to the spot she seemed unable to move but then she grabbed hold of the telephone and dialled frantically.

'Veronica, it's me, Helen,' she said through intermittent sobs. 'I've had some dreadful news. I must go to Charles. Sorry I can't discuss it over the phone but it's serious.'

Veronica asked no questions and her immediate response was that Helen should leave as soon as Gloria and Pam arrived at the shop.

She left and was completely oblivious to the traffic on the journey back home.

'I can't believe it Mary,' she whispered, tears

353

stealing gently down her cheeks as she thought of the heavy cloud hanging over her future together with Charles.

'Calm down, love. You're not in a fit state to drive anywhere just yet.'

'Sorry Mary I can't seem to think straight,' she confessed absently. 'Thanks for being so considerate. But I do need to get off straight away.'

'I'll pack some things,' Mary offered soothingly.

'I don't know what I'd do without you,' Helen said, throwing her arms around Mary.

'That's what friends are for,' she said comfortingly. 'Now stop your worrying. It can't possibly be the doctor. He's too kind and caring.' Helen wished she could adopt such optimism.

It was eleven o'clock by the time Helen was ready to leave for the south and she followed the route Charles had given her the previous time she drove down there. The roads were reasonably clear of traffic and her progress was good. Rather than calling on Miriam, she'd decided to go directly to the police station where Charles was being held. Her main priority was to see him. She could always telephone Miriam afterwards.

Her body was taut with anticipation and the hairs on the back of her neck prickled as she felt an icy coldness rush through her veins. The officer took her into a private room, asked her to be seated and leaving momentarily returned with Charles.

The huge knot of tension inside her disappeared, but her eyes veered immediately to the handcuffs on his wrists, then his two-day growth of beard. He sat down, placing his hands on the table. Her first reaction was to place a swift, forbidden kiss on his cheek before she cupped his hands in her own.

'I'm here for you, darling. Tell me what's happened,' she begged.

In the background, the constable shuffled his feet.

'It's so reassuring to see you, my love,' he said, his face assuming an expression of gravity, 'and you've got to believe I'm innocent.'

'Absolutely, Charles without a shadow of doubt.'

'Rita called on Friday evening,' he started and recounted the full story of her visit. 'It's incredible! The police thought I'd caused the bruising and, after a finger-tip search, they found the silk stocking matching the one Rita was still wearing in my dustbin. They believe it was used to strangle her. They'd picked up a crumpled piece of paper with my address on it in her handwriting. Unfortunately it had my fingerprints all over it too. But I had handled it when she showed it to me. And would I be foolish enough to place vital evidence in my dustbin? But the police reckon it was concrete evidence.' He shook his head and sighed. 'I must have been set up, Helen.'

There were more questions she wanted to ask but enough had been said particularly when she realised the constable was listening in. 'What happens now?' she asked, squeezing his hands.

'I'm due in the magistrate's court tomorrow.' He looked directly into her eyes. 'I hope the police find this Hugh fellow. The trouble is I've no idea of his second name. He could be anyone, anywhere.'

'Stay calm, my darling. I know it's difficult but they've no proof, other than a bit of paper with your address on it, and a silk stocking you know nothing about. The evidence is all rather flimsy, and as you say, it points to a set-up. Surely they need more evidence.' She paused. 'What about a solicitor?' she said, casting an anxious glance at him.

'I have the best. Jeffrey Jordan, Miriam's husband.' He grinned but still he appeared wary. 'He's coming in shortly. If he can't get at the truth, nobody can. The police say I'm the chief suspect. They're basing their decision on both circumstantial and concrete evidence. As the last person to see Rita and, being her ex-husband, they reckon we must have been at each other's' throats.' His voice was deceptively mild.

The outrage and pain inside her fought to escape, but she managed to remain calm. 'I'm sure Jeffrey will untangle this nasty mess,' she said, relieved that a top class solicitor was to represent him. Changing the subject, she continued. 'I've travelled down alone in the car,' she told him light-heartedly, hoping Charles would relax a little. 'I'm staying overnight and I'll come to the court in the morning. Don't worry darling,' she said, lifting his face with her hands. 'We all know you're innocent,' she stressed. She leant over and kissed Charles gently on the mouth. The constable deliberately looked away. 'I've every faith in you and I believe in you implicitly,' she stressed vehemently.

Despair trickled through her as the officer

nodded that it was time to leave. She stood up. 'I'll see you tomorrow. Stay strong.'

She left the building and a cool surge of controlled anger rose inside her at the false accusations. If anything happened to him, it would be the end of her bright and hopeful dream. She had her career mapped out at the shop but she knew deep down she loved Charles with such intensity that she would forego anything for them to be together. But why had she not made that clear to him before? Why had she rambled on about buying a house? Why did she have to be so independent? A prisoner of her own thoughts, the guilt mounted and swamped her.

She moved to the front of the car, took in a deep breath and turned the starter handle. It spluttered but the engine noise died away. She cranked it again. This time it started and she set off to look for a place to stay. But on the way she rang Miriam and they arranged to meet the following day at the court.

Helen found a room. It was cheap yet comfortable, but she spent the night wide awake, worrying about the trial the following day.

Miriam tried to comfort Helen as they took their seats. 'Stay positive, Helen. Jeffrey will do his utmost to clear Charles of the charges.'

Charles stood erect coolly answering the simple questions he was asked. But it was a futile exercise; everything was apparently cut and dried. The charges were read and Charles was sent down. Helen gasped in horror.

'That's the way it goes, Helen. We have to wait now for the crown court trial.'

Once outside she couldn't think straight. The events had affected her so deeply she felt as though she were on a tightrope and about to fall off.

Miriam turned to her. 'Won't you stay with us overnight, Helen? It'll give you the chance to relax before the drive back.'

'Thank you, Miriam, but there's nothing to be gained by staying. I need to get back to my girls.'

'I understand, Helen, if you're sure.'

Helen said her goodbyes and left for home, but the journey seemed to go on forever. When she drew up in front of the house Mary came dashing down the steps to meet her, taking her case and helping her up the steps as though she were an invalid.

'Let's get you inside, Helen love, before anyone sees you. You're as white as a sheet.'

Fortunately, the girls were still at school which gave Helen time to calm down before they returned. At all costs, they must not know about this. If the case became prominent in the national newspapers, she knew she'd have to face a barrage of questions. But she would face that if it arose.

She awoke next day feeling confused and depressed. The devastating rawness inside remained, but the tears lessened. There was nothing to be done until the trial in six weeks' time. Charles was transferred to Durham where Helen would be allowed to visit but there would be no more holding each other close, not until he was set free.

Following the magistrates' hearing, the item appeared in the national newspapers. Charles was incriminated as the main suspect, not exactly by name but by his position at a hospital in the area. Helen's stomach flipped aggressively, and she felt a feeling of futility inside. If Charles were found guilty of murder he would face the death penalty, he would face the hangman. His name would be recorded in history with the likes of the notorious Crippen who, in the early part of the century, had murdered his wife and run off with his mistress. That thought was so despicable she cast it from her mind. All she had to cling on to now was hope.

Chapter 27

She threw herself into her work at the shop. It was the only way to get through her days until she could see Charles again. And the car was a godsend. Visits to Durham would have been impossible without it. She called on Mother less frequently. There was something about Mother's attitude that rankled, for although she had expressed her sorrow, Helen guessed she'd been put in her place and told by Laura to curb her waspish comments.

On her final visit to Durham, two days before the trial, the feeling of pessimism refused to leave her, but nevertheless she tried to put on a cheerful front.

'It won't be long now, darling. You're innocent, and everyone believes it. Even the newspapers are saying there's insufficient evidence. You've got to believe in yourself.'

'I hear what you say, Helen. It's not easy to be optimistic in a place like this. But I'm determined they won't get me down. I'll fight to the end.'

Helen's stomach lurched. He'd fight to the end. But how would it all end?

It was nine o'clock on the day of the trial when Helen arrived at the court. She took her seat and looked around for Miriam but there was no sign of her. It was early but the courtroom soon became crowded, the public obviously curious to witness the trial of a highly respected medical consultant. The newspapers speculated on Charles's innocence, and there were campaigns to release him.

Miriam arrived and slipped into the seat beside her, just as Charles entered the dock. He looked pale yet confident and when Helen caught his eye, she detected a look of optimism. The clerk announced the charges and the trial began. To Helen's dismay, one of Rita's friends had been summoned to give evidence of the bitterness between Charles and Rita, of Rita's unfaithful behaviour and of the eventual split between them, all of which served to establish a motive for murder. The statements provided a credible background and fuelled the case for the prosecution.

Jeffrey called upon Sir Michael Stephens to describe his meeting with Charles on the day before the murder.

'He was tired. He'd had a heavy workload of ops following a nasty road accident in which many of the passengers had been seriously injured. But

Charles being Charles was in lively mood. That's the sort of person he is, more than capable of handling pressure,' he informed the court.

He was about to continue when he was interrupted by counsel for the prosecution. 'With all due respect, my lord, we are asking for facts, not opinions.'

The judge nodded his head, but Sir Michael continued and slipped in a final comment. 'And there's something else. Charles Ravel is a healer, not a destroyer.'

The ensuing silence was broken when someone started to clap. Another spectator followed. And then it seemed the whole of the courtroom had joined in. There were cheers from the crowd, and whole place was in uproar. The judge banged his gavel down hard, threatening to have the main culprits removed if their behaviour continued, but that would have meant clearing the court completely. Momentarily, Helen felt a warmth filter through her. She knew the crowd was behind Charles. That was something to hold on to.

Once the background evidence had been established, the prosecution produced the silk stocking with which Rita had been strangled, and the paper in her handwriting which was covered with both Rita's and Charles's fingerprints. The police sergeant who had visited Charles was called to the stand. He recounted the events of his visit, and then added, 'When we stepped inside the house of the accused, his suitcase was standing in the hall packed and ready for him to leave.' Not only did all the evidence point to the fact that Charles Ravel had murdered his ex-wife, but also

361

that it had been pre-meditated.

Despite Jeffrey Jordan's valiant attempts, stressing that the evidence was insubstantial, counsel for the prosecution fought hard and by this time, things were looking bad. Jeffrey's aides had searched records and carried out extensive interviews. The elusive Hugh must exist and they needed to find him. That had been Jeffrey's only hope.

In summing up he refuted the points made by the prosecution and stressed that the case against his client was based on circumstantial evidence and nothing more. Charles Ravel was innocent. Evidence had been planted on his property. 'My client has a reputation second to none of caring in the community. He had nothing to gain by killing his ex-wife. You must find him not guilty.'

Finally, counsel for the prosecution addressed the jury. 'It is obvious Charles Ravel is guilty. The murder was pre-meditated. Charles Ravel persuaded his ex-wife to visit on some pretence or other, and then he murdered her. As for a motive, Ravel wanted her out of his life forever. Evidence has led us to believe he carried out this evil deed in the early hours of the morning, possibly at his home. Subsequently he dumped Rita Ravel in the bus shelter. After all, he is a man of stature, a strong man capable of carrying out such an act. The fellow Hugh he mentioned was obviously a figment of Charles Ravel's imagination, a character in a story he had invented to cover his own tracks. Ravel's suitcase was packed ready for him to leave. What more can I say? Ravel is guilty. He is a danger to the public. He must not be allowed his freedom ever again.'

There was an undercurrent of murmured comments from the gallery again and some shouts of protest. The judge issued his threats once more before the jury were sent away to deliberate.

Helen feared the worst, dreading that the jury would find Charles guilty. Miriam took her hand and they left the courtroom. Helen needed air. Miriam suggested they have a cup of tea and try to calm their nerves.

'It's going to be some hours before the jury return, Helen. It's no good sitting there with all the time in the world contemplating the worst before we even know the verdict. Stay optimistic. There's nothing more we can do.'

It was over four hours before the bell sounded for the return of the jury.

'Would the foreman of the jury, please stand?

A small, balding man edged from his seat.

'What is your verdict,' he was asked.

'We find the accused guilty,' he said, quickly looking away.

The judge entered the court wearing the black cap, a sign that he was about to deliver the death penalty to Charles. Helen stared in horror as she saw him lift his gavel. The black cap meant death by hanging. The scene before her faded away and all went black.

Devoid of energy and enthusiasm, Helen just about coped at the shop. She'd lost Charles forever. Apart from the girls, he was the one person she needed and loved, the one she hoped would eventually be her soul-mate. He was to be hanged, and she could see no way in which the decision could be reversed. In normal circumstances the judgement would not be reversed except in extenuating circumstances when the case could be taken to the high court if fresh evidence arose.

The girls knew there was something wrong, but Helen had given them no details. What she'd told them was that Uncle Charles wasn't available for the time being. But they would have to know some time.

She visited Charles and tried to remain optimistic, chivvying him along and trying to instil some hope that Jeffery had not given up and that maybe more evidence would reveal the name and the whereabouts of Rita's partner, Hugh. But there were times when Charles became withdrawn, at other times he was highly confident that he would gain a reprieve. He had the public's support in the form of a major petition organised by one of the national newspapers. This had been sent to the Home Secretary.

But still the mysterious Hugh was still at large and nobody knew his surname or his whereabouts. Jeffrey advertised for anyone who could throw any light on the matter to come forward. He even offered a reward. But there were no takers. No date had been set for the execution, but as the days passed, Helen became more and more frantic.

Jeffrey collected his brief case from the mahogany desk and left the office, the papers for the following day's trial complete and locked away in the safe. He pushed open the heavy door, stepped out on to the pavement and looked up at the sky. It was already six thirty and the evening was sultry. Tired, weary and despondent, he set off towards the car park. The worst had happened. Charles had been found guilty, and there had been nothing Jeffrey could do to change the verdict. Understandably Helen could not be consoled. And Jeffrey felt responsible. He knew for certain that Charles was innocent but the whereabouts of this man, Hugh continued to be a mystery. He could be anywhere in the country. He could be abroad for all they knew.

As Jeffrey was about to turn the corner to the car park at the back of the building he heard someone shouting. He turned.

'Mr. Jordan. Telephone call; it's urgent.' It was his secretary, Kath whom he recalled was collecting her things to leave when he'd passed through reception. He tutted and turned back, wondering who it could be ringing him after office hours. If ten hours a day were not sufficient, then it was time he took on another partner.

'Who is it, Kath?' he asked, his brow furrowed.

'I don't know, Mr. Jordan. But it's a woman, and she said it was extremely urgent.'

When Jeffrey picked up the telephone, he couldn't believe his luck. The woman whose name was Pat Dorkins was a nurse and one-time friend of Rita Ravel.

'I'm glad I've caught you Mr. Jordan. After the break-up of my own marriage I went off to Africa with a team of midwives. I only returned a few days ago. A colleague told me that Rita Ravel had been murdered and that her ex-husband, Charles had been arrested. You can imagine how alarmed I was, especially knowing the excellent reputation of Mr. Ravel. But what I haven't told you is that my husband Hugh left me for Rita Ravel. They went off together.'

'Hugh, that's the name of your husband?' Jeffrey was elated. 'Charles has already been convicted of the murder, but this throws a different light on the matter. It would have helped if at least we'd known the surname of this fellow Hugh. Obviously I appreciate you've only today returned from Africa, and it's lucky for us you have.' Jeffery paused. 'It's difficult to talk on the telephone. I need the full facts. Is it possible for you to come and see me? Alternatively I could meet you somewhere.'

'I don't know that I could do any more to help you if I did come up there. I could have forecast the relationship between them would fail. Hugh has suffered all his life from manic-depressive psychosis, a mental disorder responsible for his mood swings. These are extreme, ranging from deep depression when he needs to escape and hide away, to over-confidence when he thinks he can rule the world. Above all, a patient with this illness needs support and security. And that's something Rita could never give.'

'Tell me, Mrs. Dorkins, what can we do to get at the truth?'

'If Rita Ravel failed to support my husband, he would have been capable of anything. What I do know is that he'll need me right now, but I've no idea where he might be. Despite what's happened, I still love my husband, Mr. Jordan. If he

366

has committed any offence, believe me it would have been when his mind was disturbed. I would need to talk to him myself before I could make a commitment to visit you there.'

'But time is ticking by for Charles Ravel. I'll ask for a stay but we must get to the bottom of this, and quick. How about if I come down there?'

'I wouldn't like Mr. Ravel to suffer on account of Hugh. But what is to say Hugh is guilty? I'm not prepared to condemn him, not until I've talked to him.'

'Then please let me come and see you. If we talk it through we might be able to come up with a plan.'

'I must make sure Hugh is comfortable and stable before I speak with him, that's if we can find him.'

'Is that a "yes"? Are you saying I can come down there?'

'I can see no alternative, but if the police are to be involved, we must play it gently.'

Since his conviction Charles was at his most optimistic when he heard the news and he remained calm throughout. It looked as if there might be a slim chance he would not be sent to the gallows after all. If sufficient evidence could be found to give him back his freedom, then once again, he could be back with Helen. She'd been his strongest support, his crutch throughout the trial.

It was crucial the police found Hugh Dorkins pretty quickly and the search became a priority. They had his name and the connection. All they needed was the man himself.

367

Pat returned to her home and was kept under police protection in the hope that she could help them with their enquiries.

'Throughout our marriage, I've had to monitor his condition,' she told them. 'I know exactly how to handle him. Occasionally he's needed electric shock treatment to stabilise him, but most of the time I can manage to control him through medication and support,' she said. 'If he's on the loose and becomes depressed, he might try to contact me. If he knows I'm back in the country he'll come back here. But you must promise to let me talk to him before you come storming in and arresting him, if at the end of the day he is guilty.'

In an attempt to find Hugh Dorkins, most national newspapers featured a front page item with a photograph of Pat Dorkins and the team of nurses who'd visited Africa to help teach the skills of midwifery. It was also broadcast on the wireless when the team of nurses were interviewed.

It seemed Hugh was in one of his depressive mood swings and in the depths of despair when he turned up at Pat's house less than a week later.

Aware of his low self-worth when he was in such a state, Pat knew how much he needed her to look after him. She talked to him and established that he and Rita had argued, but he confessed no more than that. He begged her to take him back and Pat agreed to support him provided he went with a police officer and gave evidence in court.

Helen and Miriam hugged each other in the gallery.

'Jeffrey's done it,' Miriam announced proudly. 'I knew he wouldn't fail.'

'Don't speak too soon, Miriam. It's not over yet,' Helen warned cautiously, apprehension mingled with joy racing through her body. 'They need an open confession before we're in the clear.'

'Wait and see,' was Miriam's complacent reply.

Hugh Dorkins appeared in court in such a state of depression, he needed a medical escort. He confirmed the story of his relationship with Rita who had failed to support him when he needed her. She had two-timed him on so many occasions and pushed him to the limit.

'Why did you hit her? Were you annoyed about something?' Jeffrey asked.

'I didn't hit her.'

'But she had bruises to prove it.'

'I didn't do it on purpose. She taunted me. I was sick of it. It was always someone else she wanted, never me. I was ill and I couldn't help it. I punched her in the chest and she ran out on me. But I didn't kill her. I felt sorry after I'd hit her. I shouldn't have done it.'

'How did you know where she was?'

'I followed her. I wanted to apologise and bring her back. I needed her.'

'What happened when you reached the house, Hugh? I expect you were furious when you saw Mr. Ravel answer the door and invite Rita inside.'

'She'd told me she was through with Ravel. I never expected her to turn up at his house. I thought they were back together again when I saw her go in there.'

'How did you know who he was? Had you met

him before?'

'I'd seen his photograph.'

'What do you think happened in the house, Hugh?'

'I don't know. I had an idea and when she came out I ran after her, begged her to come back. But she laughed at me and said I was crazy.'

'That must have upset you,' Jeffrey continued.

Jeffrey was interrupted. 'Objection, m'lord. The witness is being led.'

'Objection overruled.' The judge was willing for Jeffrey to continue in this vein.

'Were you upset, Hugh?' Jeffrey re-phrased his question.

'Yes, but I didn't touch her. It wasn't me who strangled her,' he said. 'It was Ravel.'

'Is that what happened, someone strangled her? What with, Hugh? Nothing was found near the body.'

'They say it was a silk stocking.'

'I see, and what did you do with it, Hugh?'

'I didn't do anything with it. It wasn't me,' he said, backing off.

'But the police maintained it had been found.'

'Yes I know but I didn't have it. It was in Ravel's dustbin.'

'You put it there, didn't you? You wanted the police to think it was Mr. Ravel. You were angry with him for taking Rita away from you, weren't you? You were angry because Rita wanted him, not you.'

'But she promised to stay with me,' he said. 'He took her away. I had to punish them.'

There were loud murmurs from the court. Unwittingly Hugh had confessed to Rita's murder, having been led to his own admission by Jeffrey's clever ploy.

Charles stepped out through the prison gates and made straight for Helen who was waiting to take him home. As they embraced she caught his steady, clear-eyed gaze.

'I can't believe it, darling. Together at last,' he said triumphantly squeezing her so tightly she thought he would never let her go.

Helen drove the car away from the prison car park and headed for Llanypen. The day was hot, the long summer having brought forth the profusion of flowers proudly displayed in the tiny cottage gardens as they passed through the villages on their way back home. The sun-dappled leaves of the willow and the ash trembled in the gentle breeze that came from the rolling, purple hills silhouetted against the azure skies. But the beauty of the countryside failed to register. Their minds were firmly fixed on one another.

Once at Willow House, they were met by Gladys and Joseph who stood waiting at the door, beaming delightedly.

'It's been so dreadful. He can thank his lucky stars that nurse came along,' Gladys confided to Helen.

'You're right, Gladys. I've been out of my mind. But he's ridden the storm, thank God,' she murmured picking up the tray and carrying it through.

Helen knelt at his feet, her head on his knees. 'It's been a nightmare, Charles. The relief must be tremendous.' Her eyes dulled with fatigue and her smile was a little too bright to be true.

'Helen, my love, you're the one I need to thank for pulling me through. You were there with me every step of the way.' He took her hands in his and the two of them remained silent for some time. And when he felt her body sinking into his, he joyfully recollected their intimacy, the feel of her body in his arms, the soft expression in her glowing eyes.

A debate was raging in his head. He knew he had a decision to make, one far tougher than any other he had ever made. He needed to decide whether he dare broach the subject. But he couldn't afford a rebuff, not at this stage, not after the ordeal he'd been through.

By the time he'd made a decision, he could feel her breathing heavily, regularly. But he was content to sit there, holding her close. It was half an hour later before she awoke and looked at the clock.

'Oh Charles! I'm awfully sorry. I must have dozed off. You should have given me a shake,' she told him with a look of embarrassment.

'You needed it, darling,' he said lovingly, feeling stronger now that he'd had time to think. He'd been selfish. All he was worried about was that she might turn him down. But he must take that chance. That was what life was all about, taking chances. He gently lifted her head from his knee and looked into her open, honest face. Her eyes glowed now, wide and depthless.

'You know how proud I am of you Helen, proud of the way you've pulled yourself up and made such a success of the shop. I'm not expecting you to give it up,' he explained and she looked at him in astonishment, her eyes soft and wondering. 'We can decide what to do later.' He swallowed hard. 'Marry me, Helen,' he said with spontaneity. 'Please don't turn me down.'

'I never thought I'd hear those words my darling,' she said huskily. Her bright eyes sparkled with pleasure as she drew herself up and kissed him gently on the mouth. He heard her moan in a quiet sound of surrender and, drawing herself away, she cupped his face with her hands, smiling up at him in a way that told him her answer.

The publishers hope that this book has given you enjoyable reading. Large Print Books are especially designed to be as easy to see and hold as possible. If you wish a complete list of our books please ask at your local library or write directly to:

Magna Large Print Books
Magna House, Long Preston,
Skipton, North Yorkshire.
BD23 4ND

This Large Print Book for the partially sighted, who cannot read normal print, is published under the auspices of

THE ULVERSCROFT FOUNDATION